"十三五"国家重点出版规划项目

王维诗歌全集英译

A Complete Edition of Wei Wang's Poems in Chinese and English
With Annotations

赵彦春 译·注

Translated and Annotated by Yanchun Chao

第一卷

Volume Ⅰ

上海大学出版社
·上海·

图书在版编目(CIP)数据

王维诗歌全集英译/赵彦春译、注.—上海：上海大学出版社，2020.10(2021.9重印)
ISBN 978-7-5671-3969-5

Ⅰ.①王… Ⅱ.①赵… Ⅲ.①唐诗－诗集－英文 Ⅳ.①I222.742

中国版本图书馆 CIP 数据核字(2020)第 202348 号

策　　划　　许家骏
责任编辑　　王悦生
助理编辑　　陆仕超
封面设计　　王兆琪
技术编辑　　金　鑫　钱宇坤

王维诗歌全集英译

赵彦春　译·注

上海大学出版社出版发行
(上海市上大路 99 号　邮政编码 200444)
(http://www.shupress.cn　发行热线 021-66135112)
出版人　戴骏豪

＊

南京展望文化发展有限公司排版
江苏凤凰数码印务有限公司印刷　　各地新华书店经销
开本 710mm×1000mm　1/16　印张 46　字数 753 千字
2020 年 11 月第 1 版　2021 年 9 月第 2 次印刷
ISBN 978-7-5671-3969-5/I·605　定价 580.00 元(精装全 2 册)

版权所有　侵权必究
如发现本书有印装质量问题请与印刷厂质量科联系
联系电话：025-57718474

序　言

译道之魅：赵彦春唐诗英译中的声、光、电、影
——以王维诗歌英译为例

　　作为中国山水田园诗的集大成者，唐代文学的代表人物，王维是一位在当时和后世都影响巨大的唐代诗人，他不仅工于诗文，在音乐、绘画、书法等领域皆造诣非凡。说到王维，我们就不得不提到苏轼对于他的妙评，苏轼在《东坡题跋》下卷《书摩诘〈蓝田烟雨图〉》写下了古今对于王维最著名的评论："味摩诘之诗，诗中有画；观摩诘之画，画中有诗。"从此，"诗中有画，画中有诗"成为王维最为后人所铭记的标志性艺术特色。

　　王维的诗歌涵蕴深厚，性灵浮动，读来浑然一帧帧美轮美奂、超逸淡远的水墨画面，一段段光影明灭、动静相宜的有声图像。因其自成一家，震烁古今的艺术成就，使他不仅是载入史册，彪炳千秋的文学巨匠，亦于后世成为中西学者在英译汉诗之时无法绕开的必选诗人。宇文所安、许渊冲等诸公都曾有王维诗歌精选的优秀译笔问世。此次赵彦春先生选择王维诗歌全集作为英译的选题，对于世界全面了解王维超拔的文学风格和艺术成就有着极为重要的价值。

　　赵彦春先生是一位对中华优秀传统文化对外传播有着卓越贡献的学者，凭借自身优秀的英语语言专业学术功底，加之对中国古典文学的精深钻研，他迄今已翻译出版了《英韵三字经》《诗经》《论语》《道德经》《庄子》《李白诗歌全集英译》等汉译英译著 24 部，33 卷，还有即将出版的《杜甫诗歌全集英译》《王维诗歌全集英译》亦是他的新成果。本书反映了赵教授对王维诗歌总体及多元风格的准确把握，其将王维笔下那苏轼所说的"诗中有画，画中有诗"的艺术境界用优雅精妙的英语呈现了出来，力求令西方世界的读者在没有中国传统文化背景知识的情况下也能领略到王维诗中的林泉高致，以及中国文学中那些最美的山水田园。这部译著突出反映了赵彦春唐诗英译的四大特色——

声、光、电、影。声,是赵译为韵律和音步忠于原作的和谐而近乎苛刻的追求;光,是赵译对光线和色彩与工笔兼具的精微描摹;电,是赵译对瞬间景物变化的震撼效果分毫毕现地捕捉和聚焦;影,是赵译对人内心普世性情感余韵袅袅的意绪共鸣之动人表达。这四大特色深刻地体现着赵彦春的译道之魅。赵彦春对于王维诗歌的英译可谓是这四大特色最精彩的例证。

一、声

韵律和音步是赵彦春在王维诗歌英译中极为重视的元素,赵彦春对其的追求,也到了近乎苛刻的程度。在首先考虑句意完整再现原文的情况下,句尾的押韵并不容易做到。而赵彦春的英译(以下简称赵译)做到了二者圆融,令句尾的押韵与意境的营构相得益彰。我们以王维的两首极为著名的作品为例。

"白云"是王维非常钟爱的意象,在其不同题材的作品中皆有显现,荒井健氏认为,喜欢白云是王维有盛唐人刚健之气的证明。王维最具画面感的诗中,多有白云。而说到王维的此类诗歌,则必然会令人想到《终南山》和《终南别业》,这两首也堪称是唐诗中的杰作,其中"白云回望合,青霭入看无"、"行到水穷处,坐看云起时"这样的美轮美奂,兼具内外意和"味外味"(禅意)的佳句,要准确传达其中的意境,需要对中英文的表达习惯、语境置换、诗歌音步都有着娴熟的把握。同时这四处的翻译,还承担着令这两句作为颔联,内部语意足以自洽和完整的功能。在全诗之中,也能负载起承转合,使全诗气韵生动,语义流畅的作用。且看赵彦春的翻译:

The white clouds behind merge as one;
The blue haze inside becomes none.

赵译用了至简的方式来呈现诗意,同时将其中包含的移步换景的空间感和画面感都用精要的英语词汇做了表达,既描绘出了云霭变幻的气象万千,又将朦胧虚幻,不可言说却令人神往的感受予以保留,堪为妙笔。"one"和"none"用于句尾,禅意十足,也令两句实现了语义和音律上的对偶和押韵。

而另一句《终南别业》中的名句"行到水穷处,坐看云起时",则充满了身处灵境的生命体验。怎样将这句充满中国式水墨画风格的恬淡悠远之句,化为令英语世界的读者可触可感的英文诗行,同时亦将涵蕴丰厚的千古名句所呈现的天地悠悠的空间感在遣词造句中无声地传达出来,这同样考验着译者对于中英文语感的准确捕捉和体察,赵译展示了动作先后关系,补足了语义和意境,译笔卓拔:

> Where the creek ends, I take a rest,
> To behold clouds arise white-dressed.

二句在逻辑上,是有着一个动作的先后关系的,赵译清晰地呈现了这一逻辑关系,与此同时,还兼顾着诗意的接续和情绪的延展。"white-dressed"一词的加入,不仅与上句结尾的"rest"押韵,更重要的是,这个词的补充,把作者的悠然恬静与开阔舒朗成功地带了出来,解决了完全依据原文逐字翻译而极易造成的诗行短缺的问题。

二、光

在王维的诗作中,对于光线和色彩的描绘往往是浩大雄浑,令人惊叹的,这令他的诗歌自有一番瑰丽壮美的气象,而要在英译其诗时反映出这种肃穆而不失绮绝的光彩,就需要在句子构造上细加推敲,突出画面中的光感和色感。在《使至塞上》中,被王国维称为"千古壮观"的名句"大漠孤烟直,长河落日圆",可谓古今描写塞外风光最著名的诗句之一。为了突出这种塞外边疆沙漠的浩瀚与壮丽,赵译采用了重置诗句中词汇顺序的方式,将定语"孤"(lonely)和"圆"(round)后置,令描写对象主体先行,保留了"烟"(smoke)和"日"(sun)仍为诗句中核心意象的句意逻辑,很好地烘托出原诗的荒凉和孤高气质:

> O'er the wild smoke lonely curls straight;
> To the river the sun round sets late.

而"To the River the sun round sets late"也营造出黄河的横贯感,同时亦渲染出清冷的塞外大漠中,落日余晖笼罩下沉郁苍凉的光感,避免了依照原句词语顺序以"round"结句而造成重形轻神,且情绪铺展上语义未尽的阅读缺憾。开元二十五年(737年),河西节度副大使崔希逸战胜吐蕃,唐玄宗命王维以监察御史身份出塞查访军情,对于王维而言,这意味着他被排挤出权力的中心地带,因此这首作于赴边途中的杰作背后是王维的压抑与愤懑。赵译将这种无声的中国式边塞诗魂的落寞情绪通过英诗的句义逻辑构造得以还原。

作为王维后期山水诗的杰出代表,《鹿柴》一诗可谓是通过光的意象,将全诗意涵韵味推向极致的典范。特别是后两句"返景入深林,复照青苔上",书写鹿柴附近的空山深林傍晚时分的幽静之景,更为夕照之光赋予了拟人化的温暖特质。鹿柴,是辋川的地名。这两句诗翻译的难点,在于其表现的是有光的幽暗,寒意笼罩中的一丝温暖。以落日余晖的回照反衬山中树林幽暗的深重,凸显空山之静寂,人迹之罕至,不仅需要借助凝练的描写,更需要借助景物意象之间的互动关系,才能在英译中无损原意地将原诗要表达的况味意绪和盘托出。赵译做了这样的构造:

> The deep wood sees the returned sun;
> Once again the green moss is shone.

赵译分毫毕现地呈现了原诗微妙的光的移动,以及光的变化对其它景物的影响,生动展示了光的意象给其他意象带来的变化,以拟人化的手法,令意象间的互动关系清晰分明,每一个意象都带着敏锐的生命触感,在语义的行进中交相辉映,令诗意圆满而紧贴原文。

三、电

王维的诗中,对于瞬间震撼效果的描绘和书写,在古今诗歌巨匠之中亦十分卓拔。赵彦春在王维诗歌的英译中,对此有着明确的认知,对其再现亦十分传神和到位。这突出体现在他对《观猎》和《鸟鸣涧》两首名作的翻译上。

先以《观猎》为例:

观 猎
风劲角弓鸣,将军猎渭城。

草枯鹰眼疾,雪尽马蹄轻。
忽过新丰市,还归细柳营。
回看射雕处,千里暮云平。

这首诗写的是一次狩猎活动,并以三个细节勾勒全貌。整体风格遒劲有力,激情澎湃,豪兴飞扬。而这样的风格,都是藉由带有瞬间震撼效果的形容词来体现,怎样让这些形容词在英译中获得原文中等值的高光效果,是翻译的难点。与此同时,本诗的艺术手法亦允为神来之笔,沈德潜曾惊叹道:"章法、句法、字法俱臻绝顶。盛唐诗中亦不多见。"(《唐诗别裁集》)因此,在翻译中如何综合彰显这首神作中的章法、句法、字法的高妙之所在,亦是英译中必须面对的课题。赵译对此作了精确的考量,逐个攻克了翻译中密集的难点:

Watching Hunting

Against the wind rings the horn bow;
Wei sees the general hunting go.
The hawk looks sharply thru dry grass;
The hoofs tread lightly on snow to pass.
The steeds bolting through Newrich Town
Come back to Thin Willow anon.
He looks back to where he has shot;
It's all quiet and clouds there are not.

赵译对于"角弓鸣"、"鹰眼疾"、"马蹄轻"这三个狩猎过程中扣人心弦的精彩瞬间采用了不同的句法,不但保留了诗句的原意,而且实景中的物的方位及其瞬间风驰电掣的速度和力度,也都毫无遗漏地再现于译本中。赵译以"Against the wind rings the horn bow"这一场景来展示呼啸的风使得弓箭发出鸣声,将风和角弓之间的互动关系做了清晰展示,没有割裂二者使之成为各自独立的意象。"草枯鹰眼疾"赵译采用了"The hawk looks sharply thru dry grass"的译法,将鹰的动作放置于枯草之前,语序的变化,凸显了猎鹰于枯草之上极速搜寻猎物的瞬间动态,将"鹰眼疾"化为对于对象瞬息万变的动态化描述,而非对于对象特征的简单形容,烘托出这首诗本身具有的极强画面感,令实景跃然纸上。而"马蹄轻"的翻译"The hoofs tread lightly on snow to pass",赵译则参考了"踏雪无痕"的意境构造,充分考虑到了马蹄踏雪后在雪地上留下的痕迹,从而用了"tread"这个单词,并以"to pass"结尾,呈现了马蹄踏雪的瞬间动态,及其与前句速度感截然不同的轻盈感。这句的翻译同样将"雪"后置,将马作为了整句动作的主体。可以说,赵译对于这三处精彩细节的动态影像化翻译精彩呈现了原作中"最富于孕育性的顷刻"(语出龙迪勇《空间维度的叙事学研究》,《中国社会科学报》2012年10月19日),给人以最震撼的力与美的体验。

赵彦春对王维的另一首名作《鸟鸣涧》中四句名句的翻译,亦体现出他深谙王维诗展示景物瞬间震撼效果的奇绝笔法,并熟知如何将之转换为英语中之高古雅致表达的功力。在《鸟鸣涧》一诗的翻译上,赵译充分照顾到了诗中隐含的鸟鸣空山中声效的回环效果:

鸟 鸣 涧

人闲桂花落,
夜静春山空。
月出惊山鸟,
时鸣春涧中。

Birds Twitter o'er the Brook

I idle laurel flowers to fall;
Night quiets the vernal hills o'er all.
The moon out, startled birds flutter;
At times, o'er the brook they twitter.

首句和第二句赵译采用了依据语序直译的方式,意象叠加的同时兼顾了韵律上的节奏感,在句尾也坚持了赵译一贯葆有的押韵的特色。而此诗翻译的难点,在于第三句"月出惊山鸟"的"惊"字,月光是无声的,但因为空谷的幽暗和静默,月亮缓缓升起,皎洁的光忽然普照的刹那,便惊起了山谷中鸟的鸣叫,这对于瞬间震撼效果的描写,令诗歌静中有动,以静制动,动静相宜。动与静之间,是相互契合又互相影响的,怎样通过译笔展示月出刹那给整个山谷飞鸟带来惊动的震撼效果,从而具象化地展示月光普照下山谷的声籁与回响,是此处英译制胜的关键。赵译采用了删繁就简,与原文趋同的方式,但又兼顾了翻译过程中对于文本不自足的语义补充。第三句结尾处的"flutter"补充了鸟受惊后飞来飞去的动态场景,增强了诗中画面构造的完整性。而末句将"twitter"后置,则充分考虑到了飞翔中鸣叫的鸟儿在山涧中的形象掠影和声效绵延。尽管此诗的英译看上去简洁明快,不事雕琢,但却突出体现了赵译构景状物时的时空意识和美学观照。

四、影

这里所说的"影",即作者诗中抒发的真挚炽热的情感在读者内心的投射和共鸣,其余韵袅袅,不可磨灭。特别是王维作品中那些对超越时空和跨越国界的人类共同情感题材的书写,更是成为王维流传后世的名作中最广为传诵的诗句。如何呈现这种"天涯共此时"的情感体验,赵彦春同样下了一番功夫。此处我们以此类作品中流传度最广的两首《送元二使安西》和《九月九日忆山东兄弟》的赵氏英译为例。

《送元二使安西》是一首送别诗,王维送友人去唐中央政府设在西域地区的安西都护府,在渭城相别。前两句中的"杨柳"意象在中国传统文化中即是离别的象征物,王维以此烘托渲染离别的气氛。而后两句"劝君更尽一杯酒,西出阳关无故人"是千古佳句,赵彦春采用了这样的句式来表达其中的气势:

Have one more cup of wine I do maintain;
West of Sun Pass you have no old fellows.

赵译的精彩高超之处,在于人称的明确介入,"I"和"you"的人称介入,使主客关系更加明晰,凸显了末句语意中明晰的主客友谊关系对于彼此的唯一性,构造起一种二人相向而坐,推心置腹的对话情境,并在一种动作的延宕(劝酒)之中,令盛情的琼浆蕴含着殷切的祝福,含不尽之意于言外,将原诗中王维对友人深挚的惜别再现出来。

而王维的另一首七绝作品《九月九日忆山东兄弟》,则是表达着人类更为普世的情感体验——思乡,既有佳句,更有佳篇,读之深有咀华含英之感。此诗用语朴实无华,却深深地感动着古往今来的万千读者。王维写作此诗之时,年仅十七岁。尽管此诗的诗意一目了然,但相比于其后来技巧圆熟、意境浑厚的作品,在感人程度上丝毫不逊色。而且这首作品也是王维作品中仅有的十首由其本人注明写作年龄的诗歌之一,是其早期作品中的代表作。

九月九日忆山东兄弟

独在异乡为异客,
每逢佳节倍思亲。
遥知兄弟登高处,
遍插茱萸少一人。

On the Ninth Day of the Ninth Moon,
Missing Brothers East of the Mountain
An alien land sees me a lonely soul;
I pine for my dear ones each festive day.
Far off, I know my brothers climb a knoll,
All wearing cornel sprigs but one away.

此时的王维,应是在长安谋求功名,故远离自己的家乡蒲州(今山西永济),蒲州在华山之东,因而称家乡的弟兄为"山东兄弟"。在重阳节,他思念远方的亲人,写下了这首诗。这首诗的翻译难点在于两处:对第一句两个"异"字的处理,怎样突出人物身在他乡的孤绝感;还有最后一句如何通过翻译呈现出人物思想情绪的浓烈和重阳不能归家的遗憾感。

对于"异乡"和"异客",赵译分别采用了直译和意译两种方式,深刻呈现出原诗意味,"a lonely soul"将在异乡的孤绝感受表达得直接而准确。而第二句中赵译将"亲"字处理为"my dear ones",而非"family",将"亲"的范围定位于所有与自己有密切情感牵系的亲友,突出了"亲"与主人公的情感连接而非止客观的亲缘关系。在句子的逻辑关系上与前句的"a lonely soul",形成了情绪意境上的顺承,同时又保留了此句在全诗中所承担的思绪由近及远、由目下望向家乡的语义功能。第三句赵译采用了抒情主体进一步介入,表达重阳节自己孑立他乡独自遐想倍感怅惘的心境,此处的妙笔在于用"far off"来翻译"遥"。句子的分割,造成了韵律上的叹息口吻,将故乡重阳登高风俗的背景下,远在他乡的少年游子不能参与的感受表述得生动活现。末句作为全诗最触动人心的句子,赵译将"少一人"进行了完全贴近原文的视角转换,因为原作中是以山东兄弟的视角反观自己,赵译清晰地呈现了这种视角转换,他在此处作了与一、二句反其道而行之的处理,避免了用"without me"("我不在")这样的直译将前两句中的视角贯穿到底,因为这样不仅不符合原诗中的视角转换,且错误强调了个体相对于群体的特异性。他用了"but one away"这样字面上看没有明确人称指向的表述,来呈示从诗人自己的视角到山东兄弟的视角对换,通过消解特定人称代词,来明确个体是群体中之一员,从而表现出诗中人物间跨越空间的情感互动,以及诗中蕴含的人物对于归属感的渴望。突出了诗中主人公重阳独在异乡,家乡于他距离上的远和情感上的近,赵译通过体察入微的译笔将这种矛盾性带来的深重的遗憾和怅惘表达得浓郁充盈。

结　　语

王维被称为"诗佛",皆因他笔下缔造的舒朗豁达的佛禅诗味之美,而这种美之所以千古之下依旧令人心驰神往,齿颊生香,窃以为恰恰是其最大限度地展示了诗歌这种文学体裁最动人心魄之处——纯粹与澄净。同时,这种美亦最为完满地彰显了唐诗的特色——"豪华落尽见真淳"(元好问《论诗三十首》其四)。

2020年4月6日,英国国家广播电视台BBC播放了纪录片"Du Fu: China's Greatest Poet"(《杜甫——中国最伟大的诗人》),这一片名,与洪业(William Hung)先生在哈佛大学出版社出版于1952年的著作名称完全一致。时隔近70年,作为西方有史以来第一部关于杜甫的纪录片,"Du Fu: China's Greatest Poet"沿用了洪业对于杜甫之于整个中国的文学地位的认定。在这部纪录片中,哈佛大学教授、世界著名汉学家宇文所安先生将杜甫与莎士比亚、但丁并列,认为他们创造了评判伟大诗歌的标准。这一文化事件意义非凡,这意味着洪业的著作问世并在西方学界引起反响之后,西方世界对于杜甫作为世界文明的先驱和布道者的再次承认和肯定。这部纪录片的播放不仅令杜甫在全球范围内成为新世纪最耀眼的中国文学IP,也令中国唐诗的伟大成就在新世纪进入了世界瞩目的视野。如果我们把宇文所安先生的话引申开来,可以说唐诗史上那些焰耀古今的名字正是一个个伟大诗歌评判标准的创造者。而这,也迫使我们重新思考,诞生于拥有世界上现存最古老诗歌传统的国度,唐诗作为中国文学美之极致的载体和明证,今人该如何去继续拓展其世界传播的意义及路径?毋庸置疑的是,唐诗的英译任何时候都是其中不可或缺的一环。

赵彦春先生的王维诗歌全集英译在今天全球化语境下最突出的价值,就在于它极佳地再现了唐诗至为关键的美学特征——真与淳。欧阳修在《论尹师鲁墓志》中,表达了自己在写作墓志时以无限趋近尹洙的文风来表达对于尹师鲁最高敬意的创作取向。而赵彦春的王维诗歌英译中对于无限贴近原文的执著追求,我们亦可将之视为是一位当代杰出译者与唐代巨匠诗人跨时空的心灵秘会。赵译"辞采华茂"(钟嵘《诗品》)、"秘响旁通"(刘勰《文心雕龙》)、"兴象玲珑"(胡应麟《诗薮》)、"不可凑泊"(严羽《沧浪诗话》),将王维诗歌的种种妙处再现得淋漓尽致,可以说,他的王维诗歌全集英译创造了我们判断唐诗英译经典的标准。

作为架设在不同文化间沟通和交流的桥梁,翻译从来不仅是语言的转换,它是语境的融通、语义的共鸣、传统的交汇。它是促使我们深思并破解朱利安(François Jullien)所说的不同文化的"间距与之间"并最终走向构建人类命运共同体的必由之途。我想,这也正是赵彦春先生译道之魅生成的原初动力和终极目的,它最终幻化为旖旎斑斓的声、光、电、影,贯穿古今,纵横中西,为我们还原了千年以前那光照万代的大唐气象。最后,让我尝试以英国国家广播电视台BBC的杜甫纪录片"Du Fu: China's Greatest Poet"的片头词为本文作结:"在当代,往昔以前所未有的速度离我们远去,但寻旅者仍然可以在中国当代找到古中国文化的价值。"

王　莹

中国社会科学院文学研究所研究员

Introduction

The Spell of Translation: Sound, Light, Power and Shade in Yanchun Chao's Translation of T'ang Poetry, a Scrutiny of Wei Wang's Case

A synthesizer of Chinese idyllism and a representative of T'ang Literature, Wei Wang exerted immense influence on his contemporaries and later generations. He was not only versed in poetry and prose but also accomplished in areas such as music, painting and calligraphy. We cannot but mention Shi Su's ingenious remarks on him in *Writing on Vimalakirti's A Picture of Misty Bluefield*, included in the second volume of *Shi Su's Inscriptions*, which may be the most famous of all evaluations of him: Savoring Wei's poem, you see a painting; savoring his painting, you see a poem. The dictum "poetry in painting and painting in poetry" has since been identified with Wei Wang's art.

Wei Wang's poems, exquisite, profound and spirited, offer a viewer a show of sublimated but detached water-ink paintings and a flash of sound-images between shine and shade, between motion and stillness. Because of his uniqueness and epoch-making achievements, he is the greatest literary master of all time, and accordingly a must for all translators, eastern or western. Stephen Owen, Yuanchung Hsu and others have done a good job in translating some of his best works, and now Professor Chao has translated all his poems extant. What is coming as *A Complete Edition of Wei Wang's Poems in Chinese and English* will be of great value for the world to know Wei Wang's excellent literary style and artistic achievements.

Professor Yanchun Chao is a scholar that has contributed a lot to the spread of excellent traditional Chinese culture. Equipped with solid academic training of the English language and in-depth perusals of classic Chinese Literature, he has published 33 volumes of 24 English translations of Chinese classics such as *Three Word Primer in English Rhyme*, *The Book of Songs*, *Analects*, *Sir Lush*, *The Word and the World*, *A Complete Edition of Pai Li's Poems in Chinese and English*. And we are expecting his recent works including *A Complete Edition of Fu Tu's Poems in Chinese and English* and *A Complete Edition of Wei Wang in Chinese and English* and so on. The work coming out soon reflects Chao's comprehension of all Wei Wang's poems in various styles, an elegant and exquisite representation of what Shi Su termed as "poetry in painting and painting in poetry" of Wei Wang's artistic realm so much so that a Western reader can apprehend the beauty of woods and springs in Wei's poems and what is the most idyllic in Chinese Literature even if without relevant background knowledge. This work is characterized by four features of Chao's translation, i.e., sound, light, power and shade. Sound bespeaks Chao's rigorous pursuit of the fidelity of rhyme and meter correspondent with the originals; light reveals Chao's delicate shining of radial and colorful impressionism and true-to-life realism; power exhibits Chao's minute snap of, and focus on, the shock of an instant change of scenes; shade represents Chao's moving expression of the lingering trace and echo of universal love in Wei's poems. These four features capture the spell of Chao's translation. His English translation of Wei Wang's poems is a best illustration of these four features.

Sound

Rhyme and meter are what Chao pays greatest attention to in his translation of Wei Wang's poems. Chao's pursuit of this technique is all but rigorous. When content is put in a primary position and kept intact, it is not easy to make it rhyme at the same time. But Chao is a great success in keeping both meaning and form, making the rhyme and artistic conception a perfect fit. Let us look at his rendering of Wei Wang's two most famous poems.

"White cloud" is an image Wei Wang loves most, appearing in many of his works of various themes. Kenji Harai remarks that the love for white clouds testifies to Wei Wang's robustness. White clouds often appear in Wei Wang's most picturesque poems. In the case of such poems, *The South Mountains* and *My Villa at the South Mountains* may occur to you. Let's first look at the two lines "白云回望合,青霭入看无" in *The Southern Mountains*, what counts most is his rendering of the diction of "回望" and "入看", "合" and "无", and the coherence of the lines. These four words function to form a couplet linking the first two lines while being autonomous and integral as a whole. In the whole poem, they are arranged to open, develop, transit and conclude, making the poem vivid and fluent. Now let's look at Chao's translation:

> The white clouds behind merge as one;
> The blue haze inside becomes none.

Chao uses the tersest language to represent the poetic quality and uses pithy words to express the sense of space and painting of the displacement of scenes, a vivid depiction of the changing and shifting clouds and haze while keeping the sense of ineffability and enthrallment. What a deft touch! "one" and "none" at the end of the lines while rhyming, coupled, and compatible with the meaning embodies a thick flavor of Zen.

Another example, "行到水穷处,坐看云起时", from *My Villa at the South Mountains*, is live with the experience of being in a spiritual realm. How to translate the detached Chinese painting-like aura into lines perceptible to English readers while mutely conveying the vast space embodied in the famous age-old dictum is a great challenge to a translator, who needs to have a good grasp of the nuances of both Chinese and English. Chao's treatment of the sequence of verbs and semantic supplement is superb:

> Where the creek ends, I take a rest,
> To behold clouds arise white-dressed.

These two lines show a sequence of actions and Chao explicitly reveals the logical relation and meanwhile supplements the poetic conception and milieu with "white-dressed", which is entailed in clouds. This addition, while making it rhyme with "rest" in the previous line, leads out the author's quietude and altitude as well as solving the possible problem of the inadequacy of a poetic line due to word-for-word translation.

Light

In Wei Wang's poems, the depiction of light and color is usually characterized by breath-taking immensity and magnanimity, which makes his poems magnificent ones. To successfully express this solemnity not without brilliance in its English translation, one needs to maneuver syntactical constructions to protrude the sense of light and color in the picture. In *To the Front as an Envoy*, "大漠孤烟直,长河落日圆", as was commented as a grandest sight for all time by Kuowei Wang, is one of the most famous couplets of the wild desert ever depicted. To showcase the vastness and magnificence of the wild desert, Chao adjoins attributives "lonely" and "round" to the back of the nouns "smoke" and "sun" so that the latter two are highlighted as central images, hence the bleakness or solitude of the original is well illuminated:

> O'er the wild smoke lonely curls straight;
> To the River the sun round sets late.

And "To the River the sun round sets late" creates the magnitude of the Yellow River and plays up the bleak sense of light touched with afterglow in the chillness of the wild desert and the inverted word order of "the sun round" presents a good theme-rheme relation for semantic extension.

In A.D. 737, the twenty-fifth year of the Allbegun reign, when Hsi-e Ts'ui, the vice general-governor of West Protectorate, defeated Tubo (today's Tibet), Emperor Deepsire sent Wei Wang as a royal inspector to the west for a military survey. To Wei Wang, it meant that he was expelled from the center of political power. Therefore, a sombre tone of depression and indignation permeates the poem composed en route to the front. Chao has conserved this voiceless desolation idiosyncratic to Chinese border war poems with his artful treatment of the syntactic-logic construction.

As a representative of Wei Wang's later idyllic creations, *The Deer Fence* can be regarded as a model of expressing the poetic flavor of a poem to the fullest by means of the light image. The void hills and deep woods nearby the Deer Fence create a quiet setting at dusk, and the last two lines "返景入深林，复照青苔上" in particular give the afterglow a tint of personalized warmness. The Deer Fence is a place in Rimriver. The difficulty in translating these two lines lies in the dimness of light and a feel of warmness in the veil of coldness. The last reflection of afterglow contrasting with the weightiness of the dim forest visualizes the calmness of the void hills and barrenness of the wild. Such a setting and feeling can only be conveyed intact by means of exquisite depiction, especially that of the interaction between the setting and images. Chao gives such a construction:

> The deep wood sees the returned sun;
> Once again the green moss is shone.

Chao exhaustively reveals the subtle move of light and the impact the change of light exerts on other scenes and vividly displays how the image of light affects other images and his personification explicates the interaction between images, and every image has an acute touch of life, which shines in semantic procession, fulfilling the poetic appeal while approximating the original.

Power

In Wei Wang's poems, his depiction and writing of an instant shocking effect can be ranked among the best of all greatest poets. In his translation of Wei Wang's poems, Chao, clearly aware of the poet's art, gives vivid touches and proper representations, which can be illustrated with his translation of two famous poems, that is, *Watching Hunting* and *Birds Twitter o'er the Brook*.

Let's first take *Watching Hunting* for example. This poem is about hunting, consisting of three details, with the overall style of vigor, passion and pride. This kind of style is realized with adjectives denoting an instant shocking effect. And how to achieve a high-light effect equivalent to that of the original in its English translation is a problem to tackle. Meanwhile the artistic technique of the poem is also considered supernatural, as Techien Shen once exclaimed: "This kind of consummation in text, syntax and morphology is rare even in High T'ang Poetry." (*Essays on T'ang Poetry*) Therefore, how to make full use of the intricacy of text, syntax and morphology in translation is a challenge to face. Chao, with his acute apprehension, has tackled the tricky problems one by one in his translation.

Watching Hunting

Against the wind rings the horn bow;
Wei sees the general hunting go.
The hawk looks sharply thru dry grass;
The hoofs tread lightly on snow to pass.
The steeds bolting through Newrich Town
Come back to Thin Willow anon.

He looks back to where he has shot;
It's all quiet and clouds there are not.

Chao deals with the three images, i.e., "角弓鸣,鹰眼疾,马蹄轻" with different syntactical structures based on the ground-figure of the original so that the setting and the instant lightning and thundering, the speed and the force are well presented in the translation. Chao's diction of "Against the wind rings the horn bow" as the setting tells the cause and effect — the wind causes the bow to ring, so that an integration of the images is achieved. In "The hawk looks sharply thru dry grass", Chao treats the hawk as THEME to foreground the predator spotting its prey over grass and the very instant of such an action. This treatment gives a life-like eye-catching picture. In the case of "马蹄轻" translated into "The hoofs tread lightly on snow to pass", Chao may have made reference to the conception of "踏雪无痕", giving a thought to the trace on the snow, hence his wording of "tread" accompanied by "to pass" to showcase the instant of the horse treading on snow and the feel of lightness in contrast with the speed in the previous line. This line, like the previous one, treats "horse" as THEME and "snow" as RHEME for emphasis of AGENT. This dynamic cinematic translation fabulously represents "the most fecund instant" of the original (Tiyung Chiang, "A narratological study in spatial dimension", *Chinese Journal of Social Sciences*, Sept. 19, 2012.), an experience of shocking force and beauty.

Birds Twitter o'er the Brook, another famous poem translated by Chao shows the translator's unique penmanship of a shocking instant and his power of how to convert it into high-grade elegant English. His translation of this poem gives enough attention to the echoing effect entailed in the chirping of the birds in the void hills.

Birds Twitter o'er the Brook
I idle laurel flowers to fall;
Night quiets the vernal hills o'er all.

The moon out, startled birds flutter;
At times, o'er the brook they twitter.

The first two lines follow the word order and rhythm of the original, with juxtaposed images and rhyme that Chao adopts as usual. The crux of the poem is the word "惊" in the line "月出惊山鸟". The moon is soundless, and just because of the dimness and calmness of the void dale, the slow rise of the moon and its pure light shed all around startle the birds in the dale to cheep. This depiction of the instant shocking effect gives the poem a sense of motion in stillness, stillness overriding motion, and motion and stillness befitting. With motion and stillness corresponding and interacting, how a translator can capture this shocking instant that birds are startled in the dale and figuratively display this sound and echo in broad moonlight is the key to success. Chao simplifies what is redundant to reach the utmost similarity, and also gives consideration to semantic compensation in case of self-insufficiency of text. The word "flutter" at the end of line three additionally portrays the dynamic scene of startled birds flying around and enhances the completeness of its poetic environment. In the last line, fully considering the birds' flying images and lingering sounds over the brook, Chao puts "twitter" at the end. Though natural and concise in wording of the translated poem, it still strongly shows Chao's temporal-spatial consciousness and aesthetic reflection in the case of describing landscape and objects.

Shade

Shade here refers to the ever-lasting trace or resonance of a poet's blazing passion interwoven in poetic lines projected on a reader's mind. Particularly in Wei Wang's writings, the universal theme of human emotions across time and space and across national borders has been entrenched as his most well-known poetic lines influencing posterity. As for how to trigger an English reader's similar reflection on a translated poem so that he can "share the same moment though far away", Chao has made a great endeavor as well. Below are two examples of Chao's translations, namely *Seeing Off My Friend Yüan Two to Pacified West as an Envoy* and *On the Ninth Day of the Ninth Moon, Missing Brothers East of the Mountain*.

Seeing Off My Friend Yüan Two to Pacified West as an Envoy is a farewell poem by Wei Wang for sending off his friend Yüan Two at Wei Town to Pacified West, a protectorate set up by the T'ang central government in the west regions of China. The image of "willow" appearing in the first two lines symbolizes farewell in Chinese traditional culture, so Wei Wang used it to create an atmosphere of parting with his friend. When translating the last two time-honored lines, namely"劝君更尽一杯酒,西出阳关无故人" to represent the original's vibe, Chao renders them into English as follows:

> Have one more cup of wine I do maintain;
> West of Sun Pass you have no old fellows.

The very excellency of Chao's translation lies in the clear intervention of English personal pronouns. The appearance of "I" and "you" forms a clearer guest-host relation and highlights the clear and unique friendship between them in the last line. Thus, in the translated text, it forms a one-to-one intimate dialogue, represents the poet's repetitive motion of asking his friend to drink one more cup and expresses the poet's sincere wishes poured into the wine as well as his grief for parting by implication.

Wei Wang's another heptasyllabic quatrain *On the Ninth Day of the Ninth Moon, Missing Brothers East of the Mountain* is themed by a more universal human emotion, that is, nostalgia. The whole poem delicate in specific wording and context, brings to readers a great pleasure to savor its poetic and emotional essence. Good poetic lines, good verse indeed!

Though unpretentious in writing, it has always been a touching poem for countless readers generation after generation. Wei Wang wrote it at the age of 17. For all its plainness and explicitness, it is not at all inferior in its perspective of impressiveness to his later poems featuring mature writing techniques and complex poetic feelings. Moreover, *On the Ninth Day of the Ninth Moon, Missing Brothers East of the Mountain* is one of the 10 clearly dated poems Wei Wang left to us, and it is a representative of his early-age poetry.

On the Ninth Day of the Ninth Moon,
Missing Brothers East of the Mountain
An alien land sees me a lonely soul;
I pine for my dear ones each festive day.
Far off, I know my brothers climb a knoll,
All wearing cornel sprigs but one away.

At that time, Wei Wang should be in Long Peace to seek rank and fame, far away from Sedgeton (now Yungchi in Shanhsi Province), his hometown. He addressed his brothers back home as Brothers East of the Mountain, because Sedgeton was located in the east of Mt. Flower. On Double Ninth Day, he missed his dear ones afar and wrote this poem. There are two difficult points for translation: one is how to translate "异" that appears twice in the first line, so as to highlight the poet's loneliness; the other is how to represent the poet's strong feelings especially the great pity of not being able to go back home on Double Ninth Day.

As for "异乡" and "异客", Chao respectively applies the method of literal translation and liberal translation to represent the original's poetic taste. For the latter, "a lonely soul" is adopted to directly and accurately express the poet's loneliness in a place far off from home. For the second line, Chao translates "亲" into "my dear ones" instead of "family", defining a wider scope covering all relatives and friends emotionally close to himself, and more emphasizing an emotional connection between "亲" and the poet rather than just limiting it to kinship. In terms of logical relation among the sentences, it is well connected to "a lonely soul" above in poetic feelings and environment, and also retains the semantic function of the original line, that is, introducing readers to the following, from a close range of surroundings to a distant vision for homeland afar. When it comes to the third line, Chao adds a lyric subject "I" to further intervene, and express the poet's solitary existence and his sorrow in a remote place far away from home. The special wording "far off" for "遥" is also such a smart choice. The breaking up results in a unique rhyme like a tone of sigh, vividly manifesting a young wanderer's pity for not being able to return home to involve himself in the Double Ninth Day customs like climbing a height. As for the last line, the most touching part of the whole poem, Chao makes a shift of perspective when translating "少一人" without sacrificing the semantic content of the original. Since in the original poem, the poet wrote from the perspective of Brothers East of the Mountain to display his absence for their gatherings, Chao uses a totally different method from that applied to translating the first two lines. By avoiding literal translation like "without me", Chao does not adopt the same perspective as the first two lines, for the reason that it would fail to represent the shift of perspective in the original poem and also incorrectly emphasize an individual's distinctiveness for a group. For this concern, Chao translates "少一人" into "but one away", which literally shows no clear personal subject and then completes the shift of perspective from the poet himself to that from Brothers East of the Mountain. By hiding a specific personal pronoun, the translation clarifies the poet as part of the group, displays the emotional interaction beyond space among all figures involved in the poem, and expresses the poet's nostalgia for homeland. All in all, in Chao's translation, a lonely man in a remote place far away from home on Double Ninth Day is distinctly portrayed, and there is a sharp contrast between "far away from homeland" and "near at heart to his dear ones". Chao with his unfailing eye and attention to details, succeeds in fully and intensively expressing Wei Wang's deep sorrow and confusion brought about by the torturing ambivalence that his homeland is far and but his feeling is near.

Conclusion

Wei Wang is known as "Buddha of Poetry" for the serenity and open-minded beauty hidden between lines that delivers a sense of Zen, making his poems fascinating throughout the ages. In my opinion, it is precisely this kind of beauty that not only maximizes the most moving parts of this literary genre — purity and clarity, but also most entirely shows the characteristics of T'ang Poetry — "Simplicity shows after all flashiness is washed off" (Haowen Yuan: *On Poems: the forth poem*).

On April 6th, 2020, British Broadcasting Corporation (hereinafter, BBC) broadcast a documentary — *Du Fu: China's Greatest Poet*, which is exactly the title of Mr. William Hung's work published by Harvard University Press in 1952. Nearly 70 years later, the first documentary ever made about Fu Tu (Du Fu) in the West follows Hung's definition of Fu Tu's literary stature throughout China. In the documentary, Stephen Owen, a Harvard professor and world-renowned Sinologist, equates Fu Tu with Shakespeare and Dante, arguing that they have created the very values by which poetry is judged. This cultural event is of great significance, which means that after the publication of William Hung's work with its repercussions in the western academic circle, the Western world once again recognizes and affirms Fu Tu as the pioneer and preacher of world civilization. The broadcast of this documentary not only makes Fu Tu the most dazzling Chinese literary IP worldwide in the new century, but also brings the great achievements of Chinese T'ang Poetry to the world's attention in the new era. If we further interpret Stephen Owen's words, we can say that the brilliant names recorded in the history of T'ang Poetry are the creators of the values for appreciating great poetry. This also leads us to a reconsideration, that is, as T'ang Poetry, formed in a country with the oldest living tradition of poetry in the world, is the carrier and proof of the ultimate beauty of Chinese literature, how should we keep on expanding the significance and path of its world communication? There is no doubt that the English translation of T'ang Poetry is an indispensable part of it at any time.

In today's context of globalization, the most outstanding value of the English version of Wei Wang's complete works by Professor Yanchun Chao lies in its excellent reproduction of the most critical aesthetic features of T'ang Poetry — sincerity and purity. Hsiu Ouyang, a poet in the Sung dynasty, once expressed his highest respect for Mo Yin in *Epitaph on Mo Yin*, through closely imitating Yin's writing style. And Professor Yanchun Chao's persistent pursuit of infinite closeness to the original text in the English translation of Wei Wang's poems can also be regarded as an intertemporal meeting between an outstanding contemporary translator and a great poet of the T'ang dynasty. Language refined without redundancy, mind interweaving in underlying words, images reflecting emotion, it can be said that Chao's translation of Wei Wang's works has created the standard whereby to judge the English translations of poetry of the T'ang dynasty.

As a bridge of communication and exchange between different cultures, translation is not only a transcoding play of language, but also a fusion of context, meaning and tradition. It is an inevitable way that prompts us to think deeply and to find out what François Jullien called "l'écart et l'entre"(space and inter-space) of different cultures and finally to build a community with a shared future for mankind. I believe that this is the original power and ultimate purpose of Mr. Chao's spell in translation, which finally turns into charming sound, light, power and shade that run through time, ancient and modern, and across China and the West, restoring T'ang's atmosphere one thousand year ago. In the end, let me try to conclude with the opening words of the BBC's documentary, *Du Fu: China's Greatest Poet:* "In our time, right across the planet, the past is receding from us at an ever faster rate, and that's specially so here in China. But travelers searching for the meaning of China's ancient culture can still find it in China's present."

Ying Wang

Institute of Literature, Chinese Academy of Social Sciences

译者自序

问你：哪个朝代的诗歌最伟大？你可能毫不犹豫：唐朝。要问你谁是唐朝最伟大的诗人，你可能不好回答，因为有好几位难以取舍。如果不选冠亚军而推举几位出类拔萃者便容易得多。王维、李白、杜甫、白居易无疑是最优秀的，他们造就了唐诗的高峰。

这一高峰地球人应该有足够的认识，然而翻译绝非易事，而且误区颇多。最核心的是"道"的缺失。

"形而上者谓之道，形而下者谓之器。"这是《易经》对人类一切知识体系的高度而精准的概括，是人类知识的坐标系，是人类智慧的坐标系。然而，西方启蒙时代打开了思想的"潘多拉的盒子"，将"道"瓦解于无形——诚如《论语》所言："天下之无道也久矣。"在西方学术出现了多次转向之后，中华传统文化的复兴已然发生——集结号已经吹响，"道"的光辉已出现于东方的地平线上。

人类思想的大变革、大繁荣大多肇始于翻译——比如东方的佛经翻译、西方的《圣经》翻译，以及近代以来的西学东渐所带动的种种翻译。中华经典外译始于明朝末年，译者多是西方汉学家、外交家和教会人士。清朝末年以后出现了一些华人译者。

但我们遗憾地发现，诗性的中国经典和诗本身的神采在很大程度上被遮蔽了，正应了罗伯特·弗罗斯特那句话：诗就是翻译中丢掉的东西。

在诸多类别的翻译实践中，文学翻译是最复杂、最难以应对的一种类型，而诗歌翻译又是文学翻译中最值得关注的对象。

人是诗性的存在；诗是人类的家园；诗是人类的表征。作诗与译诗都是以诗来表征我们自身，来表征我们的世界。诗的文学特性在于以有形的文字铺排映现无形的灵魂的跃动。"有形"表现为诗的文字载体或织体特征以及押韵、节奏构成的格律，"无形"即意外之意。诗应和着宇宙的递归性，可表现为符号之符号，它表达意义，又表达意义之意义，言有尽而意无穷。

中国是诗的国度。历史的遗存可以追溯到黄帝时代的《弹歌》。《弹歌》是二字格，是四言体的先驱。四言体古诗在公元前六世纪盛行，随之骚体诗、五言体古诗、七言体古诗和杂言古诗相继成型；进入唐朝，中华民族迎来了诗歌大繁荣，出现五言律体诗、七言律体诗和六言律体诗。

唐朝（公元618—907年）是盛世中的盛世，文学艺术在唐朝达到鼎盛，尤其是在诗歌方面达到了中国文学的巅峰。关于唐朝有多少诗人以及他们写了多少首诗，今人已无法统计，清朝编纂的《全唐诗》共收录四万九千四百零三首，所涉作者共有二千八百七十三人。仅从这些遗存，我们也可以看到唐代文人以体量巨大的诗歌记录了文人风骨和浩荡的盛唐气象。王维、李白、杜甫、白居易无疑是唐朝灿如明珠的诗人中最为耀眼的四人。闲逸如"诗佛"王维，寄情山水，禅意尽见于遣词造句中。浪漫如"诗仙"李白，才情恣意挥洒于诗行间；深刻、沉郁如现实主义诗人杜甫，忧国忧民之思倾注在一字一句中；真诚、清醒如白居易，所思所感皆可见于诗行。四人所作唐诗传世甚多，各领风骚，向后人展示了大唐气象和时代特征。这四位诗人能够代表中国诗歌的高度，在世界文学中也享有崇高的地位。为此，我觉得很有必要把他们留下的六千首诗完整地译成英诗。

西方最早大力进行唐诗英译的是18世纪英国汉学家、诗人詹尼斯（S. Jenyns），译作有《唐诗三百首选读》（*Selections from the 300 Poems of the Tang Dynasty*）和《唐诗三百首选读续集》（*A Further Selections from the 300 Poems of the Tang Dynasty*）。小畑薰良（S. Obata）最早英译了唐代诗人专集，比如1922年在纽约出版的《李白诗集》（*The Works of Li Po，the Chinese Poet*）。其他为唐诗英译做出贡献的英译家还有戴维斯爵士、翟理斯、理雅各、韦利、柳无忌、欧文等等。反观国内，自二十世纪八十年代以来，我国学者、翻译家翻译的唐诗译本有杨宪益与戴乃迭（Gladys）合译的《唐宋诗文选译》（*Poetry and Prose of the Tang and Song*）、徐忠杰翻译的《唐诗二百首新译》（*200 Chinese Tang Poems in English Verse*）、王守义与诺弗尔（J. Neville）合译的《唐宋诗词英译》（*Poems from Tang and Song Dynasties*）、吴钧陶翻译的《杜甫诗英译（一百五十首）》（*Tu Fu One Hundred and Fifty Poems*）、许渊冲翻译的《唐诗三百首新译》（*English-Chinese 300 Tang Poems A New Translation*）、《李白诗选译》（*Selected Poems of Li Bai*）、《唐诗一百五十首英译》（*150 Tang Poems*）等。可见，唐诗的英译版本虽然相对较多，然文言文的晦涩和唐诗独有的文学性为唐诗英译设置了重重障碍，回顾现有的翻译作品，唐诗英译成果并不成系统,译本多零散且译文质量参差不齐,偏离原文甚远,自然传播效果也不甚理想。本该灿如明星的唐诗反而由于翻译的精准程度不匹配而被拉下神坛,中华文化的神采在译文中被遮蔽、被消解。远游的诗神是一个蒙灰的形象,哲学内涵也被误解、被埋没。在当代文明大潮交汇的新形势下,唐诗英译亟待寻求新的翻译方法论作为指导,亟须开辟新思路以走出困局。

翻译虽然基本上表现于文字转换,实质上却蕴含着大学之道。翻译始终以言语系统之间的"易"即言语单位的切换与调变来传情达意,同时也以其与宇宙之间的全息律(holographics)表征着"davar""Brahma""道"。翻译是不乏理论的,但纵观形形色色的西方翻译理论,由于没有形而上的统领和关照,其认识是庞杂的、肤浅的、碎片化的,甚至有的理论竟是颠覆本原、本质以借翻译理论之名行解构翻译理论之实,而传统的准则,比如忠实、对等,乃至文本本身都成了负面的模因而被解构了,翻译成了是其所非的荒谬和无所不是的弥散。

笔者2005年著《翻译学归结论》一书,逆西方潮流而动,以《周易》指向,从众说纷纭的混沌中祭出一个明确的范式,这是摆脱混乱和无定的一个企图。它说:翻译是一个由原则统领的、译者借此进行参数调变与否决的动态系统。由此,译/易的本质是类比的、可拓逻辑的,即化矛盾为不矛盾,变不可译为可译。正如唐朝的贾公彦云:"译即易。谓换易言语使相解也。"语言符号是对抽象语义的表征,无论采取何种表征方式,只要能达到对等的目的即可。翻译的最根本的目的是要传递原汁原味的原文精髓,这绝不是改写,不是操控,更不是通过直译、意译或零翻译就能解决的。它需要译者设身处地,体会原作者的审美情调和意图,通过合理有效的调控,使译文最大限度地贴近原文,最大限度地实现形美、音美和意美的有机统一,即实现译文中各个变量间的平衡与相互制约,使译文自给自足,达致善译。译文虽然在语形和语义上与原文有所差别,但在意旨上又和原文保持高度一致。

自提出翻译学归结论后,笔者在典籍外译实践中就始终以翻译学归结论为理论指导,坚守悬置法则(ceteris paribus rule)即其他条件等同(other things being equal)下的语码转换。大道至简,这是最高效的方法论的起点。在其外围便是翻译生态——翻译伴随翻译生态环境而生。翻译与生态环境,犹如阴阳两种力量,相摩相荡,相生相克,交感成和,生生不息。

具体到诗歌翻译而言，诗的"有形"与"无形"为诗歌翻译带来了避无可避的翻译困境。在中西方诗歌体裁中，诗可以分为散体诗和格律诗两大类：散体诗强调自然、不拘束；格律诗是一种编排，照应生命的律动，在严谨中书写诗意，天各一方的民族还不约而同地造就了格律。世界范围内，英汉诗歌又占据世界诗歌的大半。英诗的格律由四种基调格（抑扬格、扬抑格、抑抑扬格和扬抑抑格）、两种变格（抑抑格和扬扬格）和不同音步数组合而成，再辅以交替韵、搂抱韵和重叠韵构成多种经典诗体。汉语古诗则以极富乐感的方块字写成，它的格律主要涉及四个方面，即押韵、节奏、平仄和歌唱或吟诵行为，通过押韵和平仄实现古诗的表情达意，或热烈欢快，或文静雅致。格律诗的诗体特征之鲜明，直接造成格律诗翻译的壁障。即使诗歌翻译艰难如此，就格律诗的翻译而言，我也是绝不含糊的——这样的诗不允许含糊，此乃格律之谓也。

虽说诗无达诂、译无定法，译者在翻译诗歌时也不可过度夸大主观能动性，更不可任意妄为、随意解构，诗人的思想性和诗的文学性需得到足够的重视，译诗必须为诗。诗歌翻译首先要受到押韵、节奏这一形式因素的制约，甚至说还要满足演唱并可以适当发挥的需要。当然，这只是一个显性的要求。为保证作品的品位，语言、美学、哲学等层面的隐性因素都需要全盘考虑。笔者近年来着力进行典籍英译，其中一大类别就是中国古代诗歌英译。在翻译时，我始终践行的翻译原则就是"以诗译诗，译经如经，是其所是"。

译诗是高度辩证的制衡机制与审美行为。关于翻译标准，我认为：所谓辩证，它是不忠而忠、不等而等的调配；所谓制衡，它是依权重而逐层否决的仲裁；所谓审美，它是以可视、可感、可唱、可听的意象营造而直入心境。翻译必须被赋予一定的自由度。译者可以根据目的或意图的需要，在不影响大体的前提下增加译文的可读性或可唱性，甚至必要时可以做些许改动或牺牲，这样反而能使译文符合原文的初衷。翻译虽然多变，但绝不是没有标准，只是它的标准不是机械的、僵死的、一成不变的，它的最高标准其实就一个字：美。

译好一首诗或一部作品首先要统摄原文要旨和神采，然后用另一种文字恰如其分地再现。何谓再现？再现不是字词的简单对应而是语篇的功能对等——译文与原文在逻辑关系、审美构成和语用意图等各个层面的对应。可见，在诗歌翻译中，逼近原则是首要的——这是翻译及评判的起点和根据；逼近的同时也为达到最佳效果进行灵活调变，以直译尽其可能，意译按其所需的辩证性为旨归。

翻译中国古代诗歌尤其是格律诗时,秉承着"以诗译诗"的翻译原则,笔者首先就要"保留"格律,绝不能以"自由"为托词对其格律任意阉割而损伤诗美。当然,我也不提倡因声损义的凑韵,或为了押韵而把句子搞得怪里怪气,这比平庸还低廉。韵律来自语义或语境,它是构成织综的重要成分,与之不可分割——分割了就不是这首诗了。它服务于整体效果,牵一发而动全身。具体来说,"译诗如诗"即译者在认识到诗的形式是诗的格式或模板的基础上,首先有必要对译文在形式上进行限定。译为无韵的散文体或有韵的参差不一的诗行不符合我的审美取向。译诗虽然无强制性的要求,但在实践中也能提取出便于操作和评估的一般准则。比如英语的一个音步一般为两个音节,而五个音步一般为十个音节,与汉语的七言在形式和内容上可以达到最佳匹配。所以为了便于操作我做了类比性的设定:将汉语三言类比为五音节;将汉语四言类比为六音节;将汉语五言类比为八音节;将汉语六言类比为九音节;将汉语七言类比为十音节;将汉语八言类比为十二音节;将汉语九言类比为十四音节。

其次,由于英汉诗歌中韵诗又占绝大比例,在译汉语韵诗时,译诗也必须押韵且有节奏,"以诗译诗,是其所是"在翻译韵诗时就包括"以韵译韵",这一点不能妥协,但如何押韵以及采用何种韵式则可以由译者自己调整。由于韵或韵式都是类比的,除了特殊的诗体,译诗中的韵式可以相对灵活。我多用偶韵和交叉韵或隔行韵;英诗绝大部分都是抑扬格,也会根据表意的需要夹杂扬抑格、抑抑扬格、扬抑抑格等,译诗也会求诸此类格律。在英译过程中,始终注重翻译的形意张力,避免因韵害义,同时又保证原诗风格的完整再现及诗歌情感、意境、意象等内涵的高度传达,最大化地实现翻译的效度与信度。英诗的格律不像中国的格律诗那样严格,总的原则是音韵和谐。好的译诗必须是不蔓不枝,自然天成的。

再者,除了对诗体、诗韵的保留与再现手段,中国古代诗歌翻译的另一重难点在于对文化名词的翻译处理。中华文化是一个复杂的大系统,内涵深厚,博大精深,可分为形形色色的模块,比如梅兰竹菊、琴棋书画、三皇五帝、三纲五常都是特定文化的产物。并且同一名词在不同文化语境中能够呈现不一样的内涵,中华风物可被赋予不同的内容。在中国古代诗歌英译实践中,一个负责任的译者不可忽视对这类名词的内涵和意义的解释和传达,因为翻译的目的就是不同文明之间的理解互通。对文化名词的妙用往往能体现并塑造文人的个人风格,李白的浪漫主义诗风瑰丽绚烂,白居易、杜甫等诗人的现实主义诗风发人深省，王维的田园山水诗风清新脱俗。译诗也重在译味（translating the taste）。如果仅是简单地释义，这便不是文学翻译而是文字翻译。因此，好的译诗也当一如原诗，文本自足，同时与原文的文学风格最大限度地映现。

对于在英语中无法完全找到对等表达的汉语文化名词时，笔者选择了以注释的形式扩展相关知识。不过，对于译文而言，注释属于副文本（paratext）即独立于译文的另一个文本，背景知识就语篇而言是缺省值（default value），尽管在一定程度上也会影响读者对文本的认知，但对于正文而言不是文本的必要成分，它只是揭示本族语者可能具有的默认知识。而对于英语读者而言，注释却可以在不影响译诗结构和表达的条件下，成为可辅助英语读者理解译文的、有效且必要的文本。作注和译诗是不同的路径，译者不需要想象，不需要发挥，不需要浪漫，但需要查阅、考证、取舍和提炼；同时译者还要借鉴最近的考古发现，如此才能做到用最简练的语言来概括某一注释所需的完整的历史文化要素。对译者而言，作注还能再次验证译文的准确程度，起到查漏、勘误作用，反过来提高翻译质量。

在翻译和作注的过程中，译者对于专有名词必然有很多纠结，担心信息会有所遗漏、扭曲或冗余。笔者认为：为了保全原文信息和可读性，译者在翻译中应尽量避免音译；即便音译，也要照顾西方的阅读习惯，可采用西方读者和海外华人熟悉的威氏拼音；更重要的是翻译要避免编码的夹生，比如中国文化的层级体系的编码是从大至小，而英语则是从小至大，比如"蓝田山石门精舍"译成英语则应该把"蓝天山"的译文置后，如 Stonegate Vihara at Mt. Blue Field，而译作 at Mt. Blue Field Stonegate Vihara 则怪异。同理，"李白"姓李名白，译作"Li Pai"就违反了英语的编码规律，正如把"卡尔·马克思"译作"马克思·卡尔"那样悖谬，而译作"Pai Li"才符合英语的规范。

对于有些特有的中华文化概念如精卫、后羿、颛顼、秀才等，如果音译过滤掉了中国文化的特有意义。译者还需要基于汉语词源和英语构词法在译文中进行合理创译，仿拟汉语的构词法，尽力把词素所表达的意义译出来，这等于向英语输入词汇，利用词汇在文化系统中的互文性，从而帮助英语读者通过上下文推断该词的意义所指。比如"秀才"译作"xiu cai"或"hsiu ts'ai"对于英文读者而言是毫无意义的，而重新编码为"showcharm"，读者则可以产生相应的联想，而随着认知语境的增强，则可以达到等同于原文的认知效果。通过以上翻译策略，译诗可以尽可能保留原诗用典情况，并用脚注形式注释其中出现的历史典故、神话传说、文化习俗等,使读者能够迅速了解诗歌中的典故及文化内涵。可见,注释文本为达成文化互通这一翻译的最终目的也起到了积极的推手作用,一定程度上弥补了语言系统客观差异所带来的文化缺省的难解现象。

言而总之,译者如若在中国古代诗歌英译实践中,贯彻"以诗译诗,是其所是"和逼近原则,尽可能在诗体、诗韵上做到还原和再现,且以注释辅助文化名词的翻译,译诗才能一如原文,做到浅而不白、质而不俗,达成形美、意美、音美的辩证统一,这便逼近等值、等效了。如此说来,在诗歌翻译实践中,译文比肩乃至超越原文是可能的——这取决于如何操控"言尽意"与"言不尽意"的悖论和如何破解翻译的斯芬克斯之谜。

目前放眼译界,译者由于欠缺形而上的元理论意识,对翻译本体论以及语言本体论认识不足,同时欠缺语言各分相学科的系统知识,大多还拘泥于话语层次的静态的语码转换,其译文难免失真、异化。纵观典籍外译,翻译之敝不仅遮蔽了中华文化的神采而且还割裂了中西文化一体性,不仅没能促进文明互通,反而还弄巧成拙,造成更大的"隔阂"。

笔者基于对翻译本体论和语言本体论的深刻认识,以扎实的中华文化经典英译实践为佐证,提出:典籍外译新局面的突破口在于方法论的革新。译者须从翻译本体论出发,将词源学、句法学、语义学乃至哲学、神学等领域融会贯通,突破机械的二元论,以整全的、全息的眼光审察翻译这一悖论性的辩证系统,系统调和可译/不可译等矛盾,在形意张力逼近与趋同当中追求文化、文本的自恰,以期翻译理论的涅槃,使经典外译焕发勃勃生机。

受惠于中华文化复兴这个伟大时代所提供的机遇,我们拥有了便于利用的知识宝库,而国学双语研究也进入了新境界,促进了经典文化翻译的创新。在此背景下,笔者多年来一直思考翻译理论的创新并付诸翻译实践。笔者希望王维、李白、杜甫、白居易的英译可以展示唐诗的面貌,也希望与笔者已出版的其他中华文化典籍和诗歌的英译作品形成呼应,继续提供经得起海内外读者检验、品读的系列译作,为中华文化"走出去"尽一份绵薄之力。

赵彦春

2020 年 9 月 1 日

于上海大学

Introduction by the Translator

If asked which dynasty is the greatest in poetry, you may reply without hesitation: the T'ang dynasty; if further asked who is the greatest poet in the T'ang dynasty, you may feel it uneasy to answer, because there are several too hard to rank. If not required to list the first or second but the best ones, it is much easier. Wei Wang, Pai Li, Fu Tu and Chü-e Pai, no doubt, are among the best. It is they who made the pinnacle of T'ang poetry.

This pinnacle should be well known to all earthlings. But translation is never an easy task and not without traps and fallacies. The most crucial of all is the loss of the Word.

"What is high above is the Word; what is down below is the vessel." This is a detached and exact recapitulation by *The Book of Changes* of the whole system of human knowledge, a coordinate of human knowledge and a coordinate of human wisdom. However, the Enlightenment in the West opened the Pandora's Box of thought and disintegrated the Word into dirt, as is said in *Analects*, "The world has gone astray from the Word for long." While after many turns in the West's academics, the renaissance of traditional Chinese culture has started off. The call to action has been tooted and the dawning of the Word has touched the horizon with a streak of red.

In a large sense, the great revolution or great prosperity of human thought began with translation, for example, the translation of Buddhist scriptures in the East, the translation of the Bible in the West and other kinds of translation brought about by the Eastward Spread of Western Culture in the modern era. The translation of Chinese classics started in the late Ming dynasty and translators at that time were mainly sinologists, diplomats and missionaries, and in the late Ching dynasty, some Chinese translators joined in this undertaking.

Unfortunately, we have come to find that the charm of poetic Chinese classics and poetry itself have been eclipsed to a very large extent, which happens to correspond to Robert Frost's dictum, "Poetry is what gets lost in translation."

Of all kinds of translation practice, literary translation is the trickiest and most complicated, and poetry translation is the most noteworthy kind of translation of all literary genres.

Humans are poetic beings, and poetry is the homeland of humans as well as a representation of humans. Poetry creation and poetry translation are both means of representing ourselves and representing our world. The literariness of poetry is a matter of mapping between the arrangement of visible words and the movement of invisible human souls: its visibility is manifested in what we can see, like words, texture and prosody formed by rhythm and rhyme; its invisibility refers to the meaning out of meaning. Poetry is in correspondence with the recursion of the universe and is embodied as a chain of signs or a sign of signs; it expresses meaning, and even expresses the meaning of meaning. As an old saying goes, words are finite but the meaning beyond words is infinite.

China is a nation of poetry. Its history of poetry can date back to *Song of the Catapult* in the age of Lord Yellow. *Song of the Catapult*, two characters or two syllables a line, is a forerunner of the four-character verse, i. e. , verse of four characters or four syllables a line. The four-character verse flourished in the sixth century B.C. , and then more types of verse came into being, such as the Woebegone form, the five-character old verse, the seven-character old verse and the varying-character old verse. By the T'ang dynasty ushered in a golden age of poetry, when there appeared metrical poems with five characters a line, six characters a line and seven characters a line.

The T'ang dynasty (A.D. 618 – A.D. 907) is the most golden period among all golden times, the pinnacle of achievements in Chinese literature and arts, especially in poetry. In regard of the quantity of poets and poems in T'ang, there is no exact number yet. While it can be seen from *A Complete Collections of T'ang Poems*, a book compiled in the Ching dynasty, there are 49,403 poems produced by 2,873 poets in the T'ang dynasty. From these remains, we can also see that litterateurs then showed their charm and recorded the magnificence of that great age in a great multitude of poems. Wei Wang, Pai Li, Fu Tu and Chü-e Pai are, no doubt, the brightest representative figures of all pearl-like poets in the T'ang dynasty. Detached and delighted in nature, Wei Wang pursued the great Word through wording line by line; romantic and unrestrained, Pai Li implanted his sentiments and talents into poetic lines; incisive and realistic, Fu Tu showed his worries over the nation and people in his poems; sober and percipient, Chü-e Pai expressed his great concerns over his kin, friends and homeland. Their abounding poems, though distinctive in style, altogether mirror the history in different stages of that age. These four poets can represent the pinnacle of Chinese poetry and should have been given a stature in world literature. For this reason, I think it necessary to render their poems, 6,000 in total, into English.

The first sinologist who took pains to translate T'ang poetry is S. Jenyns, a British poet in the eighteenth century, with the fruition of *Selections from the 300 Poems of the Tang Dynasty* and *A Further Selections from the 300 Poems of the Tang Dynasty*. The first one to translate the collected works of a T'ang poet is S. Obata, renowned for *The Works of Li Po, the Chinese Poet* published in New York in 1922. Other pioneers are Sir Davis, H. Giles, J. Legge, A. Waley, Wu-chi Liu, Owen and so on. Chinese translators began to translate T'ang poetry in the 1980s, and representative translated works include *Poetry and Prose of the Tang and Song* by Hsien-e Yang and Gladys Yang, *200 Chinese Tang Poems in English Verse* by Chungchieh Hsu, *Poems from Tang and Song Dynasties* by Shou-e

Wang and J. Neville, *Tu Fu One Hundred and Fifty Poems* by Chunt'ao Wu, *English-Chinese 300 Tang Poems: A New Translation* by Yüanch'ung Hsu, *Selected Poems of Li Bai* by Yüanch'ung Hsu, and *150 Tang Poems* by Yüanch'ung Hsu. As it can be seen, the obscurity of classical Chinese writings and the unique literariness of T'ang poems set many obstacles for the translation of T'ang poetry, existing translated works, though in a relatively large quantity, are far from ideal in quality and are fragmented rather than systematic in scale. So, these translations, too far away from their originals in form and meaning, have resulted in an obviously poor communication effect worldwide by now. T'ang poetry that should have been as luminous as bright stars is now being pulled down from its summit by bad translations, and the glory of Chinese civilization gets dimmed and diminished by bad translations. It also means that the images of Chinese Muses travelling afar are covered with a veil of dust, and that Chinese philosophy has been misunderstood and undermined. Against the background of cultural exchanges, a new methodology is in dire need to guide the rendering of T'ang poetry into English, so that translators can find a way out of the current plight.

Translation, a process of text transformation by and large, has an implication in the Word of the universe. It always includes the transformation between two linguistic systems to convey meanings and express emotions, and also mirrors the universal holographics to represent "davar", "Brahma" or the Word. Though there is no lack of translation theories, we can find no directions from metaphysics for translation studies in Western translation theories. The viewpoints expressed in the so-called theories can be judged as sprawling, shallow and fragmented. Some of them have even overthrown the thing-in-itself of translation and have actually deconstructed the basics of translation. Classic norms such as fidelity, equivalence and the text itself are regarded as negative memes and are deconstructed. Translation has run into a state of what it is not, with the dispersion of its essence into being anything but itself.

In 2005, I published a book *A Reductionist Approach to Translatology*, a book that goes in the opposite direction of Western translation theories. With the guidance of *The Book of Changes*, the book aims to set a clear paradigm out of all current chaos and melee, trying to lead translation studies out of disorder. As it proposes, translation is a dynamical system guided by principles, and translators can take advantage of the mechanism of checks and balances to modulate and veto parameters in the process. Hence, the essence of "trans" conforms to analogy and extenic logic, which means converting contradictoriness into compatibility and untranslatability into translatability. Just as the T'ang Confucian Scholar Kungyen Chia put it, "'yi' (falling tone, meaning trans) is equal to 'yi' (falling tone, meaning changing), namely changing from one parole into another to ensure mutual understanding". Linguistic symbols are just representations of abstract semantic meanings, and all representations can reach the same goal, different they may be. The fundamental purpose of translation is to convey the quintessence of the source text in an original way; and definitely, it is not merely what rewriting or manipulation can achieve, and even far beyond the scope of what is called literal translation, free translation or zero translation. According to *A Reductionist Approach to Translatology*, translators are required to be empathetic enough to comprehend the original's aesthetic perception and intention, and then to reasonably modulate parameters to make the translations approximate to the original as much as possible, so that the beauty in form, sound and meaning can be achieved to the largest extent, that is to say, checks and balances among all variables can be realized, and self-consistent as well as high-quality translations can be produced. Translations, though still different from the original in linguistic symbols, are very likely to be highly consistent with it in semantic meaning and motif.

Since the establishment of the reductionist approach to translatology, it has been the theoretical guide throughout my translation practice, especially that of Chinese classics, abiding by the ceteris paribus rule, namely, transcoding in the condition of other things being equal, and insisting that the great Word is the simplest and is the starting point of a methodology of the highest efficiency. Besides, translation also concerns outer communicative environment, in other words, translation exists, concurrent with it. Translation and the communicative environment, just like the two forces Shine and Shade, which endlessly collide with each other, reinforce each other and counteract each other, two in one and united in one.

In terms of poetry, its visible and invisible poetic features bring inevitable obstacles to translation. Chinese poetry and Western poetry can be generally classified into free verse and rhythmic verse. The former highlights naturalness and freedom in verse, while the latter is a fruit of many nations though far apart, featuring rhythmic rules to represent the rhythm of life itself and the poetic atmosphere behind this restriction of rhythmic rules. Chinese poetry and Western poetry can boast of more than half of all poems ever produced. In respect of Western poetry, there are basic meter patterns including four basic meter patterns (Iambus, Trochee, Anapaest and Dactyl) and two variant meter patterns (Pyrrhic and Spondee), metrical foot patterns and three common rhyming schemes (alternate rhyme as abab, enclosing rhyme as abba and distich as aa), which are the most adopted classical patterns. As for Chinese poetry, it is written in Chinese characters characterized by musicality, and the rhythmic verse features in four aspects, that is, rhyming, rhythm, tone pattern (piânn-tseh) and its chanting style for poets to convey meanings and express emotions, ardent or refined. These clear-cut poetic features of metrical verses directly challenge translators. Despite the difficulty and complexity, I show no perfunctoriness, and perfunctoriness is not allowed in metrical verses.

Admitting that "no final interpretation for literary texts, no definite translation of them either", while translating poetry, translators should not over-exaggerate their initiative, let alone wantonly interpreting and deconstructing original texts. An author's ideology and the literariness of a poem should be given enough emphasis, and its translation should still be a poem in itself. Poetry translation is firstly subject to the need of representing the original's poetic forms like rhyming and rhythm, and then to the needs of chanting or other purposes. Certainly, the requirements above are just overt ones, and to ensure the literariness of the original in the translation, invisible connotations of language, philosophy and aesthetics should all be considered. For years I have been devoted to English translation of Chinese classics, ancient poetry in particular. The ultimate translation principle I have long implemented is "translating poesie into poesie and classic into classic, translating it as it is".

Poetry translation is a highly dialectical system of checks and balances and an aesthetic activity. Speaking of translation criteria, as I see it, being dialectical lies in the modulation of parameters for dynamic fidelity and equivalence through seeming infidelity and in equivalence; checks and balances requires translators to decide whether an element should be preferred or sacrificed layer by layer based on its right weight; in aesthetic terms, poetry translation is expected to create visual and acoustical poetic imagery to impress readers. Translators should be given some independence, hence enabled to enhance the readability of a translated text according to pragmatic purposes without affecting the overall arrangements, and even to change or sacrifice some elements, if necessary, to better represent the original's intention. Translation, though ever-changing in the process, can never do without criteria, and criteria should not be mechanical, rigid or immutable. Its highest standard actually is just one word: beauty.

To produce a quality translation of poetry or literature in general, translators firstly need to fully comprehend the original's motif and style, and then appropriately represent it in another language. What is representation? It is not simple word-to-word equivalence but functional or dynamic equivalence in terms of discourse, namely, the equivalence of the original and the translated text in layers such as logical relationship, aesthetic component and pragmatic intention. This shows that in poetry translation, the principle of proximity is primary, which is the starting point and the basis for translation practice and translation criticism. Translators can flexibly modulate elements to achieve the best possible effect, aiming at the maxim "as literal as is possible, as free as necessary".

When translating ancient Chinese poetry, especially Chinese metrical poems, abiding by the principle of "translating poesie into poesie", I firstly retain the original's metrical features and never misuse a translator's freedom to arbitrarily abandon the original's metrical features at the expense of damaging its poetic beauty. Also, I don't advocate translators to unnaturally pile up rhymes at the cost of damaging meanings and twisting poetic structures. After all, going beyond the limit is as bad as falling short. Rhyme and rhythm are rooted in meaning or context, and as a significant part of poetic structure, they should not be sacrificed. They contribute to the overall poetic effect and will affect the whole body if ignored. Specifically speaking, "translating poesie into poesie" is in the condition that translators have realized the role of poetic form as a poem's base or template, at first fixing the translation's form as a poem. Translating a Chinese poem into an English blank verse or an English rhymed poem uneven in length does not conform to my aesthetic orientation. Though there is no compulsory limit for poetry translation, general translation techniques that are useful for specific performance and evaluation can be summarized from translation practice. For instance, in English, one foot generally consists of two syllables, and accordingly five feet equals ten syllables in English, which can tentatively match seven Chinese characters both in form and content. By analogy, I have set a set of rules below: translating a Chinese three-character line into a pentasyllabic line in English, a Chinese four-character line into a hexasyllabic line, a Chinese five-character line into an octosyllabic line, a Chinese six-character line into an enneasyllabic line, a Chinese seven-character line into a decasyllabic line, a Chinese eight-character line into a twelve-syllable line, and a

Chinese nine-character line into a fourteen-syllable line and so on.

In the second place, as rhymed poems account for the largest part of poems, when translating rhymed Chinese poems, the translations must be in rhyme, as the principle of "translating poesie into poesie, translating it as it is" entails "translating rhyme into rhyme". It is something that a translator should never make a concession to. Of course, a translator can decide which rhyme or which rhyming scheme to use. Since rhymes are something of analogy, except some unique poetic styles or subgenres, the rhyming schemes applied in a translation can be relatively flexible. The commonly used rhyming schemes in my translations include couplets (aa), alternate rhymes (abab) or interlacing rhymes (abcb). Most English poems use Iambus as the meter pattern along with auxiliaries such as Trochee, Anapaest and Dactyl, relevant to the requirement of meaning. A translation can do likewise. During the process, a translator should constantly focus on form-meaning tension, avoid the misuse of rhymes at the cost of damaging meaning, and ensure that the translated poem can possibly represent the original's style, emotion and imagery and then can achieve the validity of, and fidelity to, the original to the largest extent. Metrical patterns of English poetry, unlike those of Chinese metrical poems, are less strict. And the general principle is being harmonious in rhyme. A high-quality translation of a poem should be pithy, smooth and natural.

In the third place, apart from the representation of the original's poetic forms and metrical patterns, one more difficulty for translation is how to translate culture-loaded words. Chinese culture is an ancient civilization of great complexity, incomparable in profoundness and exclusively rich in dimension. It consists of diverse motifs such as plant images and art images, such as "wintersweets, orchids, bamboos and chrysanthemums", "zither, go, calligraphy, and painting", "Three Kings and Five Lords", and "Three Canons and Five Constants", all of which are outcomes of Chinese culture, and a single image can convey different meanings in different contexts and can be given a new content according to a certain language use. In the English translation of practice of Chinese ancient poetry, a responsible translator must never escape from interpreting these images and conveying their connotations in translation, for the reason that the purpose of translation is exactly to promote mutual understanding among all civilizations rather than a dialogue of the deaf. The use of culture-loaded words frequently manifests and shapes a poet's unique style, such as Pai Li's style of romanticism, Chü-e Pai's style of realism and Wei Wang's style of naturalism. Poetry translation also centers on the aesthetics of translating the taste. Simple literal translation is none but translation of words, not translation of literature. In this sense, excellent translations of poems should be as self-consistent as the original as well, and should mirror the original's literary style.

When faced with the occasions of culture default in the English translation of Chinese ancient poems, I choose the way of annotation to provide additional information outside the translated poems. However, in regard of translation, annotations belong to the type of paratext, namely, another text independent of the main body. For Chinese readers, background information of a Chinese ancient poem is a default value, and is not an essential part for the original though it affects Chinese readers' comprehension to some extent. Annotations in Chinese contexts can only reveal hidden knowledge some Chinese readers may need to know while reading, while for English readers, annotations in a translated text can be of great use and significance for them to comprehend the translation, which is an integral whole. Annotating is different from translating in the operational method. While providing annotations, a translator needs not to be imaginative, creative or sensitive, and instead needs to investigate and verify messages, to select those useful out of all and finally to summarize them into definitions. Meanwhile, a translator needs to refer to most recent archaeological findings to ensure that an annotation is able to contain complete and required historic and cultural elements with the most precise expressions. In turn, annotations can verify the degree of accuracy of translations, help translators to check and correct errors, and enhance the quality.

During the process of translation and annotation, translators must be concerned about culture-loaded words, lest some information be lost, distorted or redundant. As far as I can see, to ensure the fidelity to the original's information and readability of its translation, transliteration should be avoided as much as possible; if there is no better method than transliteration, translators should fully attend to westerners' reading habits, for example, I adopt the Wade-Giles romanization, for it has been popular with westerners and overseas Chinese. What is crucial is to avoid the hybridity of recodification, for example, the encoding of the hierarchy of Chinese culture is top-down while in English it is a bottom-up direction, just the opposite, for example, "Stonegate Vihara at Mt. Blue Field", which shows a bottom-up arrangement, is good English while "at Mt. Blue Field Stonegate Vihara" is absurd. Similarly, in "Pai Li", "Pai" is first name while "Li" is family name or surname, it is good English, while "Li Pai" violates the rule of English, just like the case we call Karl Marks "Marks Karl", so preposterous. So, "Pai Li" is the right address.

As for those salient and peculiar words in Chinese culture like Ching Wei, Hou E, Chuan Hsü and hsiuts'ai, considering that their cultural connotations will vanish in translations if transliteration is applied, I suggest that translators coin English words based on Chinese etymology and English word-formation, so as to reveal the original's word origin and introduce new eastern cultural connotations to the English world. This use of lexicon's intertextuality in cultural systems can assist English readers to deduce the signified of culture-loaded words from the translated context. For example, the word "xiu cai" or "hsiu ts'ai" makes no sense to English readers, while the recodification, like "showcharm" can trigger off similar associations, and as the target reader's cognitive environment is improved, he may have the same cognitive effect as source text readers. Through translation strategies mentioned above, a translator will be able to retain the original's allusions in the translated text to the largest extent, and provide annotations via footnotes to explain historical stories, myths, legends, and customs in the original and to delve into their connotations. So to speak, annotations play a positive role in achieving the goal of mutual understanding and compensating for the unintelligibility of cultural default brought about by the facsimiles of translation.

All in all, if a translator abides by the principle of "translating poesie into poesie, translating it as it is" and the principle of proximity while rendering Chinese ancient poetry into English, attempts to represent the original's poetic form and rhyming patterns, and provides annotations to assist translations of culture-loaded words, a translated poem can be concise and insightful, well-worded and refined, achieving the dialectical unity of beauty in form, meaning and musicality, just like the original. In this way, a translated poem can be approximate and equal to the original. Hence, in poetry translation, translations are likely to match and even exceed the original, and it depends on how a translator solves the explicability-unexplicability paradox and how he solves the riddle of Sphinx in translation.

Throughout the current translation studies and practices, it can be seen that most translators are still trapped in the static transformation of language codes at discourse level, due to the lack of a metaphysical metatheory, the ontology of translation and the ontology of language. Inevitably, their translations are unfaithful and distorted. Looking back at the course of translation of Chinese classics, translations at present have overshadowed the glory of Chinese civilization, split the oneness of the East and the West, failed to promote cultural exchanges and ironically turned out to be a barrier for cultural communication.

On the basis of a deep understanding of the ontology of translation and the ontology of language and taking substantial English translation of Chinese classics as solid evidences, I call for the innovation in translation methodology for finding a way out of the *status quo*. I suggest that translators start from the ontology of translation, synthetically apply etymology, syntax, semantics, philosophy and even theology in translation practice, and thus break through mechanical dualism. They are also expected to look upon translation as a dialectical system full of paradoxes from a holistic and holographic viewpoint. In this way, they may systematically reconcile contradictions like the translatability-untranslatability paradox; and they may pursue self-consistence of cultures as well as texts during the process of approximation and convergence in form and meaning. We look forward to the nirvana of translation theories and a refreshed look of translation of Chinese classics.

Thanks to the encouragement of the age, an age of the renaissance of traditional Chinese culture, we have access to the great treasures of knowledge. Along with bilingual studies of Chinese classics stepping into a new stage, we are experiencing the renewal of translation of Chinese classics. In this context, I have been committing myself to academic researches and translation practices for many years. I hope that the translated works of Wei Wang, Pai Li, Fu Tu and Chu-e Pai will give a true picture of what T'ang poetry is like, and that along with my other translated works of Chinese classics, these translations will keep on offering reliable resources for readers in China and overseas and will help Chinese culture to "go global" in a way.

Yanchun Chao
September 1, 2020
Shanghai University

卷 一

目 录
Contents

1　**序言**
　　Introduction

1　**译者自序**
　　Introduction by the Translator

1　过秦皇墓
　　A Visit to Emperor First's Grave

3　题友人云母障子
　　To a Friend's Mica Screen

4　九月九日忆山东兄弟
　　On the Ninth Day of the Ninth Moon, Missing Brothers East of the Mountain

5　洛阳女儿行
　　A Beauty in Loshine

8　西施咏
　　Ode to West Maid

10　李陵咏
　　Ode to Ridge Li

12　桃源行
　　Shangrila

15　赋得清如玉壶冰
　　As Clear as Ice in the Jade Pot

17　息夫人
　　Lady Hsi

18	从岐王过杨氏别业应教	
	A Visit to Yang's Cottage with Prince of Offset, a Poem in Reply to His Highness	
20	从岐王夜宴卫家山池应教	
	Attending a Feast with Prince of Offset at Wei's Hill Pool, in Reply to His Highness	
22	敕借岐王九成宫避暑应教	
	Spending the Summer in Green Palace with Prince of Offset at Royal Order, In Reply to His Highness	
24	送綦毋潜落第还乡	
	Adieu to Ch'ien Ch'iwu Who's Failed Grand Test	
27	燕支行	
	Marching to Mt. Rouge	
30	扶南曲歌词五首	
	Tune of Funam, Five Poems	
30	其一	
	No. 1	
31	其二	
	No. 2	
32	其三	
	No. 3	
33	其四	
	No. 4	
34	其五	
	No. 5	
35	少年行四首	
	The Lads, Four Poems	
35	其一	
	No. 1	
36	其二	
	No. 2	
37	其三	
	No. 3	

38	其四	
	No. 4	
39	被出济州	
	Exiled to Chichow	
41	登河北城楼作	
	Composed on the Tower North of the River	
42	宿郑州	
	Putting Up for the Night in Chengchow	
44	早入荥阳界	
	Rowing into Hsingshine in the Morning	
46	至滑州隔河望黎阳忆丁三寓	
	Arriving in Huachow and Looking at Lishine Across the River While Missing Sanyü Ting	
47	济上四贤咏	
	Ode to Four Sages in Chichow	
47	崔录事	
	To Secretary Ts'ui	
48	成文学	
	To Wenhsüeh Ch'eng	
50	郑霍二山人	
	To Two Immortals, Cheng and Huo	
52	寓言二首	
	Two Allegories	
52	其一	
	No. 1	
54	其二	
	No. 2	
56	和使君五郎西楼望远思归	
	Gazing Homeward on West Tower—In Reply to Prefect Boy Five	
58	渡河到清河作	
	Crossing the River to Blue River County	
60	鱼山神女祠歌二首	
	Goddess Shrine on Mt. Fish, Two Poems	

60	迎神	
	Expecting Goddess	
62	送神	
	Seeing Off Goddess	
63	济州过赵叟家宴	
	Attending Old Chao's Family Feast in Chichow	
65	寄崇梵僧	
	To Monk of Sanskrit Hall	
66	赠东岳焦炼师	
	To Great Master Chiao on Mt. East	
69	赠焦道士	
	To Master Chiao, the Wordist	
71	赠祖三咏	
	To Tsu Three	
73	喜祖三至留宿	
	Keeping Tsu Three for the Night	
74	齐州送祖三	
	Seeing Off Tsu Three at Ch'ichow	
75	寒食汜上作	
	Composed on the River Ssu on Cold Food Day	
76	观别者	
	Watching Those Parting	
78	偶然作	
	Composed Accidentally	
78	其一	
	No. 1	
80	其二	
	No. 2	
82	其三	
	No. 3	
84	其四	
	No. 4	

86	其五 No. 5	
88	淇上即事田园 The Field on the Ch'i, an Impromptu	
89	淇上别赵仙舟 Farewell to Fairyboat Chao on the Ch'i	
90	不遇咏 Ode to My Unfulfilled Life	
92	送严秀才还蜀 Sending Off Yan, a Showcharm, to Shu	
94	送孟六归襄阳 Seeing Meng Six Off to Sowshine	
95	送权二 Seeing Off Ch'üan Two	
97	华岳 Mt. Flower	
100	自大散以往深林密竹磴道盘曲四五十里至黄牛岭见黄花川 To the Depth of Bamboo from Tasan Pass, Following the Ascending Path, Which Turns and Twists for About Twenty Miles till I Arrive at Ox Ridge and See the Yellow Flower Stream	
102	青溪 A Blue Stream	
104	纳凉 Enjoying the Cool	
106	戏题盘石 Dedication to the Boulder for Fun	
107	晓行巴峡 Rowing to Pa Gorge at Dawn	
109	赠房卢氏琯 To Kuan Fang, Magistrate of Lushi	
111	送从弟蕃游淮南 Seeing Off My Cousin Fan to Huainan	

114	送崔兴宗	
	Seeing Off Hsingtsung Ts'ui	
116	归嵩山作	
	Back to Mt. Tower	
117	上张令公	
	To Chang, Premier of Privy Council	
120	东溪玩月	
	Playing with the Moon by the East Stream	
122	山中寄诸弟妹	
	To My Siblings from the Mountains	
123	献始兴公	
	To Count of Rising	
125	留别山中温古上人兄并示舍弟缙	
	To Reverent Wenku, a Hermit, and Shown to My Younger Brother, Chin Wang	
127	过乘如禅师萧居士嵩丘兰若	
	A Visit to Buddhist Hsiao Called Zen Master Yana at Grove Calm on Mt. Tower	
129	过太乙观贾生房	
	A Visit to Sheng Chia's Room at Temple of the One	
131	故南阳夫人樊氏挽歌	
	Elegies to Deceased Lady Fan, Countess of Southshine	
131	其一	
	No. 1	
133	其二	
	No. 2	
134	韦给事山居	
	The Cottage of Wei, an Imperial Inspector	
136	同卢拾遗过韦给事东山别业二十韵，给事首春休沐，维已陪游，及乎是行，亦预闻命，会无车马，不果斯诺	
	A Visit to Inspector Wei's East Hill Cottage with Advisor Lu, Twenty Couplets. I Would Accompany the Inspector Who Was On His Early Spring Leave, But I Failed to Keep My Promise Because I Was Told My Cart Was Not Available to This Trip	

140	韦侍郎山居	
	To the Cottage of Wei, a Ministerial Aide	
142	和尹谏议史馆山池	
	In Reply to Remonstrant Yin at Hill Pool of Imperial Archive	
143	赠徐中书望终南山歌	
	Gazing at the Southern Mountains, to Hsu, Vice Premier of Privy Council	
144	寄荆州张丞相	
	To Premier Chang at Chaston	
145	使至塞上	
	To the Front as an Envoy	
147	出塞作	
	Beyond the Border	
149	凉州郊外游望	
	Gazing on the Suburbs of Coolton	
151	凉州赛神	
	Racing with a God at Coolton	
152	双黄鹄歌送别(时为节度判官,在凉州作)	
	My Singing Goodbye to Two Yellow Swans (I was an assistant military governor and this poem was composed at Coolton)	
154	从军行	
	A Border War	
156	陇西行	
	A West Bulge Poem	
157	陇头吟	
	A Song at Mt. Bulge	
159	老将行	
	An Old General	
162	送崔三往密州觐省	
	Seeing Off Ts'ui Three to See His Parents	
163	灵云池送从弟	
	Seeing Off My Cousin at Soul Cloud Pool	

164	送岐州源长史归（源与余同在崔常侍幕中，时常侍已殁）	

Seeing Off Vice Governor Yüan Back to Offset (Yüan and I Are Both in the Tent Office of Royal Servant Ts'ui, Who Is Dead Now)

166 晦日游大理韦卿城南别业四首
A Visit to the Cottage of Wei, Chief of Jurisdiction on the Last Day of the First Moon, Four Poems

166 其一
No. 1

168 其二
No. 2

170 其三
No. 3

172 其四
No. 4

174 资圣寺送甘二
Seeing Off Kan Two at Aiding Saints Monastery

176 哭孟浩然
Mourning Haojan Meng

177 汉江临泛
Boating on the River Han

179 送封太守
Seeing Off Prefect Feng

181 送康太守
Seeing Off Prefect K'ang

183 送宇文太守赴宣城
Seeing Off Prefect Yüwen to Hsuan

185 登辨觉寺
Climbing to Discernment Temple

187 谒璿上人
Paying Respect to Great Master Hsuan

190 送邢桂州
Seeing Off Hsing to Cassiaton

192 千塔主人
To Host of Kilopagoda

194	赠裴旻将军	
	To General Min P'ei	
195	送赵都督赴代州得青字	
	Seeing Off Governor Chao to Taichow	
197	终南山	
	The South Mountains	
199	终南别业	
	My Villa at the South Mountains	
201	白鼋涡	
	White Soft-shell Turtle	
203	投道一师兰若宿	
	Putting Up for the Night at Grove Calm When Visiting Master Word One	
205	戏赠张五弟諲三首	
	Three Poems for Fun to Chang Five, a Brother	
205	其一	
	No. 1	
207	其二	
	No. 2	
209	其三	
	No. 3	
211	答张五弟	
	My Answer to Brother Chang Five	
212	送陆员外	
	Seeing Off Counselor Lu	
214	三月三日曲江侍宴应制	
	In Reply to Your Majesty's Call to Compose a Poem for the Feast on the Bent on the Third Day of the Third Moon	
216	送丘为落第归江东	
	Seeing Off Wei Ch'iu Back East, Who Failed Grand Test	
218	奉和圣制庆玄元皇帝玉像之作应制	
	In Reply to Your Majesty's Call to Follow Your Majesty's Poem: Celebration of the Carving of Emperor Dark One's Jade Statue	

220	和仆射晋公扈从温汤（时为右补阙）	
	In Reply to Lord of Chin Escorting His Majesty to Hotspring (Me as a Right Remonstrant)	
223	哭祖六自虚	
	Wailing Tzuhsu Tsu Six	
229	春日直门下省早朝	
	Morning Levee in Spring When I Am on Duty in Undergate Department	
231	送綦毋校书弃官还江东	
	Seeing Off Collator Ch'iwu, Who's Resigned, to the East	
233	青龙寺昙壁上人兄院集	
	Master Cloud Jade in Blue Dragon Temple	
235	酬黎居士淅川作	
	Thanking Li, a Lay Buddhist in Rustle River	
237	哭殷遥	
	Wailing Yao Yin	
239	送殷四葬	
	Back from Yin Four's Funeral	
240	班婕妤三首	
	Lady Fair, Three Poems	
240	其一	
	No. 1	
241	其二	
	No. 2	
242	其三	
	No. 3	
243	奉和圣制幸玉真公主山庄因题石壁十韵之作应制	
	In Reply to Your Majesty's Call to Follow Your Majesty's Poem: the Inscription on the Precipice by Her Imperial Highness Princess Jade True's Cottage, a Twenty-line Rhyme	
246	新秦郡松树歌	
	A Song of Pines in New Ch'in	

247	榆林郡歌	
	Song of Elm Wood Prefecture	
248	送高道弟耽归临淮作	
	Seeing Off Tan Kao, Tao Kao's Brother Going Back to Linhuai	
252	奉和圣制送不蒙都护兼鸿胪卿归安西应制	
	In Reply to Your Majesty's Call to Follow Your Majesty's Poem: Seeing Off Fumeng, Governor and Grandee, to Pacified West	
254	故西河郡杜太守挽歌三首	
	Three Elegies to Tu, Prefect of West River County	
254	其一	
	No. 1	
255	其二	
	No. 2	
256	其三	
	No. 3	
257	苑舍人能书梵字兼达梵音，皆曲尽其妙，戏为之赠	
	A Poem for Fun to Secretary Yüan, Who Can Write Sanskrit Characters and Knows Sanskrit Music	
259	重酬苑郎中	
	To Secretary Yüan Again	
260	同比部杨员外十五夜游有怀静者季	
	A Night Tour with Counselor Yang from the Inspection Office and Chi, a Monk, on the Fifteenth Night	
263	达奚侍郎夫人寇氏挽词二首	
	Two Elegies for Lady K'ou, Ministerial Aide Tahsi's Wife	
263	其一	
	No. 1	
265	其二	
	No. 2	
266	赠李颀	
	To Ch'i Li	
268	送缙云苗太守	
	Seeing Off Miao, Prefect of Redsilk to His Post	

270 大同殿产玉芝龙池上有庆云神光照殿百官共睹圣恩便赐宴乐敢书即事
Ganoderma Grows on a Column of Concord Hall and There Appear Auspicious Clouds Over Dragon Pool, As All Officials See, Hence His Majesty Grants a Feast. I Take the Liberty to Compose This Poem.

272 奉和圣制天长节赐宰臣歌应制
In Reply to Your Majesty's Call to Follow Your Majesty's Poem: To Premier on Longevity Day

274 奉和圣制登降圣观与宰臣等同望应制
In Reply to Your Majesty's Call to Follow Your Majesty's Poem: Ascending to Saint Descending Temple and Gazing with Premier

276 送张五归山
Seeing Off Chang Five Back to the Hills

277 送张五諲归宣城
Seeing Off Yin Chang Five Back to Hsuan

279 待储光羲不至
Waiting for Kuanghsi Ch'u in Vain

280 奉寄韦太守陟
To Prefect Chih Wei

282 酬比部杨员外暮宿琴台朝跻书阁率尔见赠之作
Thanking Counselor Yang from the Inspection Office, Who Puts Up for the Night at Lute Hall, Ascends to the Book Loft and Writes Me His Poem

284 故太子太师徐公挽歌四首
Four Elegies for Lord of Hsu, Crown Prince's Teacher

284 其一
No. 1

286 其二
No. 2

287 其三
No. 3

289 其四
No. 4

290	送崔九兴宗游蜀	
	Seeing Off Hsingtsung Ts'ui Nine to Travel Shu	
292	与卢员外象过崔处士兴宗林亭	
	Visiting Staff Ts'ui's Pavilion with Ministry Counselor Lu	
293	青雀歌	
	A Song of the Blue Sparrow	
294	崔九弟欲往南山马上口号与别	
	An Impromptu on My Horse to Brother Ts'ui Nine When He's Leaving for the Southern Hills	
295	奉和圣制御春明楼临右相园亭赋乐贤诗应制	
	In Reply to Your Majesty's Call to Follow Your Majesty's Poem: Climbing Spring Bright Tower Overlooking Right Premier's Pavilion, Hence a Poem for the Lords	
297	故人张諲工诗善易卜兼能丹青草隶顷以诗见赠	
	My Friend Yin Chang Good at Versification, Divination, and Writing Cursive and Square Styles Presents Me with an Impromptu	
299	秋夜独坐怀内弟崔兴宗	
	Missing Hsingtsung Ts'ui, My Cousin When I Sit Alone on an Autumn Night	
301	送徐郎中	
	Seeing Off Secretary Hsu	
303	敕赐百官樱桃	
	Offering Cherries to Officials upon the Imperial Order	
305	晚春归思	
	Her Alone in Late Spring	
307	送李睢阳	
	Seeing Off Suiyang Li	
310	送魏郡李太守赴任	
	Seeing Off Prefect Li to His Prefecture of Way	

过 秦 皇 墓

古墓成苍岭，
幽宫象紫台。
星晨七曜隔，
河汉九泉开。
有海人宁渡，
无春雁不回。
更闻松韵切，
疑是大夫哀。

A Visit to Emperor First's Grave

His mausoleum's like a hill green;
A palace it is, one might ween.
The sun, the moon, the stars align;
The Milky Way does all outshine.
The mercury stream does there flow;
The golden wild geese seem to crow.
You may hear the sough of the pine;
Is it the grandees there that whine?

---

* Emperor First: Emperor First (259 B.C.- 210 B.C.), the founding emperor of Ch'in who wiped out all the other states and established the first unified empire of China. He was universally acknowledged as a great politician, strategist, reformer, and an iron hand tyrant, who laid the political layout of China after the Ch'in dynasty till now.
* The sun, the moon, the stars align: The sun is a star, the source of light and heat of the earth, and the moon the satellite of the earth, a representative of shade or feminity of things. In a universe animated by the interaction of Shade and Shine

energies, the moon is Shade visible, the very germ or source of Shade, and the sun is the power station of Shine.

* mausoleum: the tomb of Mausolus, king of Caria, at Halicarnassus; included among the seven wonders of the ancient world, a metaphor for a large, imposing tomb or a building with vaults for the entombment of a number of bodies.
* the Milky Way: a model of the Milky Way in Emperor First's mausoleum. The Milky Way is called the Silver River in Chinese mythology, which is a luminous band circling the heavens composed of stars and nebulae visible to the naked eye; the Galaxy. As legend goes, the Milky Way maid, the granddaughter of Emperor of Heaven fell in love with a worldly cowherd and they gave birth to a son and a daughter. When their love was disclosed to Emperor of Heaven, he sent Queen Mother to take the fairy back to Heaven. While Cowherd was trying to catch up in a boat the cow had made with its horn broken, Queen Mother rived the air with her hair pin, so there appeared the Silver River, i.e., the Milky Way to keep them apart, and the fairy and the cowherd became two stars called Vega and Altair.
* the mercury stream: In Emperor First's underground palace there flow rivers filled with mercury not only for splendor but also for the protection of his body and burial objects and the precaution against tomb robbing.
* golden wild geese: sculpted wild geese of gold in Emperor First's mausoleum. A wild goose is esteemed in Chinese culture for being caring and responsible, taken as a symbol of benevolence, righteousness, good manner, wisdom and faith.
* pine: a cone-bearing tree having needle-shaped evergreen leaves growing in clusters, a symbol of longevity and solitude in Chinese culture.

题友人云母障子

君家云母障，
时向野庭开。
自有山泉入，
非因采画来。

To a Friend's Mica Screen

Your mica screen, made of stuff hard,
You often take it to your yard.
A spring from the mountains flows on;
No paint can make it so well done.

* mica screen: an exquisite screen made of mica, a mineral called silicate in various shapes and hues, having natural veins or lines like a painting, which may be colorless, jet-black, transparent or translucent.

九月九日忆山东兄弟

独在异乡为异客,
每逢佳节倍思亲。
遥知兄弟登高处,
遍插茱萸少一人。

On the Ninth Day of the Ninth Moon, Missing Brothers East of the Mountain

An alien land sees me a lonely soul;
I pine for my dear ones each festive day.
Far off, I know my brothers climb a knoll,
All wearing cornel sprigs but one away.

* the Ninth Day of the Ninth Moon: referring to Double Ninth Day, i.e., the ninth day of the ninth moon in Chinese Lunar calendar. There is a long tradition that people climb a height and enjoy chrysanthemums on this day to commemorate their ancestors.
* cornel: a kind of dogwood with hard, compact wood, whose sprays are carried or worn on Double Ninth Day to exorcise evil spirits.

洛阳女儿行

洛阳女儿对门居,
才可颜容十五余。
良人玉勒乘骢马,
侍女金盘鲙鲤鱼。
画阁朱楼尽相望,
红桃绿柳垂檐向。
罗帷送上七香车,
宝扇迎归九华帐。
狂夫富贵在青春,
意气骄奢剧季伦。
自怜碧玉亲教舞,
不惜珊瑚持与人。
春窗曙灭九微火,
九微片片飞花琐。
戏罢曾无理曲时,
妆成祗是熏香坐。
城中相识尽繁华,
日夜经过赵李家。
谁怜越女颜如玉,
贫贱江头自浣纱。

A Beauty in Loshine

A Loshine belle lives opposite my room;
She is about fifteen, just in full bloom.
Her husband rides a horse with jewels laid;

A plate of braised carp is served by a maid.
Her red tower with frescoes does at me gaze;
A twig of peach from her to the eaves sways.
Her canopied cart of incense wood fine
Sends her to her tent painted with flowers nine.
Her husband in full prime is full of pride;
The richest man he can beat and deride.
Concubines he trains how to dance and sing
And gives precious corals as a cheap thing.
His lamp goes out from the window at dawn,
With snuffs a-flying like a painting drawn.
No time to practice scores, she plays all day;
By the incense, well-dressed, she talks away.
Her relatives in the town are rich men;
One can see her powerful guests now and then.
West Maid in Yüeh, a beauty like a dream,
So poor, can but wash yarn in the Yeh Stream.

* carp: fresh water food fish (*Ciprinus carpiao*), originally of China, now widely distributed in Europe and America, a mascot in Chinese culture, symbolizing great success and harmony. A popular idiom "a carp jumping over the Dragon Gate" means climbing up the social ladder or succeeding in the imperial civil service examination.
* coral: the hard, stony skeleton secreted by certain marine polyps and often deposited in extensive masses forming reefs and atolls in tropical seas.
* peach: any tree of the genus *Prunus Percica*, blooming brilliantly and bearing fruit, a fleshy, juicy, edible drupe, considered sacred in China, a symbol of romance, prosperity and longevity.
* concubine: a female cohabitant or secondary wife. China was a polygamous society from prehistoric years till the first half of the twentieth century. An ordinary man could have three wives and four concubines and a concubine, seen as a property, could be bartered or sold or given as a gift in ancient China.
* Loshine: Loyang if transliterated, the eastern of the two great cities that often served as capitals in the early Chinese dynasties, and second city of the Empire in T'ang

times, when it had about 800,000 inhabitants.
* West Maid: once a laundry lady in the State of Yüeh, which was then a tributary to the State of Wu. Because of her beauty, West Maid was selected to be trained in a Yüeh palace, and sent to the King of Wu as a spy. She quickly won the king's affection, making him indulged in her charm. As a result, the State of Wu waned and perished.
* incense: an aromatic substance that exhales perfume during combustion, burnt before a Buddhist, Wordist or any religious or ancestral figure as an act of worship, usually offered with a prayer or vow.
* Yüeh: the State of Yüeh (2,032 B.C.- 222 B.C.), a vassal state under Hsia, Shang and Chough in Southeast China in the Spring and Autumn period. As a regime, it was founded by Nothing Left (Wuyü), King Young Health (Shaok'ang) of Hsia's born of a concubine.
* the Yeh Stream: or the Joyeh Stream, a stream in the south of present-day Shaohsing. It is said that West Maid did her laundry here.

西 施 咏

艳色天下重，
西施宁久微。
朝仍越溪女，
暮作吴宫妃。
贱日岂殊众，
贵来方悟稀。
邀人傅香粉，
不自著罗衣。
君宠益骄态，
君怜无是非。
当时浣纱伴，
莫得同车归。
持谢邻家子，
效颦安可希。

Ode to West Maid

Since beauty is by the world praised,
How can West Maid be long debased?
Dawn sees her wash yarn by the Yeh;
Dusk inside Wu's harem finds her.
When low, was she different somewhere?
Now high, she is found a belle rare.
To rouge her face girl servants bow;
She need not dress by herself now.
The king favors her for her glare;

She's right or wrong, he does not care.
Her mates who did wash yarn before
Cannot share her cart any more.
East Maid, please listen and calm down;
It's no use mimicking her frown.

* West Maid: also known as Miss West, one of the most beautiful women in Chinese history, once a laundry lady in the State of Yüeh (2032 B.C.- 222 B.C.). Because of her beauty, West Maid was selected to be trained in Yüeh's palace, and sent to the King of Wu as a spy. She quickly won the king's affection with her charm. Through her manoeuvres, the State of Wu waned and perished.
* the Yeh: the Joyeh Stream, a stream in the south of modern-day Shaohsing. It is said that West Maid used to do her laundry here.
* Wu: the State of Wu (12th Century B.C - 473 B.C.), a southern vassal state of Chough, founded by Usetwo, King Civil of Chough's uncle in the early years of Chough, and subjugated and annexed by the State of Yüeh in 437 B.C.
* East Maid: Miss West's ugly neighbor, who was sneered at for having mimicked West Maid or Miss West's frowning because she looked even uglier when frowning.

李　陵　咏

汉家李将军，
三代将门子。
结发有奇策，
少年成壮士。
长驱塞上儿，
深入单于垒。
旌旗列相向，
箫鼓悲何已。
日暮沙漠陲，
战声烟尘里。
将令骄虏灭，
岂独名王侍。
既失大军援，
遂婴穹庐耻。
少小蒙汉恩，
何堪坐思此。
深衷欲有报，
投躯未能死。
引领望子卿，
非君谁相理。

Ode to Ridge Li

The Han had a glorious name Li,
Three generals, generations three.
Ridge came of age with a great plan;

Though young, he became a great man.
To the front, ahead he did go,
Go ahead to Chanyü, the foe.
Banners and streamers made a line,
Flutes and war drums did sadly whine.
Dusk fell on the desert so vast;
The war cries stirred up dust, up cast.
The general would all terminate,
Not just the chieftain subjugate.
But in need he received no aid;
To surrender there he was made.
He'd been favored by Han since young;
With such a disgrace he was stung.
His Majesty's grace he'd repay;
He'd die for that to have his day.
He raised his eyes towards Wu Su:
Who can understand me now, who?

* the Han: the powerful Han Empire (202 B.C.- A.D. 220) founded by Pang Liu, one of the greatest empires in Chinese history, earlier than, and concurrent with, the Roman Empire (27 B.C.- A.D. 476), with an area of six million and nine square kilometers, including Korea in the east, Vietnam in the south, Mt. Wild Leek in the west and Gobi in the north.
* Ridge Li: Ling Li (134 B.C.- 74 B.C.), the grandson of the outstanding General Broad Li. Ridge Li surrendered to the Huns after defeat, and completely broke off with the Han court when Lord Martial killed his family, believing the rumor.
* Chanyü: the title of a Hun chieftain, the sovereign of alien nations.
* Wu Su: Wu Su (140 B.C.- 60 B.C.), a minister of Han. On his diplomatic mission, Su was detained. The Huns tried to make him surrender with threats and promises, only to fail. Then, he was sent to North Sea, today's Baikal Lake in Siberia, Russia, to be a shepherd. Through all kinds of hardship, Su finally came back to Han after 19 years' detention. During the 19 years, Wu Su had never surrendered.

桃 源 行

渔舟逐水爱山春,
两岸桃花夹古津。
坐看红树不知远,
行尽青溪不见人。
山口潜行始隈隩,
山开旷望旋平陆。
遥看一处攒云树,
近入千家散花竹。
樵客初传汉姓名,
居人未改秦衣服。
居人共住武陵源,
还从物外起田园。
月明松下房栊静,
日出云中鸡犬喧。
惊闻俗客争来集,
竞引还家问都邑。
平明闾巷扫花开,
薄暮渔樵乘水入。
初因避地去人间,
及至成仙遂不还。
峡里谁知有人事,
世中遥望空云山。
不疑灵境难闻见,
尘心未尽思乡县。
出洞无论隔山水,
辞家终拟长游衍。
自谓经过旧不迷,

安知峰壑今来变。
当时只记入山深,
青溪几度到云林。
春来遍是桃花水,
不辨仙源何处寻。

Shangrila

A fishing boat rows twixt the hills in spring;
Peach flowers to the old ford a new life bring.
He forgets the distance, watching pink trees;
Now at the end of the stream none he sees.
He tip-toes in from the hill to a nook;
The cliffs part to a plain, a sunny look.
Afar, the trees tower to merge with the blue;
At hand, all homes thrive with blooms and bamboo.
Baffled at a folk's garment still of Ch'in,
The fisher tells reigns, from Han to begin.
Of yore they came to Marsridge to abide
And opened fields, off from the world outside.
The moon sieves thru pines to huts and pens quiet;
The sun drives the clouds, dogs and fowls run riot.
Surprised that someone's come, to him they run;
All ask him to the hometown what's been done.
At dawn, early risers off streets blooms broom;
In dusk, fishermen by water come home.
Their forebears fled the outrages of the time;
They never returned from this godly clime.
In this vale who knows if others exist;
Maybe a world's beyond the mounts in mist.

No doubt this blessed place is the best to dwell;
But sometimes his nostalgia does repel.
So he goes out and goes back the old way;
Soon he'll come back and longer he will stay.
He's sure the path he's taken he knows well;
But peaks and vales change, more than he can tell.
He but remembers it's deep in hills then
And the stream bends and twists to the peach glen.
The water's strewn with peach blooms near and far;
He knows not how to get to Shangrila.

* Shangrila: an idyllic utopia, a land free of tyranny and exploitation, also known as Peach Blossom Source in Chinese culture as this poem shows.
* peach: any tree of the genus *Prunus Percica*, blooming brilliantly and bearing fruit, a fleshy, juicy, edible drupe, considered sacred in China, a symbol of romance, prosperity and longevity.
* Han: the powerful Han Empire (202 B.C.- A.D. 220) founded by Pang Liu, Emperor Highsire of Han, one of the greatest empires in Chinese history, earlier than, and concurrent with, the Roman Empire (27 B.C.- A.D. 476), with an area of six million and nine square kilometers, including Korea in the east, Vietnam in the south, Mt. Wild Leek in the west and Gobi in the north.
* Marsridge: the location of Peach Blossom Source, as is described by Poolbright T'ao.
* dog: a domesticated carnivorous mammal (*Canis familiaris*), of worldwide distribution and many varieties, noted for its adaptability and its devotion to man. The dog was domesticated in China at least 8,000 years ago and was often used as a hunter, as a poem in *The Book of Songs* says: "The dog bells clink and clink; / The hunter's handsome, a real pink."
* fowl: the common domestic cock, hen or chicken, poultry in general. The domestication of the fowl in China was begun more than 5,000 years ago according to archaeological finds.
* Ch'in: the Ch'in State or the State of Ch'in (905 B.C - 206 B.C.), enfeoffed as a dependency of Chough by King Piety of Chough in 905 B.C and enfeoffed as a vassal state by King Peace of Chough in 770 B.C. In the ten years from 230 B.C. to 221 B.C., Ch'in wiped out the other six powers and became the first unified regime of China, i.e., the Ch'in Empire.

赋得清如玉壶冰

玉壶何用好,
偏许素冰居。
未共销丹日,
还同照绮疏。
抱明中不隐,
含净外疑虚。
气似庭霜积,
光言砌月馀。
晓凌飞鹊镜,
宵映聚萤书。
若向夫君比,
清心尚不如。

As Clear as Ice in the Jade Pot

What's the best use of a jade pot?
It's best for ice, for others not.
It does not thaw beneath the sun,
As if the window's brightly shone.
It's transparent and clear throughout;
There is nothing in, one may doubt.
It's pure as if there gathers frost,
As can outshine the steps so glossed.
At morn, it's like a mirror bright;
At night, it offers fireworm light.
If we compare you with the ice,

You are far better, clear and nice.

* jade pot: also called ice pot that is transparent and crystal clear, a pot usually alluding to the integrity or purity of the holder's heart and sometimes referring to the pure world of immortality, where elixirs are concocted.
* sun: the heavenly body that is the center of attraction and the main source of light and heat in the solar system, a representation of Shine in contrast with Shade, the moon, in Chinese culture, a symbol of hope, life, strength, vigor and youth.
* fireworm: also called firefly or glowworm, which appears in or over grass at night in summer and can be put in a transparent bottle or jade pot to offer light.

息 夫 人

莫以今时宠,
能忘旧日恩。
看花满眼泪,
不共楚王言。

Lady Hsi

Your favor now, don't you believe,
Can't eclipse His grace yestereve?
The blossoms filled her eyes with rue;
She'd never talk with King of Ch'u.

* Lady Hsi: formerly Marquise of Hsi during the Spring and Autumn period. In 680 B.C., King Civil of Ch'u conquered the State of Hsi and took the beautiful queen as his wife. Though Lady Hsi bore him two children, she had never spoken to him ever since she was taken captive.
* King of Ch'u: King Civil of Ch'u (? - 677 B.C.), who conquered the State of Hsi and took the marquise as his wife. King Civil of Ch'u is best remembered for moving his capital from Red Sun to Ying and capturing Lady Hsi.

从岐王过杨氏别业应教

杨子谈经所,
淮王载酒过。
兴阑啼鸟换,
坐久落花多。
径转回银烛,
林开散玉珂。
严城时未启,
前路拥笙歌。

A Visit to Yang's Cottage with Prince of Offset, a Poem in Reply to His Highness

It's Yang's abode in solitude;
Prince of Huai sent me wine and food.
Merry, birds' changing shift they found
And flowers fallen all o'er the ground.
They turned about thru candlelight
That lit up the forest trail bright.
The town still shut, they played along,
While ringing in mind a flute song.

* Yang: referring to Man Yang (53 B.C.– A.D. 18), Hsiung Yang if transliterated, a great scholar, *euph* (rhymed prose) writer and official in the Han dynasty, whose *The Great One* has had a deep influence on works of later generations. According to *History of the Han Dynasty*, when other officials flattered those in power, only Man Yang kept to himself to write his philosophy work, *The Great One*.

* Prince of Offset: a title of nobility, begun from the T'ang dynasty. This Prince of

Offset was probably Fan Li (A.D. 686 - A.D. 726), the third son of Emperor Sagesire of T'ang (A.D. 662 - A.D. 716).
* Prince of Huai: King of Huai, An Liu (179 B.C.- 122 B.C.), who loved wine and versification, a metaphor for Prince of Offset in this poem.
* wine: one of the most important beverages in Chinese culture, of which brown wine was brewed more than three thousand years ago and white wine (spirit) became popular in the Sung dynasty. Wine has an important position in Chinese life, such as literary creation, cultural activities, health care, cookery and so on.
* flute: a tubular wind instrument of small diameter with holes along the side.

从岐王夜宴卫家山池应教

座客香貂满，
宫娃绮幔张。
涧花轻粉色，
山月少灯光。
积翠纱窗暗，
飞泉绣户凉。
还将歌舞出，
归路莫愁长。

Attending a Feast with Prince of Offset at Wei's Hill Pool, in Reply to His Highness

At the feast the guests shine in mink;
The maids serve them in the tent bright.
The flowers feel shy before cheeks pink;
The moon's outshone by candlelight.
The green invades the gauzy screen;
The spring unto the door does fly.
More performance comes to the scene;
On your way back, please do not sigh.

* Prince of Offset: a title of nobility, begun from the T'ang dynasty. Prince of Offset in this poem was probably Fan Li (A.D. 686 – A.D. 726), the first one so entitled in history, and the third son of Emperor Sagesire of T'ang (A.D. 662 – A.D. 716).
* Wei's Hill Pool: unidentified.

* mink: soft, thick glossy, brown fur from an amphibious, slender-bodied mammal called mink. Mink has been used in China and is a sign of richness and power, as is shown in *Fathers* from *The Book of Songs*, "Colored carts wrapped with mink, / The quartet eight bells clink."

敕借岐王九成宫避暑应教

帝子远辞丹凤阙，
天书遥借翠微宫。
隔窗云雾生衣上，
卷幔山泉入镜中。
林下水声喧语笑，
岩间树色隐房栊。
仙家未必能胜此，
何事吹笙向碧空。

Spending the Summer in Green Palace with Prince of Offset at Royal Order, In Reply to His Highness

The prince sets off from the capital town;
The royal edict to Green Palace comes down.
Mist enters the room to dye his robe green;
A spring flies to his mirror thru the screen.
The water giggles through the wood;
The rocks are shaded and roofs hued.
With this place no fairyland can vie;
Why play your flute to the blue sky?

* Prince of Offset: a title of nobility. In this poem, it probably refers to Fan Li (A.D. 686 - A.D. 726), the first one so entitled in history, the third son of Emperor Sagesire of T'ang (A.D. 662 - A.D. 716).

* edict: a public ordinance emanating from a sovereign and having the force of law.

* Green Palace: probably referring to Perfect Palace, a royal summer resort on Mt. Sky Height in Sha'anhsi, which was in the green hills, hence so called.
* fairyland: an ideal legendary abode for immortals, sometimes thought of as being in the middle of East Sea, sometimes in the sky.
* flute: a tubular wind instrument of small diameter with holes along the side.

送綦毋潜落第还乡

圣代无隐者,
英灵尽来归。
遂令东山客,
不得顾采薇。
既至君门远,
孰云吾道非?
江淮度寒食,
京洛缝春衣。
置酒临长道,
同心与我违。
行当浮桂棹,
未几拂荆扉。
远树带行客,
孤村当落晖。
吾谋适不用,
勿谓知音稀。

Adieu to Ch'ien Ch'iwu Who's Failed Grand Test

A good age does no hermit find;
There comes to court many a mind.
Recluses like you no more hide,
Or pick ferns on the mountainside.
Unlucky, in Grand Test you fail;
Who can say you are off the trail?

You passed Midland last Cold Food Day;
This year in Capital you stay.
Now on Broad Way I drink to you,
Because we will soon say adieu.
Down south you will row with an oar;
Before long, you'll ope your chaste door.
The trees afar will follow you,
Your village tinted with eve hue.
It's nothing that you are laid by;
You still have friends, no need to sigh.

* Ch'iwu Ch'ien: Ch'ien Ch'iwu (A.D. 692 – A.D. 749), a famous T'ang poet, who retired to be a recluse after Lushan An's Rebellion.
* Grand Test: also called Court Test or Court Examination, the highest level of the civil-service examinations aiming at selecting qualified officials, instituted by Emperor Highsire of T'ang (A.D. 628 – A.D. 683), held every three years and the final decision of ranking was made by an emperor himself. The system of imperial civil-service examinations for selecting talents to serve as governmental officials began as early as the Han dynasty, flourished in the T'ang and Sung dynasties and was annulled in the late Ch'ing dynasty. Those who passed the enteree (chinshih) level were indeed given upper-echelon government appointments, and as a perk, they were generally allied by marriage to upper-crust families. In the eighteenth century, the Jesuits and their friend Voltaire recommended such a system for Europe as a safety valve for Europe's ossified social structure, which was soon overthrown by waves of aristocratic blood.
* pick ferns on the mountainside: referring to the story of Bowone and Straightthree. As they failed to admonish King Martial of Chough, they left Chough and refused to take crops reaped under the reign of Chough. They lived on fungi on Mt. Headshine and finally starved to death.
* Cold Food Day: one or two days before Pure Brightness Day (the third day of the third moon each year), the festival in memory of Chiht'ui of Chieh (? – 636 B.C.) observed without cooking for a day. In the Spring and Autumn period, Double Ear, a prince of Chin, escaped from the disaster in his state with his follower Chiht'ui. In great deprivation, Double Ear almost starved to death, and Chiht'ui fed him with flesh cut off his thigh. When Double Ear was crowned as Lord Civil of Chin, Chiht'ui retreated to Mt. Silk Floss with his mother when feeling neglected. To have him out, Lord Civil

set the mountain on fire, but Chiht'ui did not give in and was burned with his mother, hugging a tree.
* Capital: Long Peace or Ch'ang'an if transliterated, the metropolis of gold, the capital of the T'ang Empire with 1,000,000 inhabitants, the largest walled city ever built by man, the center of world religions, Buddhism, Confucianism, Wordism, Nestorianism, Zoroastrianism, and even Islamism represented by Saracens, and the center of education — There were colleges of various grades and special institutes for calligraphy, arithmetic, music, astronomy and so on.
* Broad Way: also known as Long Peace Way.

燕 支 行

汉家天将才且雄,
来时谒帝明光宫。
万乘亲推双阙下,
千官出饯五陵东。
誓辞甲第金门里,
身作长城玉塞中。
卫霍才堪一骑将,
朝廷不数贰师功。
赵魏燕韩多劲卒,
关西侠少何咆勃。
报仇只是闻尝胆,
饮酒不曾妨刮骨。
画戟雕戈白日寒,
连旗大旆黄尘没。
叠鼓遥翻瀚海波,
鸣笳乱动天山月。
麒麟锦带佩吴钩,
飒沓青骊跃紫骝。
拔剑已断天骄臂,
归鞍共饮月支头。
汉兵大呼一当百,
虏骑相看哭且愁。
教战虽令赴汤火,
终知上将先伐谋。

Marching to Mt. Rouge

The Han general with great talent and flair
Calls on His Majesty at Palace Glare.
Most High pushes his cart out Phoenix Gate;
East of Five Tombs courtiers for farewell wait.
He makes an oath and leaves his golden hall;
At the fortress he will be a great wall.
He'll outdo Watch and Huo, commanders best
And General Li, who did foes and steeds arrest.
He's many gallants from Chao, Yan, Han and Way,
And those strongmen from West, who boldly sway.
He'd taste bitter bile to revenge the land
And drink while bone-scraping pain he could stand.
Halberds and spears wave, and the sun looks cold;
The sand kicked off will drown the flags, behold.
The war drum beaten hard the desert shakes;
The Hun flute sadly played the pass moon quakes.
The unicorn belt and Wu hook both shine;
Black steeds gallop, brown horses neigh, all fine.
Swiftly sword swayed, a Hun arm is chopped off;
Drinking out of skulls, at Jouchih they scoff.
Han soldiers fight o'erwhelmingly and shout;
Hun dragoons cry wretchedly, what a rout.
When ordered to attack, fighters will burst,
But a good general should plot the fight first.

* Mt. Rouge: the Rouge Mountains, a range of mountains in today's Ope-arms (Changyeh), Kansu Province, lush with pines and cypresses and various kinds of plants

and grass, and inhabited by Huns in the Han dynasty.
* Palace Glare: a Han palace built in the fourth year of Emperor Martial's reign, that is, 101 B.C.
* Phoenix Gate: the gate of the imperial palace with five phoenix towers on it.
* Five Tombs: five mausoleums of five Han emperors on the north bank of the Wei.
* Watch and Huo: referring to two famous generals in the Han dynasty, Blue Watch (? - 106 B.C.), Ch'ing Wei if transliterated, and Swift Huo (140 B.C.- 117 B.C.). Both generals were the first-ranking generals in the Han dynasty.
* General Li: Broad Li (? - 119 B.C.) in full name, Kuang Li if transliterated, a renowned general who won many battles against the Huns in the Han dynasty, called Flying General by the Huns.
* Chao: the State of Chao (403 B.C.- 222 B.C.), a vassal state in the Spring and Autumn period, one of the Seven Powers in the Warring States period.
* Yan: the State of Yan (1044 B.C.- 222 B.C.), a vassal state in the Spring and Autumn period, one of the Seven Powers in the Warring States period.
* Han: the State of Han (403. B.C.- 230 B.C.) a vassal state in the Spring and Autumn period, one of the Seven Powers in the Warring States period.
* Way: the State of Way (403 B.C.- 225 B.C.), a vassal state of Chough, one of the Seven Powers in the Warring States period.
* taste bitter bile: alluding to King Kouchien of Yüeh (520 B.C.- 465 B.C.) who slept on brushwood and tasted gall every night to remind himself of the shame of his subjugation by the State of Wu.
* West: alias Western Regions, the areas inhabited by Huns and other nomadic people governed by China, for example, the Han Empire and the T'ang Empire, generally stretching from Jade Gate Pass and Sun Pass to Pamir Plateau and Balkhash Lake, and sometimes even to Caspian Sea and Black Sea.
* Hun: war-like nomadic peoples occupying vast regions from Mongolia to Central Asia in Chinese history, especially during the Han dynasty. They were a constant menace on China's western and northern borders.
* Jouchih: indicating an area around Hohsi Corridor and the nationality or language bearing the name.

扶南曲歌词五首
Tune of Funam, Five Poems

其 一

翠羽流苏帐，
春眠曙不开。
羞从面色起，
娇逐语声来。
早向昭阳殿，
君王中使催。

No. 1

The tent is adorned with plumes bright;
It is still shut in dawning light.
The shyness of her face charms one;
The softness with her voice wafts on.
Now she'd hurry up to Glare Hall;
The Lord has sent eunuchs to call.

* Funam: probably Bnam in origin, an ancient kingdom in Indochina, which existed from the first century to the eleventh century, a once large and influential kingdom in Southeast Asia.
* Glare Hall: a Han palace, where Virtues Combined (Hote) Chao, who was Flying Swallow Chao's sister and rival, lived in Emperor Complete of Han's reign.
* eunuch: an emasculated man working for a special purpose, for example, a castrated official in the court or a castrated servant in a harem.

其 二

堂上动青弦,
堂前绮席陈。
齐歌卢女曲,
双舞洛阳人。
倾国徒相看,
宁知心所亲。

No. 2

Inside the hall green strings are played
Before the hall, a feast is laid.
All sing aloud Lady Lu's Air;
The Loshine beauties dance in pair.
The Lord enjoys the belles' best art;
Who has now won His loving heart?

* *Lady Lu's Air*: a conservatoire tune. Lady Lu was a courtesan in Lord Martial of Way's harem, good at zither playing. A courtesan was then a professional woman entertainer like *geisha* in Japan, who was good at singing, dancing or traditional Chinese arts such as zither playing, go playing, calligraphy and painting.
* the Loshine beauties: the beauties from Loshine, the eastern capital of T'ang.

其 三

香气传空满，
妆华影箔通。
歌闻天仗外，
舞出御楼中。
日暮归何处，
花间长乐宫。

No. 3

Her scent through the air can be seen;
Her dress casts a shade to the screen.
The song does royal guards entrance;
And in the tower goes on a dance.
Where are they going for the night?
Amid flowers is House of Delight.

* screen: a curtain which separates or cuts off, shelters or protects as a light partition, usually made of bamboo and decorated with pearls, a common image in Chinese literature. Two lines from a Sung lyric by Haowen Yüan reads like this: "The drizzle falls before my tower's sill; / 'Broidered with crabapples, the screen's chill."
* House of Delight: a Han palace, a residence for dowagers, designated after Emperor Boon of Han's reign (195 B.C.- 188 B.C.).

其 四

宫女还金屋，
将眠复畏明。
入春轻衣好，
半夜薄妆成。
拂曙朝前殿，
玉墀多珮声。

No. 4

The belle retreats to Golden House;
She'll sleep, afraid of dawning light.
It's spring; one can wear a thin blouse;
She's dressed up at the depth of night.
The frontal hall sees dawn appear;
Her pendants the jade steps can hear.

* Golden House: Lord Martial of Han once loved Petite, his cousin, and promised her a golden house when they were young. But Petite lost his love and moved to Long Gate Palace after being deposed. Now Golden House is used as a metaphor for any palace or an abode for the fair sex.
* jade steps: the steps before, and leading to, a palace hall or a harem, usually built with marble, jade being a metaphor for good quality, often used as a metonymy for the court. A verse titled *Pear Blossoms in the Left Office* by another T'ang poet mentions the steps jade white, as reads: "The chill of theirs bullies the frost; / Their fragrance soaks into the night. / As spring wind blows, tossing and tossed, / They fly over the steps jade white."

其 五

朝日照绮窗，
佳人坐临镜。
散黛恨犹轻，
插钗嫌未正。
同心勿遽游，
幸待春妆竟。

No. 5

The morning sun lights up her screen;
She looks into her mirror sheen.
She hates her rouge is a bit light
And her hairpin is not placed right.
For a tryst, we don't have to run;
For springtime, my hair should be done.

* sun: the heavenly body that is the center of attraction and the main source of light and heat in the solar system, a representation of Shine in contrast with Shade, the moon, in Chinese culture, a symbol of hope, life, strength, vigor and youth.
* screen: a curtain or blind, usually made of bamboo, most often used for a lady' room, which separates or cuts off, shelters or protects as a light partition, a common image in Chinese literature. Two lines from a Sung lyric by Haowen Yüan reads like this: "The drizzle falls before my tower's sill; / 'Broidered with crabapples, the screen's chill."
* rouge: any cosmetic used for coloring the cheeks and lips pink or red, usually in the form of paper in ancient China.

少年行四首
The Lads, Four Poems

其 一

新丰美酒斗十千，
咸阳游侠多少年。
相逢意气为君饮，
系马高楼垂柳边。

No. 1

The Newrich wine is as precious as gold;
The Allshine lads all have a resolve bold.
They take a long swallow to show their pride,
Their horses tied to the willows inn-side.

---

* the Newrich wine: the best and most expensive wine in the T'ang dynasty. Newrich was an old town of Han, in today's Lintung County, Sha'anhsi Province, well known for its good wine. The town was built by Pang Liu in imitation of his hometown Rich County, i.e., today's Rich County, Chiangsu Province.
* the Allshine lads: boys in Allshine. Allshine, Hsienyang if transliterated, was the capital of the Ch'in Empire. It is so called because all its rivers and mountains can get sunshine from all around.

其 二

出身仕汉羽林郎，
初随骠骑战渔阳。
孰知不向边庭苦，
纵死犹闻侠骨香。

No. 2

He leaves home to be an Armed Escort guard;
And follows Swift to Fishshine and fights hard.
The frontier life is hard, everyone knows;
E'en if he dies, he'll smell of a sweet rose.

* Armed Escort: imperial guarding Corps, established by Emperor Martial in Western Han.
* Swift: Swift Huo (140 B.C.- 117 B.C.), P'iaoyao Huo if transliterated, a renowned general, prominent strategist and patriotic hero in the Han dynasty. He made his first show at 17, leading 800 fierce cavalrymen to penetrate the enemy lines and defeat the Huns. Swift fought against the Huns in three major wars and each time returned with victory. He died of a disease at 24, leaving his achievements as the highest glory for Chinese military commanders.
* Fishshine: Fishshine Prefecture, approximately today's Chi District, Tientsin.

其 三

一身能擘两雕弧，
虏骑千重只似无。
偏坐金鞍调白羽，
纷纷射杀五单于。

No. 3

He draws a carved bow, vigorous with might;
The swarming horsemen are nothing at all.
Astride his steed, he adjusts the plume white
And all those Hun chieftains are shot to fall.

* Hun chieftains: leaders of the Hun troops.
* steed: a horse; especially a spirited war horse. The use of horses in war can be traced back to the Shang dynasty (1600 B.C.- 1046 B.C.), when a department of horse management was established. A verse from *The Book of Songs* tells of Lord Civil of Watch's industriousness: "In state affairs he leads; / He has three thousand steeds."
* the plume white: referring to an arrow with a plume attached to the end.

其 四

汉家君臣欢宴终，
高议云台论战功。
天子临轩赐侯印，
将军佩出明光宫。

No. 4

Lord and peers celebrate their feat of war;
On Cloud Mound they judge who's done less or more.
His Majesty confers Seal of Marquis;
The general's prize shines out of the palace.

* Cloud Mound: a peak of Mt. Flora, which is one of the Five Mountains in China, representing the west.
* Seal of Marquis: a gold seal with a purple ribbon, representing the power or status of a marquis.

被 出 济 州

微官易得罪，
谪去济川阴。
执政方持法，
明君无此心。
闾阎河润上，
井邑海云深。
纵有归来日，
各愁年鬓侵。

Exiled to Chichow

I'm prone to fall, as I am low;
Exiled to Chichow, I now row.
The judge must have sentenced me right,
As His Majesty's heart is bright.
By the Yellow River I'll be;
The town sees thick clouds from the sea.
I will come back to work one day;
My hair then may be touched with gray.

* Chichow: an old town on the Peking-Hangchow Canal, which is, present-day Ch'ip'ing, Liaoch'eng, Shantung Province.
* the Yellow River: the second longest river in China, flowing across Loess Plateau, hence yellow water all the way. It is 5,464 kilometers long, with a drainage area of 752,443 square kilometers. It has nurtured the Chinese nation, hence regarded as the cradle of Chinese civilization. As legend goes, the river derived from a yellow dragon that, couchant on Midland Plain, ate yellow soil, flooded crops, devoured people and

stock, and was finally tamed by Great Worm, the First King of Hsia (21 B.C.- 16 B.C.). Its fertile valleys were turned into fields of rice, barley and oscillating corn, amid gleaming streams and lakes.

登河北城楼作

井邑傅岩上,
客亭云雾间。
高城眺落日,
极浦映苍山。
岸火孤舟宿,
渔家夕鸟还。
寂寥天地暮,
心与广川闲。

Composed on the Tower North of the River

A village dwells on Fu's Rock high;
A station dons haze from the sky.
The high town basks in the eve sun;
The water reflects the hill shone.
The lonely boat sways the bank fire;
The fishers with the birds retire.
The vast heaven and earth please me;
The broad river's calm and I'm free.

* Fu's Rock: the rock where Yüeh Fu built walls by stamping earth between a board frames. Yüeh Fu was a noble minister of high reputation in the Shang dynasty. Historic records say that the King of Shang dreamed of a sage, and he sent people out to search for him and found Yüeh Fu.
* Heaven: the space surrounding or seeming to overarch the earth, in which the sun, the moon, and stars appear, popularly the abode of God, his angels and the blessed, and in most cases suggesting supernatural power or sometimes signifying a monarch.
* the broad river: referring to the Yellow River.

宿 郑 州

朝与周人辞，
暮投郑人宿。
他乡绝俦侣，
孤客亲僮仆。
宛洛望不见，
秋霖晦平陆。
田父草际归，
村童雨中牧。
主人东皋上，
时稼绕茅屋。
虫思机杼悲，
雀喧禾黍熟。
明当渡京水，
昨晚犹金谷。
此去欲何言，
穷边徇微禄。

Putting Up for the Night in Chengchow

I take leave of Loshine at dawn
And at dusk reach Cheng, a small town.
I've no friend out of home I fear,
So my boy servant I hold dear.
Loshine I can no longer see;
The fall rain dims all about me.
From grass comes back a farmer old;

A boy tends sheep in the rain cold.
My host abides by the east lane;
Around his hut you see his grain.
The crickets the busy loom mourn;
The sparrows chirrup to the corn.
Tomorrow the Ching I will wade,
Though last night in Gold Dale I stayed.
Now I'm leaving, what shall I say?
I'll go down there for a small pay.

* Loshine: Loyang if transliterated, the second largest city and the eastern capital in the T'ang dynasty, on the north bank of the River Lo, a central region of Hsia culture.
* sheep: a medium-sized domesticated ruminant of the genus *Ovis*, highly prized for its flesh, wool and skin, regarded as meek and mild, a symbol of beauty and purity, used as a sacrifice in both Western and Eastern cultures.
* Cheng: Chengchow, a prefecture in the T'ang dynasty, present-day Chengchow, Honan Province.
* cricket: a leaping orthopterous insect, with long antennae and three segments in each tarsus, the male of which makes a chirping sound by friction of forewings, a common image of a quiet night in Chinese literature.
* sparrow: a small, plain-colored passerine bird related to the finches, grosbeaks and buntings, a very common bird in China, a symbol of insignificance.
* the Ching: the upper reach of the Chialu River, near present-day Chengchow, Honan Province.
* Gold Dale: originally a creek located west of Loshine in present-day Honan Province, where Ch'ung Shih (A.D. 249 - A.D. 300), a rich litterateur in the Western Chin dynasty, built a park and often held feasts there.

早入荥阳界

泛舟入荥泽，
兹邑乃雄藩。
河曲间阎隘，
川中烟火繁。
因人见风俗，
入境闻方言。
秋野田畴盛，
朝光市井喧。
渔商波上客，
鸡犬岸旁村。
前路白云外，
孤帆安可论。

Rowing into Hsingshine in the Morning

Now to Hsing Lake my boat I run;
The fiefdom there is a great one.
The river flows to bend and crook;
A veil of smoke hangs o'er the brook.
I see different use and wont here,
And an alien tongue you may hear.
The autumn enjoys bumper grains;
The morning lights noise in all lanes.
Fishers, merchants float on the stream;
Dogs shoo off fowls ashore to scream.
Towards the clouds white I now row;

With my lone sail where could I go?

* Hsingshine: a county on the south bank of the Yellow River, that is modern-day Hsingshine, Honan Province.
* Hsing Lake: a lake that had run dry in the Han dynasty, probably a metaphor for a river in Hsingshine.
* Dogs shoo off fowls: a common scene in country life. Dogs are a domesticated carnivorous mammal (*Canis familiaris*), of worldwide distribution and many varieties, noted for their adaptability and their devotion to man, and fowls are the common domestic cocks, hens, or chickens.

至滑州隔河望黎阳忆丁三寓

隔河见桑柘，
蔼蔼黎阳川。
望望行渐远，
孤峰没云烟。
故人不可见，
河水复悠然。
赖有政声远，
时闻行路传。

Arriving in Huachow and Looking at Lishine Across the River While Missing Sanyü Ting

Across the stream mulberries stand,
Lush, lush the Lishine's sunny land.
Far, far I go away from here
Until the peaks all disappear.
My old friend I can see no more;
The river calms down like before.
So lucky, the world's far from me;
I can enjoy my course, so free.

* Huachow: a prefecture in the T'ang dynasty with its seat of government in White Horse.
* Lishine: a county of T'ang, on the north bank of the Yellow River, faced with Huachow across the river.
* mulberry: a kind of tree of the genus *Morus*, *Morus alba Linn* in Latin, whose leaves are food for silkworms, and whose berries are served as a human delicacy.

济上四贤咏
Ode to Four Sages in Chichow

崔录事

解印归田里，
贤哉此丈夫。
少年曾任侠，
晚节更为儒。
遁迹东山下，
因家沧海隅。
已闻能狎鸟，
余欲共乘桴。

To Secretary Ts'ui

Demobilized, thus he'd retire;
A great man, he's high and gets higher.
Young, he was gallant, doing right;
Old, he turns gentle, so polite.
From mountaintop to mountainside
He tours and he ashore does bide.
I hear birds he can entertain;
Take a raft with him I would fain.

---

* Chichow: an ancient prefecture whose administrations had moved several times due to floods, most probably today's Liaoch'eng under Shantung Province.

成文学

宝剑千金装，
登君白玉堂。
身为平原客，
家有邯郸娼。
使气公卿坐，
论心游侠场。
中年不得意，
谢病客游梁。

To Wenhsüeh Ch'eng

His sword in a gold sheath awes all;
He often goes to White Jade Hall.
He's a hanger-on of P'ing Yüan
And has concubines from Hantan.
With grandees he can proudly stalk;
With gallants he will freely talk.
Middle aged, he is unfulfilled;
So he oars in the stream, free-willed.

* White Jade Hall: a term borrowed from a Han Cconservatoire verse — Gold makes your door and white jade makes your hall.
* P'ing Yüan: Prince of Chao who was later crowned Lord Plain of Chao, one of the Four Childes in the Warring States period, generous and noble enough to attract many hangers-on to his house.
* concubine: a female cohabitant or secondary wife. China was a polygamous society from prehistoric years till the first half of the twentieth century. A man could have three wives and four concubines and a concubine could be bartered or sold or given as a gift in ancient China.

* Hantan: a city more than 3,100 years old, the capital of the State of Chao (403 B.C.- 222 B.C.) in the Eastern Chough dynasty (770 B.C.- 256 B.C.), located in present-day Hopei Province. This city was built in the Shang dynasty (cir. 1600 B.C.- cir. 1046 B.C.) and an imperial palace was built here for King Chow (cir. 1105 B.C.- 1046 B.C.) according to *Lonely Bamboo Annals*. The legacies and ruins bespeak the splendor of its glorious past.

郑霍二山人

翩翩繁华子,
多出金张门。
幸有先人业,
早蒙明主恩。
童年且未学,
肉食鹜华轩。
岂乏中林士,
无人荐至尊。
郑公老泉石,
霍子安丘樊。
买药不二价,
著书盈万言。
息阴无恶木,
饮水必清源。
吾贱不及议,
斯人竟谁论。

To Two Immortals, Cheng and Huo

You are so handsome and so bold,
Both of you from a house of gold.
Because of what your sires had done,
His Majesty's grace you soon won.
In childhood you learned well and wide;
Meat you did eat, cars you did ride.
But to forests you would retire;
To serve the court you'd no desire.
Cheng, to Old Spring Stone you did wend;

Huo, to Hill Forest you did tend.
At fixed price medicine you sold,
And wrote books to mean manifold.
Beneath no bad wood you would rest;
Of all springs you would drink the best.
Of your merits I can't praise well;
On your qualities who can dwell?

* a house of gold: a metonymy for a rich and powerful family or an influential official, alluding to the Changs and the Chins, two powerful families in the Han dynasty, which prospered for seven generations.
* Old Spring Stone: probably a boulder by a fountain spring.
* Hill Forest: a forest or wood in the hills.

寓 言 二 首
Two Allegories

其 一

朱绂谁家子，
无乃金张孙。
骊驹从白马，
出入铜龙门。
问尔何功德，
多承明主恩。
斗鸡平乐馆，
射雉上林园。
曲陌车骑盛，
高堂珠翠繁。
奈何轩冕贵，
不与布衣言。

No. 1

Who is he in red robe so bright?
Isn't he from a house so great?
His horse black follows his horse white
Into or out of Dragon Gate.
Whate'er has he, what has he done?
Much favor has he from Most High.
He's in Merry Playhouse for fun
Or shoots pheasants in High Park nigh.
He drives or rides through lanes, so free,

Jewels and emeralds in his hall.
Out of a noble pedigree,
He talks not with commons at all.

* Dragon Gate: Mt. Dragon Gate, located in present-day Sha'anhsi Province, where the Yellow River runs through.
* Merry Playhouse: name of a palace in the Han dynasty, built in Emperor Higsire's reign andamended in Emperor Martial's reign, located in High Park.
* pheasant: a long-tailed gallinaceous bird noted for the gorgeous plumage of the male.
* High Park: an imperial park that Lord Martial of Han built on the site of a discarded park of Ch'in. It was vast and splendid with palaces and woodlands, having various functions and recreational facilities, rolling about 340 kilometers.

其 二

君家御沟上,
垂柳夹朱门。
列鼎会中贵,
鸣珂朝至尊。
生死在八议,
穷达由一言。
须识苦寒士,
莫矜狐白温。

No. 2

Beside Royal Trench you abide;
Willows shade your scarlet door wide.
You treat guests to tripods displayed;
Your horse to court sways clinking jade.
You've Eight Pardons, sinning a sin;
One word may make you fail or win.
You should take care of those in need,
Not boasting your mink warm indeed.

* Royal Trench: also known as Willow Trench or Forbidden Trench flowing from the Southern Hills and through the palace complex in Long Peace.
* willow: any of a large genus of shrubs and trees related to the poplars, widely distributed in China and most of the world, having generally smooth branches, and often long, slender, pliant, and sometimes pendent branchlets, which seem to be waving to a friend.
* scarlet door: door of a palace or of a mansion, referring to a family of royals, nobles and powerful worthies.
* tripod: a cooking utensil or cauldron with three feet or legs, usually cast with bronze,

popular in ancient China, a symbol of a powerful family.
* Eight Pardons: eight kinds of abatement from penalty for peerage, those who are relatives of the royal family, those who are an emperor's old friends; those who are moral and virtuous, those who are capable artists, those who have performed meritorious service, those who have high-ranking titles, those who are devoted to, and have done the most for, the empire, and those who are former sovereigns.
* mink: a kind of precious fur which is soft, thick glossy, brown, from an amphibious, slender-bodied mammal called mink.

和使君五郎西楼望远思归

高楼望所思，
目极情未毕。
枕上见千里，
窗中窥万室。
悠悠长路人，
暖暖远郊日。
惆怅极浦外，
迢递孤烟出。
能赋属上才，
思归同下秩。
故乡不可见，
云水空如一。

Gazing Homeward on West Tower
—In Reply to Prefect Boy Five

On the tower I'd see what I miss;
Eye-strained, I drown in tear like this.
My railings can see countless miles;
My window can see farthest tiles.
The long road has passengers run;
The vast fields bask in the warm sun.
Beyond the moor I cast my eyes;
Over there lonely smoke does rise.
Best poetry I can well compose;
Homesick, I'm like low folks, all those.

Howe'er, I can't see my land, my town;
Vacant, the blue up, the blue down.

* sun: the heavenly body that is the center of attraction and the main source of light and heat in the solar system, a representation of Shine in contrast with Shade, the moon, in Chinese culture, a symbol of hope, life, strength, vigor and youth.
* the blue up, the blue down: the blue up is the color of the sky and the blue down is the color of the river.

渡河到清河作

泛舟大河里,
积水穷天涯。
天波忽开拆,
郡邑千万家。
行复见城市,
宛然有桑麻。
回瞻旧乡国,
渺漫连云霞。

Crossing the River to Blue River County

On the river, my oar I ply;
Waves roll to the end of the sky.
The blue suddenly opens wide:
A thousand households by the tide.
As I row on, I see a town
And a mulberry field looms down.
As I glance back to my old land,
The breakers to the clouds expand.

* the River: referring to the Yellow River, the second largest river in China, the cradle of Chinese civilization. As legend goes, the river derived from a yellow dragon that, couchant on Midland Plain, ate yellow soil, flooded crops, devoured people and stock, and was finally tamed by Great Worm, the First King of Hsia (21 B.C.- 16 B.C.). Its fertile valleys were turned into fields of rice, barley and oscillating corn, amid gleaming streams and lakes.

* Blue River County: present-day Blue River County in the southeast of Hopei Province.
* mulberry: the edible, berry-like fruit of a tree (genus *Morus*) whose leaves are valued for silkworm culture, and the tree itself.

鱼山神女祠歌二首
Goddess Shrine on Mt. Fish, Two Poems

迎 神

坎坎击鼓，
鱼山之下。
吹洞箫，
望极浦。
女巫进，
纷屡舞。
陈瑶席，
湛清酤。
风凄凄兮夜雨，
不知神之来兮不来，
使我心兮苦复苦。

Expecting Goddess

Thump, thump, the drum I beat
At the foot of Mt. Fish.
The holed flute I play;
For Nature I wish.
The girl witch comes in
To reel, once again.
A feast does begin;
The pure wineI drain.
The chilly wind chills the night rain;
Will my Goddess come or not, I don't know,

  As reduces me to a great, great pain.

* Mt. Fish: also known as Mt. Mine, 10 kilometers from Tung-o County, in today's Liaoton, Shantung Province.
* holed flute: a wind musical instrument, the most popular in folk music, made of nine-node-long bamboo, black or white, played with a troupe or independently.
* witch: a female official in charge of rites and sacrifices according to *Rites of Chough*, able to exorcize spirits and communicate with gods and say prayers for a rain and so on.
* wine: one of the most important beverages in China. Wine-drinking plays an important part in the lives of most Chinese, especially Chinese poets, acting as a form of enlightenment comparable to Zen practice. Wine is a must at a feast, as is said, without wine, there will be no feast.

送 神

纷进舞兮堂前,
目眷眷兮琼筵,
来不言兮意不传。
作暮雨兮愁空山,
悲急管兮思繁弦,
神之驾兮俨欲旋。
倏云收兮雨歇,
山青青兮水潺潺。

Seeing Off Goddess

She dances and dances in the hall,
To the nectar feast casting her eyes.
She remains silent, o speechless at all,
But thru the dusk drizzle to the hills sighs.
The band is so fast and the strings so tense;
The goddess boards her cart, o there she goes.
The clouds vanish, o the rain stops hence;
The mountain looks green, o the water flows.

---

* nectar feast: a fabulous banquet, which is held for a happy reunion or to celebrate an anniversary in Chinese culture, sometimes also called hawksbill feast or banquet.

济州过赵叟家宴

虽与人境接，
闭门成隐居。
道言庄叟事，
儒行鲁人馀。
深巷斜晖静，
闲门高柳疏。
荷锄修药圃，
散帙曝农书。
上客摇芳翰，
中厨馈野蔬。
夫君第高饮，
景晏出林间。

Attending Old Chao's Family Feast in Chichow

Although close to the worldly din,
You are a recluse once shut in.
In the Word, with Sir Lush you talk;
For rituals, with Lu Man you walk.
The deep lane receives afterglow;
The high gate sees willows droop low.
You farm curing herbs with a hoe,
And read farm books, loose your hair-do.
To guests you waves your writing brush
And in your kitchen cook greens lush.

O in great altitude you drink;
Of immortals you are the pink

* the Word: referring to Tao if transliterated, the most significant and profoundest concept in Chinese philosophy. According to Laocius's *The Word and the World*: "The Word is void, but its use is infinite. O deep! It seems to be the root of all things." The Word is identifiable with the Word or Logos in the West, as there is an enormous amount of common ground in the two cosmologies and the doctrines concerning the most fundamental matters such as "the Word is the One" and "God is the One", and the personalization of Being, the progenitor of finite spirits, which are subordinate kinds of Being or merely appearances of the Divine, the One.
* Sir Lush: Chuangtzu if transliterated, an important philosopher in the Warring States period, one of the representatives of Wordism (Taoism). One of the most important Chinese classics is *Sir Lush*, philosophical fables written by Sir Lush.
* Lu Man: referring to Confucius (551 B.C.- 479 B.C.) from Lu. Confucius was a renowned thinker, educator and statesman in the Spring and Autumn period, born in the State of Lu, and as the founder of Confucianism, he has exerted profound influence on Chinese culture.
* willow: any of a large genus (*Salix*) of shrubs and trees related to the poplars, having generally smooth branches, and often long, slender, pliant, and sometimes pendent branchlets, which seem to be waving good-bye, or weeping amorously, or drooping for nostalgia.
* writing brush: also called Chinese brush or brush for short, which is used for writing or painting. It is one of the four treasures in a Chinese study, the other three stationeries being ink, paper and inkslab.

寄崇梵僧

崇梵僧,崇梵僧,
秋归覆釜春不还。
落花啼鸟纷纷乱,
涧户山窗寂寂闲。
峡里谁知有人事,
郡中遥望空云山。

To Monk of Sanskrit Hall

Monk of Sanskrit Hall, Monk of Sanskrit Hall,
Spring gone, to Reversed Pot autumn does fall.
Flowers falling, birds calling, what a big rout;
The creek door, the hill window, quiet about.
Who knows what has happened in the dale there?
From the town to the void mountains I stare.

---

* Sanskrit Hall: a temple in Tung-o, today's Tung-o, in present-day Shantung Province.
* Reversed Pot: a village in the mountains near Sanskrit Hall, a monastery.

赠东岳焦炼师

先生千岁馀，
五岳遍曾居。
遥识齐侯鼎，
新过王母庐。
不能师孔墨，
何事问长沮。
玉管时来凤，
铜盘即钓鱼。
竦身空里语，
明目夜中书。
自有还丹术，
时论太素初。
频蒙露版诏，
时降软轮车。
山静泉逾响，
松高枝转疏。
支颐问樵客，
世上复何如。

To Great Master Chiao on Mt. East

Master, you're a thousand years old,
Having lived in Five Mounts, as told.
Marquis of Ch'i's tripod you've seen,
And to Queen Mother's lodge you've been.
As you won't do Confucius' task,

The worldly way you need not ask.
Your flute lures phoenixes to stay;
With a copper plate fish you may.
If rising, you can wing your flight,
And read at midnight without light.
You know how cinnabar's refined,
And talk on the birth of mankind.
Your act's moved His Majesty's heart;
He'd treat you to a cushioned cart.
Mountains quiet, the spring louder flows;
Leafage sparse, the pine taller grows.
You ask a woodman, propped your chin:
"What's happened to the worldly din?"

* Mt. East: Mt. Arch in today's Shantung Province, one of the Five Mountains in China. It is the most sacred of the five, because 72 sovereigns in prehistoric China made sacrifices to the god of the mountain and 12 emperors made sacrifices from the Ch'in dynasty to the Ch'ing dynasty, clearly recorded in history books.
* Five Mounts: the Five Mountains in China, including Mount Ever in Shanhsi, Mount Scale in Hunan, Mount Arch in Shantung, Mount Flora in Sha'anhsi, and Mount Tower in Honan, which symbolizes the unity of the Chinese nation from north, south, east, west and center.
* Queen Mother: referring to Mother West, a sovereign goddess living on Mt. Queen in Chinese myths. She was originally described as human-bodied, tiger-toothed, leopard-tailed and hoopoe-haired, regarded as a goddess in charge of women protection, marriage and procreation, and longevity. According to *Sir Lush*, with the Word, Queen Mother sat on Mt. Young Broad.
* Confucius: Confucius (551 B.C.- 479 B.C.), a renowned thinker, educator and statesman in the Spring and Autumn period, born in the State of Lu, who was the founder of Confucianism and who had exerted profound influence on Chinese culture. Confucius is one of the few leaders who based their philosophy on the virtues that are required for the day-to-day living. His philosophy centered on personal and governmental morality, correctness of social relationships, justice and sincerity.

* cinnabar: a crystallized red mercuric sulfide, the raw material for elixir in Wordist alchemy.
* pine: an evergreen tree with needle-shaped leaves, a symbol of longevity and rectitude in Chinese culture.

赠 焦 道 士

海上游三岛，
淮南预八公。
坐知千里外，
跳向一壶中。
缩地朝珠阙，
行天使玉童。
饮人聊割酒，
送客乍分风。
天老能行气，
吾师不养空。
谢君徒雀跃，
无可问鸿濛。

To Master Chiao, the Wordist

You surf to Three Isles on the blue
And meet in Huainan Eight Men true.
Shut in, you know all, where and what;
To rise, you jump into a pot.
Shrinking distance, to court you fly,
And order sprites to cruise the sky.
Toasting, you cleft the cup and brew;
To guests, you split wind into two.
Like Sky Old, you run air employed;
You need not contemplate the void.
Like a sparrow you leap ahead,

No need to ask Blackgoose instead.

* Three Isles: referring to the three fairy islands in East Sea, which is called East China Sea now, having an area of more than 700,000 square kilometers.
* Huainan: an area in the drainage basin of the Huai River, first an eastern barbarian area governed by a vassal state of Chough called Choulai in Western Chough period, enfeoffed as Kingdom of Huainan in the Han dynasty.
* Eight Men true: eight alchemists invited by King of Huainan. When they arrived, the porter was disappointed at their old age and would not admit them. The eight men said:"You discriminate our age, now we'll be young." So saying, they turned into children. King of Huainan, so surprised, bowed to them as their disciple. The eight men could make all kinds of miracles, and later rose to the Heavens, taking King of Huainan with them.
* jump into a pot: an allusion to a legend, which goes like this — Ch'angfang Fei, a market monitor, once saw an old man selling medicine, his pot hung at the entrance of the market. When business was over, the old man jumped into his pot.
* Sky Old: Lord Yellow's advisor as is recorded in *Bamboo Book Annals* and *Lord Yellow Cartshaft*.
* sparrow: a small, plain-colored passerine bird related to the finches, grosbeaks and buntings, a very common bird in China, a symbol of insignificance.
* Blackgoose: an immortal in Sir Lush's fable, who seems to know nothing but leaping happily.

赠 祖 三 咏

蟏蛸挂虚牖，
蟋蟀鸣前除。
岁晏凉风至，
君子复何如。
高馆阒无人，
离居不可道。
闲门寂已闭，
落日照秋草。
虽有近音信，
千里阻河关。
中复客汝颍，
去年归旧山。
结交二十载，
不得一日展。
贫病子既深，
契阔余不浅。
仲秋虽未归，
暮秋以为期。
良会讵几日，
终日长相思。

To Tsu Three

Spiders hang on the window bare;
Crickets to the steps sing an air.
The year ends with a chilly sough;

How are you getting along now?
Your cottage so quiet, there is none;
Isolated, where are you gone?
Your door is closed to the small pass;
The late sun chills the autumn grass.
You are here as I have been told,
Barred by the rivers manifold.
You once toured Ru and Ying from here
And came back to the hills last year.
We've been friends twenty years or so,
But I have no means to see you.
You have been so poor and ill now,
And to hard work I deeply bow.
Mid-autumn now, you're still away.
Shall we make late autumn our day?
It won't be long before we meet;
Longing is long, bitterly sweet.

* spider: a wingless arachnid having an unsegmented abdomen and capable of spinning silk in the construction of webs for the capture of prey such as flies and insects, regarded as a mascot in China, a symbol of good luck or good news to come.
* cricket: a leaping orthopterous insect, with long antennae and three segments in each tarsus, the male of which makes a chirping sound by friction of forewings, a common image of a quiet night in Chinese literature.
* Ru and Ying: the Ru River and the Ying River. The upper reach of the Ru is what is called the North Ru, and it flows into the Surging River. The Ying River originates from Ying Dale and flows into the Huai River in today's Anhui Province.

喜祖三至留宿

门前洛阳客，
下马拂征衣。
不枉故人驾，
平生多掩扉。
行人返深巷，
积雪带馀晖。
早岁同袍者，
高车何处归。

Keeping Tsu Three for the Night

A guest from Loshine comes to me；
Dismounting, his clothes he does pat.
With my friend how glad I can be!
My door has long been closed like that!
All folks go back to their deep lane，
Where snow is touched with afterglow.
My friend, stay with me I maintain；
With you high cart, where will you go?

---

* Loshine: Loyang if transliterated, the eastern capital and the second largest city, a metropolitan, in the T'ang dynasty, with a population of about 0.8 million.

齐州送祖三

送君南浦泪如丝,
君向东州使我悲。
为报故人憔悴尽,
如今不似洛阳时。

Seeing Off Tsu Three at Ch'ichow

You going south, my tears drip like a string;
You going east, the grief does my heart sting.
For you I'm sick, for you I pine away;
That day in Loshine, different from today.

* Ch'ichow: an old town in the T'ang dynasty, no longer existent now, in approximately present-day Ch'ip'ing, Shantung Province.
* Loshine: Loyang if transliterated, the eastern of the two great cities that served as capitals in the early Chinese dynasties, and second city of the Empire in T'ang times, when it had about 800,000 inhabitants.

寒食汜上作

广武城边逢暮春，
汶阳归客泪沾巾。
落花寂寂啼山鸟，
杨柳青青渡水人。

Composed on the River Ssu on Cold Food Day

It is late spring now in Broadmartial Town;
Back from the Wen, I feel tears dripping down.
To the flowers fallen the mountain birds cheep;
To me who'll cross the Ssu the willows sweep.

* the River Ssu: the river that originates from the southeast of Honan and flows north to the Yellow River at Ssu Water in Hsingshine.
* Cold Food Day: one or two days before Pure Brightness Day (the third day of the third moon each year), a festival in memory of Chiht'ui of Chieh (? - 636 B.C.) without cooking for a day.
* Broadmartial Town: two towns bearing this name on Mt. Broadmartial in today's Hsingshine, Honan Province.
* the Wen: the Wen River, 12 kilometers north of Mid-town in today's Honan Province.
* willow: any of a large genus (*Salix*) of shrubs and trees related to the poplars, widely distributed in China and most of the world, having generally smooth branches, and often long, slender, pliant, and sometimes pendent branchlets, which seem to be waving good-bye, or weeping amorously, or drooping for nostalgia. It is a significant image in Chinese literature because of its litheness and charm.

观 别 者

青青杨柳陌,
陌上别离人。
爱子游燕赵,
高堂有老亲。
不行无可养,
行去百忧新。
切切委兄弟,
依依向四邻。
都门帐饮毕,
从此谢亲宾。
挥涕逐前侣,
含凄动征轮。
车徒望不见,
时见起行尘。
吾亦辞家久,
看之泪满巾。

Watching Those Parting

On the road green, green willows sway,
Sway to the one who'll go away.
The dear son will in Yan-Chao roam,
Leaving his dear parents at home.
At home he cannot them sustain;
Now leaving, he feels a new pain.
He tells his brothers what to do

And bids all his neighbors adieu.
In the Town Gate tent he's drunk now,
So to kin and friends he does bow.
He catches up with mates in tears;
Sadly he starts to push the rears.
Cart and groom vanish from my eyes,
Except the dust kicked up there flies.
For long out of home, I've been here;
The sight moves me to shed my tear.

* willow: any of a large genus of shrubs and trees related to the poplars, having lancet-like green leaves, generally smooth branches, and often long, slender, pliant, and sometimes pendent branchlets, which seem to be waving good-bye, or weeping amorously, or drooping for nostalgia. It is a significant image in Chinese literature because of its litheness and appeal. The best image is in *Vetch We Pick*, a verse in *The Book of Songs*, which is like this: When we left long ago, / The willows waved adieu. / Now back to our home town, / We meet snow falling down.
* Yan-Chao: referring to northern areas of China, the place once belonging to the State of Yan (1044 B.C.- 222 B.C.) and the State of Chao (403 B.C.- 222 B.C.), a place often associated with knight-errants, assassins, and martyrs that lit up the sky of magnanimity in Chinese history.

偶 然 作
Composed Accidentally

其 一

楚国有狂夫,
茫然无心想。
散发不冠带,
行歌南陌上。
孔丘与之言,
仁义莫能奖。
未尝肯问天,
何事须击壤。
复笑采薇人,
胡为乃长往。

No. 1

A mad man in the State of Ch'u
Thinks of nothing, nothing he'll do.
No cap he'll wear, but unkempt hair;
On the south lane, he sings an air.
Confucius would with him converse;
To him virtues are but perverse.
He's never asked the sky, the blue;
There's no need to strike wooden shoe.
He jeers at those who gathered fern
Integrity is what he'll spurn.

* A mad man: referring to Cart Joiner, a hermit in the State of Ch'u, who spurned all traditional values, actually any doctrine.
* the State of Ch'u: a vassal state of Chough, one of the powers in the Warring States period, conquered and annexed by Ch'in in 223 B.C.
* Confucius: Confucius (551 B.C.- 479 B.C.), born into a declining aristocrat family in a chaotic revolutionary age, a great educationalist, ideologist and the founder of Confucianism from the State of Lu (770 B.C.- 476 B.C.). Through his righteousness, optimism and enterprising spirit he has greatly influenced the character of the Chinese people from generation to generation.
* wooden shoe: a game in ancient China. He who manages to strike the targeted wooden shoe with another wooden shoe wins.
* fern: any of a widely distributed class of flowerless, seedless pteridophytic plants, having roots and stems and feathery leaves (fronds) which carry the reproductive spores in clusters of sporangia called *sori*. Its young stems and root starch are table delicacies to Chinese now as well as in the past.

其 二

田舍有老翁，
垂白衡门里。
有时农事闲，
斗酒呼邻里。
喧聒茅檐下，
或坐或复起。
短褐不为薄，
园葵固足美。
动则长子孙，
不曾向城市。
五帝与三王，
古来称天子。
干戈将揖让，
毕竟何者是。
得意苟为乐，
野田安足鄙。
且当放怀去，
行行没馀齿。

No. 2

In the farmland there's an old man,
The man with white hair in his shack.
He'd shout to neighbors for a drink
When farming work is o'er or slack.
Under his thatched eaves he makes noise,
Sometimes to sit, sometimes to rise,
His linen shirt he always wears,

And is content with mallow nice.
He works just to rear children there,
Never having to go to town.
Five Emperors or else Three Kings
Were called Son of Heaven, the Crown.
There they fight and here they resign,
What are they doing, what the hell?
If we're happy, happy we are;
Farming life is nice, here I dwell.
O make merry, go marry, cheers
So that I'll finish my last years.

* linen: yarn, thread or cloth made of flax, used as material for the making of shirts, tablecloths, sheets, etc.
* mallow: Malva verticillata or any plant of the genus *Malva* with roundish leaves, the first of the five popular vegetables in ancient China.
* Five Emperors: the five mythical emperors or lords in prehistorical China are Lord Yellow (Huang Ti) (2717 B.C.- 2599 B.C.), Lord Alarm (Ti K'u) (2480 B.C.- 2345 B.C.), Dark Crown (Chuanhsu) (2342 B.C.- 2245 B.C.), Mound (Yao) (cir. 2377 B.C.- 2259 B.C.), and Hibiscus (Shun) (2277 B.C.- 2178 B.C.)
* Three Kings: the first kings of the three dynasties, Worm of Hsia, Hotspring of Shang and King Civil of Chough.
* Son of Heaven: a metaphor for a king or emperor to suggest divine kingship.

其 三

日夕见太行，
沉吟未能去。
问君何以然，
世网婴我故。
小妹日成长，
兄弟未有娶。
家贫禄既薄，
储蓄非有素。
几回欲奋飞，
踟蹰复相顾。
孙登长啸台，
松竹有遗处。
相去讵几许，
故人在中路。
爱染日已薄，
禅寂日已固。
忽乎吾将行，
宁俟岁云暮。

No. 3

Mt. Great Go I can see all day,
But never have I chance to go.
You may ask me why, why like this;
The world's a net that holds me so.
My little sister has grown up;
My brothers are not yet married.
No much saving do I have now,

Poor, ill-provided, so harried.
Several times I have tried to fly,
But hesitant, I look to and fro.
Teng Sun's Roaring Mound you find here;
The relics are in the bamboo.
Is an immortal far from here?
My old friend is now on the way.
Temptations are waning from me;
In calmness for long I will stay.
Right now get up and go from here;
Why wait till the end of the year?

* Mt. Great Go: Mt. T'aihang if transliterated, meandering on the border of Shanhsi, Honan and Sha'anhsi, an important mountain range in East China and a geographic dividing line.
* Teng Sun: a hermit in the Way and Chin dynasties, from whom Chi Juan and Kuang Chi once learned the Word.
* Roaring Mound: a mound on Mt. Su Gate, where Teng Sun used to live in reclusion.
* bamboo: a tall, tree-like or shrubby grass in tropical and semi-tropical regions, a symbol of integrity and altitude, one of the four most important botanical images in Chinese literature, which are wintersweet, orchid, bamboo and chrysanthemum. Bamboo shoots, fresh or dried, are widely used in Chinese cuisine, bamboo rats and bamboo worms are regarded as table delicacies.

其 四

陶潜任天真，
其性颇耽酒。
自从弃官来，
家贫不能有。
九月九日时，
菊花空满手。
中心窃自思，
傥有人送否。
白衣携壶觞，
果来遗老叟。
且喜得斟酌，
安问升与斗。
奋衣野田中，
今日嗟无负。
兀傲迷东西，
蓑笠不能守。
倾倒强行行，
酣歌归五柳。
生事不曾问，
肯愧家中妇。

No. 4

Ch'ien T'ao, naïve, naïve as such,
By nature he loved wine so much.
Since from his office he resigned,
So poor, no more gold could he find.
Double Ninth Day came around, and,

He held chrysanthemum in hand.
Deep in his mind he might opine:
Maybe someone will send me wine.
A man in white carried a pot;
It was wine he held for the sot.
He drank, and drank a lot with cheer;
One cup is fine, two cups are dear.
His clothes he waved up to the field:
Can we pass the day unfulfilled?
He, drunk, swayed east and west to peep;
His cap and cape he could not keep.
He stumbled on and went along;
To Five Willows he sang a song.
"I have ne'er e'er cared about life;
Need I feel shame before my wife?"

* Ch'ien T'ao: referring to Poolbright T'ao (A.D. 352 – A.D. 427), a verse writer, poet, and litterateur in the Chin dynasty, and the founder of Chinese idyllism, who was once the magistrate of P'engtse. Pure and lofty, T'ao resigned from official life several times to live a life of simplicity. There were five willow trees planted in front of his house, so he called himself Mr. Five Willows.
* Double Ninth Day: the ninth day of the ninth moon in Chinese Lunar calendar. There is a long tradition that people climb a height on this day, carrying chrysanthemums for their deceased dear ones and sprigs of cornel to exorcize evil spirits.
* chrysanthemum: any of a genus of perennials (*Chryanthemum*) of the composite family, some cultivated varieties of which have large heads of showy flowers of various colors, a symbol of purity or longevity in Chinese culture.
* Five Willows: Ch'ien T'ao's nickname.

其 五

赵女弹箜篌,
复能邯郸舞。
夫婿轻薄儿,
斗鸡事齐主。
黄金买歌笑,
用钱不复数。
许史相经过,
高门盈四牡。
客舍有儒生,
昂藏出邹鲁。
读书三十年,
腰间无尺组。
被服圣人教,
一生自穷苦。

No. 5

The Chao lady could Kunghou play
And dance a Hantan roundelay.
Her husband, flighty, all ignored,
But did cockfights to serve the Lord.
He squandered gold all for fun;
Money through his fingers did run.
He got on with peers and those great,
Who had four-steed carts by their gate.
In the guesthouse scholars there are,
Each of them is a shining star.
They may have learned for thirty years,

But on their waist no sash appears.

By saints and sages they have been taught,

But they have been poor, having naught.

* Chao: the State of Chao (403 B.C.- 222 B.C.), a vassal state in the Spring and Autumn period, one of the Seven Powers in the Warring States period.
* *Kunghou*: a stringed musical instrument looking like a large bow or a triangle, usually played by a female.
* Hantan: one of the earliest cities in China, with a history of 3,100 years. As the capital of the State of Chao, it prospered for 180 years until it was subjugated in 228 B.C and annexed in 221 B.C. by Ch'in.
* cockfights: cockfighting has a long history in China, a main recreational and gaming activity throughout history. The earliest cock fighting in China recorded in *Historical Records* was in 770 B.C.

淇上即事田园

屏居淇水上，
东野旷无山。
日隐桑柘外，
河明间井间。
牧童望村去，
猎犬随人还。
静者亦何事，
荆扉乘昼关。

The Field on the Ch'i, an Impromptu

Alone on the Ch'i I abide;
The east field looks so far and wide.
Beyond the mulberries sets the sun;
The river through the lanes is shone.
To the village the shepherds peer,
Followed by hunters in the rear.
Why does the hermit do that way,
His chaste door shut during the day?

* the Ch'i: the Ch'i River, a branch of the Yellow River in ancient times. Now it is in today's Honan Province. It appeared many times in *The Book of Songs*, like *In the Woods*: In the park we enjoyed a date; / By the Ch'i she saw me off late.
* chaste door: a door made of chaste tree branches, a symbol of country life or hermitage.

淇上别赵仙舟

相逢方一笑,
相送还成泣。
祖帐已伤离,
荒城复愁入。
天寒远山净,
日暮长河急。
解缆君已遥,
望君犹伫立。

Farewell to Fairyboat Chao on the Ch'i

We smile at our encounter, glad;
Now you leave, I can't help but cry.
The farewell feast is o'er, so sad;
To the bleak town, once more I sigh.
The hills are clean on the cold day;
The river flows in afterglow.
Unanchored, you're now far away;
For long I stand, eyes cast to you.

* the Ch'i: the River Ch'i, in today's Honan Province, a branch of the Yellow River in the past.
* the bleak town: referring to a border town in Chinese literature.

不　遇　咏

北阙献书寝不报，
南山种田时不登。
百人会中身不预，
五侯门前心不能。
身投河朔饮君酒，
家在茂陵平安否。
且共登山复临水，
莫问春风动杨柳。
今人作人多自私，
我心不说君应知。
济人然后拂衣去，
肯作徒尔一男儿。

Ode to My Unfulfilled Life

At North Gate unanswered is my advice;
In South Hills, I can reap no corn or rice.
A hundred gather, I can take no part;
To bow to the lords I've no humble heart.
North of the river with you I drink wine;
My family's in Lushridge, are they fine?
Climb high to o'erlook water, here we go;
Let spring wind to the moving willows blow.
No people on earth can have a square deal;
You should know how unhappy I may feel.
No, I must go, the world I will sustain;

How the hell can I be a man in vain?

* North Gate: One of the gates of No-end Palace.
* South Hills: a name borrowed from a verse in *The Han Book*: The field on South Hills yon, / Has no weeding e'er done.
* Lushridge: one of Five Mausoleums of Western Han, the tomb of Emperor Martial of Han, the largest of all Han mausoleums, located in Lush Township, hence the name.
* willow: any of a large genus of shrubs and trees related to the poplars, having glossy green brow-like leaves, generally smooth branches, and often long, slender, pliant, and sometimes pendent branchlets, which seem to be dancing with a wind, waving good-bye, weeping amorously, or drooping for nostalgia.

送严秀才还蜀

宁亲为令子，
似舅即贤甥。
别路经花县，
还乡入锦城。
山临青塞断，
江向白云平。
献赋何时至，
明君忆长卿。

Sending Off Yan, a Showcharm, to Shu

Kind to your parents you're good son;
Your uncle and you are like one.
You'll pass Flower County on your track,
As to Silkton you now go back.
At Green Pass there the mountains stop;
The river draws clouds from atop.
To Lord you can offer your rhyme;
Hsiangju's remembered all the time.

* showcharm: a talent recommended for official use through the imperial civil-service examination, or a well-learned person in ancient China. A showcharm was very well respected in the traditional meritocratic and bureaucratic Chinese society.
* Flower County: referring to Rivershine County, in present-day Honan Province.
* Silkton: the ancient name for Ch'engtu, for it was a town famous for silk and brocade.
* Green Pass: a border pass lush with green grass.

* Hsiangju: referring to Hsiangju Ssuma (179 B.C.-118 B.C.) in full name, a representative verse writer in Chinese literary history. He and his wife, Wenchün, a brilliant woman poet, were equally famous in Chinese history.

送孟六归襄阳

杜门不复出，
久与世情疏。
以此为良策，
劝君归旧庐。
醉歌田舍酒，
笑读古人书。
好是一生事，
无劳献子虚。

Seeing Meng Six Off to Sowshine

Now shut, I stay inside my door;
With the world I have zest no more.
It's the best policy I'd say;
You may as well go home to stay.
Drink country wine to pass your while
And read ancient books with a smile.
This is best for life all the time;
You need not offer Lord your rhyme.

* Sowshine: a famous historic city, about 2,800 years old, a birthplace of Ch'u, Han and Three Kingdom cultures, and a city of economic and military importance, in the northwest of present-day Hupei Province.

送 权 二

高人不可有,
清论复何深。
一见如旧识,
一言知道心。
明时当薄宦,
解薜去中林。
芳草空隐处,
白云馀故岑。
韩侯久携手,
河岳共幽寻。
怅别千馀里,
临堂鸣素琴。

Seeing Off Ch'üan Two

A great savant's hard to come by;
We talk to explore how and why.
We seem to have been friends before;
We seem to have seen a lot more.
Now we should serve the multitude;
Come back to the world from the wood.
The grass in the grove does lush grow;
O'er the hills white clouds freely flow.
My dear friend, let's go hand in hand
To see the splendor of our land.
Hundreds of miles, it's a long way;

For your trip, the zither I'll play.

* zither: a simple form of a stringed instrument, having a flat sounding board and from thirty to forty strings that are played by plucking with a plectrum. Zither, together with chess, calligraphy and painting are four skills that a traditional litterateur is expected to master.

华　岳

西岳出浮云，
积翠在太清。
连天凝黛色，
百里遥青冥。
白日为之寒，
森沉华阴城。
昔闻乾坤闭，
造化生巨灵。
右足踏方止，
左手推削成。
天地忽开拆，
大河注东溟。
遂为西峙岳，
雄雄镇秦京。
大君包覆载，
至德被群生。
上帝伫昭告，
金天思奉迎。
人祇望幸久，
何独禅云亭？

Mt. Flower

Floating clouds from Mt. West arise,
Like snow piled up all o'er the skies.
The blueness gathers to accrue,

And touches Mt. West all with blue.
It causes the sun to feel cold,
And will the town, Flowershade, enfold.
Of yore, formed were Heaven and earth,
And then Giant Soul was given birth.
He stood with his right leg on land,
And split the range with his left hand.
Two mountains were formed from the one;
To East Sea the river could run.
Henceforth Mt. West began to tower,
And guard Ch'in's capital with power.
Son of Heaven had all to last
And brought virtues to cover the vast.
God on high declared from the blue
And told Gold Sky what he would do.
Earth Man waited long for the throne;
Why stuck at Zen Cloud Kiosk alone?

* Mt. Flower: also known as Mt. West or Mt. Flora, one of the Five Mountains in China, representing the west, regarded as the steepest and saintly mountain in China as it is one of the progenitors of Chinese culture, the shrine of Wordism and the abode of God of Mt. Flora, located in today's Flowershade, Sha'anhsi Province.
* sun: the heavenly body that is the center of attraction and the main source of light and heat in the solar system, a representation of Shine in contrast with Shade, the moon, in Chinese culture, a symbol of hope, life, strength, vigor and youth.
* Flowershade: a town at the foot of Mt. Flower, 120 kilometers from Long Peace, a gateway leading to eight provinces, with a history of more than 2,300 years.
* Giant Soul: River God.
* East Sea: what is known as East China Sea today, with an area of 770 thousand square kilometers.
* Ch'in: the Ch'in State or the State of Ch'in (905 B.C.- 206 B.C.), one of the most powerful vassal states in the Chough dynasty, which was enfeoffed as a dependency of Chough by King Piety of Chough in 905 B.C. and enfeoffed as a vassal state by King

Peace of Chough in 770 B.C. In the ten years from 230 B.C. to 221 B.C., Ch'in wiped out the other six powers and became the first unified regime of China, i.e., the Ch'in Empire.

* Son of Heaven: a metaphor for a king or emperor to suggest divine kingship.
* God: the one Supreme Being, ever-existing and eternal; the infinite creator, sustainer and ruler of the cosmos with the attributes of being omniscient, omnipotent and omnipresent, or else called Father in Heaven or with a natural propensity, the Word, the One, Heaven and so on.
* Gold Sky: God of Mt. Flower.
* Earth Man: God of Earth.

自大散以往深林密竹磴道盘曲四五十里至黄牛岭见黄花川

危径几万转，
数里将三休。
回环见徒侣，
隐映隔林丘。
飒飒松上雨，
潺潺石中流。
静言深溪里，
长啸高山头。
望见南山阳，
白露霭悠悠。
青皋丽已净，
绿树郁如浮。
曾是厌蒙密，
旷然销人忧。

To the Depth of Bamboo from Tasan Pass, Following the Ascending Path, Which Turns and Twists for About Twenty Miles till I Arrive at Ox Ridge and See the Yellow Flower Stream

The high trail has ten thousand turns;
Within a mile three times I rest.
Looking back, my servants I see,
Lagging behind, by the wood pressed.
A gurgling creek on pebbles flow,

While a drizzle swishes from pines.
Over the quietude of the creek,
The height of the mountaintop whines.
On the southern slope of the ridge,
I find a large stretch of white frost.
There shines the brilliance of the marsh,
And the green of trees seems embossed.
The carpet of verdure looks dense,
My worries all disappear hence.

* Tasan Pass: name of an old pass, on Tasan Ridge, 26 kilometers from today's Precious Rooster (Paochi), Sha'anhsi Province.
* Ox Ridge: near Oxpolis (Huangniupao), about 57 kilometers from today's Phoenix County (Fenghsien), Sha'anhsi Province.
* the Yellow Flower Stream: a stream northeast of Phoenix County receiving water from Tasan Ridge.

青　溪

言入黄花川，
每逐清溪水。
随山将万转，
趣途无百里。
声喧乱石中，
色静深松里。
漾漾泛菱荇，
澄澄映葭苇。
我心素已闲，
清川澹如此。
请留盘石上，
垂钓将已矣。

A Blue Stream

In the Yellow Flower Stream I row,
Chasing blue ripples on the go.
Turning with the hills it does run,
For thirty miles, a trip of fun.
Against heaped rocks, it makes a noise;
Among deep pines, calm it enjoys.
The ripples push the water weed;
The pondlet mirrors the lush reed.
My simple heart is now at ease;
The blueness like this does me please.
Oh, on the boulder I would stay

And angle to finish my day!

* the Yellow Flower Stream: a stream northeast of Phoenix County receiving water from Tasan Ridge, in today's Sha'anhsi Province.
* pine: any of a genus (*Pinus*) of evergreen trees of the pine family, a cone-bearing tree having bundles of two to five needle-shaped leaves growing in clusters, an important image in Chinese literature, a symbol of rectitude, solitude, longevity and so on.
* reed: the slender, frequently jointed stem of certain tall grasses growing in wet places like a pond or marsh, or in grasses themselves.

纳　　凉

乔木万馀株，
清流贯其中。
前临大川口，
豁达来长风。
涟漪涵白沙，
素鲔如游空。
偃卧盘石上，
翻涛沃微躬。
漱流复濯足，
前对钓鱼翁。
贪饵凡几许，
徒思莲叶东。

Enjoying the Cool

There stand myriads of trees so tall,
Through which a limpid river flows.
In front you face the river mouth
So open that a long wind blows.
The ripples carry some white sand
Over which white sturgeons swim free.
On the stone I lie on my back,
While the water splashes to me.
The waves go thru between my feet,
To the fisher and what's near him.
How many fish will bite the bait?

East of the lotus leaves they swim.

* sturgeon: a large genoid fish of northern regions, with coarse, edible flesh. Sturgeons are the common source of of isinglass and caviar.
* lotus: one of the various plants of the waterlily family, noted for their large floating leaves and showy flowers, a symbol of purity and elegance in Chinese culture and a common topic in Chinese literature, unsoiled though out of soil, so clean with all leaves green.

戏 题 盘 石

可怜盘石临泉水，
复有垂杨拂酒杯。
若道春风不解意，
何因吹送落花来。

Dedication to the Boulder for Fun

The lovely boulder is faced with a spring;
The drooping willow flies to stroke my cup.
If vernal wind does not understand me,
Why does it send me flowers to cheer me up?

---

* willow: any of a large genus of shrubs and trees related to the poplars, having glossy green brow-like leaves, generally smooth branches, and often long, slender, pliant, and sometimes pendent branchlets, which seem to be waving good-bye, or weeping amorously, or drooping for nostalgia.

晓 行 巴 峡

际晓投巴峡，
馀春忆帝京。
晴江一女浣，
朝日众鸡鸣。
水国舟中市，
山桥树杪行。
登高万井出，
眺迥二流明。
人作殊方语，
莺为故国声。
赖多山水趣，
稍解别离情。

Rowing to Pa Gorge at Dawn

At daybreak to Pa Gorge I row;
Late spring now, Long Peace I miss so.
On the Ching a maid washes yarn;
All roosters crow unto the dawn.
In floating boats, they sell and buy;
On the plank bridge, they walk on high.
I climb and see many rocks rise,
And to the two flows cast my eyes.
The folks speak a different tongue here;
The orioles chirp just like ours there.
The hills and rills please me as such;

I don't miss hometown mine so much.

* Pa Gorge: On the Long River there are many gorges bearing this name; this is one of the gorges in the area of Pa.
* Long Peace: Ch'ang'an if transliterated, the capital of the T'ang Empire, with 1,000,000 inhabitants, the largest walled city ever built by man, and a cosmopolis of world religions, Buddhism, Confucianism, Wordism, Nestorianism, Zoroastrianism, and even Islamism represented by Saracens. It saw the wonder of the age that reached the pinnacle of brilliance in Emperor Deepsire's reign: The main castle with its nine-fold gates, the thirty-six imperial palaces, pillars of gold, innumerable mansions and villas of noblemen, the broad avenues thronged with motley crowds of townsfolk, gallants on horseback, and mandarin cars drawn by yokes of black oxen, countless houses of pleasure, which opened their doors by night all made this city a kaleidoscope of miracles.
* the Ching: the Ching River, the largest branch of the Yellow River, originating from Kansu and flowing into the Yellow River in Sha'anhsi, and also a branch of the Wei River originating from Ninghsia.
* rooster: the male of the chicken, which struts with pride and crows at dawn.
* oriole: golden oriole, one of the family of passerine birds, which looks bright yellow with contrasting black wings and sings beautiful songs.

赠房卢氏琯

达人无不可，
忘己爱苍生。
岂复少十室，
弦歌在两楹。
浮人日已归，
但坐事农耕。
桑榆郁相望，
邑里多鸡鸣。
秋山一何净，
苍翠临寒城。
视事兼偃卧。
对书不簪缨。
萧条人吏疏，
鸟雀下空庭。
鄙夫心所尚，
晚节异平生。
将从海岳居。
守静解天刑。
或可累安邑。
茅茨君试营。

To Kuan Fang, Magistrate of Lushi

A talent can everything do;
He loves all souls under the blue.
He does care Lushi is so small;

He can manage well in the hall.
The vagrants come back day by day;
To do farm work they all will stay.
Mulberries and elms luxuriant grow;
In the fiefdom here roosters crow.
The autumn mountains are so clean;
The cold town's veiled with vivid green.
At rest, his mind for work does run;
He reads a book with hair undone.
No disputes, no lawsuit at all;
Birds fly into the empty hall.
It's what I like to see the best:
Now as the past all are well blessed.
I'd live in hills or by the sea,
Freed of all worries, so care-free.
You may retire now from the town;
A thatched hut may settle you down.

* Kuan Fang: originally from Honan County, Honan Prefecture, an official of Privy Council, and then the magistrate of Lushi.
* Lushi: today Lushi County, established in 113 B.C. in the Western Han dynasty, in today's Three-door Gorge, Honan Province.
* mulberry: a kind of tree of the genus *Morus*, *Morus alba Linn* in Latin, whose leaves are food for silkworms, and whose berries are served as a delicacy for humans.
* elm: a deciduous shade tree of America, Europe and Asia (genus *Ulmus*), with a broad, spreading, or overarching top, whose sweet pods look like coins and are delicious.
* rooster: the male of the chicken, which struts with pride and crows at dawn.
* a thatched hut: a metonymy for hemitage in Chinese culture.

送从弟蕃游淮南

读书复骑射,
带剑游淮阴。
淮阴少年辈,
千里远相寻。
高义难自隐,
明时宁陆沉。
岛夷九州外,
泉馆三山深。
席帆聊问罪,
卉服尽成擒。
归来见天子,
拜爵赐黄金。
忽思鲈鱼鲙,
复有沧洲心。
天寒蒹葭渚,
日落云梦林。
江城下枫叶,
淮上闻秋砧。
送归青门外,
车马去骎骎。
惆怅新丰树,
空馀天际禽。

Seeing Off My Cousin Fan to Huainan

You love books, riding, shooting and

Will tour Huaishade, a sword in hand.
The boys in Huaishade will come now
From far away and to you bow.
Your altitude can't itself hide;
It's good time, how can you subside?
The isles and nine realms you may sweep
And wipe Spring Inn in mountains deep.
You will put up a sail to surge
And barbarian brown shirts you purge.
When you're back, you bow to the Lord,
To win peerage, gold and all reward.
Don't try to retire to eat perch;
To guard the land you may still search.
The reeds and shoal freeze in cold days;
In Cloud Dream dews reflect sun rays.
The maple leaves there fall aground;
From the river comes pelting sound.
I will welcome you at Green Gate,
With carts and horses at high rate.
To the Newrich trees I now sigh;
The birds cruise the end of the sky.

* Huainan: an area in the drainage basin of the Huai River, first an eastern barbarian area governed by a vassal state of Chough called Choulai in Western Chough period, enfeoffed as Kingdom of Huainan in the Han dynasty.
* Huaishade: the birthplace of Hsin Han, a founding commander of Han, in the hinterland of the northern plain of Chiangsu, on the southern bank of the Huai River, hence the name.
* Spring Inn: a house that Fishman (who has a human body having a fish tail) lives in Chinese mythology.
* reed: the slender, frequently jointed stem of certain tall grasses growing in wet places like ponds or lakes or in grasses themselves.

* Cloud Dream: a great marshland, south of Lake Cavehall in present-day Hunan Province.
* maple: any of a large genus (*Acer*) of deciduous trees of the north temperate zone, with opposite leaves that turn red in autumn frost and a fruit of two joined samaras. The maple is a symbol of cordial love and good luck in Chinese culture owing to its bright fiery color.
* Newrich: a county, built by Pang Liu in imitation of his hometown Rich County, in today's Lintung County, Sha'anhsi Province, famous for its wine, the best wine in the T'ang dynasty. Pang Liu, Emperor Highsire, born in Rich in East China, rose from grassroots, wiped out Hsiang's army and established Han, with Long Peace as its capital. As his father missed the beauty and wine of his hometown, Pang Liu made a copy of his hometown and moved the best brewers here, and ever since then Newrich wine has been well-known, attracting generations of litterateurs to sing praise of it.

送 崔 兴 宗

已恨亲皆远，
谁怜友复稀。
君王未西顾，
游宦尽东归。
塞迥山河净，
天长云树微。
方同菊花节，
相待洛阳扉。

Seeing Off Hsingtsung Ts'ui

Our relatives all keep away;
Friends are few, not friendly the least.
His Majesty has not come west;
All go-getters rush to the east.
The pass far off, the land is calm;
The sky high, the clouded trees sway.
Chrysanthemum Day is now near;
Let's meet in Loshine, come on pray.

* Hsingtsung Ts'ui: a T'ang poet from Broadridge (today's Tingchow, Hopei Province), who lived in reclusion in the South Mountains south of Long Peace in his early life and used to hang out with Wei Wang, our poet and painter, drinking, writing and playing the zither. The position he held in the dynasty was Left Alternate and he finished his career as Secretary of Jaochow Prefecture, which is approximately today's Chianghsi Province.

* Chrysanthemum Day: referring to Double Ninth Day, the ninth day of the ninth moon

in Chinese Lunar calendar. There is a long tradition that people climb a height and enjoy chrysanthemums on this day to commemorate their ancestors.
* Loshine: Loyang if transliterated, the eastern of the two great cities that served as capitals in the early Chinese dynasties, and second city of the Empire in T'ang times, when it had about 800,000 inhabitants.

归 嵩 山 作

清川带长薄，
车马去闲闲。
流水如有意，
暮禽相与还。
荒城临古渡，
落日满秋山。
迢递嵩高下，
归来且闭关。

Back to Mt. Tower

The stream girdles the bog oblong;
My horse and cart move on, so free.
The gurgle loving flows along,
While the homing birds chirp to me.
The bleak town near the ferry old
Sees fall peaks in the setting sun.
Mt. Tower looms far, rolling and rolled,
Now back home, I'm a lonely one.

* bog: wet and spongy ground; marsh; morass.
* Mt. Tower: located in the west of present-day Honan Province, one of the Five Sacred Mountains in Chinese culture. It is one of the five sanctuaries of Wordism, and the abode of God of Mt. Tower worshipped by Han Chinese, with an area of 450 square kilometers, consisting of Mt. Greatroom and Mt. Smallroom, having 72 peaks, 350 meters above sea level at the lowest and 1,512 meters at the highest.

上 张 令 公

珥笔趋丹陛,
垂珰上玉除。
步檐青琐闼,
方幰画轮车。
市阅千金字,
朝闻五色书。
致君光帝典,
荐士满公车。
伏奏回金驾,
横经重石渠。
从兹罢角抵,
且复幸储胥。
天统知尧后,
王章笑鲁初。
匈奴遥俯伏,
汉相俨簪裾。
贾生非不遇,
汲黯自堪疏。
学易思求我,
言诗或起予。
当从大夫后,
何惜隶人馀。

To Chang, Premier of Privy Council

You go up the steps with your brush;

Your trinkets clink as you flush.
Thru aisles and wicket doors you walk;
By His Dragon Sedan you stalk.
Each of your words is like gold bright;
On five-dyed silks, edicts you write.
To zenith you help Lord ascend;
Many great talents you commend.
You admonish and He does turn;
You read, you teach, and more you learn.
Henceforth Lord pleasures does abstain,
And comes back to hard work again.
His reign is better than Mound's reign;
The gain outdoes the Lu State's gain.
You prostrate the Huns from afar;
How solemn and how great you are!
Like Ee Chia, not well blessed I am;
Estranged, downcast, I do feel shame.
Perhaps with *Changes* I may aid you,
And from *Songs* better we may know.
My lord, I'll follow you behind,
One of the slaves, one of the kind.

* Chang: Chiuling Chang (A.D. 678 – A.D. 740), a famous and capable premier and poet in the T'ang dynasty, a descendant of Liang Chang (cir. 250 B.C.– 186 B.C.) in the Han dynasty and Hua Chang (A.D. 232 – A.D. 300) in the Chin dynasty.
* brush: writing brush, also called Chinese brush or brush for short, which is used for writing or painting. It is one of the four treasures in a Chinese study, the other three stationeries being ink, paper and inkslab.
* wicket door: a side door used by officials coming into or going out of a palace.
* edict: a public ordinance emanating from a sovereign and having the force of law.
* zenith: the point directly overhead in the sky or on the celestial sphere, opposed to the nadir.

* Mound: Mound (2377 B.C.- 2259 B.C.), Yao if transliterated. Divine and noble, Mound has been regarded as one of Five Lords in ancient China.
* the Lu State: the State of Lu, the state enfeoffed to Prince of Chough, inherited by his son Firstling Bird, exterminated by Ch'u in 256 B.C.
* Hun: one of barbaric nomadic Asian peoples who frequently invaded China, a general term referring to all northern or western invaders or aliens; Hun, as an adjective or attributive, refers to something about or of Huns.
* Ee Chia: Ee Chia (200 B.C.- 168 B.C.), a political commentator, litterateur, who gained his fame when he was young. When he served as an official, he was envied by those higher-ranking ministers.
* *Changes*: one of the five Confucian classics, that is, *The Book of Songs*, *The Book of Documents*, *Changes*, *Rites*, *Spring and Autumn Annals*. It is a philosophical book based on observations of all things that change or run according to a natural rule of binary opposition and mutual identification.
* *Songs*: referring to *The Book of Songs*, which consists of *Airs of the States*, *Psalms*, and *Odes*, compiled by Confucius, the first collection of poems in Chinese history.

东 溪 玩 月

月从断山口，
遥吐柴门端。
万木分空霁，
流阴中夜攒。
光连虚象白，
气与风露寒。
谷静秋泉响，
岩深青霭残。
清灯入幽梦，
破影抱空峦。
恍惚琴窗里，
松溪晓思难。

Playing with the Moon by the East Stream

From the split crag the moon does sheen
And sends light to the bramble door.
All trees beneath the sky stand clean,
While Luna at night does shine pour.
The light seems pale to link a star;
A wind whirls and churns up cold air.
The vale quiet takes a spring afar;
The crag deep holds haze from light rare.
The light blue enters my dream green,
Where broken shades in dales I seek.

The lute is played beneath a screen;
My thought strolls along the pine creek.

* the East Stream: also known as the Ying River or the Sandy Ying River, originating from the east peak of Mt. Tower, 620 kilometers long, which is the biggest branch of the Huai River.
* bramble door: a door made of brambles, a symbol of country life.
* Luna: the moon, which has an important position in Chinese literature, the most frequent image of coolness, loneliness, and hope for a happy reunion. It is the goddess of the moon and of months in Roman mythology, and in Chinese culture the imperial concubine of Lord Alarm (2480 B.C.- 2345 B.C.), one of five mythical emperors in prehistorical China.
* screen: a curtain which separates or cuts off, shelters or protects as a light partition, usually made of bamboo, a common image in Chinese literature. A poem in *The Book of Songs* reads like this:"You wait for me before the screen; / Your hat-rings white do tinkle clean, / And your rubies brilliantly sheen."

山中寄诸弟妹

山中多法侣，
禅诵自为群。
城郭遥相望，
唯应见白云。

To My Siblings from the Mountains

In the mountains monks and priests troop;
They muse or recite in a group.
The town can be seen from afar;
Clouds float above and free they are.

* my siblings: referring to Wei Wang's six siblings: four younger brothers and two younger sisters. Wei Wang's brother Chin Wang, a vice minister of the Pivy Council (the Secretariat), was famous as an official, poet and calligrapher.

献 始 兴 公

宁栖野树林，
宁饮涧水流。
不用坐梁肉，
崎岖见王侯。
鄙哉匹夫节，
布褐将白头。
任智诚则短，
守仁固其优。
侧闻大君子，
安问党与雠。
所不卖公器，
动为苍生谋。
贱子跪自陈：
可为帐下不？
感激有公议，
曲私非所求。

To Count of Rising

I would rather live in wild wood,
I would rather drink the creek flow.
I need not for dainties sit there
Or please lords and peers, bowing low.
A simple rural man I'd be
In brown clothes till white hair I grow.
Wit and wisdom I fall short of;

To keep faith is what I can do.
I hear you are so fair and square
With your sworn foe or bosom friend.
Public interests you do not sell;
To serve the masses is your end.
Now I fall on my knees to ask:
Can I give service in your tent?
I'll be gratified with your trust,
And do my best, not false or bent.

* Count of Rising: referring to Chiuling Chang (A.D. 678 – A.D. 740), a famous premier and poet in the T'ang dynasty, a descendant of Liang Chang (cir. 250 B.C.- 186 B.C.) in the Han dynasty and Hua Chang (A.D. 232 – A.D. 300) in the Chin dynasty.
* brown clothes: coarse clothes of, or a metonymy for, a commoner.
* tent: tent office, usually used as headquarters in time of war.

留别山中温古上人兄并示舍弟缙

解薜登天朝，
去师偶时哲。
岂惟山中人，
兼负松上月。
宿昔同游止，
致身云霞末。
开轩临颍阳，
卧视飞鸟没。
好依盘石饭，
屡对瀑泉渴。
理齐小狎隐，
道胜宁外物。
舍弟官崇高，
宗兄此削发。
荆扉但洒扫，
乘闲当过歇。

To Reverent Wenku, a Hermit, and Shown to My Younger Brother, Chin Wang

Out of the hills I come to court
And make friends with all those divine.
I let you down, my master dear
And let down the moon o'er the pine.
We used to saunter side by side
And with mist and clouds we would play.

We drove to the bank of the Ying,
Where we lay while birds flew away.
On the boulder we would oft dine
And by a fountain drink the spring.
Buddhism and nature as the One
Prevails o'er any worldly thing.
My brother's now mayor of Sublime,
And you're tonsured as a monk blessed.
I'll broom my room and open my door;
When you're free, please come for a rest.

* the moon o'er the pine: an image of solitude and rectitude, a metaphor for the hermit in this poem.

* the Ying: the Ying River, a river derived from Mt. Tower. The River Ying has been regarded as one of the origins of Chinese culture.

* the One: a philosophical concept of Wordism, the beginning of all things, as is defined in *Sir Lush*, "In the beginning was the None, having nothing, having no name. Then there arose the One, and nothing was formed yet." Similarly, in the West, God is the One, Self-subsisting Reality. The One in the West and the One in the East are actually one.

* Sublime: a county of three hundred households in the Han dynasty, what is now called Tengfeng, which means offering sacrifices on a mountain.

过乘如禅师萧居士嵩丘兰若

无著天亲弟与兄,
嵩丘兰若一峰晴。
食随鸣磬巢乌下,
行踏空林落叶声。
迸水定侵香案湿,
雨花应共石床平。
深洞长松何所有,
俨然天竺古先生。

A Visit to Buddhist Hsiao Called Zen Master Yana at Grove Calm on Mt. Tower

Non Fame and Sky Dear are two brothers fine;
Mt. Tower and Grove Calm face the peak in shine.
The crows fly down for food at chime stone sound,
Stirring leaves from the trees to fall aground.
Water is splashed to the incense, there spread,
Like flowers rained to all, even the stone bed.
How is the tall pine there by the deep cave?
Much like Master Old from India, so grave.

* Zen: a kind of performance of quietude in a form of meditation or contemplation. When Sanskrit jana was spread to China, it was translated as Zan or Zen for this kind of practice. In the T'ang dynasty, Zen had become very influential among the intellectuals, many of whom were associated with Zen monks and spent time in Zen monasteries.

* Grove Calm: a grove good for meditation.

* Non Fame: name of a Buddhisattava.
* Sky Dear: name of a Buddhisattava.
* Mt. Tower: located in the west of present-day Honan Province, one of the Five Mountains in Chinese culture.
* crow: an omnivorous, raucous, oscine bird of the genus *Corvus*, with glossy black plumage. It is regarded as an ominous bird, a metaphor for death because it is a scavenger, feeding on carrion.
* chime stone: an inverted stone or bronze bell, usually a Buddhist percussion instrument.
* incense: an aromatic substance in the form of a stick that exhales perfume during combustion, burnt before a Buddhist, Wordist or any religious or ancestral figure as an act of worship, usually offered with a prayer or vow.
* flowers rained: a shower of flowers like thorn apples or angel's trumpets.
* pine: a cone-bearing tree having needle-shaped evergreen leaves growing in clusters, a symbol of longevity and rectitude in Chinese culture.
* Master Old from India: referring to Buddha in this poem.

过太乙观贾生房

昔余栖遁日，
之子烟霞邻。
共携松叶酒，
俱簪竹皮巾。
攀林遍岩洞，
采药无冬春。
谬以道门子，
征为骖御臣。
常恐丹液就，
先我紫阳宾。
夭促万涂尽，
哀伤百虑新。
迹峻不容俗，
才多反累真。
泣对双泉水，
还山无主人。

A Visit to Sheng Chia's Room at Temple of the One

When I fled as a hermit then,
Amid mist and clouds you did dwell.
We did both carry pine-leaf wine,
And did both wear a bamboo shell.
We climbed and sought all crags and caves
And gathered wild herbs of all sort.

When I practiced the Word in the hills,
I was thought a page from the court.
I'd oft fear nectar was soon made
That earlier you'd join Purple Sun.
But you rushed to Hades too soon;
From all my pains grew a new one.
Solitude repels the vain world;
Learnedness may obstruct the true.
Now to the two fountains I cry;
Their host is gone, so much I rue.

* Sheng Chia: unidentified.
* the One: a philosophical concept of Wordism, the beginning of all things, as is defined in *Sir Lush*, "In the beginning was the None, having nothing, having no name. Then there arose the One, and nothing was formed yet." Similarly, in the West, God is the One, Self-subsisting Reality. The One in the West and the One in the East are actually one, identifiable though in different languages.
* the Word: referring to Tao if transliterated, the most significant and profoundest concept in Chinese philosophy. According to Laocius's *The Word and the World*: "The Word is void, but its use is infinite. O deep! It seems to be the root of all things." the Creator, the beginning of everything. It is identifiable with the Word or Logos in the West, as there is an enormous amount of common ground in the two cosmologies and the doctrines concerning the most fundamental matters such as "the Word is the One" and "God is the One", and the personalization of Being, the progenitor of finite spirits, which are subordinate kinds of Being or merely appearances of the Divine, the One.
* nectar: in Chinese and Greek mythologies, the drink of the gods or fairies and in botany the saccharine substance secreted by some plants and forming the base of natural honey.
* Purple Sun: a renowned Wordist in the T'ang dynasty.
* Hades: the abode of the dead, and a euphemism for hell. It is called Yellow Spring in Chinese culture, because deep down earth water is yellow, and Yellow Spring belongs in the Nine Hells and Nine Springs.

故南阳夫人樊氏挽歌

Elegies to Deceased Lady Fan, Countess of Southshine

其 一

锦衣馀翟茀，
绣毂罢鱼轩。
淑女诗长在，
夫人法尚存。
凝笳随晓旆，
行哭向秋原。
归去将何见，
谁能返戟门。

No. 1

Her plumed chariot does here remain;
Her fish-skinned cart stands there in vain.
The fair lady's poems will long last;
The great madam's rites have been cast.
The flute tune moves the flags with pain;
The mourners cry to the cold plain.
She is gone from her world ornate;
Will she come back to Halberd Gate?

---

* Southshine: Nanyang if transliterated, an alternative name for South Town, which had nurtured the Five Sages of Southshine — Great Grand, Sage of Wisdom in the Shang and Chough dynasty, Li Fan (530 B.C.- 443 B.C.), Sage of Commerce in the Spring

and Autumn period, Heng Chang (A.D. 78 – A.D. 139), Sage of Science in the Eastern Han dynasty, Chungching Chang, Sage of Medicine in the Eastern Han dynasty, and Liang Chuke (A.D. 181 – A.D. 234), Sage of Strategy in the Eastern Han dynasty.
* flute: a tubular wind instrument of small diameter with holes along the side.
* Halberd Gate: a noble's gate lined with guards holding halberds.

其 二

石窌恩荣重，
金吾车骑盛。
将朝每赠言，
入室还相敬。
叠鼓秋城动，
悬旌寒日映。
不言长不归，
环佩犹将听。

No. 2

You were enfeoffed with the Lord's grace,
With all carts and garrison ace.
When husband left, you gave advice;
Him back, you would show respect nice.
The drums the town in autumn quake;
The flags the cold of sunshine shake.
You won't come back you did not say;
Your trinkets seem to clink to ray.

* enfeoffed: being enfeoffed in the T'ang dynasty was an honor together with a good amount of remuneration instead of land, given to royal family members and those who had done significantly for the T'ang Empire.

韦给事山居

幽寻得此地，
讵有一人曾？
大壑随阶转，
群山入户登。
庖厨出深竹，
印绶隔垂藤。
即事辞轩冕，
谁云病未能？

The Cottage of Wei, an Imperial Inspector

I've found this place as I explore;
Travelers visiting there'd be more.
Following the steps, you see dales great;
The mountains would enter the gate.
A kitchen's found in bamboo deep;
Rattan vines o'er their ribbons sweep.
When giving up positions fat,
Who will say it's hard to do that?

* bamboo: a tall, tree-like or shrubby grass in tropical and semi-tropical regions, a symbol of integrity and altitude, one of the four most important images in Chinese literature, which are wintersweet, orchid, bamboo and chrysanthemum. Plankbridge Cheng (A.D. 1693 - A.D. 1765), A Ching poet, speaks of its character in a poem Bamboo Rooted in the Rock: "You bite the green hill and ne'er rest. / Roots in the broken crag, you grow, / And stand erect although hard pressed. /East, west, south, north, let the wind blow."

* rattan: the long, tough, flexible stem of a palm (genera *Calamus* and *Daemonorops*) growing in Asia, Africa and Australia, which can be used as material for the making of chairs and a variety of other furniture.

同卢拾遗过韦给事东山别业二十韵，给事首春休沐，维已陪游，及乎是行，亦预闻命，会无车马，不果斯诺

托身侍云陛，
昧旦趋华轩。
遂陪鹓鸿侣，
霄汉同飞翻。
君子垂惠顾，
期我于田园。
侧闻景龙际，
亲降南面尊。
万乘驻山外，
顺风祈一言。
高阳多夔龙，
荆山积玙璠。
盛德启前烈，
大贤钟后昆。
侍郎文昌宫，
给事东掖垣。
谒帝俱来下，
冠盖盈丘樊。
闺风首邦族，
庭训延乡村。
采地包山河，
树井竟川原。
岩端回绮槛，
谷口开朱门。
阶下群峰首，

云中瀑水源。
鸣玉满春山，
列筵先朝暾。
会舞何飒沓，
击钟弥朝昏。
是时阳和节，
清昼犹未暄。
蔼蔼树色深，
嘤嘤鸟声繁。
顾已负宿诺，
延颈惭芳荪。
蹇步守穷巷，
高驾难攀援。
素是独往客，
脱冠情弥敦。

A Visit to Inspector Wei's East Hill Cottage with Advisor Lu, Twenty Couplets. I Would Accompany the Inspector Who Was On His Early Spring Leave, But I Failed to Keep My Promise Because I Was Told My Cart Was Not Available to This Trip

With a full heart you serve the crown
And rush to court at early dawn.
You and your colleagues make a crowd,
Like the Milky Way turn to cloud.
You turned around and looked at me,
Expecting we'd have a day free.

I hear that day you had great grace;
His Majesty came to your place.
The Lord stopped out of the hill there
And would ask for your word to share.
High Sun boasts unicorns divine;
Mt. Chaste hoards jewelries to shine.
Your forefathers were great indeed
And lots of your sons the age lead.
Your brother holds Execution,
And your duty is inspection.
The levee o'er, you come along,
Lo, hats and caps here and there throng.
Your house canons benefit all;
Your hall teaching is a great call.
Your cottage has a vista broad;
Behold, a field, a plain, a ford.
Around the rock are railings great;
Before the vale stands a red gate.
Below the steps are peaks aghast;
Among the clouds runs water fast.
Hark, jade and jewels clink to ring;
Lo, feast is laid in sunlit spring.
The party goes on, on the way,
Bells and drums and strings all the day.
It's February, early spring still;
The dawning light feels a bit chill.
Lush, lush, the trees are in green deep;
Love, love, you hear the warblers cheep.
But I cannot make it, my lord,
I feel so sorry, my heart gnawed.
In my poor lane, I do feel lame;

Your cart I could not ride, a shame.
A recluse I was then, so free;
Out of court, better I could be.

* the Milky Way: the Silver River in Chinese mythology, a luminous band circling the heavens composed of stars and nebulae; the Galaxy.
* High Sun: the capital of Dark Crown's kingdom, in modern-day Hopei Province, also Dark Crown's alias when he reigned in High Sun. Dark Crown (2342 B.C.- 2245 B.C.), Chuanhsu if transliterated, was one of Five Emperors in prehistoric China.
* unicorn: a fabulous deer-like animal with one horn, a symbol of saintliness in Chinese culture. Confucius lamented the death of a unicorn captured and hence stopped compiling *The Spring and Autumn Annals* and died before long.
* Mt. Chaste: a mountain in Hupei Province, located on the west bank of the River Han. It's said to be the mountain where Ho Pien found the jade.
* Execution: referring to the Executive or Administration Department of T'ang's Triune Dais, which consists of privy council (Central Secretariat Department), censorate (Undergate Department) and executive (Administration Department).
* And your duty is inspection: suggesting Inspector Wei's job at Undergate Department.

韦侍郎山居

幸忝君子顾，
遂陪尘外踪。
闲花满岩谷，
瀑水映杉松。
啼鸟忽归涧，
归云时抱峰。
良游盛簪绂，
继迹多夔龙。
讵枉青门道，
胡闻长乐钟。
清晨去朝谒，
车马何从容。

To the Cottage of Wei, a Ministerial Aide

I stroll with you out of the world,
So favored I feel at your call.
Free flowers bloom all over the dale,
The pines splashed by the waterfall.
Some warblers fly down to the creek,
The peaks by homing clouds entwined.
There cloud companions' hats and caps
Followed by unicorns behind.
How can we let down Blue Gate Way?
Here we can hear a long-life toll.
Tomorrow we'll go see our Lord;

<h1 style="text-align:center">How gracefully our carts will roll!</h1>

* pine: any of a genus (*Pinus*) of evergreen trees of the pine family, a cone-bearing tree having bundles of two to five needle-shaped leaves growing in clusters, an important image in Chinese literature, a symbol of rectitude, fortitude, longevity and so on.
* unicorn: a divine animal that is like a deer with one horn, a symbol of saintliness in Chinese culture. Confucius lamented the death of a unicorn captured and hence stopped compiling *The Spring and Autumn Annals* and died before long.
* Blue Gate Way: the way leading from and to Blue Gate, the southern gate of the three gates on the east wall of Long Peace.

和尹谏议史馆山池

云馆接天居,
霓裳侍玉除。
春池百子外,
芳树万年馀。
洞有仙人箓,
山藏太史书。
君恩深汉帝,
且莫上空虚。

In Reply to Remonstrant Yin at Hill Pool of Imperial Archive

Imperial Archive near Bliss Room,
In a rainbow gown you serve Him.
Spring Pool is better than Cent Pool;
The age-old balmy tree looks trim.
Amulets there are in your cave;
In the hills history books are stored.
Do not fly high into the void;
You should be grateful to our Lord.

* Imperial Archive: an organization in charge of the compilation of historical records, instituted by Emperor Grandsire of T'ang (599 B.C.- 649 B.C.), located in Great Bright Palace.
* Bliss Room: the emperor's residence.
* Spring Pool: a pool in the court of Imperial Archive.
* Cent Pool: a pool in Han's palace.
* amulet: anything worn about one's person to protect from witchcraft, accident, or ill luck; a charm.

赠徐中书望终南山歌

晚下兮紫微,
怅尘事兮多违。
驻马兮双树,
望青山兮不归。

Gazing at the Southern Mountains, to Hsu, Vice Premier of Privy Council

I come back from office so late;
O the world frets me in many ways.
Neath the Borneo twin trees I stop;
O not back, at the hills I gaze.

* the Southern Mountains: also known as Mt. Great One, Mt. Earthlungs, the South Hills, the mountains south of Long Peace, a great stronghold of the capital, towering in the middle of Ch'in Ridge and rolling about 100 kilometers.
* Privy Council: also known as Central Secretariat Department, the most important governmental department in the T'ang dynasty, one of the three departments called Triune Dais.
* the Borneo twin trees: the twin trees where Buddhist monks or nuns achieve nirvana.

寄荆州张丞相

所思竟何在,
怅望深荆门。
举世无相识,
终身思旧恩。
方将与农圃,
艺植老丘园。
目尽南飞雁,
何由寄一言?

To Premier Chang at Chaston

Where is the one whom I admire?
To Chaston I look and look higher.
None does me recognize on earth;
I keep in mind your grace and worth.
To the farmland there I will go;
Till old I will uphill crops grow.
I gaze at the south flying bird;
How can you send to him my word?

* Premier Chang: Chiuling Chang (A.D. 678 – A.D. 740), a famous premier and poet in the T'ang dynasty, a descendant of the famous strategist Liang Chang (cir. 250 B.C.- 186 B.C.) in the Han dynasty.
* Premier Chang at Chaston: Chiuling Chang was deposed to be secretary to the governor of Chaston.
* Chaston: Chaste, Chingchow if transliterated, an old town on the Long River or a geographical region including areas of present-day Hupei and Hunan provinces.

使 至 塞 上

单车欲问边，
属国过居延。
征蓬出汉塞，
归雁入胡天。
大漠孤烟直，
长河落日圆。
萧关逢候骑，
都护在燕然。

To the Front as an Envoy

To inspect the front I drive down,
Now thru the vassal's Chüyan Town.
Thistledown past Han Fortress flies;
Wild geese fleet into the Huns' skies.
O'er the wild smoke lonely curls straight;
To the river the sun round sets late.
At Hsiao Pass I meet a scout; the man
Tells me the general's at Yanjan.

* Chüyan Town: also known as Chüyan Sea, in today's Inner Mongolia, 80 kilometers from Ope-arms, that is, today's Changyeh, Kansu Province.
* thistledown: the pappus of a thistle, which is a prickly plant with cylindrical or globular heads of tubular purple flowers or the ripe silky fibers from the dry flower of a thistle. It is a common metaphor for drifting or wandering of an aimless vagrant.
* Han Fortress: a general term referring to any border pass of Han.
* wild goose: an undomesticated goose that is caring and responsible, taken as a symbol

of benevolence, righteousness, good manner, wisdom and faith in Chinese culture.
* Hun: one of barbaric nomadic Asian peoples who frequently invaded China, a general term referring to all northern or western invaders and aliens.
* Hsiao Pass: name of an old pass, southeast of today's Firm Plain (Kuyüan), Ninghsia Hui's Autonomous Region
* Yanjan: Mt. Yanjan, a mountain located in modern-day Mongolia. It is usually used to imply an enemy with military threat.

出　塞　作

居延城外猎天骄，
白草连天野火烧。
暮云空碛时驱马，
秋日平原好射雕。
护羌校尉朝乘障，
破虏将军夜渡辽。
玉靶角弓珠勒马，
汉家将赐霍嫖姚。

Beyond the Border

Out of Chüyan, the Huns are hunting game;
Dried grass rolling to the sky is aflame.
On dust-lit sand I give my horse free rein;
It's time to shoot hawks on the autumn plain.
Ch'iang Governor climbs up the barring height;
Beat Foe General crosses the Liao at night.
Inlaid sword, horned bow and pearled steed, behold
Will be granted to those like Swift so bold.

* Chüyan: also known as Chüyan Sea, in today's Inner Mongolia, 80 kilometers from Ope-arms, that is, today's Changyeh, Kansu Province.
* Hun: one of barbaric nomadic Asian peoples who frequently invaded China, a general term referring to all northern or western invaders and aliens.
* Ch'iang: a nationality living in the west of China, having the same origin as Chinese.
* hawk: a diurnal bird of prey, notable for keen sight and strong flight, usually used as a metaphor for one who takes military means in contrast with a dove, one who tries to

find peaceful solutions.
* Beat Foe General: title of a military commander in ancient China.
* Liao: the Liao River, mainly in today's Liaoning Province.
* steed: a horse; especially a spirited war horse. The use of horses in war can be traced back to the Shang dynasty (1600 B.C.- 1046 B.C.), when a department of horse management was established. A verse from *The Book of Songs* tells of Lord Civil of Watch's industriousness: "In state affairs he leads; / He has three thousand steeds."
* Swift: Swift Huo (140 B.C.- 117 B.C.), P'iaoyao Huo if transliterated, a renowned general, prominent strategist and patriotic hero in the Han dynasty. He made his first show at 17, leading 800 fierce cavalrymen to penetrate the enemy lines and defeat the Huns. Swift fought against the Huns in three major wars and each time returned with victory. He died of a disease at 24, leaving his achievements as the highest glory for Chinese military commanders.

凉州郊外游望

野老才三户，
边村少四邻。
婆娑依里社，
箫鼓赛田神。
洒酒浇刍狗，
焚香拜木人。
女巫纷屡舞，
罗袜自生尘。

Gazing on the Suburbs of Coolton

Households of farmers are so few;
To the border few neighbors come.
By the sacrifice tree they dance;
To please Field God they beat the drum.
They splash spirit to the straw dog;
Incense burned, to dryads they pray.
The witches dance and dance again
And kick up all dust while they play.

* Coolton: a prefecture of T'ang or referring to the town where the government was, approximately today's Martial Might (Wuwei), Kansu Province.
* To please Field God: farmers beat drums to express their thanks to Field God after a harvest.
* straw dog: a dog made of straw, used in sacrifice.
* incense: an aromatic substance in the form of a stick that exhales perfume during combustion, burnt before a Buddhist, Wordist or any religious or ancestral figure as an

act of worship, usually offered with a prayer or vow.
* dryad: a wooden figure used in sacrifice.
* witch: a female official in charge of rites and sacrifices according to *Rites of Chough*, able to exorcize spirits and communicate with gods and say prayers for a rain and so on.

凉 州 赛 神

凉州城外少行人,
百尺峰头望虏尘。
健儿击鼓吹羌笛,
共赛城东越骑神。

Racing with a God at Coolton

Out of Coolton few travelers on the way,
On beacon tower at Hun dust you may gaze.
The fighters beat drums and the flute they play;
With Dragoon God east they will have a race.

* Coolton: a prefectural city located in present-day Kansu Province, built by Emperor Martial of Han (156 B.C.- 87 B.C.) to garrison the border, so named because Swift Huo defeated Huns and thus showed the martial might of the great Han Empire. It has been prosperous as the hub of the Silk Road and famous for wine brewage, hence styled Grape Wine Town.
* beacon tower: a prominent building set on a wall or hill or a similar position, as a guide or warning to garrison generals or others.
* Hun: one of barbaric nomadic Asian peoples who frequently invaded China, a general term referring to all northern or western invaders and aliens; when used as an adjective, it denotes something of or about Huns.
* flute: a tubular reed musical instrument of small diameter with holes along the side.
* Dragoon God: god in charge of riding and shooting.

双黄鹄歌送别（时为节度判官，在凉州作）

天路来兮双黄鹄，
云上飞兮水上宿，
抚翼和鸣整羽族。
不得已，忽分飞，
家在玉京朝紫微，
主人临水送将归。
悲笳嘹唳垂舞衣，
宾欲散兮复相依。
几往返兮极浦，
尚裴回兮落晖。
岸上火兮相迎，
将夜入兮边城。
鞍马归兮佳人散，
怅离忧兮独含情。

My Singing Goodbye to Two Yellow Swans (I was an assistant military governor and this poem was composed at Coolton)

From Heaven blue two yellow swans in flight
From clouds alight on water for the night.
They flutter and preen their plumage alright.
But they have to part, and apart they fly,
One to Capital to worship Most High.
Their host sees them off, with water nearby.

The sad flute is blown and they dance with pain;
When going separate, they fly back again.
By the marsh they fly to and fro,
Their wings tinted with afterglow.
The fire ashore welcomes them with light,
To the border town in the depth of night.
The dancers are gone, but the horse is back;
I'm stricken with sadness and love, alack.

* swan: a large web-footed, long-necked bird (subfamily *Cygninae*), allied to but heavier than the goose and noted for its grace on the water, as the whooper, the trumpeter swan, and the whistling swan.
* Heaven: the space surrounding or seeming to overarch the earth, in which the sun, the moon, and stars appear, popularly the abode of God, his angels and the blessed, and in most cases suggesting supernatural power or sometimes signifying a monarch.
* Capital: Long Peace or Ch'ang'an if transliterated, the capital of the T'ang Empire, a cosmopolis with 1,000,000 inhabitants, the largest walled city ever built by man, the center of world religions, Buddhism, Confucianism, Wordism, Nestorianism, Zoroastrianism, and even Islamism represented by Saracens, and the center of education — There were colleges of various grades and special institutes for calligraphy, arithmetic, music, astronomy and so on.
* Most High: an emperor is usually addressed as Most High.

从 军 行

吹角动行人,
喧喧行人起。
笳悲马嘶乱,
争渡黄河水。
日暮沙漠陲,
战声烟尘里。
尽系名王颈,
归来报天子。

A Border War

A conch toot starts soldiers asleep;
Quick, quick, off bed they rise to leap.
The flute tune sad, the horses cry;
To rush 'cross the River they vie.
The eve sunlight does the sand shroud;
Drowned in the dust is their shouts loud.
Go and get the head of the foe;
To report to Lord we can go.

* conch: any of various large marine gastropod mollusks, (family *Strombidae*) having heavy, colorful, spiral shells, which are used as trumpets.
* flute: a tubular wind instrument of small diameter with holes along the side.
* the River: the Yellow River, the second longest river in China, flowing across Loess Plateau, hence yellow. It is 5,464 kilometers long, with a drainage area of 752,443 square kilometers, having nurtured the Chinese nation, regarded as the cradle of

Chinese civilization. After being tamed by Great Worm, the First King of Hsia (21 B.C.- 16 B.C.), its fertile valleys were turned into fields of rice, barley and oscillating corn, amid gleaming streams and lakes.

陇 西 行

十里一走马，
五里一扬鞭。
都护军书至，
匈奴围酒泉。
关山正飞雪，
烽戍断无烟。

A West Bulge Poem

Four miles the horse does run in haste,
Two miles finished at one whip raised.
The governor's order comes then:
Wine Spring's besieged by the Hun men.
Snow flies over pass and mountain,
No more smoke from any beacon.

* West Bulge: Lunghsi if transliterated, the name of a shire in the Warring States period and the T'ang dynasty, located in the southeast of present-day Kansu Province, covering Lanchow, West Buldge and Lint'ao.
* Wine Spring: a city called Chiuch'üan if transliterated, in the western part of today's Kansu Province, as is said to have possessed a natural fountain of wine.
* Hun men: Hun invaders from north and west of China. Huns have been regarded as barbarians in Chinese history although they are of the same origin as Chinese, originating from Old Ch'iang.
* beacon: a prominent building set on a wall or hill or a similar position, as a guide or warning to garrison generals or others.

陇　头　吟

长安少年游侠客，
夜上戍楼看太白。
陇头明月迥临关，
陇上行人夜吹笛。
关西老将不胜愁，
驻马听之双泪流。
身经大小百馀战，
麾下偏裨万户侯。
苏武才为典属国，
节旄落尽海西头。

A Song at Mt. Bulge

A Long Peace lad would be a gallant knight;
On a watchtower he asks Venus at night.
The mountain and pass are paled by the moon;
A vagrant paled as well plays a flute tune.
The frontier general old stricken with woe
Stops his horse to listen and his tears flow.
He's fought a hundred small or large battles
And his men have been peered with all titles.
Wu Su was named for mere vassal affairs;
By North Sea worn off were his tally hairs!

* Mt. Bulge: a mountain located in the southeast of present-day Kansu Province, 2,928 meters above sea level and about 240 kilometers long from north to south, the

borderline between Sha'anhsi Loess Plateau and West Bulge Loess Plateau.
* Long Peace: Chang'an if transliterated, the capital of China in the T'ang dynasty, with 1,000,000 inhabitants, the largest walled city ever built by man, and perhaps the most cultivated and cosmopolitan in human history, with T'ang civilization at its peak. As the starting point of the Silk Road and the birthplace of Chinese civilization, it has been a capital for thirteen dynasties, enjoying the privilege of the Museum of Chinese History, and it is now the capital of Sha'anhsi Province.
* watchtower: a tower upon which a sentinel is stationed.
* Venus: the planet closest to the sun, as is called Morning Star in the morning and Evening Star in the evening. Chinese ancients believed that Venus could predict military affairs.
* the moon: the satellite of the earth, a representation of feminity in contrast with the sun, a presentation of masculinity. In a universe animated by the interaction of Shade (female) and Shine (male) energies, the moon is literally Shade visible.
* Wu Su: Wu Su (140 B.C.- 60 B.C.), a minister of Han. On his diplomatic mission, Su was detained. The Huns tried to make him surrender with threats and promises, only to fail. Then, he was sent to North Sea to be a shepherd. Through all kinds of hardship, Su finally came back to Han after 19 years' detention. During the 19 years, Wu Su had never surrendered.
* North Sea: present-day Lake Baikal, the deepest lake in the world, in today's Siberia, Russia.

老 将 行

少年十五二十时,
步行夺得胡马骑。
射杀山中白额虎,
肯数邺下黄须儿。
一身转战三千里,
一剑曾当百万师。
汉兵奋迅如霹雳,
虏骑崩腾畏蒺藜。
卫青不败由天幸,
李广无功缘数奇。
自从弃置便衰朽,
世事蹉跎成白首。
昔时飞箭无全目,
今日垂杨生左肘。
路旁时卖故侯瓜,
门前学种先生柳。
苍茫古木连穷巷,
寥落寒山对虚牖。
誓令疏勒出飞泉,
不似颍川空使酒。
贺兰山下阵如云,
羽檄交驰日夕闻。
节使三河募年少,
诏书五道出将军。
试拂铁衣如雪色,
聊持宝剑动星文。
愿得燕弓射大将,

耻令越甲鸣吾君。
莫嫌旧日云中守,
犹堪一战取功勋。

An Old General

When fifteen, twenty or so, a young one,
On foot, I could catch a horse from a Hun.
In hills I'd shoot tigers with a white head;
Is the rash boy from Yeh the best, as said?
For a thousand miles I've fought for the Lord;
I could brave a million troops with my sword.
So fast like thunder the Han soldiers sped;
The cavalrymen fell as thorns they tread.
Blue Watch won, who was helped by Heaven great;
Broad Li lost, as was haunted by ill fate.
Thrown on the scrapheap, I grew weak in plight;
With the elapse of time, my hair's turned white.
With eyes shut, a target I'd shoot of yore;
Now my left arm aches like a tumor sore.
I'd sell melons by a road like the mean;
Or by my door plant gleeful willows green.
My poor lane sees pines and cypresses old;
My window faces the bleak mountains cold.
I swear to make Shule's spring spurt again,
Not like General Kuan, who drank in vain.
The soldiers at Mt. Holan swarm like cloud;
Urgent orders rush day and night, so loud.
Envoys urge the army to recruit more;
Edits start generals to march to the fore.

The general strokes his mail to shine like snow;
The seven stars on his sword seem to glow.
I'd have a Yan bow to shoot the foes awed;
Ne'er to let armored Huns frighten our Lord.
The deposed general is now coming back;
He will glorify our land with one smack.

* Hun: war-like nomadic peoples occupying vast regions from Mongolia to Central Asia in Chinese history, especially during the Han dynasty. They were a constant menace on China's western and northern borders.
* tiger: a large carnivorous feline mammal of Asia, with vertical black wavy stripes on a tawny body and black bars or rings on the limbs and tail, praised as king of all animals.
* Yeh: one of the eight most famous capitals in Chinese history, in today's Linchang County, Hopei Province.
* Han: China or Chinese, a metonymy adopted because of the powerful Han Empire founded by Pang Liu, King of Han before he won the war and reunified China.
* Blue Watch: Blue Watch (? - 106 B.C.), Ch'ing Wei if transliterated, a renowned commander in the Western Han dynasty.
* Broad Li: Broad Li (? - 119 B.C.), Kuang Li if transliterated, a renowned general fighting against the Huns in the Han dynasty, called Flying General by the Huns.
* melon: a trailing plant of the gourd family, or its fruit. There are two genera, the muskmelon and the watermelon, each with numerous varieties, growing in both tropical and temperate zones.
* gleeful willows: an allusion to Lord Glee, that is, Poolbright T'ao (A.D. 352 - A.D. 427), a verse writer, poet, and litterateur in the Chin dynasty, and the founder of Chinese idyllism, who was once the magistrate of P'engtse. Pure and loft, T'ao resigned from official life several times to live a life of simplicity. There were five willow trees planted in front of his house, so he called himself Mr. Five Willows.
* pines and cypresses: two kinds of similar evergreen trees, a symbol of rectitude, nobility and longevity in Chinese culture.
* Shule: name of an old kingdom, in today's Kashgar, New Land (Hsinchiang).
* General Kuan: Fu Kuan (? - 131 B.C.), an official and general in Western Han.
* Mt. Holan: a mountain on the border between Ninghsia and Inner Mongolia.
* Yan: the State of Yan (1044 B.C.- 222 B.C.), a vassal state in the Spring and Autumn period, one of the Seven Powers in the Warring States period.

送崔三往密州觐省

南陌去悠悠，
东郊不少留。
同怀扇枕恋，
独念倚门愁。
路绕天山雪，
家临海树秋。
鲁连功未报，
且莫蹈沧洲。

Seeing Off Ts'ui Three to See His Parents

The southern road rolls on afar;
The eastern field would keep you more.
To wait on parents we both yearn;
My mum alone peers by the door!
Mt. Heaven here is deep with snow;
Trees in your home sweep the shore.
Your mission has not been fulfilled;
You should not retreat to the moor.

* Mt. Heaven: one of the seven largest mountains in the world, rolling in the hinterland of Eurasia, 2,500 kilometers long, 250 - 350 kilometers on average, and more 800 kilometers at the widest.
* retreat to the moor: a metonymy, which is a roundabout way of saying the action to seek quietude as a recluse.

灵云池送从弟

金杯缓酌清歌转，
画舸轻移艳舞回。
自叹鹡鸰临水别，
不同鸿雁向池来。

Seeing Off My Cousin at Soul Cloud Pool

A gold cup we sip, the clear songs we hear;
The pleasure boat sways dancers in the cool.
We sigh like wagtails by water we'll part;
But there, wild geese fly along to the pool.

* Soul Cloud Pool: a pool in Coolton, that is, in today's Martial Might (Wuwei), Kansu Province.
* wagtail: any of several small singing birds (genus *Motacilla*), named from their habit of jerking the tail.
* wild goose: an undomesticated goose that is caring and responsible, taken as a symbol of benevolence, righteousness, good manner, wisdom and faith in Chinese culture.

送岐州源长史归（源与余同在崔常侍幕中，时常侍已殁）

握手一相送，
心悲安可论。
秋风正萧索，
客散孟尝门。
故驿通槐里，
长亭下槿原。
征西旧旌节，
从此向河源。

Seeing Off Vice Governor Yüan Back to Offset (Yüan and I Are Both in the Tent Office of Royal Servant Ts'ui, Who Is Dead Now)

I now see you off hand in hand;
How sad we feel, sad a lot more.
The autumn wind blows now to sough,
Sough to those leaving Mengch'ang's door.
The post road rolls to Locust Tree;
The large kiosk's at Hibiscus Plain.
You'll follow our general's long trek
To River Source that's roiled again.

* Offset: a prefecture of T'ang, with its government in Yung County, south of today's Phoenix Flying County.
* Tent Office: West Tent Office: the organization governing four towns in the western

border of China.
* Mengch'ang: Lord of Mengch'ang of Ch'i, one of the Four Gallants in the Warring States period.
* Locust Tree: the name of an old county and the name of a post.
* Hibiscus Plain: unidentified, probably name of an old place or post.
* River Source: another way of saying the West Regions.

晦日游大理韦卿城南别业四首
A Visit to the Cottage of Wei, Chief of Jurisdiction on the Last Day of the First Moon, Four Poems

其 一

与世澹无事，
自然江海人。
侧闻尘外游，
解骖鞿朱轮。
平野照暄景，
上天垂春云。
张组竟北阜，
泛舟过东邻。
故乡信高会，
牢醴及佳辰。
幸同击壤乐，
心荷尧为君。

No. 1

You're serene, by nothing worn,
Loving nature, a hermit born.
I hear to tour out dust you start,
Untying your steeds from your cart.
The plain enjoys the sunlit hue;
Spring clouds hang about in the blue.
In the north tents are set for fun;

In the east boats float to the sun.
In your hometown all come to meet;
Beef, pork, wine, e'en pages have a treat.
For merriment Wood Shoe you play,
Back home to Mound's age, the best day.

* beef, pork: In ancient China, of all kinds of meat, beef ranked the first, mouton the second, pork the third, and then chicken and fish.
* Wood Shoe: a kind of game in prehistoric China. A wood piece in the shape of shoe is laid sidelong on the ground, and the one who hits it with another piece from thirty or forty feet away wins the game.
* sun: the heavenly body that is the center of attraction and the main source of light and heat in the solar system, a representation of Shine in contrast with Shade, the moon, in Chinese culture, a symbol of hope, life, strength, vigor, and youth.
* Mound's age: a heyday in Chinese history, when China was reigned by Mound (2377 B.C.-2259 B.C.).

其 二

郊居杜陵下，
永日同携手。
仁里霭川阳，
平原见峰首。
园庐鸣春鸠，
林薄媚新柳。
上卿始登席，
故老前为寿。
临当游南陂，
约略执杯酒。
归欤绌微官，
惆怅心自咎。

No. 2

You cottage's at Birchleaf Pear Ridge;
I yearn to join you hand in hand.
The village is by the lush stream;
The plain can see the peak high stand.
Turtledoves warble in your yard;
The meadow charms your willows new.
When you ascend to a grand feast,
All guests will toast good health to you.
That day I was touring South Pond,
So I could not with you drink wine.
I blame myself with much regret;
From office mine I should resign!

* Birchleaf Pear Ridge: 10 kilometers from Wannian County, in today's Hsi-an, Sha'anhsi Province.
* turtledove: a kind of dove (genus *Streptopelia*), noted for its affection for mate and young.
* willow: any of a large genus of shrubs and trees related to the poplars, having glossy green leaves in the shape of a girl's eye-brow, and generally having smooth branches, and often long, slender, pliant, and sometimes pendent branchlets, which seem to be waving good-bye, or weeping amorously, or drooping for nostalgia.
* South Pond: name of a pond, unidentified.

其 三

冬中馀雪在,
墟上春流驶。
风日畅怀抱,
山川多秀气。
雕胡先晨炊,
庖脍亦云至。
高情浪海岳,
浮生寄天地。
君子外簪缨,
埃尘良不霑。
所乐衡门中,
陶然忘其贵。

No. 3

The winter sees remaining snow;
The village feels spring tidings flow.
The fresh brisk wind you can embrace,
While mountains and rivers show grace.
As breakfast water oats you eat,
To be followed by various meat.
You surf all mounts and seas with pride;
Life is just a place to abide.
Crowns and sashes for which all lust
Are nothing to you, only dust.
With simple huts you are well pleased,
And forget ranks and wealth, so eased.

* water oats: a water cereal looking like pampas grass, usually known as wild rice, the stem of which is used as a vegetable and the seeds as rice, regarded as a table delicacy now.
* mounts and seas: a metonymy for hermitage or love for nature.
* crowns and sashes: a metonymy for powerful officials or a rich and dignified life.

其 四

高馆临澄陂，
旷望荡心目。
淡荡动云天，
玲珑映墟曲。
鹊巢结空林，
雉雏响幽谷。
应接无闲暇，
徘徊以踯躅。
纡组上春堤，
侧弁倚乔木。
弦望忽已晦，
后期洲应绿。

No. 4

Your cottage o'erlooks your clear pond;
You feel enlightened while you gaze.
The ripples move clouds in the sky;
Their charm joins the village thru rays.
Magpies build their nest in the wood;
Pheasants' coos with dales resonate.
You seem short of insights for all,
So in some trance you hesitate.
The courtiers go up the spring dyke;
Their caps askew, on trees they lean.
The waning moon will lose her sheen;
Our next date will see the shoal green.

* magpie: a jaylike passerine corvine bird, having a long and graduated tail and featured with black-and-white coloring, which often makes loud chirps to report good news, as is believed by many Chinese.
* pheasant: a long-tailed gallinaceous bird noted for the gorgeous plumage of the male.

资圣寺送甘二

浮生信如寄，
薄宦夫何有。
来往本无归，
别离方此受。
柳色蔼春馀，
槐阴清夏首。
不觉御沟上，
衔悲执杯酒。

Seeing Off Kan Two at Aiding Saints Monastery

Life's only a journey to take;
What if we cannot have a post?
To go or come, you reach nowhere;
Only parting do you feel most.
Willow leaves turn lush in late spring;
Early summer sees locusts shine.
Unawares, Royal Trench turns blue;
Sadly, I lower my cup of wine.

* willow: any of a large genus of shrubs and trees related to the poplars, having generally smooth branches, and often long, slender, pliant, and sometimes pendent branchlets, which seem to be waving good-bye, or weeping amorously, or drooping for nostalgia.
* locust: a tree of the bean family, with a rough bark, odd-pinnate leaves, and loose, slender racemes of fragrant, white flowers, which are a seasonal delicacy.

* Royal Trench: also known as Willow Trench or Forbidden Trench flowing from the Southern Hills and through the palace complex in Long Peace. Water is important to an estate according to Chinese geomancy, for example, one could find something like Great One Pool or Nectar Pool in a palace.

哭 孟 浩 然

故人不可见，
汉水日东流。
借问襄阳老，
江山空蔡洲。

Mourning Haojan Meng

My friend I can no longer see;
The Han blue flows and flows again.
A folk in Sowshine I would ask:
Why do mounts and rivers remain?

* Haojan Meng: Haojan Meng (A.D. 689 - A.D. 740), a renowned pastoral poet, Wei Wang and Pai Li's good friend, ranking next to Pai Li and Fu Tu in the entire galaxy of the poets of the glorious Tang Empire, but unfulfilled officially, he lived in reclusion almost all his life. There is a story that one day when he was in a room at the Palace with Wang Wei the Emperor suddenly materialized. Meng was so frightened that he hid under a couch. But as soon as Meng's name was mentioned, the Emperor said he would see him and asked him to recite one of his poems. When Haojan came to the line "As I'm no talent, our Lord turned me down", the emperor interrupted him, exclaiming: "You've never applied to me for a job. How can you talk about my turning you down? It's a libel! Go back to where you hail from!" Haojan Meng returned to hometown and some accounts read as though he lived there in retirement till his death in A.D. 740.

* the Han: the Han River, which is the longest branch of the Long River, having an important position in Chinese history.

* Sowshine: Hsiangyang if transliterated, a famous historic city, about 2,800 years old, a birthplace of Ch'u, Han and Three Kingdom cultures, and a city of economic and military importance, in the northwest of present-day Hupei Province.

汉 江 临 泛

楚塞三湘接，
荆门九派通。
江流天地外，
山色有无中。
郡邑浮前浦，
波澜动远空。
襄阳好风日，
留醉与山翁。

Boating on the River Han

It flows back to Three Hsiangs from Ch'u
And through Chastegate to the Nine blue.
The waters outrun earth and sky;
The misty hills heave low or high.
The town ashore seems there to drown;
The dome shakes as if to fall down.
O Sowshine's good sights do please me;
I will drink with Hillman, care-free.

* the River Han: the Han River, the longest branch of the Long River, having an important position in Chinese history.
* Three Hsiangs: Hsiang for short, referring to present-day Hunan Province. The Hsiang River flows into three rivers, the Li, the Cheng and the Hsiao, hence the name Three Hsiangs.
* Ch'u: a vassal state of Chough, one of the powers in the Warring States period, conquered and annexed by Ch'in in 223 B.C.

* Chastegate: Chingmen if transliterated, an important city in today's Hupei Province.
* the Nine: the Nine Rivers, that is, Bankshine, today's Chiuchiang, Chianghsi Province or the nine rivers in this area, after which the city was named.
* Sowshine: a famous historic city, about 2,800 years old, a birthplace of Ch'u, Han and Three Kingdom cultures, and a city of economic and military importance, in the northwest of present-day Hupei Province.
* Hillman: referring to the fifth son of T'ao Shan (A.D. 205 – A.D. 283), one of the Seven Sages of the Bamboo Grove in the Chin dynasty. He was as gentle and graceful as his father. When he was an official, the nation was falling apart and other officials were worried and depressed. Hillman, however, lived a casual life. When he hanged out, he used to hold a banquet and get drunk at the High Sun Pool.

送 封 太 守

忽解羊头削，
聊驰熊首轓。
扬舲发夏口，
按节向吴门。
帆映丹阳郭，
枫攒赤岸村。
百城多候吏，
露冕一何尊。

Seeing Off Prefect Feng

From military you resign
And soon become a prefect great.
Quickly you row from Summermouth
And rush to your post in Wu Gate.
Your sail reflects and moves Redshine;
Maples dye hamlets by Red Bank.
Guards of honor stand there in line;
How stately you are with your rank!

* Summermouth: an ancient town, in present Wuhan, Hupei Province, so named because of its location at the river mouth of the Summer River, that is, the lower reach of the Han River.
* Wu Gate: modern-day Soochow, an important city in Chiangsu, rich in historical relics and well-developed economically.
* Redshine: Redshine County, in present-day Chiangsu Province, a county instituted by Emperor First in 221 B.C. and its long history has left us a long list of celebrities and

cultural legacies.
* Red Bank: Mt. Red Bank, in present-day Chiangsu Province.
* maple: any of a large genus (*Acer*) of deciduous trees of the north temperate zone, with opposite leaves that turn flaming red in autumn and a fruit of two joined samaras, a symbol of cordial love and good luck because of its bright fiery color.

送 康 太 守

城下沧江水，
江边黄鹤楼。
朱阑将粉堞，
江水映悠悠。
铙吹发夏口，
使君居上头。
郭门隐枫岸，
候吏趋芦洲。
何异临川郡，
还劳康乐侯。

Seeing Off Prefect K'ang

The Blue rushes under the wall;
Riverside is Yellow Crane Tower.
The red railings and parapets
See the stream in its serene hour.
Cymbals loud, you start from the town,
And you sit down there in the fore.
Town Gate's lost from the maple bank;
Welcomers to Reed Shoal will oar.
Your county will boom one may see,
And you will work hard like Lord Glee.

---

* the Blue: the Blue River, an unidentified river in this poem or probably a common river.

* Yellow Crane Tower: a famous tower built by Wu in A.D. 223, located on the top of Mt. Snake, overlooking the Long River, one of the three historical attractions (the other two being Shine River Pavilion and the Old Lute Platform) of today's Wuhan, Hupei Province.
* cymbal: one of a pair of platelike metallic (usually brass) musical instruments played by being clashed together.
* the town: referring to Summermouth, an ancient town that is a district under today's Wuhan.
* welcomers: official receptionists designated to welcome a new official like a magistrate.
* Reed Shoal: a shoal lush with reeds near Southridge garrison, under today's Hsuan, Anhui Province.
* Lord Glee: the court title of Poolbright or Lingyün Hsieh (A.D. 385 – A.D. 433), a Buddhist and traveler in the Northern and Southern dynasties, and a representative topographical poet in Chinese history.

送宇文太守赴宣城

寥落云外山，
迢递舟中赏。
铙吹发西江，
秋空多清响。
地迥古城芜，
月明寒潮广。
时赛敬亭神，
复解罟师网。
何处寄相思，
南风摇五两。

Seeing Off Prefect Yüwen to Hsuan

Out the clouded hills it's so calm;
While you row you enjoy the view.
Cymbals send you at the West Stream,
Ringing across the autumn blue.
The distance makes the town look bleak;
And it feels cold while the moon glares.
The fisher's thanking Chingt'ing gods,
For they have ridden him of cares.
Where can I send my greetings, ay?
South wind does the weathercock sway.

---

* Hsuan: a county instituted in the early years of the Ch'in Emperor under the Prefecture of Redshine. It became a prefecture in A.D. 281 during the Chin dynasty. It is well

known for rich historical legacies, and best remembered for its high-quality rice paper.
* cymbal: one of a pair of platelike metallic (usually brass) musical instruments, bulgy like half a ball in the middle, played by being clashed together.
* the moon: the satellite of the earth, a representative of shade or feminity of things, alluding to the belle in this poem. In a universe animated by the interaction of Shade and Shine energies, the moon is Shade visible, the very germ or source of Shade, and the sun is its Shine counterpart.
* weathercock: a vane, properly one in the semblance of a cock, which turns to indicate the direction of thewind.
* Chingt'ing: a mountain with many cultural attractions, located nearby Hsuan in today's Anhui Province.

登 辨 觉 寺

竹径从初地，
莲峰出化城。
窗中三楚尽，
林上九江平。
软草承趺坐，
长松响梵声。
空居法云外，
观世得无生。

Climbing to Discernment Temple

The bamboo forest links with First Place,

Lotus Peak out of Transmission good.

From the window you see the land;

The Nine looks level on the wood.

The monks sit cross-legged on soft grass;

Buddhist sutras ring thru pine trees.

Alone out the sphere of Dharma,

You may obtain Non-life at ease.

* Discernment Temple: a temple probably in today's Hupei or Chianghsi, on the bank of the Long River.
* First Place: Place of Happiness, the first of the twelve places in Dharma.
* Lotus Peak: a peak in the shape of a lotus in Buddhist illusion.
* Transmission: Transmission Town in Buddhist terms, that may come into being in a second.
* good: satisfactory in quality and kind. Etymologically, "good" is derived from "God".

As is universally taught, "Doing good brings up good fortune", and as is termed in Buddhist karma, "What goes around, comes around".

* The Nine: the River Nine or Bankshine, a river town in present-day Chianghsi Province.
* sutra: a formulated doctrine, often so short as to be unintelligible without a key; literally a rule or a precept. In Buddhism, it is an extended writing usually in verse, and often in dialogue form, embodying important religious and philosophical propositions, sometimes directly, sometimes in highly allegorical or metaphorical language.
* Dharma: truth and righteousness in Buddhist terms.
* Non-life: the ideal state of freedom like Nirvana in Buddhist terms.

谒璿上人

上人外人内天,不定不乱。舍法而渊泊,无心而云动。色空无碍,不物物也。默语无际,不言言也,故吾徒得神交焉。玄关大启,德海群泳。时雨既降,春物具美。序于诗者,人百其言。

少年不足言,
识道年已长。
事往安可悔,
馀生幸能养。
誓从断荤血,
不复婴世网。
浮名寄缨佩,
空性无羁鞅。
夙承大导师,
焚香此瞻仰。
颓然居一室,
覆载纷万象。
高柳早莺啼,
长廊春雨响。
床下阮家屐,
窗前筇竹杖。
方将见身云,
陋彼示天壤。
一心在法要,
愿以无生奖。

Paying Respect to Great Master Hsuan

A great master regards humans as external and Heaven as internal, neither serene nor disturbed. Out of Dharma, one is placid , unintentional like clouds floating. Form is nothing, and when one is free, he is not had by a thing. Speechless without bound, one speaks without speech, therefore I communicate with my soul. Profound Gate is open, and virtue is a sea for all to swim in. A timely rain falls and all grow fine in spring. What is written in this preface is but one hundredth of what people say.

In youth I knew nothing of speech;
As I came to the Word, I was old.
How can I regret what is past?
Myself lefto'er I could uphold.
Cut off meat and blood I must be;
Ne'er should I fall into a snare.
A vain name depends on high ranks,
While thusness is free of whate'er.
Before a master I'd learn from
And burned incense to seek the true.
In meditation in my room,
All in the world I could see through.
Orioles on the tall willow chirp;
The veranda hears a swishing rain.
Juan's sandals are under the bed;
Near the sill is a bamboo cane.
You are to see all things thru clouds;
Sir Kettle's vision's all too low.
I'd have the essence of Dharma,

Hence into Non-life I could go.

* Dharma: truth and righteousness in Buddhist terms.
* Profound Gate: a breakthrough in the understanding of the Word, as is said in *The Word and the World*: The profoundest of the profound is the entrance to all subtleties.
* the Word: referring to Tao if transliterated, the most significant and profoundest concept of cosmology and axiology in Chinese philosophy. The Word is fully elucidated in *The Word and the World*, the single book that Laocius wrote all his wisdom into. Its importance can be seen in this verse: "The Word is void, but its use is infinite. O deep! It seems to be the root of all things."
* thusness: the being, Tathatā or Bhūtatathatā, what exists, as for ever exists, a similar notion to the Word, God or Void.
* oriole: golden oriole, one of the family of passerine birds, which looks bright yellow with contrasting black wings and sings beautiful songs.
* Juan's sandals: a token of a hermit's life. Fu Juan, Chi Juan's grandnephew loved a free life, so he cherished sandals instead of riches and ranks.
* Sir Kettle: a Wordist from the State of Cheng, Sir Line's teacher, one of the Wordist representatives in the Spring and Autumn period.
* Non-life: a state of Nirvana, a "blowing out" of the spark of life; hence spiritual reunion with Brahma.

送 邢 桂 州

铙吹喧京口，
风波下洞庭。
赭圻将赤岸，
击汰复扬舲。
日落江湖白，
潮来天地青。
明珠归合浦，
应逐使臣星。

Seeing Off Hsing to Cassiaton

Cymbals at Townmouth sound loud,
Send you to Cavehall and more.
You sail from Brown Shore to Red Bank,
Propelling water with your oar.
The sun sets into the lake white;
The tide sets the sky and land blue.
Pearls will appear in Union Shore;
The prefect to come will best do.

* Cassiaton: present-day Cassia Wood or Kuilin if transliterated.
* cymbal: one of a pair of platelike metallic musical instruments played by being clashed together, bulgy in the middle like half a ball, widely used in China and the West.
* Townmouth: present-day Chenchiang, Chiangsu Province.
* Cavehall: Lake Cavehall, a large lake with an area of 2,740 square kilometers, a lake of strategic importance since ancient times, a place of many resources for today's Hunan Province.

* Brown Shore: an ancient town in modern-day Anhui Province.
* Red Bank: Mt. Red Bank, in present-day Chiangsu Province.
* pearl: a lustrous, calcareous concretion deposited in layers around a central nucleus in the shells of various mollusks, and largely used as a gem.
* Union Shore: Hopu if transliterated, in modern-day Kuanghsi Province.

千 塔 主 人

逆旅逢佳节，
征帆未可前。
窗临汴河水，
门渡楚人船。
鸡犬散墟落，
桑榆荫远田。
所居人不见，
枕席生云烟。

To Host of Kilopagoda

The festival comes to the inn；
You cannot now set sail to go.
The window overlooks the Pien；
The door sees boats rowing from Ch'u.
In the village cocks and dogs stroll；
To far fields mulberries and elms spread.
No dwellers here one can see now，
But mist seems to rise from their bed.

* Kilopagoda：name of a temple or a place.
* Pien：referring to the Pien River in present-day Honan Province.
* Ch'u：a vassal state of Chough, one of the powers in the Warring States period, conquered and annexed by Ch'in in 223 B.C.
* cock：the male, usually full grown and full of pride, of the domesticated fowl, having a high red crown, hence an image of a leader or champion.
* dog：a domesticated carnivorous mammal (*Canis familiaris*), of worldwide distribution

and many varieties, noted for its adaptability and its devotion to man. The dog was domesticated in China at least 8,000 years ago and was often used as a hunter, as a poem in *The Book of Songs* says: "The dog bells clink and clink; / The hunter's handsome, a real pink."

* mulberry: a kind of tree of the genus *Morus*, *Morus alba Linn* in Latin, whose leaves are food for silkworms, and whose berries are served as a human delicacy.
* elm: a deciduous shade tree of America, Europe and Asia (genus *Ulmus*), with a broad, spreading, or overarching top, whose sweet pods look like coins and are delicious.

赠裴旻将军

腰间宝剑七星文，
臂上雕弓百战勋。
见说云中擒黠虏，
始知天上有将军。

To General Min P'ei

The seven-starred sword you carry does sheen;
The carved bow on your arm has all wars seen.
As said, an old man's caught a crafty foe;
A Swift Huo from the Heavens now I know!

* A Swift Huo: a metaphor used in praise of General Min P'ei, a great general like Swift Huo (140 B.C.- 117 B.C.) in the Han dynasty, one of the greatest generals in Chinese history.
* Heavens: a state or place of complete happiness or prefect rest, attained by the good after death.

送赵都督赴代州得青字

天官动将星，
汉地柳条青。
万里鸣刁斗，
三军出井陉。
忘身辞凤阙，
报国取龙庭。
岂学书生辈，
窗间老一经。

Seeing Off Governor Chao to Taichow

Check Star above will start a war;
Han soldiers see willows lush grow.
The wot-pots go a thousand miles,
And to the battlefield they go.
Leaving Phoenix Gate, they march on,
And will take Dragon Court, behold.
How can we learn from the book worms
Reading by the window till old?

* Check Star: a constellation. According to *Historical Records*, there are five star generals in the Heavens, and Check Star, in charge of warfare, is one of the five.
* Han: of the Han Empire or nationality.
* willow: any of a large genus of shrubs and trees related to the poplars, widely distributed in China and most of the world, having glossy green leaves resembling a girl's eye-brow, and generally having smooth branches, and often long, slender, pliant, and sometimes pendent branchlets, which seem to be waving good-bye, or

weeping amorously, or drooping for nostalgia.
* wot-pot: a pot used for cooking and telling time by striking when the holder is on night patrol.
* Phoenix Gate: the gate of the imperial palace with five phoenix towers on it. The phoenix is the king of all birds, an auspicious sign in Chinese civilization. In Egyptian mythology it is a legendary bird of great beauty, unique of its kind, which was supposed to live five or six hundred years before consuming itself by fire, rising again from its ashes to live through another cycle, a symbol of immortality. In Chinese mythology, the phoenix is the most beautiful bird that only perches on phoenix trees, i.e. firmiana, only eats firmiana fruit, and only drinks sweet spring water, and this mythic bird appears only in times of peace and sagacious rule.
* Dragon Court: also known as Dragon Town, the place where Chanyü, the chieftain of Huns made sacrifices to Heaven and earth, gods and demons, in present-day Qaidam Lake, Mongolian People's Republic.

终 南 山

太乙近天都，
连山接海隅。
白云回望合，
青霭入看无。
分野中峰变，
阴晴众壑殊。
欲投人处宿，
隔水问樵夫。

The South Mountains

Great One does near Capital soar;
The ranges stretch onto the shore.
The white clouds behind merge as one;
The blue haze inside becomes none.
The main peak's a dividing line;
The dales are in shade or in shine.
Here I would put up for the night,
Asking a logger across: Right?

* the Southern Mountains: also known as Mt. Great One or Mt. Earthlungs, the mountains south of Long Peace, one of the mountains of Ch'in Ridge, a great stronghold of the capital, rolling about 100 kilometers. It is the birthplace of Wordist culture, Buddhist culture, Filial Piety culture, Longevity culture, Bellheads culture and Plutus culture and is praised as the Capital of Fairies, the crown of Heavenly Abode and the Promised Land of the World.
* Great One: Mt. Great One, i.e., the Southern Mountains; also a Wordist term, the

One, indicating natural changes or the unification of everything. As *The Word and the World* says: The Word begets one, one begets two, two beget three, and three beget everything.

* Capital: Long Peace or Ch'ang'an if transliterated, a capital of sixteen dynasties in Chinese history. When the T'ang Empire adopted it as its capital, it reached its fullest glory as a cosmopolis with 1,000,000 inhabitants, the largest walled city ever built by man. It was the center of world religions, Buddhism, Confucianism, Wordism, Nestorianism, Zoroastrianism, and even Islamism represented by Saracens, and the center of education and academy — There were colleges of various grades and special institutes for calligraphy, arithmetic, music, astronomy and so on.

终 南 别 业

中岁颇好道，
晚家南山陲。
兴来每独往，
胜事空自知。
行到水穷处，
坐看云起时。
偶然值林叟，
谈笑无还期。

My Villa at the South Mountains

Middle aged, I worshiped Buddha;
Now old, I've a mountain villa.
Once in good mood, I stroll alone;
The good scenes are to myself known.
Where the creek ends, I take a rest;
To behold clouds arise white-dressed.
Sometimes a woodsman I may see
And forget time while talking free.

* the South Mountains: one of the mountains of Ch'in Ridge, where dwelt many hermits, located to the south of Long Peace, Sha'anhsi Province. It is the birthplace of Wordist culture, Buddhist culture, Filial Piety culture, Longevity culture, Bellheads culture and Plutus culture and is praised as the Capital of Fairies, the crown of Heavenly Abode and the Promised Land of the World.
* Buddha: Literally, the Enlightened; an incarnation of selflessness, virtue and wisdom; specifically, Gautama Siddhartha (cir. 563 B.C.- cir. 483 B.C.), the founder of

Buddhism, regarded by his followers as the last of a series of deified religious teachers of central and eastern Asia.
* woodsman: usually referring to a hermit. Words like fisher, Hillman, farmer and so on are often used like this to suggest reclusion.

白　鼋　涡

南山之瀑水兮，
激石滈瀑似雷惊，
人相对兮不闻语声。
翻涡跳沫兮苍苔湿，
藓老且厚，
春草为之不生。
兽不敢惊动，
鸟不敢飞鸣。
白鼋涡涛戏濑兮，
委身以纵横。
王人之仁兮，
不网不钓，
得遂性以生成。

White Soft-shell Turtle

The South Hills water does down pour,
Rushes on rocks and like thunder does there roar.
We face each other, but can't each other hear.
A whirlpool throws up foams and wets the moss near.
The moss is old and thick;
The spring grass choked by it is sick.
The beasts dare not go;
The birds dare not crow.
The turtle plays with eddies on the flow,
And floats on ripples to and fro.

> A saint with all virtues there
> Falls not into a snare,
> Here by nature he enjoys free air.

* the South Hills: the Southern Mountains, also known as Mt. Great One, Mt. Earthlungs, the mountains south of Long Peace, a great stronghold of the capital, towering in the middle of Ch'in Ridge and rolling about 100 kilometers.
* moss: a tiny, delicate green bryophytic plant growing on damp decaying wood, wet ground, humid rocks or trees, producing capsules which open by an operculum and contain spores. Under a poet's writing brush, this tiny, insignificant plant may arouse a poetic feeling or imagination, as was written by Mei Yüan, a poet in the Ching dynasty: "Where the sun does not arrive, /Springtime does on its own thrive. / The moss flowers like rice tiny, / Rush to bloom like the peony."
* Here by nature he enjoys free air: an ideal state in Wordist terms, as is said in *Sir Lush*: Keeping the property endowed by nature is called law.

投道一师兰若宿

一公栖太白，
高顶出风烟。
梵流诸壑遍，
花雨一峰偏。
迹为无心隐，
名因立教传。
鸟来远语法，
客去更安禅。
昼涉松路尽，
暮投兰若边。
洞房隐深竹，
清夜闻遥泉。
向是云霞里，
今成枕席前。
岂唯暂留宿，
服事将穷年。

Putting Up for the Night at Grove Calm When Visiting Master Word One

Atop Mt. Venus you abide,
Where a wind with haze does arise.
Buddhist music flows o'er all vales;
A flower rain down the One peak flies.
No trace is left 'cause of no craft;
As you teach, your fame carries on.

Birds come along, free of Dharma;
It's more serene, the travelers gone.
The day sees you go your pine way;
The night finds you sleep in Grove Calm.
The deep cave is in deep bamboo;
You hear gurgles thru night, thru balm.
You have cloud and haze for the day;
For the night you have quilt and bed.
You're not here just for a short stay,
For all life, you'll be here instead.

* Grove Calm: a Buddhist temple or a calm grove for meditation.
* Master Word One: a Zen master in Chianghsi See, which is approximately today's Chianghsi Province.
* Mt. Venus: the highest peak of Ch'in Ridge and also the highest peak in China east of Blue Sea-Tibetan Plateau, a Wordist sanctuary, known for its height, coldness, dangerousness, strangeness and bountifulness.
* Dharma: truth and righteousness in Buddhist terms.
* bamboo: a tall, tree-like or shrubby grass in tropical and semi-tropical regions, a symbol of integrity and altitude, one of the four most important botanical images in Chinese literature, which are wintersweet, orchid, bamboo and chrysanthemum. Bamboo shoots, fresh or dried, are widely used in Chinese cuisine; bamboo rats and bamboo worms are regarded as table delicacies.

戏赠张五弟諲三首

Three Poems for Fun to Chang Five, a Brother

其 一

吾弟东山时,
心尚一何远。
日高犹自卧,
钟动始能饭。
领上发未梳,
床头书不卷。
清川兴悠悠,
空林对偃蹇。
青苔石上净,
细草松下软。
窗外鸟声闲,
阶前虎心善。
徒然万象多,
澹尔太虚缅。
一知与物平,
自顾为人浅。
对君忽自得,
浮念不烦遣。

No. 1

My brother, oh, on this east hill,
How broad your mind, how far your soul!

The whole morning you lie in bed,
And have your breakfast at lunch toll.
Over your collar your hair's uncombed,
And on your bed your book unclosed.
The blue brook gurgles on afar
And you lie on in the grove, reposed.
On the boulder the moss is clean,
And by the pine grass is refined.
To the window birds chirp with love;
And on the steps tigers are kind.
For all the bustle of the world,
You are calm and so calm you are.
In and of nature you have been;
While I find myself not to par.
I feel enlightened before you,
No more worries and no more rue.

* Chang Five: Yin Chang, a hermit good at poetry, calligraphy and divination, who lived at Mt. Smallroom With Wei Wang for more than ten years.
* moss: a tiny, delicate green bryophytic plant growing on damp decaying wood, ground, rocks or trees, producing capsules which open by an operculum and contain spores. Under a poet's writing brush, it may arouse a poetic feeling or imagination.
* pine: any of a genus (*Pinus*) of evergreen trees of the pine family, a cone-bearing tree having bundles of two to five needle-shaped leaves growing in clusters, an important image in Chinese literature, a symbol of rectitude, longevity and so on.
* tiger: a large carnivorous feline mammal of Asia, with vertical black wavy stripes on a tawny body and black bars or rings on the limbs and tail, praised as king of all animals.

其 二

张弟五车书,
读书仍隐居。
染翰过草圣,
赋诗轻子虚。
闭门二室下,
隐居十年馀。
宛是野人野,
时从渔父渔。
秋风自萧索,
五柳高且疏。
望此去人世,
渡水向吾庐。
岁晏同携手,
只应君与予。

No. 2

My brother you are widely read;
In nature you read and recline.
The great cursive saint you outmatch;
The prose *None-Being* you outshine.
Under two Rooms you live, there shut;
For more than ten years you are free.
You are like a farmer on farm;
You follow a fisher at sea.
The five willows are tall and clean,
While autumn wind to them does sough.
While I watch you go out the world,

To my lodge I cross the stream now.
When the year's o'er, I'll come again,
So hand in hand we will remain.

* The great cursive saint: Chih Chang (? – cir. A.D. 192), a great calligrapher in Eastern Han, whose handwriting in cursive style has been regarded as the best in Chinese history.
* *None-Being*: a Wordist piece of classic prose by Hsiangju Ssuma (179 B.C.– 118 B.C.), a great prose writer in Western Han, when he was touring Liang.
* the two Rooms: referring to Mt. Smallroom and Mt. Greatroom, two main mountains that make Mt. Tower.
* the five willows: an allusion to Poolbright T'ao (A.D. 352 – A.D. 427), a verse writer, idyllist, and litterateur in the Chin dynasty. Pure and lofty, T'ao resigned from official life several times to live a life of simple leisure. There were five willow trees planted in front of his cottage, and he called himself Mr. Five Willows.

其 三

设置守狡兔，
垂钓伺游鳞。
此是安口腹，
非关慕隐沦。
吾生好清净，
蔬食去情尘。
今子方豪荡，
思为鼎食人。
我家南山下，
动息自遗身。
入鸟不相乱，
见兽皆相亲。
云霞成伴侣，
虚白侍衣巾。
何事须夫子，
邀予谷口真。

No. 3

You set up a trap for sly hares;
You dangle your line for smart fish.
This is just to please your stomach;
This is not nature as you wish.
I'd love to be clean as I do;
Food and vegetables I douse.
Now you feel so high, full of pride,
As you come from a noble house.
I live under the southern hill,

So free wheth'r I move or repose.
Unstirred, the birds don't fly away;
So dear, the beasts to me are close.
Clouds and mist have become my friends;
Light in my room does on me wait.
Why should I stay with you like now;
I'll go to Cheng, the hermit great.

* hare: a rodent (genus *Lepus*) with cleft upper lip, long ears, and long hind legs: characterized by its timidity and swiftness, habitating woodland, farmland or grassland.
* Cheng: Sirtruth by given name, Dalemouth Sirtruth by nick name, a hermit from Dalemouth in the late Western Han dynasty, tilling and reading in the hills, aloof from politics and material pursuits.

答 张 五 弟

终南有茅屋，
前对终南山。
终年无客长闭关，
终日无心长自闲。
不妨饮酒复垂钓，
君但能来相往还。

My Answer to Brother Chang Five

In South End a thatched hut have I,
With the South Mountains eye to eye.
I have no guests, so it's closed all year round,
And all day I feel free, free without bound.
Why not have a drink or angle for fish?
You may come along or go as you wish.

* South End: the southern urban area of Long Peace.
* the South Mountains: the Southern Mountains, also known as Mt. Great One, the mountains south of Long Peace, a great stronghold of the capital, towering in the middle of Ch'in Ridge and rolling about 100 kilometers. It is the birthplace of Wordist culture, Buddhist culture, Filial Piety culture, Longevity culture, Bellheads (Chungk'ui) culture and Plutus culture and is praised as the Capital of Fairies, the crown of Heavenly Abode and the Promised Land of the World.

送陆员外

郎署有伊人，
居然古人风。
天子顾河北，
诏书除征东。
拜手辞上官，
缓步出南宫。
九河平原外，
七国蓟门中。
阴风悲枯桑，
古塞多飞蓬。
万里不见虏，
萧条胡地空。
无为费中国，
更欲邀奇功。
迟迟前相送，
握手嗟异同。
行当封侯归，
肯访商山翁。

Seeing Off Counselor Lu

In Staff Office is such a one
With the manner of ancient sages.
The Lord looks north of the river;
At His edict, a war he wages.
He paces out of South Palace,

Having said bye to the heads great.
Nine rivers flow out of the plain,
Seven states within Thistle Gate.
The old pass sees thistledown fly
While wind blows mulberries to sough.
Thousands of miles, no foes seen,
The Hun land is deserted now.
No need to waste national power,
He wants to do more for the state.
Slowly, slowly, I'll see you off;
I sigh we have a different fate.
When you're entitled as a peer,
Will you visit a grey head here?

* edict: a public ordinance emanating from a sovereign and having the force of law.
* South Palace: alias of Privy Council or Central Secretariat Department, a palace already existing in the Han dynasty.
* Thistle Gate: name of an old place, today's Thistle Gate in Peking.
* thistledown: the pappus of a thistle; the ripe silky fibers from the dry flower of a thistle, a metaphor for drifting or wandering.
* mulberry: a kind of tree of the genus *Morus*, *Morus alba Linn* in Latin, whose leaves are food for silkworms, and whose berries are served as a human delicacy.
* the Hun land: west and north of China, the land of Hun barbarians.

三月三日曲江侍宴应制

万乘亲斋祭,
千官喜豫游。
奉迎从上苑,
祓禊向中流。
草树连容卫,
山河对冕旒。
画旗摇浦溆,
春服满汀洲。
仙籞龙媒下,
神皋凤跸留。
从今亿万岁,
天宝纪春秋。

In Reply to Your Majesty's Call to Compose a Poem for the Feast on the Bent on the Third Day of the Third Moon

Most High lights on Flow Sacrifice;
All officials like such a go.
They escort the Lord from High Park;
All filth will be gone with the flow.
Trees and grass link the royal guards;
To our view move tassel and crown.
Flags painted shade the waterfront;
The banks see tides of sash and gown.
The Bent welcomes His sedan great

Accompanied by carts all the way.
Our land will live a trillion years
From Heaven Bliss, our greatest day.

* Most High: referring to Deepsire (Hsuan Tsung) the emperor (A.D. 685 - A.D. 762), the ninth emperor of the T'ang dynasty. When a prince, he was regarded as wise and valiant, a sportsman accomplished in all knightly exercises and a master of all elegant arts. He established Pear Garden, an operatic school, where actors and actresses were trained, and the prototype of the modern Chinese drama was developed.
* the Bent: name of a pool, also known as Lotus Park, in southeast of Long Peace, which is present-day Hsi-an.
* Flow Sacrifice: sacrifice made on a river to ward off evils on the third day of the third moon.
* High Park: an imperial park that Lord Martial of Han built on the site of a discarded park of Ch'in. It was vast and splendid with palaces and woodlands, having various functions and recreational facilities, rolling about 340 kilometers.
* Heaven Bliss: a pun: blessings from Heaven and a reign title of Emperor Deepsire, which began in the first moon of A.D. 742 to the seventh moon of A.D. 756.

送丘为落第归江东

怜君不得意，
况复柳条春。
为客黄金尽，
还家白发新。
五湖三亩宅，
万里一归人。
知祢不能荐，
羞为献纳臣。

Seeing Off Wei Ch'iu Back East, Who Failed Grand Test

I feel so sad you Grand Test you failed;
E'en the green willows worry you.
Outside, you have spent all your gold;
Back home, your grey hair will accrue.
You have a small farm on the lake,
Awaiting you there far away.
You are so talented I know well.
My recommendation failed, ay!

* Grand Test: also called Court Test or Court Examination, the highest level of of the imperial civil-service examinations for selecting talents to serve as governmental officials, a system and practice initiated in the Han dynasty (202 B.C.- A.D. 220), formally begun in the Sui dynasty (A.D. 581 - A.D. 619), well-developed in the T'ang dynasty (A.D. 618 - A.D. 907) and abolished in the Late Ch'ing dynasty (A.D. 1636 - A. D. 1912). In the eighteenth century, the Jesuits and their friend Voltaire

recommended such a system for Europe as a safety valve for Europe's ossified social structure, which was soon overthrown by waves of aristocratic blood.
* willow: any of a large genus of shrubs and trees related to the poplars, widely distributed in China and most of the world, having glossy green leaves resembling a girl's eye-brow, and generally having smooth branches, and often long, slender, pliant, and sometimes pendent branchlets, which seem to be waving good-bye, or weeping amorously, or drooping for nostalgia.

奉和圣制庆玄元皇帝玉像之作应制

明君梦帝先，
宝命上齐天。
秦后徒闻乐，
周王耻卜年。
玉京移大像，
金箓会群仙。
承露调天供，
临空敞御筵。
斗回迎寿酒，
山近起炉烟。
愿奉无为化，
斋心学自然。

In Reply to Your Majesty's Call to Follow Your Majesty's Poem: Celebration of the Carving of Emperor Dark One's Jade Statue

Your Majesty dreamed of Dark One,
Who said you'd enjoy your great bliss.
Ch'in's lord just listened to music;
King of Chough's long reigns could but miss.
His Great Statue to Capital comes;
For sacrifice all priests light there.
Royal offerings tune with blessed dew;
A grand feast's held in open air.
The Southern Dipper turns for wine;

Stove smoke curls up the mountainside.
Into non-action we would go,
And in Nature we would abide.

* Your Majesty: referring to Emperor Deepsire or Hsuan Tsung the emperor (A.D. 685 – A.D. 762), the ninth emperor of the T'ang dynasty. When a prince, he was regarded as wise and valiant, a sportsman accomplished in all knightly exercises and a master of all elegant arts. He established Pear Garden, an operatic school, where actors and actresses were trained, and the prototype of the modern Chinese drama was developed. Under his enthusiastic patronage, arts and letters flourished. Indeed, his reign is often considered the pinnacle of Chinese cultural achievement.
* Dark One: Laocius (571 B.C.– 471 B.C.), who was posthumously crowned as emperor in the T'ang dynasty. Laocius was the founder or one of the most influential philosophers of Wordism in the Spring and Autumn period, the author of one of the most important books in the world, that is, *The Word and the World*. Laocius's ideas, quietism in particular, have had a great influence on the development of Chinese philosophy as well as social and political development.
* Ch'in: the Ch'in State or the State of Ch'in (905 B.C.– 206 B.C.), enfeoffed as a dependency of Chough by King Piety of Chough in 905 B.C. and enfeoffed as a vassal state by King Peace of Chough in 770 B.C. In the ten years from 230 B.C. to 221 B.C., Ch'in wiped out the other six powers and became the first unified regime of China, i.e., the Ch'in Empire.
* Chough: the State of Chough (1046 B.C – 256 B.C.) the regime established after Shang perished, the last slavery society in China. There were two periods in the Chough dynasty, the Western Chough (1046 B. C. – 771 B. C.) and the Eastern Chough (770 B.C.– 256 B.C.). The Eastern Chough consists of two periods: the Spring and Autumn period and the Warring States period.
* the Southern Dipper: a southern constellation having six stars in the form of a dipper.
* non-action: the attitude of quietism proposed by Laocius, as is said in *The Word and the World*: Therefore, the sages leave things as they are. They teach without inculcation, let things arise instead of raising them; they work without deliberation, achieve without crediting themselves; just because they do not credit themselves, they have nothing to lose.

和仆射晋公扈从温汤（时为右补阙）

天子幸新丰，
旌旗渭水东。
寒山天仗外，
温谷幔城中。
奠玉群仙座，
焚香太乙宫。
出游逢牧马，
罢猎见非熊。
上宰无为化，
明时太古同。
灵芝三秀紫，
陈粟万箱红。
王礼尊儒教，
天兵小战功。
谋犹归哲匠，
词赋属文宗。
司谏方无阙，
陈诗且未工。
长吟吉甫颂，
朝夕仰清风。

In Reply to Lord of Chin Escorting His Majesty to Hotspring (Me as a Right Remonstrant)

His Majesty to Newrich lights;

和仆射晋公扈从温汤（时为右补阙） / 221

Along the Wei flags flutter on.
Camps set up round Hotspring Dale;
His guards beyond hills coldly shone.
Jade laid in front of fairy seats;
Incense burned in Great One Hall there.
His Majesty meets a sky horse,
Like King Civil saw a cat-bear.
The grandee goes for non-action;
The age outshines the age long past.
Lucid ganoderma looks great;
Millets in big chests, ne'er surpassed.
Confucianism's worshiped by royals;
Royal troops despise the small den.
Great strategies belong to sages;
Poems count on literary men.
For admonishment there's no room,
And my poem is not yet well done.
I would sing Chifu's song for long;
May the cool breeze blow and blow on.

* Newrich: a county, known for wine brewed there. The county was built by Pang Liu in imitation of his hometown Rich County. Newrich is in today's Lintung County, near Hsi-an, Sha'anhsi Province.
* the Wei: the River Wei, the biggest tributary of the Yellow River.
* Hotspring Dale: the name of a hotspring, an old resort, probably on Mt. Black Steed.
* incense: an aromatic substance in the form of a stick that exhales perfume during combustion, burning bit by bit like a candle before a Buddhist, Wordist or any religious or ancestral figure as an act of worship, usually offered with a prayer or vow.
* Great One Hall: the building where sacrifices are made to Lord Great One, that is, Lord of Heaven.
* sky horse: according to historical records, the sky horse from Kusana is a precious kind. As it sprints, its shoulders swell and it sweats as if bleeding.
* King Civil: King Civil (1152 B.C.- 1056 B.C.), a wise monarch of high reputation and

the founder of Chough.
* cat-bear: non-existent auspicious animal that is unlike a tiger or bear, unlike a dragon or unicorn.
* lucid ganoderma: *Ganoderma Lucidum Karst* in Latin, a grass with an umbrella top, a pore fungus, used as medicine and tonic in China.
* millet: a member of the foxtail grass family, or its seeds, tiny and yellow, cultivated as a cereal, used as a stable food in ancient times, having been cultivated in China for more than 7,300 years, one of the earliest crops in the world.
* Chifu's song: "Chifu sings a song to please,/As refreshing as a breeze." Chifu was a great grandee who helped the Chough House to prosper.

哭祖六自虚

否极尝闻泰，
嗟君独不然。
悯凶才稚齿，
赢疾至中年。
馀力文章秀，
生知礼乐全。
翰留天帐览，
词入帝宫传。
国讶终军少，
人知贾谊贤。
公卿尽虚左，
朋识共推先。
不恨依穷辙，
终期济巨川。
才雄望羔雁，
寿促背貂蝉。
福善闻前录，
歼良昧上玄。
何辜铩鸾翮，
底事碎龙泉。
鹏起长沙赋，
麟终曲阜编。
域中君道广，
海内我情偏。
乍失疑犹见，
沉思悟绝缘。
生前不忍别，

死后向谁宣。
为此情难尽,
弥令忆更缠。
本家清渭曲,
归葬旧茔边。
永去长安道,
徒闻京兆阡。
旌车出郊甸,
乡国隐云天。
定作无期别,
宁同旧日旋。
候门家属苦,
行路国人怜。
送客哀难进,
征途泥复前。
赠言为挽曲,
奠席是离筵。
念昔同携手,
风期不暂捐。
南山俱隐逸,
东洛类神仙。
未省音容间,
那堪生死迁。
花时金谷饮,
月夜竹林眠。
满地传都赋,
倾朝看药船。
群公咸属目,
微物敢齐肩。
谬合同人旨,
而将玉树连。

不期先挂剑，
长恐后施鞭。
为善吾无矣，
知音子绝焉。
琴声纵不没，
终亦断悲弦。

Wailing Tzuhsu Tsu Six

A pain brings in a gain, I hear,
But it is not your case, alack.
In childhood, you were often sick;
Middle-aged, you bore all attack.
You wrote articles wonderful;
You were a born musician best.
The palace now all chant your verse;
The Lord enjoys your scripts at crest.
You're like Chung, a talent so rare,
And like Chia, sagacious and bright.
All grandees show respect to you,
And colleagues to you are polite.
You didn't care you were thwarted;
To serve the land you'd a great plan.
Though you hoped to be recruited,
Unfulfilled were you, a great man.
Virtue has good returns as said,
But you fell against Heaven's will.
Why break the wings of a phoenix?
Why break Dragon Spring into nil?
An owl flew in, hence *The Owl In*,

For the annals, Unicorn cried.
In the realm you had a broad mind,
While I am inclined to one side.
Though gone, you seem to be with me;
But you are gone for e'er, I rue.
Ere you passed, I would with you stay;
With whom can I talk now? Oh, woe.
I cannot tear myself from you;
More and more I fall into gloom.
Though I come from beside the Wei,
I would be buried by your tomb.
We'd be out of Long Peace for e'er;
In vain there lies Capital Lane.
Streamers and carts are out suburbs;
In clouds our town seems to remain.
I'd rather you strayed out for aye,
Going, going neath the old sun.
How sad your kin are by the door;
How keenly the passengers run!
It's hard for mourners to proceed,
And there's too much mud all the way.
Words are well weighed for elegies;
The feast is for you, gone away.
Then we used to walk hand in hand;
Your good bearing never decreased.
Hermits teem in the Southern Hills,
And there are nymphs in Loshine east.
So short we have been together,
And we are apart for e'er, woe.
In blooms we'd drink in golden dales
And sleep in the moonlit bamboo.

The whole town recited your verse
While you stayed away out of view.
You had all the lords' attention;
How dared I stand to be with you!
By mistake we were together;
Indeed with you I was aligned.
Your favor left me all too soon;
You advanced, and I was behind.
Alone I'd do good as before,
Although we are apart for e'er.
Your lute has suddenly broken,
But a sad string rings in the air.

* Chung: Chün Chung (133 B.C.- 112 B.C.), a famous politician and diplomat in Western Han.
* Chia: Ee Chia (200 B.C.- 168 B.C.), a political commentator, litterateur, who gained his fame when he was young. When he served as an official, he was envied by those higher-ranking ministers.
* Dragon Spring: a legendary sword made by Yehtzu Ou, a renowned swordsmith.
* owl: a predatory nocturnal bird, having large eyes and head, short, sharply hooked bill, long powerful clawks, and a circular facial disk of radiating feathers, regarded as ominous in Chinese culture.
* *The Owl In*: a piece of *euph*, a euphuist prose-like essay composed by Ee Chia when he was Teacher of Prince in Long Sand. An owl is an ominous sign in Chinese culture.
* Unicorn: a divine deer-like animal with one horn, a symbol of saintliness in Chinese culture. Confucius lamented the death of a unicorn captured and hence stopped compiling *The Spring and Autumn Annals* and died before long.
* Long Peace: Ch'ang'an if transliterated, the capital of the T'ang Empire, a cosmopolis with 1,000,000 inhabitants, the largest walled city ever built by man, the center of world religions, Buddhism, Confucianism, Wordism, Nestorianism, Zoroastrianism, and even Islamism represented by Saracens, and the center of education — There were colleges of various grades and special institutes for calligraphy, arithmetic, music, astronomy and so on.
* Capital Lane: the way leading from Long Peace to Lushridge, a site of Han

mausoleums.
* the Southern Hills: a sight of great significance located in Sha'anhsi Province, and a holy place for Wordism and Buddhism.
* Loshine: Loyang if transliterated, the eastern capital and the second largest city in the T'ang dynasty, with a population of about 0.8 million.

春日直门下省早朝

骑省直明光,
鸡鸣谒建章。
遥闻侍中珮,
闇识令君香。
玉漏随铜史,
天书拜夕郎。
旌旗映闻阖,
歌吹满昭阳。
官舍梅初紫,
宫门柳欲黄。
愿将迟日意,
同与圣恩长。

Morning Levee in Spring When I Am on Duty in Undergate Department

On night shift in the department;
Hark, to the palace roosters crow.
I hear the premier's trinkets clink,
And balm from the courtiers does flow.
The hourglass urges the bronze man;
The edict's for secretary there.
Flags flutter on Gate of Heaven;
While songs are played in Palace Glare.
In the yard wintersweets smell sweet;
By the gate willows' new sheen sways.

I wish the sun could longer last,
As long as His Majesty's grace.

* levee: a morning reception or an assembly at the court of a sovereign or at the house of a great personage. In ancient China, a levee at court was held every five days.
* Undergate Department: One of the three departments under an emperor in the T'ang dynasty, which was in charge of reviewing edicts and orders, remonstration, inspection and other services. Other two departments were Central Privy Department, which was responsible for making plans and decisions and writing edicts, policies, regulations and so on, and Executive Department, which was to carry out what had been decided or approved by other two departments.
* rooster: the male of the chicken that struts with pride and crows at dawn.
* hourglass: a vessel made of glass or some similar material, which is used for measuring time by the running of water or sand from the upper into the lower compartment, also used as metaphor for the elapse of time.
* edict: a public ordinance emanating from a sovereign and having the force of law.
* Gate of Heaven: the gate of the imperial palace.
* Palace Glare: an empress's residence in the T'ang dynasty.
* sun: the heavenly body that is the center of attraction and the main source of light and heat in the solar system. In Chinese culture, it is a representation of Shine in contrast with Shade, the moon, a symbol of hope, life, strength, vigor, and youth, and sometimes it may refer to a sovereign.

送綦毋校书弃官还江东

明时久不达,
弃置与君同。
天命无怨色,
人生有素风。
念君拂衣去,
四海将安穷。
秋天万里净,
日暮澄江空。
清夜何悠悠,
扣舷明月中。
和光鱼鸟际,
澹尔兼葭丛。
无庸客昭世,
衰鬓日如蓬。
顽疏暗人事,
僻陋远天聪。
微物纵可采,
其谁为至公。
余亦从此去,
归耕为老农。

Seeing Off Collator Ch'iwu, Who's Resigned, to the East

If it does not clear up ere long;
To follow you, I will resign.

Heaven does not complain at all;
Life should be simple, should be fine.
I care you now go straight away;
In nature you live a life true.
In autumn all the land is clean;
The river at dusk is sky blue.
The night so quiet rolls on and on;
In moonlight you tap on your boat.
Birds and fish bask in Luna fair;
And 'mid clusters of reeds you float.
Of no use, you live in great gleam,
With your loose hair like thistledown.
Too simple to trouble the world,
You're dirt, unknown to the crown.
Although cheap ferns all can gather,
Who can be of self-interest free?
I'd resign from office hereby
And an old farmer I would be.

* Luna: the moon, the goddess of the moon and of months in Roman mythology, and in Chinese culture the imperial concubine of Lord Alarm (2480 B.C.- 2345 B.C.), one of five mythical emperors in prehistorical China. Luna or the moon is an important image in Chinese literature as it can give rise to many associations such as solitude, purity, brightness and happy reunions.
* reed: the slender, frequently jointed stem of certain tall grasses growing in wet places or in grasses themselves.
* thistledown: the pappus of a thistle; the ripe silky fibers from the dry flower of a thistle, a metaphor for drifting or wandering of an aimless vagrant.
* fern: any of a widely distributed class of flowerless, seedless pteridophytic plants, having roots and stems and feathery leaves (fronds) which carry the reproductive spores in clusters of sporangia called *sori*. Its young stems and root starch are table delicacies to Chinese now as well as in the past.

青龙寺昙璧上人兄院集

吾兄大开荫中,明彻物外。以定力胜敌,以惠用解严。深居僧坊,傍俯人里。高原陆地,下映芙蓉之池;竹林果园,中秀菩提之树。八极氛霁,万汇尘息。大虚寥廓,南山为之端倪;皇州苍茫,渭水贯于天地。经行之后,跌坐而闲。升堂梵筵,饵客香饭。不起而游览,不风而清凉。得世界于莲花,记文章于贝叶。时江宁大兄持片石命维序之,诗五韵,坐上成。

> 高处敞招提,
> 虚空讵有倪。
> 坐看南陌骑,
> 下听秦城鸡。
> 眇眇孤烟起,
> 芊芊远树齐。
> 青山万井外,
> 落日五陵西。
> 眼界今无染,
> 心空安可迷?

Master Cloud Jade in Blue Dragon Temple

You, my brother, disenchanted and illuminated, overwhelm the enemy with composure and enter nirvana with wisdom. Living in your Zen room, you overlook the lanes, and your height envisages the lotus pool below. Between the bamboo grove and orchard, there stands a bodhi tree. It's clear in all directions, free of any dust. In this great serene void loom the South Hills; in the greenness of the land flows the Wei under the blue. After your meditation, you sit cross-legged at ease. You treat us with a

Buddhist feast in the hall, all clean foods and drinks. Seated, we see scenic sights; without wind, enjoy the cool. We find a world in a lotus flower and write sutra on a pattra leaf. Now, a brother from Riverpeace offers a tablet and bids me to write down this occasion, hence the poem in ten lines, finished at feast.

> A temple stands on the broad height;
> Is there a way to Void to go?
> I, seated, see a horseman south
> And hear roosters in Ch'in Town crow.
> Far there, a curl of smoke does rise;
> So lush, the trees with yon trees link.
> Green hills appear beyond the fields;
> The eve sun west of Five Ridges sink.
> Your sight is now clean, free of dust;
> How can you be misled by lust?

* Blue Dragon Temple: Emperor Secret of T'ang's ashram, 4 kilometers from Long Peace County, in today's Hsi-an, Sha'anhsi Province.
* Void: the truth of nature or a state of nothingness. According to *The Word and the World*, "The Word is void. Void, it's used without end; moved, the more it will send."
* rooster: the male of the chicken that struts with pride and crows at dawn. The rooster is often a theme of literature, as is shown in *A Rooster in the Painting* by Pohu T'ang (A.D. 1470 – A.D. 1524), a Ming painter, "Untailored, naturally made its red crown, / The pure snow tiptoes, donning a white gown. / It dare not call, now timid as before; But at its crow all households ope their door."
* Ch'in Town: old town. Many palaces and towns of Ch'in and Han remained in T'ang.
* Five Ridges: the Five Ridges, the five hills south of Mt. Scale in today's Hunan Province, rolling east to the sea.

酬黎居士淅川作

依家真个去，
公定随侬否。
著处是莲花，
无心变杨柳。
松龛藏药裹，
石唇安茶臼。
气味当共知，
那能不携手。

Thanking Li, a Lay Buddhist in Rustle River

I will go out of the world now;
Are you sure you will follow me?
Lo, lotus blossoms here and there,
In Nature, like nature we'll be.
Tea mortar placed beside the rock;
Herbal bag stored in the pine shrine.
The taste, the flavor we both know;
Why don't we join hands to combine?

* lay Buddhist: one who believes in Buddhist doctrines and practises Buddhism in the form of meditation at home instead of being a professional monk in a temple.
* Rustle River: a county named Rustle River, Hsichuan if transliterated, in today's Southshine, Honan Province.
* lotus blossom: flower of a plant of the waterlily family blooming in red or white, an important image in Chinese culture and in many cases associated with Buddhism as a

sign of holiness and divinity.

* tea: an evergreen Asian shrub or small tree (*Thea sinensis*), having a compact head of leathery, toothed leaves and white or pink flowers. The cured leaves of this plant or an infusion of them are used as a beverage.

哭殷遥

人生能几何，
毕竟归无形。
念君等为死，
万事伤人情。
慈母未及葬，
一女才十龄。
泱漭寒郊外，
萧条闻哭声。
浮云为苍茫，
飞鸟不能鸣。
行人何寂寞，
白日自凄清。
忆昔君在时，
问我学无生。
劝君苦不早，
令君无所成。
故人各有赠，
又不及生平。
负尔非一途，
恸哭返柴荆。

Wailing Yao Yin

How long is life, how long is it?
All will become dust, become dirt.
You died, the same as people do,

But still everything seems so hurt.
Your mother's not been buried yet,
And your daughter's but ten years old.
In the vast expanse of the wild,
Wails can be heard in the wind cold.
The clouds float in the blue expanse;
Flying birds cannot chirp or shrill.
How lonesome the passengers are!
The white sun by itself feels chill.
I recall when you were alive,
You asked me what non-life did mean.
I tried to lead you to the way,
But nothing you did or had been.
Now all friends would give you a gift,
But you live in this world no more.
I have not done my best to help you,
So, wailing, I'm back to my door.

* sun: the heavenly body that is the center of attraction and the main source of light and heat in the solar system, a representation of Shine in contrast with Shade, the moon, in Chinese culture, a symbol of hope, life, strength, vigor and youth.
* Non-life: nirvana in Buddhist terms, a "blowing out" of the spark of life, complete freedom from all mental, emotional and psychic tension.

送 殷 四 葬

送君返葬石楼山，
松柏苍苍宾驭还。
埋骨白云长已矣，
空馀流水向人间。

Back from Yin Four's Funeral

Your funeral's been held at Mt. Stone Tower;
Pines and cypresses see the mourners back.
Buried neath white clouds, you'll be there for e'er;
The water flows to the world in vain, alack.

* Mt. Stone Tower: When Nestle came into power, he moved the capital to Mt. Stone Tower, a holy land in the north and he held office in a cave dug by his order on the mountain, northeast of present-day Rising (Hsing) County, Sha'anhsi Province.
* pines and cypresses: two similar kinds of evergreen trees, having durable timber, a symbol of rectitude, nobility and longevity in Chinese culture.

班婕妤三首
Lady Fair, Three Poems

其 一

玉窗萤影度，
金殿人声绝。
秋夜守罗帷，
孤灯耿不灭。

No. 1

Fireflies to the screen their light cast;
From the harem all voice has gone.
Her net's so cold this autumn night,
And her lonely lamp flickers on.

* firefly: also known as fireworm or glowworm, which appears in or over grass at night and can be put in a transparent bottle or jade pot to offer light.
* screen: a curtain which separates or cuts off, shelters or protects as a light partition, usually made of bamboo, a common image in Chinese literature. Two lines from a Sung lyric by Haowen Yüan reads like this: "The drizzle falls before my tower's sill; / 'Broidered with crabapples, the screen's chill."
* harem: a imperial palace for wives and concubines in Chinese history. A harem could be very large. In the harem in the age of Emperor Martial (156 B.C.- 87 B.C.) or Emperor Vital (74 B.C.- 33 B.C.), there were 3,000 concubines in a hierarchical structure of fourteen ranks. And in the Chin dynasty, Emperor Martial of Chin (A.D. 236 - A.D. 290) had 10,000 beauties and Emperor Deepsire of T'ang (A.D. 685 - A.D. 762) had 40,000.

其 二

宫殿生秋草，
君王恩幸疏。
那堪闻凤吹，
门外度金舆。

No. 2

Her harem wild with autumn grass,
The Lord's no interest any more.
How could she bear the flute tune that
Escorts His gold cart out of door.

* harem: an imperial palace reserved for wives and concubines in Chinese history. A T'ang harem could boast as many as 40,000 beauties, like that of Emperor Deepsire.
* flute tune: a tune of the flute, a tubular wind instrument of small diameter with holes along the side, often a cold or sad tune when played at night.
* gold cart: gold sedan cart, an enclosed vehicle for the emperor, usually drawn by goats to visit his concubines in the harem.

其 三

怪来妆阁闭，
朝下不相迎。
总向春园里，
花间笑语声。

No. 3

No wonder she makes up no more;
The Lord does not come to her room.
In the spring garden over there,
Their laughter can bend a bloom.

* their laughter: referring to the imperial concubines' laughter. It was common that an emperor abandoned the old for the new because he had too many beauties in the harem.

奉和圣制幸玉真公主山庄因题石壁十韵之作应制

碧落风烟外,
瑶台道路赊。
如何连帝苑,
别自有仙家。
比地回鸾驾,
缘溪转翠华。
洞中开日月,
窗里发云霞。
庭养冲天鹤,
溪流上汉查。
种田生白玉,
泥灶化丹砂。
谷静泉逾响,
山深日易斜。
御羹和石髓,
香饭进胡麻。
大道今无外,
长生讵有涯。
还瞻九霄上,
来往五云车。

In Reply to Your Majesty's Call to Follow Your Majesty's Poem: the Inscription on the Precipice by Her Imperial Highness Princess Jade True's Cottage, a Twenty-line Rhyme

Blue Dome is beyond mist and clouds;
Jade Mound is far and far away.
The cottage's a royal abode,
Where immortal fairies may stay.
Now her sedan turns up and down
Along the brook to somewhere green.
The cave is lit up by the sun,
And clouds float on out of the screen.
A Rising Crane's reared in the court;
The creek sends a raft to afar.
From the field one may crop white jade;
In clay stovesthey melt cinnabar.
The dale calm, the spring gurgles loud;
The hills deep, the sun does incline.
One may eat stalactites as soup
And on sesame food one may dine.
The great Word extends without end,
And longevity has no bound.
Raise your head to Nine Skies above,
Five colored carriages may be found.

* Her Imperial Highness Princess of Jade True: Emperor Deepsire of T'ang's sister.
* Princess Jade True: Princess Jade True (A.D. 692 - A.D. 762), Upmost Truth by Wordist name, a princess and Wordist in the T'ang dynasty, Emperor Sagacious of

T'ang's daughter and Emperor Deepsire of T'ang's sister.
* Blue Dome: the first layer of sky in Wordist terms.
* Jade Mound: Mt. Queen, Mt. Kunlun if transliterated, the most sacred mountain in China. It starts from the Eastern Pamir Plateau, stretches across New Land (Hsinchiang) and Tibet, and extends to Chinghai, with an average altitude of 5,500 - 6,000 meters. In Chinese myths, Mt. Queen is where Mother West dwells.
* sun: the heavenly body that is the center of attraction and the main source of light and heat for the earth. It is a representation of Shine in contrast with Shade, the moon, in Chinese culture, a symbol of hope, life, strength, vigor, and youth.
* Rising Crane: an allusion to Prince of Front, who rode a crane to the sky as an immortal.
* stalactite: an elongated, downward hanging form in which certain minerals, especially calcium carbonate, are sometimes deposited by slow dripping, as in a cave.
* sesame: an East Indian herb, containing seeds which are used as food and as a source of the pale yellow sesame oil, used as salad oil or an emollient, introduced from Ferghana by Ch'ien Chang (164 B.C.- 114 B.C.), a diplomat, traveler, explorer, and the initiator of the Silk Road.
* the great Word: the Word or Tao if transliterated, the most significant and profoundest concept in Chinese philosophy, comparable to God, the Word or the Logos in Western culture. According to Laocius's *The Word and the World*: "The Word is void, but its use is infinite. O deep! It seems to be the root of all things."
* Nine Skies: the profound sky in Wordist terms.

新秦郡松树歌

青青山上松，
数里不见今更逢。
不见君，
心相忆，
此心向君君应识。
为君颜色高且闲，
亭亭迥出浮云间。

A Song of Pines in New Ch'in

The green pines on the mountains there,
Not more than a mile, loom to me once more.
You out of my sight,
You inside my heart,
Don't you know your heart and love I long for?
High above in solitude you are free;
Amid clouds floating high you seem to be.

* pine: any of a genus (*Pinus*) of evergreen trees of the pine family, a cone-bearing tree having bundles of two to five needle-shaped leaves growing in clusters, an important image in Chinese literature, a symbol of rectitude, longevity and so on.
* New Ch'in: a prefecture founded in the first year of Heaven Bliss (A.D. 742 - A.D. 756), changed to Unicorn Town the first year of Gen Begun (A.D. 758 - A.D. 760).

榆 林 郡 歌

山头松柏林，
山下泉声伤客心。
千里万里春草色，
黄河东流流不息。
黄龙戍上游侠儿，
愁逢汉使不相识。

Song of Elm Wood Prefecture

On the mountainside grow pine trees;
The fountain spring below adds to my woe.
For myriads of miles spring grass with hue shines;
The Yellow River eastward does non-stop flow.
The gallant at the front of Yellow Dragon
In sadness sees me but does not me know.

* Elm Wood Prefecture: what was Shengchow in the Sui dynasty, made a prefecture in the first year of Heaven Bliss (A.D. 742 – A.D. 756) and changed to Shengchow in the first year of Gen Begun (A.D. 758 – A.D. 760), its seat of administration in today's Inner Mongolia.
* the Yellow River: the second longest river in China, the cradle of Chinese civilization. It is 5,464 kilometers long, with a drainage area of 752,443 square kilometers. As legend goes, the river derived from a yellow dragon that, couchant on Midland Plain, ate yellow soil, flooded crops, devoured people and stock, and was finally tamed by Great Worm, the First King of Hsia (21 B.C.– 16 B.C.). Its fertile valleys were turned into fields of rice, barley and oscillating corn, amid gleaming streams and lakes.
* Yellow Dragon: name of an old town in today's Morn Sun (Chaoyang), Liaoning Province.

送高道弟耽归临淮作

少年客淮泗,
落魄居下邳。
遨游向燕赵,
结客过临淄。
山东诸侯国,
迎送纷交驰。
自尔厌游侠,
闭户方垂帷。
深明戴家礼,
颇学毛公诗。
备知经济道,
高卧陶唐时。
圣主诏天下,
贤人不得遗。
公吏奉纁组,
安车去茅茨。
君王苍龙阙,
九门十二逵。
群公朝谒罢,
冠剑下丹墀。
野鹤终踉跄,
威凤徒参差。
或问理人术,
但致还山词。
天书降北阙,
赐帛归东菑。
都门谢亲故,

行路日逶迟。
孤帆万里外，
淼漫将何之。
江天海陵郡，
云日淮南祠。
杳冥沧洲上，
荡漭无人知。
纬萧或卖药，
出处安能期。

Seeing Off Tan Kao, Tao Kao's Brother Going Back to Linhuai

When young, you traveled to Huai-Ssu;
In Hsiap'i you were out and out.
You made lots of friends in Lintzu,
And in the north you loafed about.
The six states east of the mountains
All treated you with zest galore.
Then you were tired of playing out,
And got down to read in the door.
You well studied *Rites* by the Tai's
And *Book of Songs* prefaced by Mao.
You learned how to manage the state
And traced back to the Time of T'ao.
Most High issued the edict then
To recruit sages all o'er the land.
The officials rode to your place
With jade, sash and all gifts so grand.
The Lord's Gates, Blue Dragons by name,

Start twelve boulevards rolling down.
The morning levee o'er, the lords
Came down the red steps, sword and gown.
A wild crane cannot walk so well;
A phoenix confined flaps in vain.
When asked about how to govern,
You answered you'd live out again.
Most High's edict fell on North Gate,
To granting you silk as you'd go back.
At Town Gate you said bye to friends;
The setting sun gilt your long track.
Your lone sail disappeared beyond;
With the billows where would you go?
The river flew to Sea Ridge there;
The sun to Huainan Fane did glow.
So dim and so far loomed Blue Shoal;
The water rolled away to swell.
Weaving grass screens or selling herbs,
Where you would abide who could tell?

* Huai-Ssu: the drainage area of the Huai River and the Ssu River. The Huai River is one of the seven rivers in China, between the Long River and the Yellow River, 1,000 kilometers long. The Ssu River is a river originating from Mt. Black Dale and flowing into Lake Four (Sir Wei Hill Lake), 169 kilometers long, a major river in today's Shantung Province.
* Hsiap'i: a place tracing back to the Warring State period, a fief, then the capital of a prefecture early in the Han dynasty, a vassal state enfeoffed to Hsin Han in 202 B.C. and a kingdom in the Emperor Bright of Han reign, a place of strategic importance.
* Lintzu: the capital of the State of Ch'i, a prefecture in T'ang, an area of today's Tzupo, Shantung Province.
* Rites: one of the *Five Books*, i.e. the five Confucian classics, that is, *The Book of Songs*, *The Book of Documents*, *Changes*, *Rites*, *Spring and Autumn Annals*, the oldest books of Chinese civilization, which have been well kept till today.

* *Book of Songs*: the earliest collection of Chinese poems including folk songs, psalms and odes, compiled by Confucius.
* the Time of T'ao: the age of Mound (2377 B.C.- 2259 B.C.), Yao if transliterated. Divine and noble, Mound has been regarded as one of Five Lords in ancient China.
* edict: a public ordinance emanating from a sovereign and having the force of law.
* Blue Dragons: name of T'ang's gates of the Imperial Palace.
* levee: a morning reception or an assembly at the court of a sovereign or at the house of a great personage. In ancient China, a levee at court was held every five days.
* red steps: the steps, painted in red, leading up to an imperial palace or an official or monastic hall, frequently occurring in classic Chinese literature.
* crane: one of a family of large, long-necked, long-legged, heronlike birds allied to the rails, a symbol of integrity and longevity in Chinese culture, only second to the phoenix in cultural importance.
* phoenix: a legendary bird of great beauty, unique of its kind, which was supposed to live five or six hundred years before consuming itself by fire, rising again from its ashes to live through another cycle, a symbol of immortality. In Chinese mythology, the phoenix only perches on phoenix trees, i.e. firmiana, only eats firmiana fruit, and only drinks sweet spring water, and this mythic bird appears only in times of peace and sagacious rule.
* Sea Ridge: an old prefecture founded in the Chin dynasty and annulled in the Sui dynasty, its administration office in today's T'aichow, Chiangsu Province.
* Huainan Fane: an old temple in today's Hillshine (Shanyang) County, Ch'angsu Province.
* Blue Shoal: any place of reclusion for hermits or immortals.

奉和圣制送不蒙都护兼鸿胪卿归安西应制

上卿增命服,
都护扬归旆。
杂虏尽朝周,
诸胡皆自郐。
鸣笳瀚海曲,
按节阳关外。
落日下河源,
寒山静秋塞。
万方氛祲息,
六合乾坤大。
无战是天心,
天心同覆载。

In Reply to Your Majesty's Call to Follow Your Majesty's Poem: Seeing Off Fumeng, Governor and Grandee, to Pacified West

A grandee in brighter costume,
The governor in flags goes west.
The barbarians rush to worship;
All Huns feel lowly, as addressed.
His army have marched past Sun Pass;
The flute tune does the desert thrill.
The sun has set at River Source,
The mountains cold, the autumn still.

From all directions it is great peace;
The cosmos is vast, filled with worth.
No war's a call from Most High's heart;
Most High's heart fills Heaven and earth.

* Huns: a nationality that has the same origin as Chinese. In approximately 16th century B.C., a branch of the Hsia family fled to the north and annexed other tribes, hence the formation of the Hun nationality.
* Sun Pass: an old pass built in Han, in today's Tunhuang, Kansu Province, an important pass to the west regions in ancient China.
* flute tune: a tune of the flute, which is a tubular wind instrument of small diameter with holes along the side, often sounding cold or sad when it is played at night.
* River Source: another way of saying the West Regions dwelt by Huns and Turks in general.
* cosmos: the world or universe considered as a harmonious system, perfect in order and arrangement, opposed to chaos.

故西河郡杜太守挽歌三首
Three Elegies to Tu, Prefect of West River County

其 一

天上去西征，
云中护北平。
生擒白马将，
连破黑雕城。
忽见刍灵苦，
徒闻竹使荣。
空留左氏传，
谁继卜商名。

No. 1

You finished west expedition;
You guarded the northern front town.
White Horse General you did catch live;
Black Teeth Tattoos you did crash down.
The straw men and steeds are aligned;
Your envoy tally none will read.
Your essays remain in the world;
To your teaching who will succeed?

* White Horse General: the title of a Hun general.
* Black Teeth Tattoos: barbarians on the borders of China, with their teeth painted black and their foreheads tattooed.
* straw men and steeds: figures of men and steeds made of straw for a funeral, which are set on fire when the funeral is over.

其 二

返葬金符守，
同归石窌妻。
卷衣悲画翟，
持翣待鸣鸡。
容卫都人惨，
山川驲马嘶。
犹闻陇上客，
相对哭征西。

No. 2

Back to east with your tally gold,
You'll be buried in your wife's tomb.
The funeral starts when roosters crow,
To your folded soul robe in gloom.
The procession moves, the crowd sad;
The horses to the mountains neigh.
Cries for you, prefect, are now heard
From farmland there and from the way.

* tally gold: a tiger tally of gold, a token issued to generals for troop movement. It is usually tiger-shaped, with one half kept by the Monarch and the other by local generals, and generals can send troops only if the two halves are matched.
* rooster: the male of the chicken that struts with pride and crows at dawn. The funeral in this poem starts early as it is time when roosters crow.

其 三

涂刍去国门，
秘器出东园。
太守留金印，
夫人罢锦轩。
旌旗转衰木，
箫鼓上寒原。
坟树应西靡，
长思魏阙恩。

No. 3

Now your hearse leaves the town gate
And your coffin goes out East Lane.
Your gold seal is left to the world,
And your wife's car stays there in vain.
Banners and flags sway the old trees;
Bamboo flutes and drums quake the plain.
The tomb trees should look to the west,
As thankful to Lord they remain.

* hearse: an unvarnished four-wheeled vehicle carrying the dead usually in a coffin to his grave.
* coffin: the case or box made of various types of wood such as pine, cypress, Phoebe zhennan and so on, in which a dead body is laid to be buried in a tomb.
* East Lane: an office for funeral management.
* gold seal: In ancient China, the seal for a premier, a general or prefect was a gold one.
* bamboo flute: a tubular wind instrument of small diameter with holes along the side, made of bamboo.

苑舍人能书梵字兼达梵音，
皆曲尽其妙，戏为之赠

名儒待诏满公车，
才子为郎典石渠。
莲花法藏心悬悟，
贝叶经文手自书。
楚词共许胜扬马，
梵字何人辨鲁鱼。
故旧相望在三事，
愿君莫厌承明庐。

A Poem for Fun to Secretary Yüan, Who Can Write Sanskrit Characters and Knows Sanskrit Music

While famous showcharms wait to be recruits,
You're Secretary and also Sage Scholar.
You contemplate in Dharma so profound,
And can well compose a palm-leaf sutra.
In brilliance of art you outshine those best;
In Sanskrit who can judge the wrong or right?
You'll be one of the three premiers at court;
Just be patient on your shift for the night.

* Sanskrit: the ancient and classical language of the Hindus of India, belonging to the Indic branch of the Indo-Iranian subfamily of the Indo-European languages. It includes Vedic Sanskrit, the language of the Vedas and the later classical Sanskrit of India's

great religious, philosophical and poetic literature, still used for sacred and learned writings.
* showcharm: hsiuts'ai if transliterated, a talented candidate recommended for official use through official civil-service examinations usually held every three years or a well-learned person in ancient China. A showcharm was well respected in the traditional and meritocratic Chinese society.
* Sage Scholar: one of the scholars in the Sages' College, who was appointed to help the premier.
* Dharma: truth and righteousness in Buddhist terms.
* palm-leaf sutra: a Buddhist sutra copied on a palm leaf. A sutra is a formulated doctrine, often so short as to be unintelligible without a key; literally it is a rule or a precept. In Buddhism, it is an extended writing usually in verse, and often in dialogue form, embodying important religious and philosophical propositions, sometimes directly, sometimes in highly allegorical or metaphorical language.

重酬苑郎中

何幸含香奉至尊，
多惭未报主人恩。
草木尽能酬雨露，
荣枯安敢问乾坤。
仙郎有意怜同舍，
丞相无私断扫门。
扬子解嘲徒自遣，
冯唐已老复何论。

To Secretary Yüan Again

With balm in mouth you report to the crown;
Ashamed, I have done nothing for Most High.
Plants and grass do have the same rain and dew;
If one goes dry, how can it blame the sky?
I'm lucky that we have been colleagues here;
Our premier is selfless, so clean his door.
Yang wrote *Fun of Me* to amuse himself;
Now old and useless, I should talk no more.

* balm in mouth: referring to the elegant language and original thought of a scholar or official.
* *Fun of Me*: the *euph* or euphuistic prose Man Yang composed in A.D. 5. With a survey of, and comments on, the rises and falls, gains and losses of the past dynasties, he ridiculed the malfeasances of the society and the malfunctions of the system in a tone of ridiculing himself.

同比部杨员外十五夜
游有怀静者季

承明少休沐，
建礼省文书。
夜漏行人息，
归鞍落日馀。
悬知三五夕，
万户千门辟。
夜出曙翻归，
倾城满南陌。
陌头驰骋尽繁华，
王孙公子五侯家。
由来月明如白日，
共道春灯胜百花。
聊看侍中千宝骑，
强识小妇七香车。
香车宝马共喧阗，
个里多情侠少年。
竞向长杨柳市北，
肯过精舍竹林前。
独有仙郎心寂寞，
却将宴坐为行乐。
傥觉忘怀共往来，
幸沾同舍甘藜藿。

A Night Tour with Counselor Yang from the Inspection Office and Chi, a Monk, on the Fifteenth Night

The one on night shift has few leaves;
In Rite Hall, o'er writs he does run.
Dusk falling now, all have gone out.
I ride back 'gainst the fading sun.
On this fifteenth night you don't know,
Most of the households close their door.
Outside, they will spend the whole night;
Lo, to south fields the townsfolk pour.
Steeds gallop in the fields, what a great sight!
Lords, grandees, peers swarm to enjoy their hours.
As e'er, the moon is as bright as the sun;
They all say their spring lanterns outshine flowers.
Lo, the royal servant on his high steed
Accosts a young belle in her balmy cart.
Her balmy cart and her horses bump out,
Wondering at the young man gallant and smart.
He runs to Willow House and Sallow Fair,
And then to the temple and bamboo wood.
But you, Counselor, stay in solitude
And take meditation as better food.
You forget what comes and goes, free of care;
I'm so happy that sweet goosefoots we share.

* Rite Hall: an office or hall where a Privy Council secretary worked on night shift in the T'ang dynasty.

* south fields: a metonymy for fields. As a slope facing south is good for farming, ancient Chinese usually reclaimed farmland facing south, hence the term.
* steed: a horse; especially a spirited war horse. The use of horses in war can be traced back to the Shang dynasty (1600 B.C. - 1046 B.C.), when a department of horse management was established. A verse from *The Book of Songs* tells of Lord Civil of Watch's industriousness: "In state affairs he leads; / He has three thousand steeds."
* Willow House: name of a Ch'in palace, in which there was an acre of willows, refurbished in the Han dynasty.
* Sallow Fair: name of a market in Long Peace in the Han dynasty.
* goosefoot: any plant of a widely distributed genus (*Chenopodium*) of mealy-leaved shrubs and herbs with small green flowers, the pigweed.

达奚侍郎夫人寇氏挽词二首
Two Elegies for Lady K'ou, Ministerial Aide Tahsi's Wife

其 一

束带将朝日，
鸣环映漏辰。
能令谏明主，
相劝识贤人。
遗挂空留壁，
回文日覆尘。
金蚕将画柳，
何处更知春。

No. 1

You dressed up for morning levee；
Your loops clank to the rising sun.
She'd make you admonish the throne
And recognize a sagacious one.
Her scripts are still hung on the wall，
Her palindrome collects dust there.
The gold silkworms laid on her hearse，
Where can you find a spring, o where?

* levee：a morning reception or an assembly at the court of a sovereign or at the house of a great personage. In ancient China，a levee at court was held every five days.
* hearse：a vehicle which has four wheels and is unvarnished，used to carry the dead

usually in a coffin to his grave.
* her scripts: referring to the fact that she was a calligrapher.
* palindrome: a poem with the words arranged that read the same forward or backward or make sense when read from both ends of a line.
* silkworm: the larva of a moth that produces a dense silken cocoon, especially the common silkworm from whose cocoon commercial silk is made. The silkworm was cultivated in 3,000 B.C. when Lace Mum, who was Lord Yellow's concubine began to raise silkworms and made silk.

其 二

女史悲彤管，
夫人罢锦轩。
卜茔占二室，
行哭度千门。
秋日光能淡，
寒川波自翻。
一朝成万古，
松柏暗平原。

No. 2

The woman scribe mourns her red brush,
As your wife's death makes her rue.
Two Rooms have been divined for her;
Many gates the mourners go through.
The autumn sun turns palely light;
The river cold sobs in thin brume.
One day for her runs endless now;
The cypresses will shade her tomb.

* brush: writing brush, also called Chinese brush or brush for short, which is used for writing or painting. It is one of the four treasures in a Chinese study, the other three stationeries being ink, paper and inkslab.
* Two Rooms: referring to two mountains, Mt. Greatroom and Mt. Smallroom, that make Mt. Tower, where Lady K'ou would be buries.
* cypress: an evergreen tree of the family *Cypressaseae*, having durable timber, a symbol of rectitude, nobility and longevity in Chinese culture.

赠李颀

闻君饵丹砂，
甚有好颜色。
不知从今去，
几时生羽翼。
王母翳华芝，
望尔昆仑侧。
文螭从赤豹，
万里方一息。
悲哉世上人，
甘此膻腥食。

To Ch'i Li

I hear cinnabar you oft eat
And have a complexion so great.
When from today I do not know
A pair of plumed wings you will grow.
Queen Mother has best herbs for you
And hopes to Mt. Queen you will go.
Leopards red, hornless dragons blessed
Run ten thousand miles without rest.
O humans in this world, so sad,
Like to eat them, as is their fad.

* cinnabar: a crystallized red mercuric sulfide, HgS, the chief ore of mercury, the raw mineral material for elixir in Wordist alchemy.

* Queen Mother: referring to Mother West, a sovereign goddess living on Mt. Queen in Chinese myths. She was originally described as human-bodied, tiger-toothed, leopard-tailed and hoopoe-haired, regarded as a goddess in charge of women protection, marriage and procreation, and longevity.
* Mt. Queen: Mt. Kunlun if transliterated, the most sacred mountain in China. It starts from the eastern Pamir Plateau, stretches across Hsinchiang and Tibet, and extends to Ch'inghai, with an average altitude of 5,500 – 6,000 meters. In Chinese myths, Mt. Queen is where Mother West dwells. And Mother West is a sovereign goddess.
* leopard: a ferocious carnivorous mammal of the cat family of Asia and Africa, of a pale fawn color, spotted with dark brown or black, praised as King of Forest, regarded as an auspicious animal in Chinese culture.
* dragon: Though variously understood as a large reptile, a marine monster, a jackal and so on in Western culture, it has been esteemed as a fabulous serpent-like giant winged animal that can change its girth and length, a symbol of benevolence and sovereignty in Chinese culture and the totem of all Chinese across the world.

送缙云苗太守

手疏谢明主，
腰章为长吏。
方从会稽邸，
更发汝南骑。
按节下松阳，
清江响铙吹。
露冕见三吴，
方知百城贵。

Seeing Off Miao, Prefect of Redsilk to His Post

Having written to thank Most High,
Now you're prefect, seal on your side.
From Long Peace, you'll go to your post;
Behold, the granted horse you ride.
You gallop to Pineshine, your town,
Where cymbals shake the river clear.
All know your dignity and grace
When in Southern Land you appear.

* Redsilk: a prefecture in the T'ang dynasty, west of today's Bellewater (Lishui) County, Chechiang Province.
* Long Peace: Ch'ang'an if transliterated, the capital of the T'ang Empire, with 1,000,000 inhabitants, the largest walled city ever built by man, and the center of world religions, Buddhism, Confucianism, Wordism, Nestorianism, Zoroastrianism, and even Islamism represented by Saracens, and the center of education — There were

colleges of various grades and special institutes for calligraphy, arithmetic, music, astronomy and so on. It saw the wonder of the age that reached the pinnacle of brilliance in Emperor Deepsire's reign. As the starting point of the Silk Road and the birthplace of Chinese civilization, it has witnessed the full glory of China's past and has been a capital for thirteen dynasties, enjoying the privilege of the nickname of the Museum of Chinese History, and it is now the capital of Sha'anhsi Province.

* Pineshine: a county in the T'ang dynasty under Chinyün Prefecture, today's Suich'ang, Chechiang Province.
* cymbal: one of a pair of platelike metallic musical instruments played by being clashed together.
* Southern Land: the land south of the Yangtze River, where the State of Wu was in general.

大同殿产玉芝龙池上有庆云神光照殿百官共睹圣恩便赐宴乐敢书即事

欲笑周文歌宴镐,
遥轻汉武乐横汾。
岂知玉殿生三秀,
讵有铜池出五云。
陌上尧樽倾北斗,
楼前舜乐动南薰。
共欢天意同人意,
万岁千秋奉圣君。

Ganoderma Grows on a Column of Concord Hall and There Appear Auspicious Clouds Over Dragon Pool, As All Officials See, Hence His Majesty Grants a Feast. I Take the Liberty to Compose This Poem.

At King Civil's feast held in Hao I laugh;
At Lord Martial's banquet at Fen I sneer.
How great, at Jade Hall ganoderma grows
And over Copper Pool five clouds appear.
Granted cups raised to the Dipper on high
Hibiscus's tune moves the sunlit air.
Man and Heaven have the same heart, all blessed;
May our Holy Lord live long and for e'er.

* ganoderma: *Ganoderma Lucidum Karst* in Latin, a grass with an umbrella top, a pore fungus, used as medicine and tonic in China.
* Dragon Pool: probably Copper Pool in the poem proper.
* King Civil: King Civil (1152 B.C.- 1056 B.C.), a wise monarch of high reputation and the founder of Chough.
* Hao: one of the twin capitals of Chough, the other being Rich (Feng) on the other bank of the River Rich, northwest of Long Peace, used for nearly three hundred years from 1046 B.C. to 771 B.C.
* Lord Martial: King Martial of Chough (? - 1043 B.C.), the Founder of Chough, the second son of King Civil (1152 B.C.- 1056 B.C.). He inherited the throne when King Civil died in 1050 B.C.
* Jade Hall: the other way of saying palace.
* Copper Pool: name of a pool in the palace.
* the Dipper: a constellation composed of seven bright stars, and looks like a spoon in the sky.
* Hibiscus's tune: Hibiscus made a five-stringed zither wherewith to eulogize parental love.

奉和圣制天长节赐宰臣歌应制

太阳升兮照万方，
开阊阖兮临玉堂，
俨冕旒兮垂衣裳。
金天净兮丽三光，
彤庭曙兮延八荒。
德合天兮礼神遍，
灵芝生兮庆云见。
唐尧後兮稷契臣，
匝宇宙兮华胥人。
尽九服兮皆四邻，
乾降瑞兮坤献珍。

In Reply to Your Majesty's Call to Follow Your Majesty's Poem: To Premier on Longevity Day

The sun does rise and does spread light to all;
The gate opens and does face the jade hall.
Great, Your Majesty rules with grace and love;
The autumn sky does wash Tri-lights above.
The sunlight from court does warm all the land;
Virtues from the Word can make people stand.
Ganoderma great and clouds auspicious,
Kings are saintly and lords are sagacious,
In this cosmos all men become gracious.
From four bounds come nations in clothes diverse,

A heyday with blessings and jewels occurs.

* Your Majesty: referring to Deepsire (Hsuan Tsung) the emperor (A.D. 685 – A.D. 762), the ninth emperor of the T'ang dynasty. When a prince, he was regarded as wise and valiant, a sportsman accomplished in all knightly exercises and a master of all elegant arts. He established Pear Garden, an operatic school, where actors and actresses were trained, and the prototype of the modern Chinese drama was developed.
* Longevity Day: Emperor Deepsire's birthday, the fifth day of the eighth moon, celebrated all over the nation for three days.
* sun: the heavenly body that is the center of attraction and the main source of light and heat in the solar system. It is a representation of Shine in contrast with Shade, the moon, in Chinese culture, a symbol of hope, life, strength, vigor, and youth, and sometimes it may stands for an emperor or his power and grace.
* Tri-lights: referring to the sun, the moon and the stars.
* the Word: referring to Tao if transliterated, the most significant and profoundest concept in Chinese philosophy. According to Laocius's *The Word and the World*: "The Word is void, but its use is infinite. O deep! It seems to be the root of all things." The Word is identifiable with the Word or Logos in the West, as there is an enormous amount of common ground in the two cosmologies and doctrines concerning the most fundamental matters of creation and human nature.
* Ganoderma: Lucid Ganoderma, a magic herb with an umbrella top, a pore fungus, used as herbal medicine and held dear as a tonic in China.
* cosmos: the world or universe considered as a harmonious system, perfect in order and arrangement, opposed to chaos.

奉和圣制登降圣观与宰臣等同望应制

凤宸朝碧落，
龙图耀金镜。
维岳降二臣，
戴天临万姓。
山川八校满，
井邑三农竟。
比屋皆可封，
谁家不相庆。
林疏远村出，
野旷寒山净。
帝城云里深，
渭水天边映。
佳气含风景，
颂声溢歌咏。
端拱能任贤，
弥彰圣君圣。

In Reply to Your Majesty's Call to Follow Your Majesty's Poem: Ascending to Saint Descending Temple and Gazing with Premier

Phoenix Screen faces the blue sky;
Hexagram shines to Mirror Gold.
Mt. Tower offers You a premier,
Who does the multitude behold.
The farmers have finished their work;

All's guarded by garrisons eight.
Everyone's chance to be knighted,
All households this age celebrate.
A village's beyond the wood sparse;
The field's vast and the hills serene.
Clouds hang o'er the capital town;
To the skyline flows the Wei green.
It's great everywhere, every sight,
Filled with songs and music fine.
Inaction leads to a great reign
That makes Your Majesty more shine.

* Your Majesty: referring to Emperor Deepsire or Hsuan Tsung the emperor (A.D. 685 – A.D. 762), the ninth emperor of the T'ang dynasty. When a prince, he was regarded as wise and valiant, a sportsman accomplished in all knightly exercises and a master of all elegant arts. He established Pear Garden, an operatic school, where actors and actresses were trained, and the prototype of the modern Chinese drama was developed. Under his enthusiastic patronage, arts and letters flourished. Indeed, his reign is often considered the pinnacle of Chinese cultural achievement.
* Saint Descending Temple: a temple in Floral Clean Palace.
* Phoenix Screen: the screen with a phoenix embroidered on it in the court, a partition between door and window, also a metonymy for the court or emperor.
* Hexagram: a diagram formed with eight trigrams representing eight directions. Eight phenomena or eight elements are used in divination, referring to the emperor's strategies and blueprints in this poem.
* Mirror Gold: the bright Way or the great Word.
* Mt. Tower: located in the west of present-day Honan Province, one of the Five Sacred Mountains in Chinese culture.
* the Wei: the Wei River, the largest branch of the Yellow River, originating from today's Mt. Birdmouse in Kansu Province, flowing through the major cities of today's Sha'anhsi Province, namely Precious Rooster, Allshine, Long Peace, and meeting the Yellow River at T'ung Pass.
* inaction: a major philosophical doctrine of quietism in Wordism.

送 张 五 归 山

送君尽惆怅，
复送何人归。
几日同携手，
一朝先拂衣。
东山有茅屋，
幸为扫荆扉。
当亦谢官去，
岂令心事违。

Seeing Off Chang Five Back to the Hills

Seeing you off, I can but sigh;
Who's the next to bid me good-bye?
Just a few days, now you go back,
From your office to hills, alack.
At Mt. East a cot you dwell in;
Wait for me and your wicket clean.
From office I will soon resign;
How can one his free will confine?

* Mt. East: the place where Chang Five lives in reclusion. Mt. East was originally where An Hsieh lived in reclusion and it is often used as a metonymy for a hermitage.
* wicket: a side door for everyday use beside a main gate usually opened on special occasions.

送张五諲归宣城

五湖千万里，
况复五湖西。
渔浦南陵郭，
人家春谷豀。
欲归江淼淼，
未到草萋萋。
忆想兰陵镇，
可宜猿更啼。

Seeing Off Yin Chang Five Back to Hsuan

Five Lakes are myriads of miles off,
Let alone west of them you sail.
Beyond the shoal there looms Southridge;
Some households are found in the dale.
I'd go but the water's too vast,
Although the grass is so lush there.
Now I recall Orchidridge Town,
But monkey shrieks I cannot bear.

* Hsuan: a county instituted in the early years of the Ch'in Emperor under the Prefecture of Redshine. It became a prefecture in A.D. 281 during the Chin dynasty. It is well known for rich historical legacies, and best remembered for its high-quality rice paper.
* the Five Lakes: referring to Lake T'ai and the other four lakes around. As legend goes, Li Fan (536 B.C.- 448 B.C.), a renowned statesman, strategist, economist and Wordist in the Spring and Autumn period, changed his name to live in seclusion among the Five Lakes after he helped the State of Yüeh wipe out Wu.

* Southridge: Southridge County under Hsuan Prefecture, today's Southridge County under Wuhu, Anhui Province
* Orchidridge Town: an old town 45 kilometers from today's Wuchin County, Chiangsu Province.
* monkey: any of a group of primates having elongate limbs, hands and feet adapted for grasping, and a highly developed nervous system, including marmosets, baboons, and macaques, but not the anthropoid apes, though monkeys and apes are used alternatively in Chinese.

待储光羲不至

重门朝已启，
起坐听车声。
要欲闻清佩，
方将出户迎。
晚钟鸣上苑，
疏雨过春城。
了自不相顾，
临堂空复情。

Waiting for Kuanghsi Ch'u in Vain

The gates open one after one;
I sit up to hark to your cart.
To listen to your trinkets clink,
Out my door to meet you I start.
There passes a toll from High Park,
While a drizzle blows past the town.
You're too busy to come along;
In my hall in sadness I drown.

---

* High Park: an imperial park that Lord Martial of Han built on the site of a discarded park of Ch'in. It was vast and splendid with palaces and woodlands, having various functions and recreational facilities, rolling about 340 kilometers.

奉寄韦太守陟

荒城自萧索，
万里山河空。
天高秋日迥，
嘹唳闻归鸿。
寒塘映衰草，
高馆落疏桐。
临此岁方晏，
顾景咏悲翁。
故人不可见，
寂寞平陵东。

To Prefect Chih Wei

The lonely town is cold and bleak;
The land looks void from rill to hill.
The sky's high, the autumn sun's far;
There linger wild geese trills so shrill.
The cold pondlet reflects grass dry;
To the house fall parasol leaves.
It's time the year comes to an end;
Glancing back, I croon *Old Man Grieves*.
Your friend is not here, out of sight;
East of Level Wood you're in plight.

* wild goose: an undomesticated goose that is caring and responsible, taken as a symbol of benevolence, righteousness, good manner, wisdom and faith in Chinese culture.

* parasol leaves: leaves of the Chinese parasol tree (*Firmiana simplex*), of the hibiscus family native to Asia, growing as tall as 12 meters, having deciduous leaves and small greenish white flowers that are borne in clusters.
* *Old Man Grieves*: the title of a verse in Chi Lu's prose *Percussion*, borrowed by the poet to express his loneliness.
* Level Wood: the name of a wood on a level ground.

酬比部杨员外暮宿琴台朝跻书阁
率尔见赠之作

旧简拂尘看，
鸣琴候月弹。
桃源迷汉姓，
松树有秦官。
空谷归人少，
青山背日寒。
羡君栖隐处，
遥望白云端。

Thanking Counselor Yang from the Inspection Office, Who Puts Up for the Night at Lute Hall, Ascends to the Book Loft and Writes Me His Poem

I stroke the dust off the book read
And play the lute for Luna's shine.
In Shangrila one knows not Han,
And there is the canonized pine.
In the vale few people remain;
No sunlight, the green hill feels cold.
The place where you dwell I admire;
The clouds above I can behold.

* Lute Hall: also known as Lute Mound, a place where Puch'i Mi, Confucius's student, played the lute when he was the mayor there, in today's Shan County, Shantung

Province.
* Luna: the moon, an important image in Chinese literature as it can give rise to many associations such as solitude, purity, brightness and happy reunions.
* Shangrila: often referring to Peach Blossom Source described by Poolbright T'ao, which is an ideal land free of tyranny and exploitation.
* Han: the powerful Han Empire (202 B.C.- A.D. 220) founded by Pang Liu, one of the greatest empires in Chinese history, earlier than, and concurrent with, the Roman Empire (27 B.C.- A.D. 476), with an area of six million and nine square kilometers, including Korea in the east, Vietnam in the south, Mt. Wild Leek in the west and Gobi in the north.
* pine: a cone-bearing tree having needle-shaped evergreen leaves growing in clusters, a symbol of longevity and rectitude in Chinese culture.

故太子太师徐公挽歌四首
Four Elegies for Lord of Hsu, Crown Prince's Teacher

其 一

功德冠群英，
弥纶有大名。
轩皇用风后，
傅说是星精。
就第优遗老，
来朝诏不名。
留侯常辟谷，
何苦不长生。

No. 1

Your merits outshine those of all;
For governance famous you are.
Lord Yellow employed Aeolus
And Master Joy who was a star.
You like them have been treated well,
At court no need to tell your name.
Like Liang Chang you oft went fasting;
Why so short-lived, now missed your aim?

* Lord Yellow: alias Cartshaft, the first of the five heavenly gods in myth and the earliest ancestor of Chinese people. It was said that Lord Yellow made a tripod in the Chaste Hills. As the tripod was done, a dragon came down to visit him. He and his 70 or more officials and consorts all rode on the dragon and flew to the sky. In myth, when Lord Yellow and his retinue rode the dragon away, they left some junior officials on earth, who could but pull the dragon's beard in vain. All they got was only a strand of beard and the sword dropped from Lord Yellow.

* Aeolus: Lord of Wind, a minister in charge of weather forecast under Lord Yellow.
* Master Joy: Yüeh Fu if transliterated, a noble minister of high reputation in the Shang dynasty. Historic records say that the King of Shang dreamed of a sage, and he sent people out to search for him and found Master Joy.
* Liang Chang: Liang Chang (250 B.C.- 186 B.C.), a renowned strategist in Chinese history and one of the Three Standouts of the early Han. Polite and respectful, he won the legendary Wordist Yellow Stone's trust and received *The Art of War* from him. By studying the book, Liang Chang became a wise and resourceful brain truster. After the reign of Han was stabilized, he asked for retirement and followed Red Pine to be an immortal. The poet takes Liang Chang as a symbolic figure of his own to imply his hidden talent and ambition.

其 二

谋猷为相国，
翊赞奉宸舆。
剑履升前殿，
貂蝉托后车。
齐侯疏土宇，
汉室赖图书。
僻处留田宅，
仍才十顷馀。

No. 2

You made plans for the great empire
And helped Most High with a full heart.
Sword and shoes on, you went to court
And would follow Lord's sedan cart.
You were knighted as Duke of Land;
And Like Han borrowed books from Ch'in.
In remote place you had your farm
Just a few hundred *mu*, so thin.

* Duke of Land: a metaphor for Lord of Hsu, Crown Prince's Teacher. In the T'ang dynasty, kings, dukes or counts were not granted a fief but the title and a quantity of appropriate pay.
* Han: the powerful Han Empire (202 B.C.- A.D. 220) founded by Pang Liu, one of the greatest empires in Chinese history, earlier than, and concurrent with, the Roman Empire (27 B.C.- A.D. 476), with an area of six million and nine square kilometers, including Korea in the east, Vietnam in the south, Mt. Wild Leek in the west and Gobi in the north.
* Ch'in: Ch'in (221 B.C.- 207 B.C.), the first unified empire in Chinese history founded by the State of Ch'in in the late Warring States period.
* *mu*: a measure of land, commonly 666.67 square meters or 0.16 acres.

其 三

旧里趋庭日，
新年置酒辰。
闻诗鸾渚客，
献赋凤楼人。
北首辞明主，
东堂哭大臣。
犹思御朱辂，
不惜污车茵。

No. 3

Like Confucius you taught so well;
For Spring Festival you served wine.
You wrote poems like poets of the best,
And offered our Lord your verse fine.
Your were tombed with head towards north,
And mourned by our Lord in East Hall.
Your groom would still drive your red cart,
Not caring about filth at all.

* Confucius: Confucius (551 B.C.- 479 B.C.), born into a declining aristocrat's family, a renowned thinker, educator and statesman in the Spring and Autumn period, born in the State of Lu, who was the founder of Confucianism and who had exerted profound influence on Chinese culture. Confucius is one of the few leaders who based their philosophy on the virtues that are required for the day-to-day living. His philosophy centered on personal and governmental morality, correctness of social relationships, justice and sincerity.
* Spring Festival: New Year, the fifteen days of the first moon, formally begun in the Han dynasty and celebrated every year till now.

* East Hall: east of the emperor's bedroom, where funerals were held for lords of the royal family while funerals for lords out of the royal family were held at court. Hsu's funeral was held in East Hall because he was particularly favored and honored by the emperor.

其 四

久践中台座，
终登上将坛。
谁言断车骑，
空忆盛衣冠。
风日咸阳惨，
笳箫渭水寒。
无人当便阙，
应罢太师官。

No. 4

For long a premier's post you held,

And then climbed up General Mound.

Unexpected, you passed away;

How fully you were clad and crowned!

Your hearse went past Allshine, so sad

And the flutes played made the Wei cold.

Your office should now be dissolved,

As nobody can your post hold.

* General Mound: Lord of Hsu was the general-governor of Hohsi (West of the River).
* hearse: an unvarnished four-wheeled vehicle carrying the dead usually in a coffin to his grave.
* Allshine: Hsienyang if transliterated, the capital of the Ch'in Empire. It is so called because all its rivers and mountains can get sunshine from all around. It was built in 350 B.C. and Ch'in moved its capital here the next year from Oakshine (Liyang).
* flute: a tubular wind instrument of small diameter with holes along the side, usually made of bamboo in China.
* the Wei: the River Wei, the biggest tributary of the Yellow River.

送崔九兴宗游蜀

送君从此去，
转觉故人稀。
徒御犹回首，
田园方掩扉。
出门当旅食，
中路授寒衣。
江汉风流地，
游人何岁归。

Seeing Off Hsingtsung Ts'ui Nine to Travel Shu

I see you departing hereby,
And feel I've no friends left, no more.
Your retinue turn back to look;
The farmstead will soon close its door.
Out there, do sleep and dine on time
Midway, a cold season it'll be.
The Long and the Han roll afar;
Which year will you come back to me?

* Shu: an area covering approximately today's Ssuch'uan Province, one of the earliest kingdoms in China, founded by Silkworm and Fishbuck according to legend. In the Three Kingdoms period, a new Shu was established by Pei Liu, hence one of the three kingdoms in that period.
* the Long: the Long River, a cradle of Chinese civilization. It is the longest river in China, originating from the T'angkula Mountains on Tibet Plateau, flowing through 11

provincial areas, more than 6,300 kilometers long, the third longest river in the world.
* the Han: the Han River: the longest branch of the Long River, having an important position in Chinese history.

与卢员外象过崔处士兴宗林亭

绿树重阴盖四邻,
青苔日厚自无尘。
科头箕踞长松下,
白眼看他世上人。

Visiting Staff Ts'ui's Pavilion with Ministry Counselor Lu

The green trees shade the houses all around;
The moss grows thicker, free of dust aground.
Hairbun raised, it sits under the pine trees
And casts a cold look at the world it sees.

* moss: a tiny, delicate green bryophytic plant growing on damp decaying wood, wet ground, humid rocks or trees, producing capsules which open by an operculum and contain spores. Under a poet's writing brush, this tiny, insignificant plant may arouse a poetic feeling or imagination, as was written by Mei Yüan, a poet in the Ching dynasty: "Where the sun does not arrive, /Springtime does on its own thrive. / The moss flowers like rice tiny, / Rush to bloom like the peony."

青　雀　歌

青雀翅羽短，
未能远食玉山禾。
犹胜黄雀争上下，
唧唧空仓复若何。

A Song of the Blue Sparrow

The blue sparrow spreads its wings short
And can't eat grain from the mountains afar.
It challenges yellow sparrows in their sport;
Chirp, chirp, to the void barn crying they are.

* blue sparrow: a bird looking like a sparrow or a little turtle. A verse in *The Book of Songs* reads like this: The blue sparrow cries / And darts towards the skies.
* yellow sparrow: a small passerine bird, *Carduelis spinus* in Latin, having yellow wings and a yellow tail.

崔九弟欲往南山马上口号与别

城隅一分手，
几日还相见。
山中有桂花，
莫待花如霰。

An Impromptu on My Horse to Brother Ts'ui Nine When He's Leaving for the Southern Hills

We say good-bye outside the town;
When can we gather now you go?
Laurel trees grow among the hills;
Don't wait till their flowers blow like snow.

* laurel: *laurus nobilis*, an evergreen shrub with aromatic, lance-shaped leaves, yellowish grain-like small flowers, and succulent, cherry-like fruit, a symbol of glory usually in the form of a crown or wreath of laurel to indicate honor or high merit, especially when one had passed Grand Test in ancient China. In Chinese mythology, there is a giant laurel tree on the moon, and it would never fall even though Kang Wu, a banished immortal, kept cutting it.

奉和圣制御春明楼临右相园亭赋乐贤诗应制

复道通长乐,
青门临上路。
遥闻凤吹喧,
暗识龙舆度。
褰旒明四目,
伏槛纡三顾。
小苑接侯家,
飞甍映宫树。
商山原上碧,
浐水林端素。
银汉下天章,
琼筵承湛露。
将非富人宠,
信以平戎故。
从来简帝心,
讵得回天步。

In Reply to Your Majesty's Call to Follow Your Majesty's Poem: Climbing Spring Bright Tower Overlooking Right Premier's Pavilion, Hence a Poem for the Lords

The suspension road to Long Glee
Sees Blue Gate there across the way.
We know Your Majesty comes on,

As we hear the Phoenix Flute play.
Our tassel raised, we can well see;
By the rail we look as we please.
The royal park links with Duke's house;
The high eaves greet the palace trees.
Mt. Shang extends to fields so green;
The Ch'an by the wood shimmers white.
Your Majesty's poem shines above;
The grand feast receives dewdrops bright.
This is held for our country's wealth
Or for peace with the Huns, perhaps.
The world Your Majesty knows well,
Steering our nation from all traps.

* Right Premier: in contrast with Left Premier. Right Premier is prime minister while Left Premier is a deputy prime minister.
* Long Glee: name of a palace, probably referring to Rise-Laud (Hsingch'ing) Palace.
* Blue Gate: the east gate of Long Peace, the capital of T'ang.
* Your Majesty: referring to Deepsire (Hsuan Tsung) the emperor (A.D. 685 - A.D. 762), the ninth emperor of the T'ang dynasty. When a prince, he was regarded as wise and valiant, a sportsman accomplished in all knightly exercises and a master of all elegant arts. He established Pear Garden, an operatic school, where actors and actresses were trained, and the prototype of the modern Chinese drama was developed.
* the Phoenix Flute: the flute that sounds like a phoenix sings; a praise of a flute tune.
* Mt. Shang: a mountain where the Four Grey Heads, Pang Liu's royal think tank, once lived in reclusion, in today's Shanglo, Sha'anhsi Province.
* the Ch'an: the Ch'an River, originating from Ch'inridge southwest of Blue Field (Lantien), Sha'anhsi Province.
* Hun: one of barbaric nomadic Asian peoples who frequently invaded China, a general term referring to all northern or western invaders or aliens; Hun, as an adjective or attributive, refers to something about or of Huns.

故人张諲工诗善易卜兼能丹青草隶顷以诗见赠

不逐城东游侠儿，
隐囊纱帽坐弹棋。
蜀中夫子时开卦，
洛下书生解咏诗。
药阑花径衡门里，
时复据梧聊隐几。
屏风误点惑孙郎，
团扇草书轻内史。
故园高枕度三春，
永日垂帷绝四邻。
自想蔡邕今已老，
更将书籍与何人。

My Friend Yin Chang Good at Versification, Divination, and Writing Cursive and Square Styles Presents Me with an Impromptu

You don't chase with gallants east of the town;
Capped in gauze and cushioned, the game you play.
Like best fortune tellers, you oft divine,
And like Loshine chanters, you sing your lay.
Medicine herbs, flowers reach the bramble gate;
You struck the lute strings at desk now and then.
Your ink stain can make one think it's a fly;
Your scripts challenge all literary men.
In your garden you will o'ersleep in spring,

Secluded all day from your neighborhood.
You, like Yung Tsai, the scholar, is old now;
Then who would inherit your books, who could?

* Loshine: Loyang if transliterated, one of the four ancient capitals in China, along with Long Peace (Hsi'an), Gold Hill (Nanking) and Peking, and it was the second largest city in the T'ang dynasty.
* medicine herbs: herbs gathered from the wild or cultivated play an important part in Chinese medicare, usually called Chinese medicine.
* fly: one of various small dipterous insects (family *Musidae*), especially the common housefly. The fly, especially the bluebottle, is a nasty slanderer in Chinese culture, like a section of a verse from *The Book of Songs* reads:"Upon the hazels o'erthere, / Alight the buzzing flies. / Those mean men you trust ne'er, / They estrange us with lies."
* Yung Tsai: Yung Tsai (A.D. 133 – A.D. 192), a famous minister, litterateur and calligrapher in the Eastern Han dynasty, Wenchi's father.

秋夜独坐怀内弟崔兴宗

夜静群动息，
蟋蛄声悠悠。
庭槐北风响，
日夕方高秋。
思子整羽翰；
及时当云浮。
吾生将白首，
岁晏思沧洲。
高足在旦暮，
肯为南亩俦。

Missing Hsingtsung Ts'ui, My Cousin When I Sit Alone on an Autumn Night

Night quiet, all creatures are at rest;
But cicadas make their long trill.
The yard locust soughs to north wind;
When late, you feel the autumn chill.
I think you're now spreading your wings
To cruise the sky, and thereby rise.
I'm in my last years of my life,
Now to the wild I'd cast my eyes.
You will soon fly high, going great;
How can you be my farming mate?

* cicada: a homopterous insect that sings its song of summer and shrills in autumn, a symbol of death and resurrection in Chinese culture because of its metamorphosis and recycle. Therefore, in ancient China, a jade miniature cicada was put in the mouth of a dead body with such an intention of eternal life.

* locust: a tree (*Robinia pseudoacasia*) of the bean family widely distributed in the north temperate zone, with a rough bark, odd-pinnate leaves, and loose, slender racemes of fragrant, white flowers, which are a seasonal delicacy.

送徐郎中

东郊春草色，
驱马去悠悠。
况复乡山外，
猿啼湘水流。
岛夷传露版，
江馆候鸣驺。
卉服为诸吏，
珠官拜本州。
孤莺吟远墅，
野杏发山邮。
早晚方归奏，
南中才忌秋。

Seeing Off Secretary Hsu

Spring grass east of the town does sheen;
Galloping, far and far you go.
And now beyond the mountains there
Monkeys cry and the Hsiang does flow.
The isle barbarians crave you there;
The inn waits for your horse to rest.
Those in grass hope you'll recruit them;
The pearlers treat you as their guest.
An oriole to the villa chirps;
Apricots by the hill post blush.
Now you're going back to the court;

In the south autumn falls to hush.

* monkey: any of a group of primates having elongate limbs, hands and feet adapted for grasping, and a highly developed nervous system, including marmosets, baboons, and macaques, but not the anthropoid apes, though monkeys and apes are used alternatively in Chinese.
* the Hsiang: the Hsiang River, a river in today's Hunan Province, the major source of Lake Cavehall.
* oriole: a small golden bird, one of the family of passerine birds, which looks bright yellow with contrasting black wings and sings beautiful songs.
* apricot: a tree or the fruit of the tree of the rose family, intermediate between the peach and the plum. It often appears in Chinese poetry, as a line by Chun Kou (A.D. 961 – A.D. 1023) says:"To the slanting sun apricot blooms fly."

敕赐百官樱桃

芙蓉阙下会千官,
紫禁朱樱出上兰。
才是寝园春荐后,
非关御苑鸟衔残。
归鞍竞带青丝笼,
中使频倾赤玉盘。
饱食不须愁内热,
大官还有蔗浆寒。

Offering Cherries to Officials upon the Imperial Order

Under Lotus Gates there officials meet;
In Forbidden Orchids cherries look sweet.
In Rest Yard the spring sacrifice ends now;
In High Park red cherries weigh down the bough.
All ride back with a full load in skeps blue;
Full-loaded red jade plates the courtiers show.
Eat more, no inner heat you need to care;
Sugar cane juice the great chefs will prepare.

* Lotus Gates: the gate towers looking like lotus flowers.
* Forbidden Orchids: the name of a Han Wordist temple in High Park.
* Rest Yard: the name of a graveyard or an imperial mausoleum.
* High Park: an imperial park that Lord Martial of Han built on the site of a discarded park of Ch'in. It was vast and splendid with palaces and woodlands, having various functions and recreational facilities, rolling about 340 kilometers.

* cherry: any of various trees (genus *Prunus*) of the rose family, related to the plum and the peach and bearing small, round or heart-shaped drupes enclosing a smooth pit, red, purple or yellow in color; especially the sweet cherry, the sour cherry and the wild black cherry.
* sugar cane: a tall, stout, perennial grass of tropical regions with a solid jointed stalk rich in sugar, from which juice can be extracted.

晚 春 归 思

新妆可怜色,
落日卷罗帷。
淑气清珍簟,
墙阴上玉墀。
春虫飞网户,
暮雀隐花枝。
向晚多愁思,
闲窗桃李时。

Her Alone in Late Spring

Her blouse new gives a lovely hue;
The sun set, she rolls up her shade.
A gentle air soothes the pearled mat;
A wall shade creeps on the steps jade.
Spring insects fly to the door checks;
Sparrows for the night hide neath sprays.
Alone, she feels sick for her man
While to her pane a peach twig sways.

* steps jade: usually called jade steps, the steps before, and leading to, a palace hall or a harem, usually built with marble, jade being a metaphor for good quality, often used as a metonymy for the court. A verse titled *Pear Blossoms in the Left Office* by another T'ang poet mentions the steps jade white, as reads: "The chill of theirs bullies the frost; / Their fragrance soaks into the night. / As spring wind blows, tossing and tossed, / They fly over the steps jade white."
* sparrow: a small, plain-colored passerine bird related to the finches, grosbeaks and

buntings, a very common bird in China, a symbol of insignificance.
* peach: any tree of the genus *Prunus Percica*, blooming brilliantly and bearing fruit, a fleshy, juicy, edible drupe, considered sacred in China, a symbol of romance, prosperity and longevity.

送李睢阳

将置酒,
思悲翁。
使君去,
出城东。
麦渐渐,
雉子斑。
槐阴阴,
到潼关。
骑连连,
车迟迟,
心中悲。
宋又远,
周间之。
南淮夷,
东齐儿。
碎碎织练与素丝,
游人贾客信难持。
五谷前熟方可为,
下车闭阁君当思。
天子当殿俨衣裳,
大官尚食陈羽觞。
彤庭散绶垂鸣珰,
黄纸诏书出东厢,
轻纨叠绮烂生光。
宗室子弟君最贤,
分忧当为百辟先。
布衣一言相为死,

何况圣主恩如天。
鸾声哕哕鲁侯旗,
明年上计朝京师。
须忆今日斗酒别,
慎忽富贵忘我为。

Seeing Off Suiyang Li

Set there is wine;
The man does pine.
Prefect goes down
East of the town.
The wheat is lush;
The pheasants rush.
Locust trees sway,
To T'ung Pass way.
The horses slow
Make the carts go.
How sad you are!
Sung is too far,
Barred by Chough's bar
South Huai's hither;
East Ch'i's thither.
Cloth, silk, yarns, weavings, all such things they sell;
Passengers, travelers, merchants can't hold well.
When grains are ripe, you may go for success;
Dismounting, you should think twice in recess.
Most High on the throne, dressed in full array;
The chefs prepared a feast and cups did lay;
In Red Hall, sashes and trinkets did sway.

A yellow edict came from the east room;
Gauze, silk, brocade, damask, all seemed in bloom.
Of all royal sons you've been the most kind;
For the nation, you'd lead vassals behind.
To keep faith a commoner may well die,
Let alone you with the grace of Most High.
"The flags fly as Marquess of Lu comes nigh";
Reports you write and report to Most High.
Remember today we drink here and part;
Despite wealth and ranks, bear me in your heart.

* wheat: a grain yielding an edible flour, the annual product of a cereal grass (genus *Triticum*), introduced to China from West Asia more than 4,000 years ago, used as a staple food in China and most of the world. In its importance to consumers, it is second only to rice.
* pheasant: a long-tailed gallinaceous bird noted for the gorgeous plumage of the male.
* locust tree: a tree (*Robinia pseudoacasia*) of the bean family widely distributed in the temperate zone, with a rough bark, odd-pinnate leaves, and loose, slender racemes of fragrant, white flowers, which are a seasonal delicacy.
* T'ung Pass: an old pass at the east of the West of Pass Plain (Kuan-chung).
* Sung: the State of Sung (cir. 1039 B.C.- 286 B.C.), a vassal state of Chough, a dukedom, its capital being Shang Knoll (Shangch'iu).
* Chough: Chough (1046 B.C.- 256 B.C.), the regime established after Shang perished, the last slavery society in China. There were two periods in the Chough dynasty, Western Chough (1046 B.C.- 771 B.C.) and Eastern Chough (770 B.C.- 256 B.C.). Eastern Chough consists of two periods: the Spring and Autumn period and the Warring States period.
* South Huai: the area south of the Huai River.
* East Ch'i: the area east of Suishine.
* Red Hall: the Han Court was in red, hence the name.
* yellow edict: a rescript from an emperor, usually written on yellow silk, which is a public ordinance having the force of law.
* Marquess of Lu comes nigh: a metaphor used for the procession.

送魏郡李太守赴任

与君伯氏别,
又欲与君离。
君行无几日,
当复隔山陂。
苍茫秦川尽,
日落桃林塞。
独树临关门,
黄河向天外。
前经洛阳陌,
宛洛故人稀。
故人离别尽,
淇上转骖騑。
企予悲送远,
惆怅睢阳路。
古木官渡平,
秋城邺宫故。
想君行县日,
其出从如云。
遥思魏公子,
复忆李将军。

Seeing Off Prefect Li to His Prefecture of Way

To your brother I said good-bye;
Now to you I will say adieu.

A few days after you depart,
You'll be barred by hills green, rills blue.
The Ch'in Plain rolls far, far away;
The peach wood basks in the eve sun.
A tree stands alone by the pass;
The River out the sky does run.
Ahead you go through Loshine fields;
On the river few friends you'll see.
When all friends have gone out of sight,
You get on your cart by the Ch'i.
On tiptoe, I watch you away;
While towards Suishine you do sigh.
In Kuantu the barracks are gone;
The palaces in Yeh waste lie.
When counties of yours you inspect,
Your retinue's like clouds behind.
Now I miss Prince of Way far back,
And General Li comes to my mind.

* the Ch'in Plain: the area north of Ch'inridge that rolls in today's Sha'anhsi and Kansu, which belonged to the State of Ch'in in the past, geographically, the center of China.
* the River: referring to the Yellow River, the second longest river in China, flowing through Loess Plateau, hence yellow water all the way. 5,464 kilometers long, with a drainage area of 752,443 square kilometers, it has been regarded as the cradle of Chinese civilization.
* Loshine: Loyang if transliterated, one of the four ancient capitals in China, along with Long Peace (Hsi'an), Gold Hill (Nanking) and Peking, and it was the second largest city in the T'ang dynasty.
* The Ch'i: an ancient affluent of the Yellow River.
* Suishine: a county south of the Sui River, now in Shangch'iu, Honan Province.
* Kuantu: an old battlefield where Ts'ao Ts'ao decisively defeated Shao Yüan's army, in today's Chungmou, Honan Province.
* Yeh: one of the eight most famous capitals in Chinese history, in today's Linchang

County, Hopei Province.

* Prince of Way: Faithridge (? - 243 B.C.), the youngest son of King Glare of Way, a famous militarist and politician in the Warring States period. He was courteous to talents, attracting 3,000 hangers-on. Hai Chu, a butcher, and Ying Hou, a porter, were treated with great courtesy and became his hangers-on.

* General Li: Broad Li (? - 119 B.C.) in full name, Kuang Li if transliterated, a renowned general who won many battles against the Huns in the Han dynasty. Two of his descendants left deep footprints in Chinese history, Hao Li (A.D. 351 - A.D. 417), King Martial Glare of West Cool (A.D. 400 - A.D. 421) and Yüan Li (A.D. 566 - A.D. 635), the founder and first emperor of T'ang.

"十三五"国家重点出版规划项目

王维诗歌全集英译

A Complete Edition of Wei Wang's Poems in Chinese and English
With Annotations

赵彦春　译·注

Translated and Annotated by Yanchun Chao

第二卷

Volume II

上海大学出版社
·上海·

卷 二

目　录
Contents

313　送秘书晁监还日本国
Seeing Off Heng Ch'ao, Secretariat Censor, Home to Japan

319　同崔兴宗送衡岳瑗公南归
Seeing Off Master Yüan Back to the South, with Hsingtsung Ts'ui

321　同崔员外秋宵寓直
On Duty with Counselor Ts'ui on an Autumn Night

323　与苏卢二员外期游方丈寺而苏不至因有此作
Appointment Made to Tour Abbot Temple with Counselors Su and Lu, But Su Does Not Make It, Hence the Poem

325　过卢四员外宅看饭僧共题七韵
A Visit to Ministry Counselor Lu's Estate to View Food Offering, a Fourteen-line Rhyme

327　与卢象集朱家
Visiting Chu with Hsiang Lu

329　春过贺遂员外药园
A Visit to Ministry Counselor's Medicine Herb Garden in Spring

331　送贺遂员外外甥
Seeing Off Ministry Counselor's Nephew

333　赠从弟司库员外絿
Seeing Off My Cousin Ch'iu Wang, Ministry Counselor of War Ministry

335　过崔驸马山池
A Visit to Adjunct Groom Ts'ui's Hillpool

337　送丘为往唐州
Seeing Off Wei Ch'iu to T'angchow

339	问寇校书双溪	
	Asking Collator K'ou About Twain Brooks	

| 340 | 春日与裴迪过新昌里访吕逸人不遇 |
| | A Visit with Ti P'ei to Lu, a Hermit in New Boom Lane, Whom We Fail to See |

| 342 | 奉和圣制从蓬莱向兴庆阁道中留春雨中春望之作应制 |
| | In Reply to Your Majesty's Call to Follow Your Majesty's Poem: Viewing Spring in the Rain Along the Booming Suspension Road from Great Bright Palace |

| 344 | 酬郭给事 |
| | To Kuo, Secretary of the Court |

| 346 | 别綦毋潜 |
| | Good-bye to Wuch'ien Ch'i |

| 348 | 冬夜书怀 |
| | Remarks on a Winter Night |

| 349 | 过沈居士山居哭之 |
| | Visiting the Villa of Shen, a Lay Buddhist, and Crying |

| 351 | 夏日过青龙寺谒操禅师 |
| | Paying Respects to Zen Master Zen Holder at Blue Dragon Fane on a Summer's Day |

| 352 | 和太常韦主簿五郎温汤寓目之作 |
| | In Reply to Wei Five, Deputy Governor of Rite Department, Who Tours Hotspring |

| 354 | 奉和圣制暮春送朝集使归郡应制 |
| | In Reply to Your Majesty's Call to Follow Your Majesty's Poem: Seeing Off Finance Reporters Back to Their Prefectures in Late Spring |

| 356 | 冬日游览 |
| | Touring in Winter |

| 358 | 奉和圣制与太子诸王三月三日龙池春禊应制 |
| | In Reply to Your Majesty's Call to Follow Your Majesty's Poem: Offering Spring Sacrifice at Dragon Pool with Crown Prince and Other Princes on the Third Day of the Third Moon |

360	奉和圣制重阳节宰臣及群官上寿应制	

360 奉和圣制重阳节宰臣及群官上寿应制
In Reply to Your Majesty's Call to Follow Your Majesty's Poem: To My Premier and Ministers Who Wish Ourself Longevity

362 三月三日勤政楼侍宴应制
Waiting upon Your Majesty at the Feast in Administration Hall the Third Day of the Third Moon

364 奉和圣制赐史供奉曲江宴应制
In Reply to Your Majesty's Call to Follow Your Majesty's Poem: the Inspector Attending a Feast at the Bend

366 奉和圣制十五夜然灯继以酺宴应制
In Reply to Your Majesty's Call to Follow Your Majesty's Poem: Viewing Lanterns on the Fifteenth Night and Granting a Feast

368 奉和圣制上巳于望春亭观禊饮应制
In Reply to Your Majesty's Call to Follow Your Majesty's Poem: Viewing a Feast at Spring-Gazing Pavilion on the Third Day of the Third Moon

370 登楼歌
Song of Climbing the Tower

373 送友人归山歌二首
Seeing Off My Friend Back to Hills, Two Poems

373 其一
No. 1

375 其二
No. 2

377 叹白发
Sighing to My Gray Hair

378 送李太守赴上洛
Seeing Off Prefect Li to His Position in Shanglo

380 送熊九赴任安阳
Seeing off Hsiung Nine to His Position in Peaceshine

382 送张判官赴河西
Seeing Off Judge Chang to His Position in Hohsi

384 送宇文三赴河西充行军司马
Seeing Off Yüwen Three to His Post as a Vice Commander

| 386 | 送韦评事
Seeing Off Judge Wei |
|---|---|
| 387 | 送刘司直赴安西
Seeing Off Justice Liu to Pacified West |
| 389 | 送平淡然判官
Seeing Off Judge Tanran P'ing |
| 391 | 送元二使安西
Seeing Off My Friend Yüan Two to Pacified West as an Envoy |
| 392 | 相思
The Love Bean |
| 393 | 伊州歌
An Eechow Song |
| 394 | 辋川集二十首
A Rimriver Collection, Twenty Poems |
| 395 | 孟城坳
Meng's Planeton |
| 396 | 华子冈
Floral Mound |
| 397 | 文杏馆
Ginkgo Pavilion |
| 398 | 斤竹岭
Axe Bamboo Ridge |
| 399 | 鹿柴
The Deer Fence |
| 400 | 木兰柴
The Magnolia Fence |
| 401 | 茱萸沜
The Cornel Riverside |
| 402 | 宫槐陌
Palace Locust Lane |
| 403 | 临湖亭
The Lakeside Pavilion |

404	南垞 The South Mound
405	欹湖 Bed-tilting Lake
406	柳浪 Willows Wave
407	栾家濑 The Gushing Rapids
408	金屑泉 Gold Dust Spring
409	白石滩 The White Gravel Shoal
410	北垞 The North Mound
411	竹里馆 Bamboo Grove Villa
412	辛夷坞 The Lily Magnolia Grove
413	漆园 The Lacquer Garden
414	椒园 The Prickly-ash Garden
415	辋川闲居赠裴秀才迪 To Showcharm P'ei from My Villa in Rimriver
417	答裴迪辋口遇雨忆终南山之作 Reminiscing the South Hills Caught in a Rain at the Mouth of the Rim, In Reply to Ti P'ei
418	赠裴十迪 To Ti P'ei Ten
420	黎拾遗昕裴秀才迪见过秋夜对雨之作 Composed on a Raining Autumn Night When Counselor Hsin Li and Showcharm Ti P'ei Visit Me

422	裴迪	
	To Ti P'ei	
423	登裴秀才迪小台作	
	Climbing onto Showcharm P'ei's Platform	
424	酌酒与裴迪	
	Drinking with Ti P'ei	
425	闻裴秀才迪吟诗因戏赠	
	Hearing Showcharm Ti P'ei Chanting, Hence the Poem for Fun	
426	过感化寺昙兴上人山院	
	A Visit to Monk Cloud Rise's Cottage at Inspiration Temple	
427	游感化寺	
	Touring Inspiration Temple	
430	临高台送黎拾遗	
	Ascending the Height to See Off Counselor Li	
431	辋川闲居	
	Staying Idle at Rimriver	
433	积雨辋川庄作	
	Composed at Rimriver Villa in a Raining Season	
435	戏题辋川别业	
	A Poem to Rimriver Villa for Fun	
436	归辋川作	
	Composed After Going Back to Rimriver	
438	春中田园作	
	Spring Comes to the Country	
440	春园即事	
	Working in the Field in Spring	
442	山居即事	
	Notes on Mountain Abiding	
444	山居秋暝	
	The Hills Wearing Autumn Hue	
446	田园乐七首	
	Farmland Glee, Seven Poems	

446	其一 No. 1	
447	其二 No. 2	
448	其三 No. 3	
449	其四 No. 4	
450	其五 No. 5	
451	其六 No. 6	
452	其七 No. 7	
453	泛前陂 Boating on the Front Pond	
454	山茱萸 Hill Cornels	
455	酬虞部苏员外过蓝田别业不见留之作 To Counselor Su of Forestry Office Who Visits My Cottage in Blue Field but Does Not Stay	
456	蓝田山石门精舍 Stonegate Vihara at Mt. Blue Field	
459	山中 In the Hills	
460	赠刘蓝田 To Magistrate Liu of Blue Field	
462	山中送别 Parting in the Hills	
463	早秋山中作 In the Hills on an Early Autumn Day	
465	林园即事寄舍弟紞 To My Younger Brother Tan from Wood Land	

467	酬诸公见过 Thanks to the Lords Who Visit Me	
470	别辋川别业 Good-bye to My Cottage at Rimriver	
471	辋川别业 My Cottage at Rimriver	
473	郑果州相过 A Visit from Cheng, Magistrate of Kuochow	
474	酬张少府 Thanks to Chang, a County Sheriff	
475	题辋川图 Dedication to the Painting of Rimriver	
476	崔濮阳兄季重前山兴 To Brother Chichung Ts'ui, Magistrate of P'ushine, at the Front Hill, with Zest	
478	山中示弟 To My Younger Brothers in the Hills	
480	菩提寺禁裴迪来相看说逆贼等凝碧池上作音乐供奉人等举声便一时泪下私成口号诵示裴迪 I'm Jailed in Boddhi Temple and Ti P'ei Comes to See Me, Telling of Lushan An's Party at Deepblue Pool for Musicians While I Am Shaken to Tears with this Oral Impromptu To Ti P'ei	
482	口号又示裴迪 Another Oral Impromptu To Ti P'ei	
483	既蒙宥罪旋复拜官，伏感圣恩窃书鄙意，兼奉简新除使君等诸公 When Pardoned and Given Back My Post, I Fall Prostrate to Express My Gratitude to His Majesty with this Poem and Copy the Verse in Letters to the Lords Rehabilitated	
485	和贾舍人早朝大明宫之作 In Reply to Secretary Chia's Poem: the Levee at Great Bright Palace	
487	晚春严少尹与诸公见过 Visited by Shaoyin Yan and Other Lords in Late Spring	

489	酬严少尹徐舍人见过不遇	
	Thanks to Shaoyin Yan and Secretary Hsu, Who Visit but Fail to See Me	

491	同崔傅答贤弟	
	In Reply to You and Fu Ts'ui	

494	和宋中丞夏日游福贤观天长寺寺即陈左相宅所施之作	
	Touring Heaven Long Fane and Blessed Sage Temple Donated by Left Premier Ch'en with Magistrate Sung on a Summer Day	

496	春夜竹亭赠钱少府归蓝田	
	To Ch'ien, a County Sheriff, Back to Blue Field at Bamboo Pavilion on a Spring Night	

497	送钱少府还蓝田	
	Seeing Off Chien, a County Sheriff, Back to Blue Field	

499	左掖梨花	
	Pear Blossoms at Undergate Department	

500	送韦大夫东京留守	
	Seeing Off Grandee Wei to East Capital as a Stay Guard	

503	瓜园诗	
	A Poem of Melon Field	

506	送杨长史赴果州	
	Seeing Off Vice Governor Yang to Kuochow	

508	慕容承携素馔见过	
	Ch'eng Mujung's Visit with Vegetarian Food	

510	酬慕容十一	
	Thanks to Mujung Eleven	

511	饭覆釜山僧	
	Treating Monk of Reversed Pot with Food	

513	叹白发	
	Sighing to My Gray Hair	

514	和陈监四郎秋雨中思从弟据	
	In Reply to Ch'ien Ch'en Four's Missing My Cousin Chü in Autumn Rain	

516	冬晚对雪忆胡居士家	
	Reminiscing Hu, a Lay Buddhist on a Snowy Night	
518	胡居士卧病遗米因赠人	
	To Hu, a Lay Buddhist, Who Gives Me Rice When I Lie Ill	
521	秋夜独坐	
	Sitting Alone on an Autumn Night	
522	与胡居士皆病寄此诗兼示学人二首	
	To Hu, the Lay Buddhist, Who Is Ill like Me and For Other Learners, Two Poems	
522	其一	
	No. 1	
525	其二	
	No. 2	
527	恭懿太子挽歌五首	
	Five Elegies to Crown Prince of Respecting Virtue	
527	其一	
	No. 1	
529	其二	
	No. 2	
530	其三	
	No. 3	
531	其四	
	No. 4	
533	其五	
	No. 5	
535	河南严尹弟见宿弊庐访别人赋十韵	
	Yin Yan from Honan Pays Me a Visit and Stays for the Night in My Lodge, Hence the Score Lines	
538	送元中丞转运江淮	
	Seeing Off Magistrate Yüan to the Yangtze and the Huai Area as Transportation Director	
539	早春行	
	Early Spring	

541	座上走笔赠薛璩慕容损	
	To Ch'u Hsüeh and Sun Mujung as I Run My Brush Seated	
543	李处士山居	
	The Cottage of Li, a Lay Buddhist	
545	丁寓田家有赠	
	To Yü Ting Who Likes a Farming Life	
548	渭川田家	
	A Farmer on the Wei	
550	过李揖宅	
	A Visit To Chi Li's Residence	
552	奉送六舅归陆浑	
	Seeing Off My Sixth Uncle to Luhun	
554	送别	
	Good-bye	
555	送张舍人佐江州同薛璩十韵	
	Seeing Secretary Chang Off to Be Vice Prefecture of Riverton Together with Ch'u Hsüeh	
558	新晴野望	
	An Outlook after a Rain	
559	苦热	
	Smothering Heat	
561	燕子龛禅师	
	To Zen Master in Swallow Shrine	
565	羽林骑闺人	
	The Escort Guard's Wife	
567	早朝	
	Morning Levee	
569	杂诗	
	Miscellany	
571	夷门歌	
	Song of Ee Gate	
573	黄雀痴	
	The Loving Siskin	

575	赠吴官 To Officials from Wu	
577	雪中忆李揖 Missing Chi Li in Snow	
578	送崔五太守 Seeing off Prefect Ts'ui Five	
581	寒食城东即事 Notes on Cold Food Day East of the Town	
583	奉和杨驸马六郎秋夜即事 In Reply to Adjunct Groom Yang Six, Notes on an Autumn Night	
585	酬贺四赠葛巾之作 Thanks to Ho Four, Who Presents Me with a Co-hemp Scarf	
586	过福禅师兰若 A Visit to Zen Master Bliss in a Temple	
588	过香积寺 A Visit to Balm Temple	
589	送李判官赴东江 Seeing Off Judge Li to East of the River	
590	送张道士归山 Seeing Off Chang, a Wordist, Back to the Hills	
592	送李员外贤郎 Seeing Off Counselor Li's Talented Son	
593	送梓州李使君 Seeing Off Prefect Li of Tsuchow	
595	送孙秀才 Seeing Off Showcharm Sun	
597	送方城韦明府 Seeing Off Wei, Magistrate of Squareton	
599	送友人南归 Seeing Off My Friend Back South	
601	送孙二 Seeing Off Sun Two	

602	观猎	
	Watching Hunting	
604	春日上方即事	
	Notes on Your Abbot Room on a Spring Day	
606	游李山人所居因题屋壁	
	Touring Immortal Li's Abode and Writing the Dedication on His Wall	
608	戏题示萧氏甥	
	Dedication to Hsiao's Nephew for Fun	
610	听宫莺	
	Listening to Orioles in the Palace	
612	早朝	
	Morning Levee	
614	愚公谷三首	
	Fool's Dale, Three Poems	
614	其一	
	No. 1	
616	其二	
	No. 2	
617	其三	
	No. 3	
618	杂诗	
	Miscellany	
620	送方尊师归嵩山	
	Seeing Off Master Fang Back to Mt. Tower	
622	送杨少府贬郴州	
	Seeing Off Yang, a County Sheriff, Demoted to Ch'enchow	
624	听百舌鸟	
	Listening to Mocking Birds	
626	沈十四拾遗新竹生读经处同诸公之作	
	Counselor Shen Fourteen's Sutra Reading Place in New Bamboo, with Other Colleagues	

628	田家 Farmers	
630	哭褚司马 Mourning Commander Ch'u	
632	赠韦穆十八 To Mu Wei Eighteen	
633	皇甫岳云溪杂题五首 Five Miscellanies at Hill Huangfu's Cloud Creek	
633	鸟鸣涧 Birds Twitter o'er the Brook	
634	莲花坞 Lotus Cove	
635	鸬鹚堰 Cormorant Weir	
636	上平田 Upper Field	
637	萍池 Lotus Pool	
638	红牡丹 The Red Peony	
639	杂诗三首 Three Miscellanies	
639	其一 No. 1	
640	其二 No. 2	
641	其三 No. 3	
642	书事 The Sight Before Me	
643	崔兴宗写真咏 Portraying Hsingtsung Ts'ui	

644	寄河上段十六	
	To Tuan Sixteen on the River	
645	送王尊师归蜀中拜扫	
	Seeing Off Master Wang to Mid-Shu for Tomb Sweeping	
647	送沈子福归江东	
	Seeing You Off Back to East of the River	
648	剧嘲史寰	
	Jeering at Huan Shih	
649	秋夜曲	
	A Tune of Autumn	
651	**译者简介**	
	About the Translator	

送秘书晁监还日本国

　　舜觐群后,有苗不服;禹会诸侯,防风后至——动干戚之舞,兴斧钺之诛——乃贡九牧之金,始颁五瑞之玉。我开元天地大宝圣文神武应道皇帝:大道之行,先天布化;乾元广运,涵育无垠。若华为东道之标,戴胜为西门之候;岂甘心于邛杖,非征贡于苞茅。亦由呼韩来朝,舍于蒲陶之馆;卑弥遣使,报以蛟龙之锦。牺牲玉帛,以将厚意;服食器用,不宝远物。百神受职,五老告期。况乎戴发含齿,得不稽颡屈膝?

　　海东国日本为大,服圣人之训,有君子之风。正朔本乎夏时,衣裳同乎汉制。历岁方达,继旧好于行人;滔天无涯,贡方物于天子。司仪加等,位在王侯之先;掌次改观,不居蛮夷之邸。我无尔诈,尔无我虞;彼以好来,废关弛禁。上敷文教,虚至实归。故人民杂居,往来如市。晁司马结发游圣,负笈辞亲。问礼于老聃,学诗于子夏。鲁借车马,孔子遂适于宗周;郑献缟衣,季札始通于上国。

　　名成太学,官至客卿。必齐之姜,不归娶于高国;在楚犹晋,亦何独于由余。游宦三年,愿以君羹遗母;不居一国,欲其昼锦还乡。庄舄既显而思归,关羽报恩而终去。于是驰首北阙,裹足东辕。箧命赐之衣,怀敬问之诏。金简玉字,传道经于绝域之人;方鼎彝樽,致分器于异姓之国。琅邪台上,回望龙门;碣石馆前,夐然鸟逝。鲸鱼喷浪,则万里倒回;鹢首乘云,则八风却走。扶桑若荠,郁岛如萍。沃白日而簸三山,浮苍天而吞九域。黄雀之风动地,黑蜃之气成云。淼不知其所之,何相思之可寄?

　　嘻!去帝乡之故旧,谒本朝之君臣。咏七子之诗,佩两国之印。恢我王度,谕彼蕃臣。三寸犹在,乐毅辞燕而未老;十年在外,信陵归魏而逾尊。子其行乎,余赠言者。

　　　　　　积水不可极,
　　　　　　安知沧海东。
　　　　　　九州何处远,
　　　　　　万里若乘空。
　　　　　　向国唯看日,

归帆但信风。
鳌身映天黑,
鱼眼射波红。
乡树扶桑外,
主人孤岛中。
别离方异域,
音信若为通。

Seeing Off Heng Ch'ao, Secretariat Censor, Home to Japan

Hibiscus received all in audience, but the Sprouts did not submit; Worm summoned all vassals, and Windbreak was late. The saintly lords danced with shields and axes and killed with spears and halberds, so aliens all over the land sent their tributes of gold and jade. Our Allbegun Heaven and Earth Great-treasure Saintly Civil and Martial In-Word Emperor practices the Word under the Heavens; the Great One moves on, nurturing all without bound. The Word spreads east to Sunrise; Queen Mother gazes from West Gate. The aliens come not simply to offer Ch'iung canes, nor does our Lord ask for their bundled thatch. Just like Huhan who came to worship and was well treated, accommodated in Sedgepot Palace and Himiko who sent her envoy and was granted brocade embroidered with dragons. Livestock, jade and silk were given to envoys and nothing was expected of them, wearings or foods. All priests fulfill their jobs, all folks enjoy their life. How can people not bow and kowtow to our Lord?

Japan is the biggest of kingdoms east of the sea, having been cultivated with saints' teachings to have a gentlemanly bearing. Japanese are modeled on Chinese, wearing Chinese clothes. They send envoys to China and it takes them one year to arrive; having voyaged a long way on the sea, they present their specialties to the court. And accordingly, they are given the best treatment, preferential than the peerage. Since they have been well civilized, no longer barbaric or crafty or cheating, the blockades and blockages are taken off for a friendly relation. With the empire's magnanimity, they come with hopes and go back with gains. Japanese and Chinese dwell with each other, hustling and bustling as if in a market.

Commander Ch'ao left his parents for Great China in his teens, learning rites and poetry like saints such as Laocius and Sir Summer, like Confucius, who with cart and horses given by the State of Lu went on a pilgrimage to Chough and like Stripfour, who, in white clothes offered by the State of Cheng, went on a learning tour to the mother state. Having graduated from Grand College, he was appointed as a guest minister. He got married in China, never feeling lonely, though far away from his motherland. Having been a scholar and official for years, he would go back to show his kindness to his mother, so glorified and honored, like Sir Lush who missed his homeland when in prominence, like Yü Kuan chose to leave to requite his lord's grace. Therefore, Ch'ao kowtowed to the throne and started his journey back home, with gifts from the court and an edict from the Lord. The literary refinements are to be brought to the esoteric isles, and square bronzes and utensils introduced to the alien land. Atop Ivory Mound, he may look back at the capital; before Tablet Hall he may see birds fly away. The whales throw up waves and the waves wash back ten thousand miles; his ship sails through clouds and against all winds. The hibiscuses loom like water chestnuts, the green isles seem to float like duckweed. The sea splashes to the sun and quakes the mountains, licks the blue and gulps the earth; sparrows churn up air to shake the land; a black mirage changes into clouds. In the vast ocean where is he going? What great love is he yearning to express?

Ah! He has left the empire for his old land to pay his respects to the sovereign and subjects. As he has chanted the Seven's poems and has been officials for two states, he should be able to convey to his kinfolk our emperor's grace, like Ee Glee who, so brilliant and talented, left Yan when young, and like Faithridge who came back to Way with honor, having toured out for ten years. Upon his departure, I write this verse for farewell.

> The river's too far off to see,
> Let alone the east of the sea.
> What is the place that farthest lies?
> A clime hard to reach like the skies.
> If you gaze there, you'll see the sun
> And see a wind the sails o'errun.
> The turtle turns to cloud the skies;
> The fish shoots red waves from its eyes.
> Fusang's nearer than your home trees;
> Your isle's surrounded by rough seas.
> If too far off, far off indeed,
> How can we exchange news we need?

* Heng Ch'ao: Heng Ch'ao (A.D. 698 – A.D. 770), an overseas student from Japan, Abe Nakamaro by his original name. He came to China for education in A.D. 717, and having survived the shipwreck on his trip back to Japan, he served as a high-ranking official in T'ang, first made Protector-General of Tonkin and then Secretariat Censor of the Censorate, a post he held until his death in A.D. 770.
* Hibiscus: Shun if transliterated, an ancient sovereign, a descendant of Lord Yellow (2,717 B.C.- 2,599 B.C.), a son-in-law of Mound (cir. 2,377 B.C.- 2,259 B.C.), regarded as one of Five Lords in prehistoric China.
* Sprouts: Three Sprouts, often called Miao or Hmong, an ethnic minority living in the southwest of China and some Asian countries, noted for their silver crowns and trinkets as well as dancing and herbal medicine.
* Worm: the founding lord of Hsia, who took over the leadership from Hibiscus. It was said that Mound was put in jail, having lost his morality, and Hibiscus died in a moor when he was in a tour. The poet borrowed the ancient legend to imply that the reign of T'ang was in danger of being destroyed.
* Windbreak: a legendary head of a tribe in prehistorical China, a giant, about ten

meters and three tall, the founder of the Kingdom of Windbreak, killed by Worm due to his being late for the summit of vassal states.
* Allbegun Heaven and Earth Great-treasure Saintly Civil and Martial In-Word Emperor: the formal title of Emperor Deepsire, the 6th emperor of T'ang.
* Sunrise, referring to Japan, as was believed to be where the sun rises.
* Queen Mother: Mother West, a mythological being in Chinese culture.
* Huhan: Chanyu Huhanyeh (? - 31 B.C.), a sovereign of a Hun state, in power from 58 B.C. to 31 B.C.
* Ch'iung cane: a kind of bamboo growing in Shu, that is, today's Ssuch'uan Province.
* Himiko: Queen of Yamatai, an isle kingdom in the Three Kingdoms period, an ancient name of Japan.
* Laocius: one of the most influential philosophers of Wordism in China, the proponent of quietism. Laocius wrote all his wisdom into a single book of about five thousand words, which came to be known as *The Word and the World*.
* Sir Summer: formally Shang Pu (507 B.C.- 420 B.C.), a student of Confucius's, one of the Best Ten and one of the seventy two sages in Confucius's school.
* Confucius: Confucius (551 B.C.- 479 B.C.), a renowned thinker, educator and statesman in the Spring and Autumn period, born in the State of Lu, who was the founder of Confucianism and who had exerted profound influence on Chinese culture. Confucius is one of the few leaders who based their philosophy on the virtues that are required for the day-to-day living. His philosophy centered on personal and governmental morality.
* Stripfour: Stripfour(576 B.C.- 484 B.C.), Chi Cha if transliterated, or styled Sir Four of Broadridge, an honest and righteous man, who founded the State of Wu (12 Cent. B.C.- 473 B.C.).
* Yü Kuan: Yü Kuan(A.D. 161 - A.D. 220), a famous general of Shu in the Three Kingdoms period.
* Ivory Mound: Langya T'ai if transliterated, a coastal mound built by Emperor First in modern-day Shantung Province.
* Tablet Hall: the name of a hall at Mt. Tablet in today's Shangtung Province.
* the hibiscuses: referring to Japan, which was called Fusang, Hibiscus literally.
* Seven: referring to the seven famous poets of Way in the Three Kingdoms period.
* Ee Glee: referring to Ee Yüeh, a prominent military commander. In the year of 284 B.C., he commanded the five-nation allied forces to attack the State of Ch'i and set an example of the weak overcoming the strong in war history.
* Faithridge: Prince of Hsin Ling, the youngest son of King Glare of Way, a famous militarist and statesman in the Warring States period.

* the turtle: referring to a giant turtle in legend.
* Fusang: the old name of Japan, called Nippon from the age of Dowager Wu (A.D. 624 - A.D. 705), who approved a Japanese envoy's request of Japan's new name Nippon, which means "Where the Sun Rises".

同崔兴宗送衡岳瑗公南归

衡岳瑗上人者，常学道于五峰，荫松栖云，与狼虎杂处，得无所得矣。天宝癸巳岁，始游于长安。手提瓶笠，至自万里；宴居吐论，缁属高之。初，给事中房公谪居宜春，与上人风土相接，因为道友，伏腊往来。房公既海内盛名，上人亦以此增价。秋九月，杖锡南返，扣门来别。秦地草木，槭然已黄；苍梧白云，不日而见。㵲阳有曹溪学者，为我谢之。

Seeing Off Master Yüan Back to the South, with Hsingtsung Ts'ui

Master Yüan on Mt. Scale practiced the Word among the five peaks, resting under pines, reposing in clouds, and dwelling with wolves and tigers, gaining Nothing to Gain. The twelfth year of the Allbegun reign, Master Yüan came to tour Long Peace. Carrying a pot and a bamboo hat, he had travelled ten thousand *li*; the way he talked when idle was admirable. He made friends with Kuan Fang, Secretary of Inspection, who had earlier been demoted to Good Spring, adjacent to where Master Yüan lived, and they would meet in summer and winter. As Master Fang was well known, Master Yüan became renowned accordingly. It is an autumn day in the ninth moon, Master Yüan is going back to the south holding his tin staff and comes to knock on my door to bid good-bye. Now in Ch'in Land grass is withered, while in the south the clouds over Mt. Nine Doubts will see you soon. I hear there are Zen scholars called Ts'ao Stream School, please give my best regard to them.

> On the plank road on Stone Fungus
> To Solemn Ridge you go away.

And to Poolshine you walk alone,
But over the hills white clouds stay.
On this autumn day you darn clothes
And wash your bowl in the pines old.
You'll teach Dharma from heart to heart
And return with canons you hold.

* Master Yüan: a Buddhist monk, no further information available.
* Hsingtsung Ts'ui: a T'ang poet from Broadridge (today's Tingchow, Hopei Province), who lived in reclusion in the South Mountains in the south of Long Peace in his early life and used to hang out with Wei Wang, our poet and painter, drinking, writing and playing the zither. The position he held in the dynasty was Left Alternate and he finished his career as Secretary of Jaochow Prefecture, in today's Chianghsi Province.
* Mt. Scale: one of the Five Mountains in China, located in Hunan Province, along with Mt. Ever in Shanhsi, Mt. Arch in Shantung, Mt. Flora in Sha'anhsi, and Mt. Tower in Honan.
* Nothing to Gain: a naturalist state of nothingness practiced by Wordists.
* Kuan Fang: a high official, Secretary of Inspection of the T'ang Empire.
* Good Spring: Echun if transliterated, in today's Chiangsu Province.
* Stone Fungus: one of the seventy-two peaks of Mt. Scale.
* Solemn Ridge: 50 kilometers from today's Hempton (Mach'eng), Huangchow, Hupei Province.
* Poolshine: the name of an old county founded in the Han dynasty, in today's Chingshine (Chingyang), Sha'anhsi Province.
* pine: an evergreen tree with needle-like leaves and cones, a symbol of longevity and rectitude in Chinese culture.
* Dharma: the state of truth and righteousness in Buddhist teachings.
* canon: a book of Buddhist sutra, recognized as holy.

同崔员外秋宵寓直

建礼高秋夜,
承明候晓过。
九门寒漏彻,
万井曙钟多。
月迥藏珠斗,
云消出绛河。
更惭衰朽质,
南陌共鸣珂。

On Duty with Counselor Ts'ui on an Autumn Night

In Rite Hall we have an autumn night
Till the day comes with dawning light.
The Nine Gates watch hourglasses cold
Till in all the lanes bells are tolled.
Behind Big Dipper the moon pries;
From the Milky Way clouds arise.
Although weak and old as I think,
We should ride while our trinkets clink.

* Rite Hall: an office or hall where a Privy Council secretary worked on night shift in the T'ang dynasty.
* the Nine Gates: nine imperial palace gates. According to *Rites*, a palace of a king or Son of Heaven is ordained to have nine gates.
* hourglass: a vessel used for measuring time by the running of water or sand from the upper into the lower compartment, also used as metaphor for the elapse of time.

* Big Dipper: the Dipper, a constellation composed of seven bright stars, and looks like a spoon in the sky.
* the Milky Way: the Silver River in Chinese mythology in contrast with Zeus and Hera in Greek mythology. Physically, it is a luminous band circling the heavens composed of stars and nebulae visible to the naked eye; the Galaxy.
* the moon: the satellite of the earth, a representative of shade or feminity of things, alluding to the belle in this poem. In a universe animated by the interaction of Shade and Shine energies, the moon is Shade visible, the very germ or source of Shade, and the sun is its Shine counterpart.

与苏卢二员外期游方丈寺而苏不至因有此作

共仰头陀行,
能忘世谛情。
回看双凤阙,
相去一牛鸣。
法向空林说,
心随宝地平。
手巾花叠净,
香帔稻畦成。
问道邀同舍,
相期宿化城。
安知不来往,
翻得似无生。

Appointment Made to Tour Abbot Temple with Counselors Su and Lu, But Su Does Not Make It, Hence the Poem

We would both practice Shaking-off,
As we can go back to what's True.
With a glance back at Twainbird Gate,
We're close, as far as a cow moo.
Dharma speaks to a vacant wood;
At the blessed ground a heart is laid;
The handkerchief looks clean like cloth;
The balmy cassock's finely made.

For the Word my mates I invite
To Transmigration for the day.
Although you cannot make it here,
In non-life you'll manage to stay.

* Shaking-off: getting rid of worries in meditation, translated from Sanskrit Dhuta.
* True: the unsoiled state of things, for example, Princess Jade True (A.D. 692 - A.D. 762) was so named because Jade True was her motivation or the state she would achieve.
* Twainbird Gate: imperial palace gate or gate tower with two phoenixes on.
* a cow moo: a short distance, as long as one can hear a cow moo.
* Dharma: truth and righteousness in Buddhist terms.
* cassock: a close-fitting garment, reaching to the feet, worn by Catholic or Buddhist monks.
* the Word: referring to Tao if transliterated, the most significant and profoundest concept in Chinese philosophy. According to Laocius's *The Word and the World*:"The Word is void, but its use is infinite. O deep! It seems to be the root of all things." The Word is identifiable with the Word or Logos in the West, as there is an enormous amount of common ground in the two cosmologies and the doctrines concerning the most fundamental matters such as "the Word is the One" and "God is the One", and the personalization of Being, the progenitor of finite spirits, which are subordinate kinds of Being or merely appearances of the Divine, the One.
* Transmigration: name of a temple with meaning of transforming one's life.
* Non-life: nirvana in Buddhist terms, an ideal state free from mental, emotional and psychic tenstion.

过卢四员外宅看饭僧共题七韵

三贤异七圣，
青眼慕青莲。
乞饭从香积，
裁衣学水田。
上人飞锡杖，
檀越施金钱。
跌坐檐前日，
焚香竹下烟。
寒空法云地，
秋色净居天。
身逐因缘法，
心过次第禅。
不须愁日暮，
自有一灯然。

A Visit to Ministry Counselor Lu's Estate to View Food Offering, a Fourteen-line Rhyme

Third-Sage differs from Seventh-Saint,
And you admire Green Lotus so.
You provide monks with Balmy Food
And for them best cassocks you sew.
The monk flies through clouds with his staff;
The donor helps the poor with gold.
Incense smoke curls from the bamboo;
The monk sits cross-legged there, behold.

The chill sky o'er Dharma Cloud Ground,
Autumn hue tints Clean Abode Blue.
Your body after Seed-fruit Law,
Sequence Zen your heart can go through.
Darkness you need not care about;
A lamp with you will ne'er go out.

* Third-Sage differs from Seventh-Saint: In Small Wheel Buddhism, Third-Sage is the initial state of Buddhist practice and Seventh-Saint is the next to the highest stage, that is Null.
* Green Lotus: a symbol of Buddhism or a metaphor for a Buddhist temple or the other way of saying Buddha.
* Balmy Food: food that Buddhist monks eat.
* cassock: a close-fitting garment, reaching to the feet, worn by Buddhist or Catholic monks.
* incense: an aromatic substance in the form of a stick that exhales perfume during combustion, burnt before a Buddhist, Wordist or any religious or ancestral figure as an act of worship, usually offered with a prayer or vow.
* bamboo: a tall, tree-like or shrubby grass in tropical and semi-tropical regions, a symbol of integrity and altitude, one of the four most important botanical images in Chinese literature, which are wintersweet, orchid, bamboo and chrysanthemum.
* Dharma Cloud Ground: perfection, the last stage of practice in Big Wheel Buddhism.
* Clean Abode Blue: the fourth stage of Zenist meditation, a state free of food and sexual desires.
* Seed-fruit Law: cause-effect, the elucidation of the causes of all physical, social, and psychological problems in the world.
* Sequence Zen: the sequence of nine stages in Zenist meditation.

与卢象集朱家

主人能爱客,
终日有逢迎。
赊得新丰酒,
复闻秦女筝。
柳条疏客舍,
槐叶下秋城。
语笑且为乐,
吾将达此生。

Visiting Chu with Hsiang Lu

So hospitable is our host,
Receiving guests day after day.
He buys Newrich wine on credit
And the lute he lets his belle play.
Sparse willows shade his guesthouse there
And locust leaves fall to the wall.
Laughing for fun from ear to ear,
I'd free my life, no care at all.

---

* Newrich: a county, known for wine brewed there. The county was built by Pang Liu in imitation of his hometown Rich County. Newrich is in today's Lintung County, near today's Hsi-an, Sha'anhsi Province. Pang Liu, Emperor Highsire, born in Rich, rose from grassroots, wiped out Hsiang's army and established Han, with Long Peace as its capital. As his father missed the beauty and wine of his hometown, Pang Liu made a copy of his hometown and moved the best brewers here, and ever since then Newrich wine has been well-known, attracting generations of litterateurs to sing praise of it.

* willow: any of a large genus of shrubs and trees related to the poplars, widely distributed in China and most of the world, having glossy green leaves resembling a girl's eye-brow, and generally having smooth branches, and often long, slender, pliant, and sometimes pendent branchlets, which seem to be waving good-bye, or weeping amorously, or drooping for nostalgia.
* locust: a tree of the bean family, with a rough bark, prickly twigs, odd-pinnate leaves, and loose, slender racemes of fragrant, white flowers, which are a seasonal delicacy to many Chinese.

春过贺遂员外药园

前年槿篱故，
新作药栏成。
香草为君子，
名花是长卿。
水穿盘石透，
藤系古松生。
画畏开厨走，
来蒙倒屣迎。
蔗浆菰米饭，
蒟酱露葵羹。
颇识灌园意，
於陵不自轻。

A Visit to Ministry Counselor's Medicine Herb Garden in Spring

A hibiscus hedge set last year,
Now new medicine herbs grow lush.
The balmy weed's a gentleman;
The fragrant flower's a girl to blush.
Clinging to the old pine vines grow;
Water seeps from a boulder crack;
Paintings in his kitchen are stored;
He greets guests, shoes front at the back.
Sugar cane juice and wild rice meal,
Betel pepper and mallow bright.

I know what you mean with this style;
A recluse, you don't yourself slight.

* hibiscus: any of various malvaceous herbs, shrubs and trees of the genus *Hibiscus*, having large, showy flowers of various colors.
* medicine herbs: herbs gathered from the wild or cultivated play an important part in Chinese medicare, usually called Chinese medicine.
* sugar cane: a tall, stout, perennial grass of tropical regions with a solid jointed stalk rich in sugar, from which juice can be extracted.
* wild rice: a tall aquatic grass, what is *zizania aquatica* in Latin, the stem of which is used as a vegetable and the grain of which was formerly used as food, now esteemed as a table delicacy.
* betel: a climbing plant of Asia, the leaves of which are chewed by natives of Malaya and other Asian countries.
* mallow: *Malva verticillata* or any plant of the genus *Malva* with roundish leaves, the first of the five popular vegetables in ancient China.

送贺遂员外外甥

南国有归舟，
荆门溯上流。
苍茫葭菼外，
云水与昭丘。
樯带城乌去，
江连暮雨愁。
猿声不可听，
莫待楚山秋。

Seeing Off Ministry Counselor's Nephew

In the south your boat back home rows;
And in Chastegate upstream it goes.
The reeds spread till out of the blue;
Water and Glare Knoll are mates two.
Your mast carries off town wall crows;
The stream at dusk adds to your woes.
You can hardly bear monkeys' calls;
Do not wait until autumn falls.

* Chastegate: a town located on the southern bank of the Yangtze River, today's Hupei Province.
* reed: the slender, frequently jointed stem of certain tall grasses growing in wet places or in grasses themselves.
* Glare Knoll: name of a tomb, that is, the mausoleum of King Glare of Ch'in (306 B.C.- 251 B.C.).
* crow: an omnivorous, raucous, oscine bird of the genus *Corvus*, with glossy black

plumage. It is regarded as an ominous bird, a messenger from hell because it can smell those dying and feeds on carrion as a scavenger.

* monkey: any of a group of primates having elongate limbs, hands and feet adapted for grasping, and a highly developed nervous system, including marmosets, baboons, and macaques, but not the anthropoid apes, though monkeys and apes are used alternatively in Chinese.

赠从弟司库员外絿

少年识事浅，
强学干名利。
徒闻跃马年，
苦无出人智。
即事岂徒言，
累官非不试。
既寡遂性欢，
恐招负时累。
清冬见远山，
积雪凝苍翠。
浩然出东林，
发我遗世意。
惠连素清赏，
夙语尘外事。
欲缓携手期，
流年一何驶。

Seeing Off My Cousin Ch'iu Wang, Ministry Counselor of War Ministry

Shallow was I when I was young;
For fame and wealth I rushed along.
I believed in my galloping prime;
I'd no enough wisdom to climb.
My will I had not just expressed;
For officialdom I tried my best.

Of happiness I was deprived;
I was derided though I strived.
In winter far hills can be seen;
Heavy snow covers the pines green.
Out of the east wood all is white,
Which stirs up my loss and my plight.
Like Huilien, you're pure, free of lust;
We have talked how to flee world dust.
Our reclusion I would postpone,
But time flies so fast, all alone.

* pine: any of a genus (*Pinus*) of evergreen trees of the pine family, a cone-bearing tree having bundles of two to five needle-shaped leaves growing in clusters, an important image in Chinese literature, a symbol of rectitude, solitude, longevity and so on.
* Huilien: Huilien Hsieh (A.D. 406 – A.D. 433), a litterateur in the Southern Dynasties period.

过崔驸马山池

画楼吹笛妓,
金碗酒家胡。
锦石称贞女,
青松学大夫。
脱貂贳桂醑,
射雁与山厨。
闻道高阳会,
愚公谷正愚。

A Visit to Adjunct Groom Ts'ui's Hillpool

In the carved tower is a flute player;
With a gold bowl a Hun girl shines.
The hill with stripes is called Mt. Chaste,
As called grandees are the Five Pines.
He exchanges mink for laurel wine,
And will shoot down wild geese to cook.
For the Word in High Sun they meet;
Hasn't Fool's Dale a foolish look?

* Adjunct Groom: an emperor's son-in-law, usually holding the position of guarding the horses of the adjunct carts, hence the name.
* Hun girl: a northern or western nomadic young woman selling wine in her wineshop in the capital or other parts of China in the T'ang dynasty, featured with a high nose, charming eyes and blonde hair, and brimming with enthusiasm and ardor.
* Mt. Chastegate: Chingmen if transliterated, an area of military significance in the middle of present-day Hupei Province.

* the Five Pines: Mt. Five Pines, a mountain located in today's Tungling, Anhui Province, so named because there once grew five pines on the very top. According to *Geographical Wonders* compiled in the Southern Sung dynasty, "The mountain boasted old pines, five in one, a pentad, reaching high to the sky with scale-like bark on the trunk."
* mink: a kind of precious fur that is soft, thick glossy and brown, from an amphibious, slender-bodied mammal called mink.
* laurel: laurus nobilis, an evergreen shrub with aromatic, lance-shaped leaves, yellowish flowers, and succulent, cherry-like fruit, a symbol of glory usually in the form of a crown or wreath of laurel to indicate honor or high merit, especially when one had passed Grand Test in ancient China. In Chinese mythology, there is a colossal laurel tree on the moon, and it would never fall even though Kang Wu, a banished immortal, kept cutting it.
* wild goose: an undomesticated goose that is caring and responsible, taken as a symbol of benevolence, righteousness, good manner, wisdom and faith in Chinese culture.
* the Word: referring to Tao if transliterated, the most significant and profoundest concept in Chinese philosophy. According to Laocius's *The Word and the World*: "The Word is void, but its use is infinite. O deep! It seems to be the root of all things."
* High Sun: the capital of Dark Crown's kingdom, in present-day Hopei Province, also Dark Crown's alias when he reigned in High Sun. Dark Crown (2342 B.C.- 2245 B.C.), Chuanhsu if transliterated, was one of Five Emperors in prehistoric China.
* Fool's Dale: a dale that a hermit called Fool once abode.

送丘为往唐州

宛洛有风尘，
君行多苦辛。
四愁连汉水，
百口寄随人。
槐色阴清昼，
杨花惹暮春。
朝端肯相送，
天子绣衣臣。

Seeing Off Wei Ch'iu to T'angchow

Wan and Lo blow up wind and dust;
On your way bear hardship you must.
Your rues and the Han are combined;
You leave all your dear ones behind.
The locust hue shades the day bright;
The catkins stir up the spring light.
To say you bye the whole court run;
His Majesty grants you silks well-shone.

* T'angchow: an old name of Huai-an Prefecture, in today's Mishine, Honan Province.
* Wan and Lo: Southine and Loshine, two places in the T'ang dynasty, in today's Honan Province.
* the Han: the Han River, the longest branch of the Long River, having an important position in Chinese history.
* locust: a tree of the bean family, with a rough bark, prickly twigs, odd-pinnate leaves, and loose, slender racemes of fragrant, white flowers, which are a seasonal

delicacy.
* catkin: a deciduous scaly spike of flowers, as in the willow, an image of helpless drifting or wandering in Chinese literature.

问寇校书双溪

君家少室西，
为复少室东？
别来几日今春风。
新买双溪定何似？
余生欲寄白云中。

Asking Collator K'ou About Twain Brooks

Do you live west of Mt. Small Room
Or bide Mt. Small Room in its east?
Apart for few days, with spring wind you're pleased!
How are Twain Brooks you newly bought beside?
For the rest of your life, in clouds you'll bide.

* Mt. Small Room: Mt. Smallroom, a Buddhist sanctuary, one of the mountains that make Mt. Tower, located in present-day Honan Province.
* Twain Brooks: name of the villa Collator K'ou bought.

春日与裴迪过新昌里访吕逸人不遇

桃源一向绝风尘，
柳市南头访隐沦。
到门不敢题凡鸟，
看竹何须问主人。
城外青山如屋里，
东家流水入西邻。
闭户著书多岁月，
种松皆作老龙鳞。

A Visit with Ti P'ei to Lu, a Hermit in New Boom Lane, Whom We Fail to See

In Peach Source there you have no din at all;
On the sage south of Willow Market I'll call.
I dare not paint a phoenix on his door;
To see his bamboo, you need ask no more.
The green hills out of town seem like yours;
The stream to west from your east neighbor pours.
Indoors for many years you write a book;
And plant pines with dragon scales, an old look.

* Peach Source: Peach Blossom Source. According to Yüanming T'ao's writing, a group of Ch'in people fled to a cove called Peach Blossom Source to keep away from the turbulent days, and the people and their offsprings had lived an idyllic and isolated life for 500 years before a fisherman of Chin stumbled into their village.
* Willow Market: also known as East Market, a big market in Long Peace in the T'ang dynasty.

* phoenix: a legendary bird of great splendor, unique of its kind, which was supposed to live five or six hundred years before consuming itself by fire, rising again from its ashes to live through another cycle, a symbol of immortality. In Chinese mythology, this mythic bird, only perching on phoenix trees, i.e. firmiana, only eating firmiana fruit, and only drinking sweet spring water, appears only in times of peace and sagacious rule.
* pine with dragon scales: a kind of pine tree with a bark full of mottles looking like dragon scales. Both pine and dragon are positive things, the former being a sign of rectitude and longevity and the latter a symbol of benevolence and sovereignty in Chinese culture, the totem of all Chinese across the world.

奉和圣制从蓬莱向兴庆阁道中
留春雨中春望之作应制

渭水自萦秦塞曲，
黄山旧绕汉宫斜。
銮舆迥出千门柳，
阁道回看上苑花。
云里帝城双凤阙，
雨中春树万人家。
为乘阳气行时令，
不是宸游重物华。

In Reply to Your Majesty's Call to Follow Your Majesty's Poem: Viewing Spring in the Rain Along the Booming Suspension Road from Great Bright Palace

The River Wei gurgles past Ch'in's Fortress;
Mt. Yellowfoot goes around Han's palace.
Your royal sedan passes the willows there;
The high road to High Park sees blossoms fair.
Clouds hang o'er the Gate of Two Phoenixes;
A spring rain falls onto the souls and trees.
Your Majesty has come out by Nature,
Not to see good sights or seek pleasure.

* Great Bright Palace: the main palace and a symbol of politics and nation of the T'ang Empire, built at Dragonhead Plain in A.D. 634, the eighth year of Emperor Deepsire's

reign entitled Loyal View, the largest of the three main palace complexes.
* the River Wei: the biggest tributary of the Yellow River.
* Ch'in's Fortress: referring to Case Dale or the land west of Case Dale.
* Mt. Yellowfoot: also known as Mt. Yellow, where Mt. Yellow Palace was built in the Han dynasty, in today's Hsingping County, Sha'anhsi Province.
* High Park: an imperial park that Lord Martial of Han built on the site of a discarded park of Ch'in. It was vast and splendid with palaces and woodlands, having various functions and recreationalfacilities, rolling about 340 kilometers.
* Gate of Two Phoenixes: imperial palace gate or gate tower with two phoenixes on it.
* Your Majesty: referring to Deepsire (Hsuan Tsung) the emperor (A.D. 685 - A.D. 762), the ninth emperor of the T'ang dynasty. When a prince, he was regarded as wise and valiant, a sportsman accomplished in all knightly exercises and a master of all elegant arts. He established Pear Garden, an operatic school, where actors and actresses were trained, and the prototype of the modern Chinese drama was developed.

酬 郭 给 事

洞门高阁霭馀辉，
桃李阴阴柳絮飞。
禁里疏钟官舍晚，
省中啼鸟吏人稀。
晨摇玉佩趋金殿，
夕奉天书拜琐闱。
强欲从君无那老，
将因卧病解朝衣。

To Kuo, Secretary of the Court

Turrets and porticos don the dusk sun;
Catkins fly, peach and plum trees dimly shone.
You sit in your office till eve bell tolls;
Birds chirrup and the court sees few souls.
At dawn, jewels swinging, for levee you wait;
At dusk, edicts you announce at the gate.
Old, I can't follow you, though I desire,
Ill, I'll take off my court robe to retire.

* catkin: a deciduous scaly spike of flowers, as in the willow, usually an image of helpless drifting or wandering in Chinese literature, just like the scene in this poem.
* peach: any tree of the genus *Prunus Percica*, blooming brilliantly and bearing fruit, a fleshy, juicy, edible, drupe, considered sacred in China, a symbol of romance, prosperity and longevity.
* plum: a kind of plant or the edible purple drupaceous fruit of the plant which is any one of various trees of the genus *Prunus*, cultivated in temperate zones.

* levee: a morning reception or an assembly at the court of a sovereign or at the house of a great personage. In ancient China, a levee at court was held every five days.
* edict: a rescript from an emperor, usually written on yellow silk, which a public ordinance having the force of law.

别綦毋潜

端笏明光宫,
历稔朝云陛。
诏刊延阁书,
高议平津邸。
适意偶轻人,
虚心削繁礼。
盛得江左风,
弥工建安体。
高张多绝弦,
截河有清济。
严冬爽群木,
伊洛方清泚。
渭水冰下流,
潼关雪中启。
荷蓧几时还,
尘缨待君洗。

Good-bye to Wuch'ien Ch'i

You hold a hand board in Bright Hall,
And walk on the marble steps high.
You collate books in the studio,
And discuss vassals far and nigh.
You don't worry about your pay,
Or haggle o'er the trivial rite.
Riverleft style you are good at,

And Making Peace genre you write.
You play the lute so high and strong,
And your poems read like rivers clean.
Winter withers trees where you'll be;
The Lo River shimmers to sheen.
The Wei River flows down with ice
And T'ung Pass is covered with snow.
Your tassel waits for you to wash,
While into Great Nature you go.

* hand board: a board like today's notebook, held by ministers or other high ranking official for note-taking at a morning levee.
* Bright Hall: name of a Han palace, a metaphor for the court of T'ang.
* Riverleft style: the style of writing of scholars south of the lower reaches of Long River, characterized by euphuism in the period of the Southern dynasties.
* Making Peace Genre: the style adopted in Making Peace period, which is the third reign title of Emperor Hsien (A.D. 181 – A.D. 234) of the Eastern Han, when literature flourished.
* the Lo River, the river which flows through Loshine, a river of cultural significance.
* the Wei: the Wei River: the largest branch of the Yellow River, originating from today's Mt. Birdmouse in Kansu Province, flowing through Precious Rooster, Allshine, Long Peace, and meeting the Yellow River at T'ung Pass.
* T'ung Pass: an old pass at the east of the West of Pass Plain (Kuanchung).
* Great Nature: the truth or the natural state of life pursued by Wordists in China.

冬 夜 书 怀

冬宵寒且永，
夜漏宫中发。
草白霭繁霜，
木衰澄清月。
丽服映颓颜，
朱灯照华发。
汉家方尚少，
顾影惭朝谒。

Remarks on a Winter Night

A winter night is cold and long;
The palace hourglass stills the night.
The grass is tinted with white frost;
The trees are sparse neath Luna bright.
My silk robe gleams to my tired look;
The red lamp shines to my gray hair.
His Majesty's too young to rule well;
Now I glance back, laden with care.

* hourglass: a vessel used for measuring time by the running of water or sand from the upper into the lower compartment, also used as metaphor for the elapse of time.
* Luna: the moon, an important image in Chinese literature or culture, as it can give rise to many associations such as solitude, purity, brightness and happy reunions. What is "moon" in Chinese has at least two hundred names, like Jade Mound (yaot'ai), Fair Lady (ts'anchüan), Jade Hare (yüt'u), White Hare (pait'u), Silver Hare (yint'u), Ice Hare (pingt'u), Gold Hare (chint'u), Hare Gleam (t'uhui), and so on.

过沈居士山居哭之

杨朱来此哭,
桑扈返于真。
独自成千古,
依然旧四邻。
闲檐喧鸟鹊,
故榻满埃尘。
曙月孤莺啭,
空山五柳春。
野花愁对客,
泉水咽迎人。
善卷明时隐,
黔娄在日贫。
逝川嗟尔命,
丘井叹吾身。
前后徒言隔,
相悲讵几晨?

Visiting the Villa of Shen, a Lay Buddhist, and Crying

Like Chu Yang, I come here to cry;
To Great Truth you now disappear.
You have merged with nature alone;
Your neighbors as e'er are still here.
Your bed are empty, full of dust;
On your free eaves the magpies sing.

The lonely oriole cries to the moon;
With willows the hills welcome spring.
Wild flowers look sad to travelers now;
The spring sobbing does people greet.
Like Darklow you lead a poor life;
Like Shanfu to hills you retreat.
All will be gone like the stream flows;
The disused well does sigh to me.
You are in that world as I'm here;
Aggrieved, how long could I here be?

* lay Buddhist: one who believes in Buddhism and practises Buddhism at home instead of being a monk in a temple.
* Chu Yang: Chu Yang (395 B.C.- 335 B.C.), a great philosopher in the Warring States period, who advocated the thoughts of Laocius and Sir Lush. Opposite to Sir Ink, the founder of Inkism and proponent of universal love, Chu Yang put stress on keeping to one's nature. When Chu Yang came to a crossroads, unable to decide which road to take, he thought of the crossroads in life and wept for any carelessness that might lead to a wrong path.
* Great Truth: a Wordist term meaning nirvana or nature in its own sense. As is exclaimed in *Sir Lush*, "O my, Sir Mulberry! O my, Sir Mulberry! You've turned back to nature while we are still human."
* oriole: golden oriole, one of the family of passerine birds, which looks bright yellow with contrasting black wings and sings beautiful songs.
* magpie: a corvine bird, having a long and graduated tail, which often makes loud chirps.
* the moon: the satellite of the earth, a representation of feminity in contrast with the sun, a presentation of masculinity. In a universe animated by the interaction of Shade (female) and Shine (male) energies, the moon is literally Shade visible.
* Darklow: a Wordist hermit in the Spring and Autumn period, living a poor but pure life, rejecting worldly values.
* Shanfu: Father Shan, who lived in what is now Shanfu, Shantung Province after he declined Lord Mound's offer of the throne.

夏日过青龙寺谒操禅师

龙钟一老翁，
徐步谒禅宫。
欲问义心义，
遥知空病空。
山河天眼里，
世界法身中。
莫怪销炎热，
能生大地风。

Paying Respects to Zen Master Zen Holder at Blue Dragon Fane on a Summer's Day

A senile old man totters here
To pay his respects to the fane.
If you ask what's a heart in heart,
You'd know a pain is free of pain.
All on earth is in Heaven's eye;
Inside Dharma the whole world lies.
You may wonder heat can be cool,
Because from the land wind may rise.

* Zen: a kind of performance of quietude in a form of meditation or contemplation. When Sanskrit jana was spread to China, it was translated as Zan or Zen for this kind of practice. Many educated Chinese in the T'ang dynasty were associated with Zen monks and spent much time in Zen monasteries.
* Dharma: the ideal state of truth and righteousness in Buddhist terms.

和太常韦主簿五郎温汤寓目之作

汉主离宫接露台,
秦川一半夕阳开。
青山尽是朱旗绕,
碧涧翻从玉殿来。
新丰树里行人度,
小苑城边猎骑回。
闻道甘泉能献赋,
悬知独有子云才。

In Reply to Wei Five, Deputy Governor of Rite Department, Who Tours Hotspring

The Detached Palace with Dew Mound combines;
Half of Ch'in opes to the eve sun that shines.
Scarlet flags surround the green mountains all;
A lucid creek gurgles down from Jade Hall.
In Newrich trees travelers walk up and down;
Hunters come back from nearby the small town.
Like Yang you can write *Sweet Spring* for our Lord;
How could a talent like him be ignored?

* Dew Mound: the name of an observatory.
* Ch'in: Ch'in (221 B.C.– 207 B.C.), the first unified empire in Chinese history founded by the State of Ch'in in the late Warring States period.
* Jade Hall: referring to Floral Clean Palace with an allusion to two lines of an old poem: Bright gold is your gate; white jade is your hall.
* Newrich: a county, in today's Lintung County, Sha'anhsi Province. It was built by

Pang Liu in imitation of his hometown Rich County in the east of China when Liu came into power and was famous for its wine, the best wine in the T'ang dynasty.

* Yang: Man Yang (53 B.C.- A.D. 18), Hsiung Yang if transliterated, born in Silkton, present-day Chengt'u, Ssuch'uan, a great scholar, rhymed prose writer and official in the Han dynasty. His *The Great One* is a masterpiece, a literary genre between verse and prose, which can be termed as euph (a coinage based on euphuism and euphemism); it has had a deep influence on works of later generations. According to *History of the Han Dynasty*, when other officials flattered those in power, only Man Yang kept to himself to write his philosophy work, *The Great One*.
* *Sweet Spring*: a piece of prose composed by Man Yang, one of the representative works on Han palaces.

奉和圣制暮春送朝集使归郡应制

万国仰宗周，
衣冠拜冕旒。
玉乘迎大客，
金节送诸侯。
祖席倾三省，
褰帷向九州。
杨花飞上路，
槐色荫通沟。
来预钧天乐，
归分汉主忧。
宸章类河汉，
垂象满中州。

In Reply to Your Majesty's Call to Follow Your Majesty's Poem: Seeing Off Finance Reporters Back to Their Prefectures in Late Spring

All worship our capital town,
And come to pay respects to Crown.
For grandees the jade inlet way;
For vassals the gold tally ray.
Banquets the highest peers attend;
Tents with shades far away extend.
Catkins over the broad way float;
Locust green decorates the moat.
Celestial music moves the air;

Your Majesty's cares all will share.
Your poem shines like a star above,
Filling the whole land with your love.

* capital town: referring to Long Peace, the metropolis of gold, the largest walled city ever built by man, with 1,000,000 inhabitants, the center of world religions, Buddhism, Confucianism, Wordism, Nestorianism, Zoroastrianism, and even Islamism represented by Saracens, and the center of education — There were colleges of various grades and special institutes for calligraphy, arithmetic, music, astronomy and so on.
* gold tally: a tally granted to a vassal lord. According to *Rites of Chough*, tiger tallies are granted to lords of mountainous vassal states, human tallies to lords of plain vassal states and dragon tallies to lords of moorland vassal vassal states, all made of gold.
* catkin: a deciduous scaly spike of flowers, as in the willow, an image of helpless drifting or wandering in Chinese literature.
* locust: a tree of the bean family widely distributed in the temperate zone, with a rough bark, odd-pinnate leaves, and loose, slender racemes of fragrant, white flowers, which are a seasonal delicacy.
* Your Majesty: referring to Deepsire (Hsuan Tsung) the emperor (A.D. 685 – A.D. 762), the ninth emperor of the T'ang dynasty. When a prince, he was regarded as wise and valiant, a sportsman accomplished in all knightly exercises and a master of all elegant arts. He established Pear Garden, an operatic school, where actors and actress were trained, and the prototype of the modern Chinese drama was developed.

冬 日 游 览

步出城东门，
试骋千里目。
青山横苍林，
赤日团平陆。
渭北走邯郸，
关东出函谷。
秦地万方会，
来朝九州牧。
鸡鸣咸阳中，
冠盖相追逐。
丞相过列侯，
群公饯光禄。
相如方老病，
独归茂陵宿。

Touring in Winter

Now going out of East Town Gate,
My eyes would gallop, gallop on.
The green hills are covered with wood;
On the vast plain hangs the red sun.
North of the Wei to Chao I go
And in east go out of Case Dale.
Ch'in's land sees barbarians come;
Nine prefectures approach to hail.
In the capital roosters crow;

Where they chase, they run and they cry.
The premier visits the vassals;
And the lords hold feasts to say bye.
Now like Hsiangju, I'm old and ill;
I would back to live by the hill.

* sun: the heavenly body that is the center of attraction and the main source of light and heat for the sustenance of the earth, a representation of Shine in contrast with Shade, the moon, in Chinese culture, a symbol of hope, life, strength, vigor and youth.
* the Wei: the Wei River: the largest branch of the Yellow River, originating from today's Mt. Birdmouse in Kansu Province, flowing through Precious Rooster, Allshine, Long Peace, and meeting the Yellow River at T'ung Pass.
* Case Dale: an ancient pass located to the east of the capital of Ch'in, and Lint'iao to the west.
* Ch'in: Ch'in (221 B.C.- 207 B.C.), the first unified empire in Chinese history founded by the State of Ch'in in the late Warring States period.
* rooster: the male of the chicken that struts with pride and crows at dawn.
* Hsiangju: Ssuma Hsiangju (179 B.C.- 118 B.C.), a representative rhymed verse writer in the Han dynasty.

奉和圣制与太子诸王三月三日龙池春禊应制

故事修春禊，
新宫展豫游。
明君移凤辇，
太子出龙楼。
赋掩陈王作，
杯如洛水流。
金人来捧剑，
画鹢去回舟。
苑树浮宫阙，
天池照冕旒。
宸章在云表，
垂象满皇州。

In Reply to Your Majesty's Call to Follow Your Majesty's Poem: Offering Spring Sacrifice at Dragon Pool with Crown Prince and Other Princes on the Third Day of the Third Moon

We offer spring sacrifice as e'er
At New Palace and at the bend.
Your Majesty takes Sedan Cart;
Crown Prince from Dragon Pool does wend.
Your prose outshines Prince of Ch'en's art;
Your cup on the Lo downstream floats.

As golden men come to play swords,
There return the bird-painted boats.
In High Park looms the palace gate;
Heaven Pool sees arrays so grand.
Your poem shimmers onto the stars
Shedding bright light all o'er the land.

* New Palace: referring to Rise-Laud Palace linked with Great Bright Palace with a suspension road.
* Dragon Pool: a pool behind Rise-Laud Palace, so named because auspicious clouds in the shape of a dragon were often seen to hang above.
* Prince of Ch'en: Chih Ts'ao (A.D. 192 – A.D. 232), styled Making, Ts'ao Ts'ao's third son, a famous litterateur, a representative of Making Peace Literature. His *Verse to Quiet Girl* has been best remembered throughout history.
* the Lo: the Lo River, which flows through the ancient capital Loshine.
* High Park: an imperial park that Lord Martial of Han built on the site of a discarded park of Ch'in. It was vast and splendid with palaces and woodlands, having various functions and recreational facilities, rolling about 340 kilometers.
* Heaven Pool: unidentified, probably a pool in High Park.

奉和圣制重阳节宰臣及群官上寿应制

四海方无事，
三秋大有年。
百工无此日，
万寿愿齐天。
芍药和金鼎，
茱萸插玳筵。
玉堂开右个，
天乐动宫悬。
御柳疏秋景，
城鸦拂曙烟。
无穷菊花节，
长奉柏梁篇。

In Reply to Your Majesty's Call to Follow Your Majesty's Poem: To My Premier and Ministers Who Wish Ourself Longevity

This autumn, we've a good harvest,
All the land at peace, calm around.
All officials observe the day;
Long live Most High, be safe and sound.
Five herbs there are in the tripod;
Cornel is placed on the feast square.
The hall has rooms on either side;
The celestial music moves the air.
The willows cast an autumn shade;

The crows caw to the dawning light.
On every Chrysanthemum Day,
Your Majesty's poems we recite.

* Ourself: when a sovereign addresses himself, He usually uses Ourself instead of "I" or "me".
* tripod: a cooking utensil or cauldron with three feet or legs, usually cast with bronze, popular in ancient China, a symbol of a powerful family.
* cornel: a kind of dogwood carried or worn on Double Ninth Day.
* willow: any of a large genus of shrubs and trees related to the poplars, having glossy green leaves resembling a girl's eye-brow, and generally having smooth branches, and often long, slender, pliant, and sometimes pendent branchlets, which seem to be waving good-bye, or weeping amorously, or drooping for nostalgia.
* crow: an omnivorous, raucous, oscine bird of the genus *Corvus*, with glossy black plumage. It is regarded as an ominous bird, a metaphor for death because it is a scavenger, feeding on carrion.
* Chrysanthemum Day: a festival on the ninth day of the ninth moon in Chinese Lunar calendar. There is a long tradition that people, wearing or taking cornel, climb a height and enjoy chrysanthemums on this day to commemorate their ancestors.
* Your Majesty: referring to Deepsire (Hsuan Tsung) the emperor (A.D. 685 – A.D. 762), the ninth emperor of the T'ang dynasty. When a prince, he was regarded as wise and valiant, a sportsman accomplished in all knightly exercises and a master of all elegant arts. He established Pear Garden, an operatic school, where actors and actresses were trained, and the prototype of the modern Chinese drama was developed.

三月三日勤政楼侍宴应制

彩仗连宵合,
琼楼拂曙通。
年光三月里,
宫殿百花中。
不数秦王日,
谁将洛水同。
酒筵嫌落絮,
舞袖怯春风。
天保无为德,
人欢不战功。
仍临九衢宴,
更达四门聪。

Waiting upon Your Majesty at the Feast in Administration Hall the Third Day of the Third Moon

The guards of honor stay till night;
The jade palace greets dawning light.
The third moon we enjoy best hours;
Court and palace are hemmed by flowers.
King of Ch'in had not such a day;
Who could, drinking, in the Lo play?
A banquet does catkins detest;
A dancer hates her sleeves wind-pressed.
Heaven likes non-action in deed;

One who does not fight will succeed.
The Broad Way feast on, glad all are.
The Four Gates can hear from afar.

* Ch'in: the Ch'in State or the State of Ch'in (905 B.C.- 206 B.C.), one of the most powerful vassal states in the Chough dynasty, which developed into enfeoffed as a dependency of Chough by King Piety of Chough in 905 B.C. and enfeoffed as a vassal state by King Peace of Chough in 770 B.C. In the ten years from 230 B.C. to 221 B.C., Ch'in wiped out the other six powers and became the first unified regime of China, i.e., the Ch'in Empire.
* the Lo: the Lo River that flows through Loshine.
* non-action: the attitude and practice of quietism advocated by Laocius, as is said in *The Word and the World* — Therefore, the sages leave things as they are. They teach without inculcation, let things arise instead of raising them; they work without deliberation, achieve without crediting themselves; just because they do not credit themselves, they have nothing to lose.
* the Broad Way: the street that leads to all directions.
* the Four Gates: referring to the four directions.

奉和圣制赐史供奉曲江宴应制

侍从有邹枚，
琼筵就水开。
言陪柏梁宴，
新下建章来。
对酒山河满，
移舟草树回。
天文同丽日，
驻景惜行杯。

In Reply to Your Majesty's Call to Follow Your Majesty's Poem: the Inspector Attending a Feast at the Bend

Like Ts'ou and Mei I serve Most High;
A feast by water I attend.
At Cypress Banquet I serve well,
And oft from Chapter Hall descend.
Towards the mountains we drink deep;
Out of the trees some boats appear.
Your poems outshine the stars bright;
In the shade, we drink with more cheer.

* Ts'ou and Mei: Yang Ts'ou and Ch'eng Mei, lobbyists in the early Han dynasty.
* Cypress Banquet: a symposium with wine placed on Cypress Mound, where a poetry competition was often held under the orders of an emperor, and a seven-word-line

poems were favored.
* Chapter Hall: name of a magnificent Han palace built in 104 B.C.; it's probably a metaphor in this poem for Great Bright Palace.

奉和圣制十五夜然灯继以酺宴应制

上路笙歌满，
春城漏刻长。
游人多昼日，
明月让灯光。
鱼钥通翔凤，
龙舆出建章。
九衢陈广乐，
百福透名香。
仙伎来金殿，
都人绕玉堂。
定应偷妙舞，
从此学新妆。
奉引迎三事，
司仪列万方。
愿将天地寿，
同以献君王。

In Reply to Your Majesty's Call to Follow Your Majesty's Poem: Viewing Lanterns on the Fifteenth Night and Granting a Feast

A flute song fills the royal way;
The hourglass runs in the spring town.
The spectators enjoy their day;
The moon yields to the lanterns down.

Phoenix Hall opes with a fish key;
You leave Chapter in Sedan Cart.
Nine Thoroughfares are live with glee;
The halls are balmed for every part.
The belle singers Gold Hall entrance;
All viewers go round the hall in turn.
They will mimic their supple dance,
And how to make new clothes they'll learn.
The grandees ahead lead the way,
The guards of honor in their post.
Like Heaven and earth may you ray;
May you live long and be blessed most.

* flute: a tubular wind instrument of small diameter with holes along the side.
* hourglass: a vessel made of glass or some similar material, used for measuring time by the running of water or sand from the upper into the lower compartment, also used as metaphor for the elapse of time.
* Phoenix Hall: name of a Ch'in palace, a metaphor in this poem for a palace.
* Chapter: Chapter Hall, name of a Han palace, a metaphor in this poem probably for Great Bright Palace.
* Nine Thoroughfares: broad ways or busy streets, a sign of prosperity.
* Gold Hall: referring to the emperor's dwelling.

奉和圣制上巳于望春亭观禊饮应制

长乐青门外，
宜春小苑东。
楼开万井上，
辇过百花中。
画鹢移仙妓，
金貂列上公。
清歌邀落日，
妙舞向春风。
渭水明秦甸，
黄山入汉宫。
君王来祓禊，
灞浐亦朝宗。

In Reply to Your Majesty's Call to Follow Your Majesty's Poem: Viewing a Feast at Spring-Gazing Pavilion on the Third Day of the Third Moon

Out of Blue Gate one sees Long Glee;
East of the park you find Spring Hours.
Spring Gazing Pavilion is high;
Your cart passes a hundred flowers.
The pleasure boat carry the belles;
The grandees in mink there align.
The pure song invites the eve sun;
To spring wind they dance a dance fine.

The Wei shimmers out of the town;
Mt. Yellow tints the hall with hue.
Your Majesty cleans all the filth;
The Pa and the Ch'an flow to you.

* Blue Gate: the southern gate of the three gates on the east wall of Long Peace.
* Long Glee: name of an imperial palace, also called Spring Gazing Pavilion or Spring Gazing Palace, 4.5 kilometers from Long Peace, one of the twenty four imperial pavilion palaces in Long Peace area.
* Spring Hours: Spring Hours Palace, a detached imperial palace in Ch'in. East of the palace there was a park called Spring Hours Park.
* mink: a kind of precious fur which is soft, thick glossy, brown, from an amphibious, slender-bodied mammal called mink.
* the Wei: the Wei River: the largest branch of the Yellow River, originating from today's Mt. Birdmouse in Kansu Province, flowing through Precious Rooster, Allshine, Long Peace, and meeting the Yellow River at T'ung Pass.
* Mt. Yellow: located in Anhui Province. Mt. Yellow is one of the most famous mountains in China with natural, literary, cultural attractions, featured with wondrous pines, clouds and hotsprings. It is said that Lord Yellow used to make elixirs here.
* the Pa and the Ch'an: two rivers. The Pa originates from Blue Field Dale and flows into the Wei River northeast of Long Peace; the Ch'an River originates from the Ch'inridge hills and flows into the Pa River at the Pa Mausoleum.

登 楼 歌

聊上君兮高楼,
飞甍鳞次兮在下。
俯十二兮通衢,
绿槐参差兮车马。
却瞻兮龙首,
前眺兮宜春。
王畿郁兮千里。
山河壮兮咸秦。
舍人下兮青宫,
据胡床兮书空。
执戟疲于下位,
老夫好隐兮墙东。
亦幸有张伯英草圣兮龙腾虬跃,
摆长云兮掞回风。
琥珀酒兮雕胡饭,
君不御兮日将晚。
秋风兮吹衣,
夕鸟兮争返。
孤砧发兮东城,
林薄暮兮蝉声远。
时不可兮再得,
君何为兮偃蹇。

Song of Climbing the Tower

O on the high tower is the crown,

The ridge flies up and the eaves fly down.
He o'erlooks boulevards ten and two,
And in green locust trees carts come and go.
In the back Mt. Dragonhead towers;
In the front you can see Spring Hours.
Hundreds of miles round is capital land;
How grand mountains and rivers, how grand!
The secretary comes out of Blue Hall there;
Seated on the stool, he writes in the air.
Halberd holding, of lowness one may tire;
But me, an old man to East Wall will retire.
Fortunately, I can learn from Cursive Saint
   who writes like a dragon flies and a horse whirls,
To split clouds and stir up wind, furls and curls.
A wild rice meal o my amber wine,
It will be too late, o sit down to dine.
O autumn wind, to my clothes it blows;
O the birds flutter back with coos.
The pestling sound vibrates from East Town;
In the wood at dusk, cicadas shrill on.
Time goes away and will ne'er come back;
O man, why do you hang there, so slack?

* locust: a tree of the bean family widely distributed in the temperate zone, with a rough bark, odd-pinnate leaves, and loose, slender racemes of fragrant, white flowers, which are a seasonal delicacy.
* Mt. Dragonhead: the name of an old mountain north of Long Peace, gradually erased when palaces were built here in the Han and T'ang dynasties.
* Spring Hours: Spring Hours Palace, a detached imperial palace in Ch'in. East of the palace there was a park called Spring Hours Park.
* Blue Hall: Crown Prince's palace built with blue stone.
* stool: formerly called Hun stool, an armless and backless collapsible seat intended for

one person, introduced to China in the Han dynasty.
* East Wall: a cow market out of the east wall of the town. Chünkung Wang, a hermit in Eastern Han, once lived here as a cow market broker, therefore East Wall has been known as a place for reclusion.
* Cursive Saint: Chih Chang (? - cir. A.D. 192), a great calligrapher in Eastern Han, whose handwriting in cursive style has been regarded as the best in Chinese history.
* dragon: a fabulous serpent-like giant winged animal that can change its girth and length, a totem of the Chinese nation and a symbol of benevolence and sovereignty in Chinese culture.
* wild rice: a tall aquatic grass, what is *zizania aquatica* in Latin, the white thick stem of which is used as a vegetable and the brown or black grain of which was formerly used as food, now esteemed as a table delicacy.
* amber wine: wine looking translucent like the color of amber.
* East Town: referring to the east end of Long Peace.
* cicada: a homopterous insect that sings its song of summer and shrills in autumn, a symbol of death and resurrection in Chinese culture because of its metamorphosis and recycle. Therefore, in ancient China, a jade cicada figure was put in the mouth of a dead body with such an intention of eternal life.

送友人归山歌二首
Seeing Off My Friend Back to Hills, Two Poems

其 一

山寂寂兮无人,
又苍苍兮多木。
群龙兮满朝,
君何为兮空谷。
文寡和兮思深,
道难知兮行独。
悦石上兮流泉,
与松间兮草屋。
入云中兮养鸡,
上山头兮抱犊。
神与枣兮如瓜,
虎卖杏兮收谷。
愧不才兮妨贤,
嫌既老兮贪禄。
誓解印兮相从,
何詹尹兮可卜。

No. 1

The mountains are calm, o no soul,
Lots of trees o cover the glen.
The court o is full of courtiers;
Why o do you go fasting then?
Your art aloof, you're in deep thought;

The Word so hard, you walk alone.
Your shack is there in the pine trees
Hearing water gurgling on stone.
In Mid-Clouds roosters you will raise;
And on uphill a calf you will keep.
The dates you eat are melon-like,
And tigers help you cereals reap.
I'm worthless and may hinder sages;
I should not get wages, now old.
Give up my seal o I'll follow you!
Need my trip to hills be foretold?

* the Word: referring to Tao if transliterated, the most significant and profoundest concept of genesis or creation in Chinese philosophy. The Word is fully elucidated in *The Word and the World*, the single book that Laocius wrote all his wisdom into. Its importance can be seen in this verse: "The Word is void, but its use is infinite. O deep! It seems to be the root of all things."
* pine: a cone-bearing tree having needle-shaped evergreen leaves growing in clusters, a symbol of longevity and rectitude in Chinese culture.
* Mid-Clouds: a fairyland mid clouds, where, according to *Tales of Fairies* by Hsiang Liu, a chicken man raised chickens here for a hundred years. A thousand chickens he kept all had their name and a chicken could come to him if called.
* rooster: the male of the chicken that struts with pride and crows at dawn. The rooster is often a theme of literature, as is shown in *A Rooster in the Painting* by Pohu T'ang (A.D. 1470 – A.D. 1524), a Ming painter, "Untailored, naturally made its red crown, / The pure snow tiptoes, donning a white gown. / It dare not call, now timid as before; But at its crow all households ope their door."
* calf: the young of the cow or bull or various other bovine animals, also used as a metaphor for the young of other mammals, even humans.
* date: an oblong, sweet, fleshy fruit of the date palm, enclosing a single hard seed, a symbol of early fertility in Chinese culture.
* tiger: a large ferocious carnivorous feline mammal of Asia, with vertical black wavy stripes on a tawny body and black bars or rings on the limbs and tail, praised as king of all animals.

其 二

山中人兮欲归,
云冥冥兮雨霏霏。
水惊波兮翠菅靡,
白鹭忽兮翻飞,
君不可兮褰衣。
山万重兮一云,
混天地兮不分。
树晻暧兮氛氲,
猿不见兮空闻。
忽山西兮夕阳,
见东皋兮远村。
平芜绿兮千里,
眇惆怅兮思君。

No. 2

Go back to the hills o you would fain;
The clouds so dim o sends down a rain.
The water rushes o the thatch falls down,
Up and down there, o the herons fly,
You should not wade, o you should not try.
Ten thousand hills, o a cloud on high.
One can't tell o the earth from the sky.
The trees in the dark, o mist hangs there;
The monkeys unseen, o their cries you hear.
West of the hills o the eve sun glooms;
East of the marsh, o a village looms.
The green of wilds o spreads far away;

Missing you o, I scratch my hair gray.

* thatch: any of tall, coarse grasses (genus *Spatina*) widely distributed in temperate zones.
* heron: a long-necked and long-legged wading bird, a symbol of freedom, purity, longevity and happiness.
* monkey: any of a group of primates having elongate limbs, hands and feet adapted for grasping, and a highly developed nervous system, including marmosets, baboons, and macaques, but not the anthropoid apes, though monkeys and apes are used alternatively in Chinese.
* marsh: a tract of low, wet, soft land that is temporarily, or permanently, covered with water, characterized by aquatic grass-like vegetation. Natural places like marshes, moors, hills, rivers, seas and so on are often mentioned as places for reclusion in Chinese culture.

叹 白 发

我年一何长，
鬓发日已白。
俯仰天地间，
能为几时客。
怅惘故山云，
徘徊空日夕。
何事与时人，
东城复南陌。

Sighing to My Gray Hair

Into my late years I advance;
My hair day after day grows gray.
Looking up and down in this world,
How long can one on the earth stay?
I sigh to the clouds o'er the hills;
To the eve sun I pace to and fro.
Why should I go along with them?
From east they come, to south they go!

送李太守赴上洛

商山包楚邓，
积翠蔼沉沉。
驿路飞泉洒，
关门落照深。
野花开古戍，
行客响空林。
板屋春多雨，
山城昼欲阴。
丹泉通虢略，
白羽抵荆岑。
若见西山爽，
应知黄绮心。

Seeing Off Prefect Li to His Position in Shanglo

Mt. Shang does Ch'u and Teng compass;
Green and greener grows the spring grass.
On your way you find fountains flow;
Into High Pass the sun does glow.
Flowers blow by the garrison old;
Passengers stir the wood, behold.
The plank huts receive heavy rain;
The hill town's dimmed once and again.
Red Fountain leads on to Kuo's bound;
White Plumage links up with Mt. Crowned.

The cool West Mountains if you'll greet,
You should go there and Four Sages meet.

* Shanglo: once named Shangchow, a shire in the T'ang dynasty, and a district in present-day Shanglo, Sha'anhsi Province.
* Mt. Shang: the southern hills where dwelt the Four Old Men, four Wordist hermits, who were invited as Pang Liu's imperial advisors, that is, a think tank for the House of Han.
* Ch'u and Teng: the area belonging to the State of Ch'u and the State of Teng. Tengchow in today's Honan Province was a town under Ch'u, and Teng, in today's Hupei Province, was a vassal state of Chough subjugated by Ch'u in 678 B.C.
* High Pass: probably the pass at Mt. High southeast of today's Blue Field, Sha'anhsi Province.
* sun: the heavenly body that is the center of attraction and the main source of light and heat in the solar system, a representation of Shine in contrast with Shade, the moon, in Chinese culture, a symbol of hope, life, strength, vigor and youth.
* Red Fountain: name of a county in Ch'in and Han dynasties.
* Kuo: referring to the State of West Kuo (? – A.D. 655), a vassal state enfeoffed to Kuo Three, King Civil's brother as a buttress of Chough against possible barbarian invasions.
* White Plumage: name of an old place in today's West Gorge, Honan Province.
* Mt. Crowned: Mt. Chaste, where Ho Pien found the famous crude jade, in today Hu Pei Province.
* the cool West Mountains: a term borrowed from *Thus Speaks the World* (Shi Shuo Hsinyü).
* Four Sages: Four Gray Heads, that is, the four old Wordist hermits living at Mt. Shang. They were invited as a think tank for the House of Han in the 3rd century B.C. They withdrew from the world at the end of the reign of Emperor First of Ch'in and were welcomed and venerated by the new emperor of Han.

送熊九赴任安阳

魏国应刘后，
寂寥文雅空。
漳河如旧日，
之子继清风。
阡陌铜台下，
闾阎金虎中。
送车盈灞上，
轻骑出关东。
相去千馀里，
西园明月同。

Seeing off Hsiung Nine to His Position in Peaceshine

After Kingdom of Way's best time,
Literature did lose its prime.
The Chang River is clear as e'er,
I hope you'll follow the pure air.
All roads leads to Bronze Sparrow Tower;
All lanes before Gold Tiger cower.
To Pa Mouth I see off your cart;
The horses from Pass East depart.
Hundreds of miles away from here,
West Garden sees the same moon clear.

* Peaceshine: Peaceshine, Anyang if transliterated, in today's Honan Province.

* Kingdom of Way's best time: referring to the flourish of literature, which ended with Yang Ying and Chen Liu, the two famous litterateurs in Kingdom of Way (A.D. 213 - A.D. 266), one of the three kingdoms in the Three Kingdoms period.
* the Chang River: the Limpid Chang and the Turbid Chang meet at She in today Hopei Province, hence the Chang River.
* Bronze Sparrow Tower: a tower built by Ts'ao Ts'ao.
* Gold Tiger: Gold Tiger Tower south of Bronze Sparrow Tower.
* Pa Mouth: the mouth of the River Pa east of Long Peace.
* Pass East: the area east of Case Dale Pass.
* West Garden: a term borrowed from Chih Ts'ao's lines, which read: His Highness does love to play host; / The feast over, he's still with zest./ At night, in the Western Garden, / They drive around, crest after crest.

送张判官赴河西

单车曾出塞，
报国敢邀勋。
见逐张征虏，
今思霍冠军。
沙平连白雪，
蓬卷入黄云。
慷慨倚长剑，
高歌一送君。

Seeing Off Judge Chang to His Position in Hohsi

On the frontier you used to drive
Not for ranks but our land to thrive.
Out there, like Beatfoe Chang you fought;
In here, like General Huo you thought.
The great desert sees white snow fly,
While thistledown's blown to the sky.
Thrusting with my sword I sigh long;
For farewell, I chant you a song.

* Beatfoe Chang: Flying Chang (cir. A.D. 166 - A.D. 221), Prefect of Eeton, and Beatfoe General of the Kingdom of Shu, a brave fighter known for his bravery and loyalty in the Three Kingdom period.
* General Huo: P'iaoyao Huo (140 B.C.- 117 B.C.) or Swift Huo, a renowned general, prominent strategist and patriotic hero in the Han dynasty. He made his first show at 17, leading 800 fierce cavalrymen to penetrate the enemy lines and defeat the Huns.

Swift fought against the Huns in three major wars and each time returned with victory. He died of a disease at 24, leaving his achievements as the highest glory for Chinese military commanders.

* thistledown: the pappus of a thistle, which is a prickly plant with cylindrical or globular heads of tubular purple flowers or the ripe silky fibers from the dry flower of a thistle. It is a common metaphor for drifting or wandering of an aimless vagrant.

送宇文三赴河西充行军司马

横吹杂繁笳，
边风卷塞沙。
还闻田司马，
更逐李轻车。
蒲类成秦地，
莎车属汉家。
当令犬戎国，
朝聘学昆邪。

Seeing Off Yüwen Three to His Post as a Vice Commander

Hsiao and flute are mixed, like a band;
Sand's whirled up in the borderland.
As Commander Tien you admire,
For Charioteer Li you aspire.
Of Ch'in Cattail has now become;
Shache to Han's Empire will succumb.
You should make barbarians and Huns
Come to worship Lord like conquered ones.

* Yüwen Three: unidentified.
* *Hsiao*: a flute-like wind instrument, played vertically held in hands.
* flute: a tubular wind instrument of small diameter with holes along the side.
* Commander Tien: Kuangming Tien, a general in the Han dynasty, a metaphor for Yüwen Three.
* Charioteer Li: Ts'ai Li, Broad Li's cousin, a Cavalry general in the Han dynasty.

* Cattail: an ancient state in the western regions, near Barkol Lake in today's New Land (Hsinchiang).
* Shache: a Hun kingdom west of China in the Han dynasty.
* Han's Empire: the powerful Han Empire (202 B.C.- A.D. 220) founded by Pang Liu.
* Hun: a nationality that has the same origin as Chinese. In approximately 16th century B.C., a branch of the Hsia family fled to the north and annexed other tribes, hence the formation of the Hun nationality.

送 韦 评 事

欲逐将军取右贤，
沙场走马向居延。
遥知汉使萧关外，
愁见孤城落日边。

Seeing Off Judge Wei

You'd follow the general to catch Right Sage
To Chüyan the desert you gallop down.
I know afar you're now out of Hsiao Pass,
Watching the sun set by the lonely town.

* Right Sage: Prince of Right Sage in full, a title conferred upon Hun nobles. Left Sage, Right Sage, Left Dale Pest, Right Dale Pest and so on (24 all together) are titles of Hun nobility. Left Sage or Prince of Left Sage is the highest, usually conferred upon a crown prince.
* Chüyan: also known as Chüyan Town or Chüyan Sea, in today's Inner Mongolia, 80 kilometers from Ope-arms, that is, today's Changyeh, Kansu Province.
* Hsiao Pass: name of an old pass, in today's Firm Plain (Kuyüan), Ninghsia Hui's Autonomous Region.

送刘司直赴安西

绝域阳关道，
胡沙与塞尘。
三春时有雁，
万里少行人。
苜蓿随天马，
蒲桃逐汉臣。
当令外国惧，
不敢觅和亲。

Seeing Off Justice Liu to Pacified West

The Sun Pass road rolls far and far,
Full of border dust and Hun sand.
Only a few wild geese in spring,
And few people on the vast land.
Clover, Pegasus and grape seed
Will be carried back to Mid-plain.
This will deter the aliens much
From imposing marriage again.

* Pacified West: a military and political institution or a protectorate set up in the town of Link River in Turpan in A.D. 640 to pacify and govern the west regions of China.
* Sun Pass: name of an old pass in today's Tunhuang, Kansu Province, an important gateway to the western regions like Jade Gate Pass.
* Hun: war-like nomadic peoples occupying vast regions from Mongolia to Central Asia in Chinese history, especially during the Han dynasty. They were a constant menace on China's western and northern borders.

* wild goose: an undomesticated goose that is caring and responsible, taken as a symbol of benevolence, righteousness, good manner, wisdom and faith in Chinese culture.
* clover: any of several species of plants (genus *Trifolium*) of the legume family, having dense flower heads and the leaves divided into three leaflets, introduced to China from west of China by Chien Chang (164 B.C.- 114 B.C.) in the Han dynasty.
* Pegasus: a kind of horse from west of China, usually with wings in fairy tales, also known as sky-horse. In many cases it is used as a metaphor for a fine horse.
* grape: any grapevine yielding grapes, smooth-skinned, edible, juicy, berrylike fruit, introduced to China by Chien Chang (164 B.C.- 114 B.C.) in the Han dynasty.

送平淡然判官

不识阳关路，
新从定远侯。
黄云断春色，
画角起边愁。
瀚海经年到，
交河出塞流。
须令外国使，
知饮月氏头。

Seeing Off Judge Tanran P'ing

As Lord Far Pacifier was placed,
The way to Sun Pass one does know.
Yellow clouds eclipse the spring hue;
A painted horn stirs up your woe.
It takes years to reach the desert,
Where the Link out the pass does flow.
One can drink out of a Scyths's skull,
Envoys from all countries should know.

* Sun Pass: name of an old pass in today's Tunhuang, Kansu Province, an important gateway to the western regions like Jade Gate Pass.
* Lord Far Pacifier: referring to Ch'ao Pan (A.D. 32 – A.D. 102), a general-governor in the Eastern Han dynasty (A.D. 25 – A.D. 220), who pacified more than 50 kingdoms in the west regions within 31 years, hence entitled Lord Far Pacifier.
* the Link: the River River, the river flowing around the ancient town called Link River, built by a king of Jushi, in today Turpan, New Land (Hsinchiang), 8,150 li,

i.e. 4,075 kilometers from Long Peace, T'ang's capital.

* Scyths: the name of a state in the Western Regions during the Han Dynasty and the people of the state, who were nomadic and known as fiercely savage.

送元二使安西

渭城朝雨浥轻尘，
客舍青青柳色新。
劝君更尽一杯酒，
西出阳关无故人。

Seeing Off My Friend Yüan Two to Pacified West as an Envoy

Dust in the town choked with a morning rain,
The inn looks blue 'mid new weeping willows.
Have one more cup of wine I do maintain;
West of Sun Pass you have no old fellows.

* Pacified West: a military and political institution, a protectorate, set up in the town of Link River in Turpan in A.D. 640 to pacify and govern the west regions of China.
* willow: any of a large genus of shrubs and trees related to the poplars, widely distributed in China and most of the world, having glossy green leaves resembling a girl's eye-brow, and generally having smooth branches, and often long, slender, pliant, and sometimes pendent branchlets, which seem to be waving good-bye, or weeping amorously, or drooping for nostalgia.
* Sun Pass: name of an old pass in today's Tunhuang, Kansu Province, an important gateway to the western regions like Jade Gate Pass.

相　　思

红豆生南国，
春来发几枝。
愿君多采撷，
此物最相思。

The Love Bean

The red bean grows in Southern Land.
How many twigs shoot forth in spring?
Pray pick, pick more to fill your hand;
To speak for love, 'tis the best thing.

* the red bean: a kind of red seed produced by ormosia in tropical and subtropical southern areas, a symbol of love.
* Southern Land: an area south of the lower reaches of the Long River or the old name of today's Nanchung, a city under Ssuch'uan Province.

伊 州 歌

清风明月苦相思，
荡子从戎十载馀。
征人去日殷勤嘱，
归雁来时数附书。

An Eechow Song

Wind chill, moon clear, I feel drear.
I've fought out many a year.
When I left home, lots of words:
Send me news with homing birds.

* Eechow: a prefecture instituted in the Sui dynasty in A.D. 584, modern-day Hami, New Land (Hsinchiang).
* moon clear: an image of solitude and purity in Chinese culture.
* Send me news with homing birds: Birds like doves and wild geese are metonymy for letters or messengers in ancient China. Pang Liu, when besieged by Overlord Hsiang, used a dove as a messenger so that he was saved as legend goes. And Ch'ien Chang and Ch'ao Pan also used doves to send letters to the court when they were envoys of Han in the West Regions.

辋川集二十首

A Rimriver Collection, Twenty Poems

余别业在辋川山谷,其游止有孟城坳、华子冈、文杏馆、斤竹岭、鹿柴、木兰柴、茱萸沜、宫槐陌、临湖亭、南垞、欹湖、柳浪、栾家濑、金屑泉、白石滩、北垞、竹里馆、辛夷坞、漆园、椒园等,与裴迪闲暇,各赋绝句云尔。

My villa is in Rimriver Valley, where one can stroll places such as Meng's Planeton, Floral Mound, Ginkgo Pavilion, Axe Bamboo Ridge, the Deer Fence, the Magnolia Fence, the Cornel Riverside, Palace Locust Lane, the Lakeside Pavilion, the South Mound, Bed-tilting Lake, Willows Wave, the Gushing Rapids, Gold Dust Spring, the White Gravel Shoal, the North Mound, Bamboo Grove Villa, the Lily Magnolia Grove, the Lacquer Garden and the Prickly-ash Garden. When I idle my time with Ti P'ei, we both write quatrains about them.

孟城坳

新家孟城口，
古木馀衰柳。
来者复为谁？
空悲昔人有。

Meng's Planeton

To Meng's Planeton I've newly moved,
Old woods forlorn, willows down cast.
Who will come next to take my place?
In vain I mourn the one long past!

* Meng's Planeton: Meng was an old town built at a pass, also called Willow Town, and Meng's Planeton was a plane ground in the hills near the town, in today's Blue Field County, Sha'anhsi Province.
* willow: any of a large genus of shrubs and trees related to the poplars, having generally smooth branches, and often long, slender, pliant, and sometimes pendent branchlets, a symbol of farewell or nostalgia in Chinese culture. The best image is in *Vetch We Pick*, a verse in *The Book of Songs*, which is like this: When we left long ago, / The willows waved adieu. / Now back to our home town, / We meet snow falling down.

华子冈

飞鸟去不穷,
连山复秋色。
上下华子冈,
惆怅情何极。

Floral Mound

The warblers fly away non-stop,
Autumn hue dyes the mountaintop.
Up and down, it's all Floral Mound;
My sadness stretches with no bound.

* Floral Mound: a peak of Mt. Rimriver (Wangch'uan) named after the Rim River, a beautiful mountain about 5 kilometers from Blue Field (Lant'ien) County under taday's Shanhsi Province.

文杏馆

文杏裁为梁，
香茅结为宇。
不知栋里云，
去作人间雨。

Ginkgo Pavilion

Of ginkgo wood the beam is made;
With balmy thatch the roof is laid.
The clouds inside it, you don't know
Make a rain to the world below.

* Ginkgo Pavilion: one of the several pavilions with railings on the southeast mountainside of Mt. Rimriver (Wangch'uan).
* ginkgo: a deciduous resinous tree (*Ginkgo biloba*), native in China, but cultivated in the United States for its fanlike foliage; the maidenhair tree, regarded as the only surviving member of a family that have flourished millions of years ago, during the time of the dinosaurs.
* balmy thatch: a kind of thatch of the genus *Spartina*, which gives off a smell of balm, growing mainly in the Hsiang River, the Long River and the Huai River areas.

斤竹岭

檀栾映空曲，
青翠漾涟漪。
暗入商山路，
樵人不可知。

Axe Bamboo Ridge

O'er there the bamboo sways so lush,
Stirring the green ripples to rush.
From here to Mt. Shang one may go,
A place woodcutters may not know.

* Axe Bamboo Ridge: a mountain where axe bamboo grows in the southern part of Mt. Rimriver.
* bamboo: a tall, tree-like or shrubby grass in tropical and semi-tropical regions, a symbol of integrity and altitude, one of the four most important botanical images in Chinese literature, which are wintersweet, orchid, bamboo and chrysanthemum. Bamboo shoots, fresh or dried, are widely used in Chinese cuisine, bamboo rats and bamboo worms are regarded as table delicacies.
* Mt. Shang: a mountain where the Four Grey Heads, Pang Liu's royal think tank, once lived in reclusion, in today's Shanglo, Sha'anhsi Province.

鹿　柴

空山不见人，
但闻人语响。
返景入深林，
复照青苔上。

The Deer Fence

In the mountains no one is found,
But his voice is heard to resound.
The deep wood sees the returned sun;
Once again the green moss is shone.

* the Deer Fence: probably a pen where deer are kept in a hill wood.
* moss: a tiny, delicate green bryophytic plant growing on damp decaying wood, wet ground, humid rocks or trees, producing capsules which open by an operculum and contain spores. Under a poet's writing brush, it may stir up a poetic feeling or imagination, as was written by Mei Yüan, a poet in the Ching dynasty: "Where the sun does not arrive, /Springtime does on its own thrive. / The moss flowers like rice tiny, / Rush to bloom like the peony."

木兰柴

秋山敛馀照,
飞鸟逐前侣。
彩翠时分明,
夕岚无处所。

The Magnolia Fence

The autumn hills keeps afterglow;
The warblers chase their mates ahead.
The peaks their greenness fully show;
The mist at dusk has far-off fled.

* the Magnolia Fence: a magnolia grove with a fence, close to Axe Bamboo Ridge. Magnolia is any of a genus (*Magnolia*) of trees or shrubs with large, fragrant and usually showy flowers.

茱萸沜

结实红且绿，
复如花更开。
山中傥留客，
置此芙蓉杯。

The Cornel Riverside

The cornel bears fruit red and green;
As if the flowers burst once again.
I'll put their seeds in lotus cups
If in the hills my friends remain.

* cornel: a kind of dogwood carried or worn on Double Ninth Day, as it can exorcize evil spirits, as is traditionally believed.
* lotus: one of the various plants of the waterlily family, noted for their large floating round leaves and showy pink or white flowers, a symbol of purity and elegance in Chinese culture, as is often praised as "unsoiled though out of soil, so clean with all leaves green".

宫槐陌

仄径荫宫槐，
幽阴多绿苔。
应门但迎扫，
畏有山僧来。

Palace Locust Lane

The path's shaded by locust trees;
The shaded is thick with moss green.
Afraid mountain monks may come on,
The door keeper sweeps it so clean.

* Palace Locust Lane: a road lined with locust trees planted on either side, which leads from the palace to Bed-tilting Lake.
* locust: a tree of the bean family widely distributed in the temperate zone, with a rough bark, odd-pinnate leaves, and loose, slender racemes of fragrant, white flowers, which are a seasonal delicacy.
* moss: a tiny, delicate bryophytic plant growing on damp decaying wood, ground, rocks or trees, producing capsules which open by an operculum and contain spores. Under a poet's writing brush, insignificant it may be, it may arouse a poetic feeling or imagination.

临湖亭

轻舸迎上客，
悠悠湖上来。
当轩对樽酒，
四面芙蓉开。

The Lakeside Pavilion

My yacht meeting my honored guest
Rows along on the lake at ease.
In the pavilion we sit to drink
While the lotus flowers burst to please.

* the Lakeside Pavilion: the pavilion on the shore of Bed-tilting Lake.
* yacht: a small vessel specially built or fitted for private pleasure excursions.
* lotus flower: a flower pink or white of one of the various plants of the waterlily family, a symbol of purity and elegance in Chinese culture, often praised as "unsoiled though out of soil, so clean with all leaves green".

南 垞

轻舟南垞去，
北垞淼难即。
隔浦望人家，
遥遥不相识。

The South Mound

My yacht rows on to the south mound,
To the north mound it's hard to row.
I crane to gaze across the shoal
At the neighborhood I don't know.

* the south mound: referring to a mountain village on the south shore of Bed-tilting Lake.
* yacht: a small boat specially built or fitted for private pleasure excursions, distinguished from a cargo or warship.

欹 湖

吹箫凌极浦，
日暮送夫君。
湖上一回首，
山青卷白云。

Bed-tilting Lake

At dusk I bid my friend good-bye,
Playing the flute toward the shoal.
On the lake I cast back my eye,
Over the green hills white clouds roll.

* Bed-tilting Lake: a natural lake caused by floods from Mt. Rimriver, having run dry now.
* flute: a tubular wind instrument of small diameter with holes along the side.

柳 浪

分行接绮树，
倒影入清漪。
不学御沟上，
春风伤别离。

Willows Wave

The gorgeous willows stand in line
Cast their shade onto ripples there.
Unlike those by the royal trench,
They don't wave their departing care.

* Willows Wave: the name of a willow grove by Bed-tilting Lake.
* willow: any of a large genus of shrubs and trees related to the poplars, widely distributed in China and most of the world, having glossy green leaves resembling a girl's eye-brow, and generally having smooth branches, and often long, slender, pliant, and sometimes pendent branchlets, which seem to be waving good-bye, or weeping amorously, or drooping for nostalgia. The best image is in Vetch We Pick, a verse in *The Book of Songs*, which is like this: When we left long ago, / The willows waved adieu. / Now back to our home town, / We meet snow falling down.
* the royal trench: referring to Royal Trench, also known as Willow Trench or Forbidden Trench flowing from the Southern Hills and through the palace complex in Long Peace.

栾家濑

飒飒秋雨中,
浅浅石溜泻。
跳波自相溅,
白鹭惊复下。

The Gushing Rapids

Soughing, soughing, the autumn rain,
Shallow, shallow, the brook on stone.
The waves run with a splashing tone;
The heron shocked alights again.

* the Gushing Rapids: a section of rapids of the Rim River originating from Mt. Rimriver.
* heron: a long-necked and long-legged crane-like wading bird, feeding on fish, a symbol of freedom, purity, longevity and happiness.

金屑泉

日饮金屑泉，
少当千馀岁。
翠凤翊文螭，
羽节朝玉帝。

Gold Dust Spring

A drink from Gold Dust Spring a day,
A thousand years younger you grow.
On Green Phoenix or Striped Dragon,
To worship Jade Emperor you go.

* Gold Dust Spring: a natural spring in a dale of Mt. Rimriver (Wangch'uan).
* Green Phoenix: a phoenix an immortal rides in fairy tales.
* Striped Dragon: a hornless striped dragon, an immortal's guard.
* Jade Emperor: formally called Celestial Supreme Utmost Natural Wonderful Encompassing Truest Jade Emperor at Gold Gate, the deity with highest power in Chinese mythology and Wordist literature.

白石滩

清浅白石滩，
绿蒲向堪把。
家住水东西，
浣纱明月下。

The White Gravel Shoal

Flow clear, so white the pebbles seem;
The sedge springs up, a greenish sight.
The girls who live nearby the stream
Wash linen under the moon bright.

* the White Gravel Shoal: a shoal in the Rim River with white gravel or pebbles on it.
* sedge: a grasslike cyperaceous herb with flowers densely clustered in spikes; widely distributed in marshy places.
* linen: things made of linen which is yarn, thread or cloth made of flax, or of cotton, etc., as shirts, tablecoths, sheets, etc.
* the moon: the satellite of the earth, a representative of shade or feminity of things, alluding to the belle in this poem. In a universe animated by the interaction of Shade and Shine energies, the moon is Shade visible, the very germ or source of Shade, and the sun is its Shine counterpart. The moon is celebrated with mooncakes in China on Mid-autumn Day when the moon is at its full glory.

北 垞

北垞湖水北,
杂树映朱栏。
迤逦南川水,
明灭青林端。

The North Mound

The North Mound is north of the lake;
Mixed trees shade the red balustrade.
The south river zigzags down south,
Shimmering to the emerald glade.

* the North Mound: a knoll north of Bed-tilting Lake.
* emerald glade: a clearing or open space in a luxuriant wood. Natural places like coves, glades, hills, moors, rivers, mounts and seas, and so on often allude to reclusion in Chinese culture.

竹里馆

独坐幽篁里，
弹琴复长啸。
深林人不知，
明月来相照。

Bamboo Grove Villa

'Midst the bamboos I sit alone,
Plucking my lute and chanting free.
This grove is to the world unknown;
The moon comes to illustrate me.

* Bamboo Grove Villa: a villa in a bamboo grove at Mt. Rimriver (Wangch'uan).
* bamboo: a tall, tree-like or shrubby grass in tropical and semi-tropical regions, a symbol of integrity and altitude.
* lute: a Chinese lute, a stringed musical instrument, usually placed on a table, played by plucking the strings with fingers or a plectrum.
* the moon: the satellite of the earth, a symbol of solitude and purity and sometimes nostalgia in Chinese literature. The moon is celebrated with mooncakes in China on Mid-autumn Day when the moon is at its full glory.

辛夷坞

木末芙蓉花,
山中发红萼。
涧户寂无人,
纷纷开且落。

The Lily Magnolia Grove

Like lotus buds red on spays,
Uphill lily magnolias flower.
By the creek there's no human trace
But blossoms burst and petals shower.

* lily magnolia: also known as magnolia wood with blooms looking like lotus flowers, pink, purple or white.
* lotus: one of the various plants of the waterlily family, noted for their large floating round leaves and pink or white showy flowers, used as a religious symbol in Hinduism and Buddhism. The lotus is a common image in Chinese literature, as two lines of a lyric by Hsiu Ouyang (A.D. 1007 - A.D. 1072) read: "A thunder brings rain to the wood and pool, / The rain hushes the lotus, drips cool." It is a symbol of purity and elegance in Chinese culture, unsoiled though out of soil, so clean with all leaves green. And because of this, it has become a symbol of Buddhist enlightenment, which requires an alienation from the dust and noise of the world.

漆　园

古人非傲吏，
自阙经世务。
偶寄一微官，
婆娑数株树。

The Lacquer Garden

The man of yore was not defiant
But did not know how to rule well.
A low official he would be,
And by a few trees did he dwell.

* lacquer: a lacquer tree of China and Japan, from which resinous varnish can be extracted.
* The man of yore was not defiant: an allusion to Sir Lush (cir. 369 B.C.- 286 B.C.), who was once a lacquer garden manager. Detached from worldly affairs, he declined King Power of Ch'u's invitation to be the prime minister of Ch'u.

椒 园

桂尊迎帝子，
杜若赠佳人。
椒浆奠瑶席，
欲下云中君。

The Prickly-ash Garden

A cinnamon cup for Princess,
The life-flo for a lady fair.
Prickly-ash wine for a grand feast
That pleased the lord above the air.

* cinnamon cup: a cup made of cinnamon, which is the aromatic inner bark of any of several tropical trees of the laurel family.
* Princess: referring to Mound's daughter, also called Lady Hsiang.
* life-flo: a perennial grass of the genus *Pollia*, *Pollia japonica Thunb* in Latin, widely distributed in China, Japan and South Korea.
* prickly-ash: either of two shrubs or trees (genus *Zanthoxylum*) of the rue family, with pinnately compound leaves having paired spines on the base and small berry-like seeds used as condiment.

辋川闲居赠裴秀才迪

寒山转苍翠，
秋水日潺湲。
倚杖柴门外，
临风听暮蝉。
渡头馀落日，
墟里上孤烟。
复值接舆醉，
狂歌五柳前。

To Showcharm P'ei from My Villa in Rimriver

The cold mountains deeper green grow;
The autumn rills more slowly flow.
By my door I lean on my cane,
Hearing cicadas sing their strain.
The ferry's touched with afterglow;
The village sees smoke upward go.
And I have seen Cart Joiner drunk,
Who, by Five Willows sing with spunk.

* showcharm: a talent recommended for official use or a well-learned person in ancient China. A showcharm was usually well respected in the traditional meritocratic Chinese society.
* Rimriver: a place named after the Rim River south of Blue Field, which flows into the Pa River. Wei Wang, our poet, had a cottage here, which was bought from Chihwen Sung (A.D. 656 – A.D. 712), another T'ang poet.

* cicada: a homopterous insect that sings its song of summer and shrills in autumn, a symbol of death and resurrection in Chinese culture because of its metamorphosis and recycle. Therefore, in ancient China, a jade cicada figure was put in the mouth of a dead body with such an intention of eternal life.
* Cart Joiner: a hermit in Ch'u in the Spring and Autumn period. A passage from *Sir Lush* reads like this: When Confucius went to the State of Ch'u, Cart Joiner, the mad hermit, came to his door: "Phoenix, phoenix! Why is your virtue debased? The future we cannot see; the past we cannot catch hold of. When the world follows the Word, a sage completes all; when the world doesn't, he just survives. In this age, to stay free of penalty is the best. Good fortune like a feather is too thin to get; bad luck like the soil is too thick to avoid. Forget it, forget it! Do not show your virtue! Dangerous, dangerous! Scratch a path lest people go astray; brambles, brambles, do not creep and get in my way. O road, you bend and stretch away, do not bar my feet, o nay!"
* Five Willows: an allusion to Poolbright T'ao (A.D. 352 – A.D. 427), a verse writer, poet, and litterateur in the Chin dynasty. Pure and lofty, T'ao resigned from official life several times to live a life of simplicity. There were five willow trees planted in front of his house, so he called himself Mr. Five Willows.

答裴迪辋口遇雨忆终南山之作

森森寒流广，
苍苍秋雨晦。
君问终南山，
心知白云外。

Reminiscing the South Hills Caught in a Rain at the Mouth of the Rim, In Reply to Ti P'ei

Dim, so dim, the autumn rain falls;
Vast, so vast, the cold water flows.
If you ask about the South Hills,
Out of clouds they are, my heart knows.

* the South Hills: the Southern Mountains, also known as Mt. Great One, Mt. Earthlungs, the mountains south of Long Peace, a great stronghold of the capital, towering in the middle of Ch'in Ridge and rolling about 100 kilometers. It is the birthplace of Wordist culture, Buddhist culture, Filial Piety culture, Longevity culture, Bellheads culture and Plutus culture and is praised as the Capital of Fairies, the crown of Heavenly Abode and the Promised Land of the World.
* the Rim: the Rim River, originating from the north foot of Ch'in Ridge, flowing to the south of Blue Field County and then poring into the Pa River.

赠裴十迪

风景日夕佳，
与君赋新诗。
澹然望远空，
如意方支颐。
春风动百草，
兰蕙生我篱。
暧暧日暖闺，
田家来致词。
欣欣春还皋，
淡淡水生陂。
桃李虽未开，
荑萼满芳枝。
请君理还策，
敢告将农时。

To Ti P'ei Ten

A fine sight it is all day long;
With you a new verse I compose.
Quietly, I gaze at the far sky
While comfort does my cheek repose.
The vernal wind moves all the grass
While by my hedge grows orchids sweet.
The warming sun warms the farm house;
The farmer comes and does me greet.
"Springtime has come to the field now

And water on the slope does shine.
Though peaches and plums not yet bloom,
Their sprays are loaded with buds fine.
Please take your stick and go back home;
Do not miss farming season thine."

* orchids sweet: The orchid is any of a widely distributed family of terrestrial or epiphytic monocotyledonous plants having thickened bulbous roots and often very showy distinctive flowers, is one of the four most important images in Chinese literature, which are wintersweet, orchid, bamboo and chrysanthemum.
* plums and peaches: a metonymy for plants in general; a metaphor for disciples or students, and sometimes symbolizing a flashy life.
* sun: the heavenly body that is the center of attraction and the main source of light and heat in the solar system, a representation of Shine in contrast with Shade, the moon, in Chinese culture, a symbol of hope, life, strength, vigor and youth.

黎拾遗昕裴秀才迪见过秋夜对雨之作

促织鸣已急，
轻衣行向重。
寒灯坐高馆，
秋雨闻疏钟。
白法调狂象，
玄言问老龙。
何人顾蓬径，
空愧求羊踪。

Composed on a Raining Autumn Night When Counselor Hsin Li and Showcharm Ti P'ei Visit Me

The crickets cry, a hasty air:
Clad little, more clothes ye should wear.
In the high hall sits my lamp cold
That through a rain hears a bell tolled.
With Dharma the wild I subdue
And enquire into the Word true.
Now you two visit my poor shed,
I feel ashamed, like burning red.

* showcharm: one who has passed the civil-service examinations at provincial level, ready for official use, or a title of one who enjoys high prestige in a society.
* cricket: a leaping orthopterous insect, with long antennae and three segments in each tarsus, the male of which makes a chirping sound by friction of forewings, a common

image of a quiet night in Chinese literature.
* the Word: referring to Tao if transliterated, the most significant and profoundest concept in Chinese philosophy. According to Laocius's *The Word and the World*: "The Word is void, but its use is infinite. O deep! It seems to be the root of all things." It is identifiable with the Word or Logos or God in the West, as there is an enormous amount of common ground in the great religions, concerning the most fundamental matters such as the One-to-many relation and the divine nature of the Creator, whatever it may be called.
* Dharma: an ideal state of truth and righteousness in Buddhist terms.

裴　迪

不相见，
不相见来久。
日日泉水头，
常忆同携手。
携手本同心，
复叹忽分襟。
相忆今如此，
相思深不深。

To Ti P'ei

A long time has passed;
It's long time since I saw you last.
I oft recall then hand in hand,
By the spring every day we'd stand.
Hand in hand, we had the same heart,
But damn it, we again would part.
I think of you much now like this,
How I miss you, what an abyss!

* abyss: a deep fissure in the earth; bottomless gulf, a metaphor for anything too deep for measurement, especially love or feeling or sadness.

登裴秀才迪小台作

端居不出户，
满目望云山。
落日鸟边下，
秋原人外闲。
遥知远林际，
不见此檐间。
好客多乘月，
应门莫上关。

Climbing onto Showcharm P'ei's Platform

You need not go out of the door;
Clouded hills roll on to your eye.
All travelers gone, the plain is free;
Through afterglow, birds back home fly.
The distant wood I used to tour;
Now on your platform it's not far.
In moonlight I may oft come here,
Dear host, do leave your door ajar.

* showcharm: hsiuts'ai if transliterated, a talent recommended for official use through official examinations usually held every three years or a well-learned person in ancient China. A showcharm was well respected in the traditional meritocratic and bureaucratic Chinese society. Showcharms were the first grade candidates, who had passed the civil-service examinations at the provincial or state level, followed by more advanced candidates, that is, the second grade recommendees (chüjen), the third grade offerees (kungshi), and the highest grade enterees (chinshi).

酌酒与裴迪

酌酒与君君自宽,
人情翻覆似波澜。
白首相知犹按剑,
朱门先达笑弹冠。
草色全经细雨湿,
花枝欲动春风寒。
世事浮云何足问,
不如高卧且加餐。

Drinking with Ti P'ei

I pour you wine and you can feel at rest;
At changing feelings one may be distressed.
One still holds his sword on guard in old age;
Those advanced laugh at those new on the stage.
The greener grass has been moistened by rain;
When twigs sway, a cold wind will them restrain.
Worldly affairs are nasty things, ne'er mind;
We'd better eat more, reposed and reclined.

* worldly affairs: usually referring to the hustle and bustle of Vanity Fair, characterized by frivolity, snobbishness and craftiness.

闻裴秀才迪吟诗因戏赠

猿吟一何苦,
愁朝复悲夕。
莫作巫峡声,
肠断秋江客。

Hearing Showcharm Ti P'ei Chanting, Hence the Poem for Fun

How sadly the monkeys there grieve!
Grieving at dawn, grieving at eve.
Don't like Witch Gorge relieve your sigh;
Don't let boatmen in autumn cry.

* showcharm: hsiuts'ai if transliterated, a talent recommended for official use through civil-service examinations usually held every three years or a well learned person in ancient China. A showcharm was well respected in the traditional Chinese society. Showcharms are primary candidates, who have passed civil examinations at provincial level, followed by more advanced recommendees (chüjen), offerees (kungshi), and enterees (chinshi).
* monkey: any of a group of primates having elongate limbs, hands and feet adapted for grasping, and a highly developed nervous system, including marmosets, baboons, and macaques, but not the anthropoid apes, though monkeys and apes are used alternatively in Chinese.
* Witch Gorge: one of the three gorges of the Long River, that is, Big Pond Gorge, Witch Gorge, and Westridge Gorge. A metonymy for Witch Gorge monkeys or gibbons in this poem.

过感化寺昙兴上人山院

暮持筇竹杖，
相待虎谿头。
催客闻山响，
归房逐水流。
野花丛发好，
谷鸟一声幽。
夜坐空林寂，
松风直似秋。

A Visit to Monk Cloud Rise's Cottage at Inspiration Temple

At dusk you walk there with your stick
And by Tiger Ford wait for me.
The creek makes a sound to urge us
And we go back by the stream free.
The wild flowers give off a fresh balm;
A dale bird gives out a long crow.
We sit in peace in the calm grove;
An autumn wind to pines does blow.

* Inspiration Temple: name of a temple, which is probably on Mt. Blue Field.
* Tiger Ford: name of a ferry on the Tiger Stream, near East Wood Temple. As is said, tigers could be heard in the hills when one sees off a guest by the stream.
* pine: an evergreen tree with needle-like leaves, a symbol of longevity and rectitude in Chinese culture.

游 感 化 寺

翡翠香烟合，
琉璃宝地平。
龙宫连栋宇，
虎穴傍檐楹。
谷静唯松响，
山深无鸟声。
琼峰当户拆，
金涧透林鸣。
郢路云端迥，
秦川雨外晴。
雁王衔果献，
鹿女踏花行。
抖擞辞贫里，
归依宿化城。
绕篱生野蕨，
空馆发山樱。
香饭青菰米，
嘉蔬绿笋茎。
誓陪清梵末，
端坐学无生。

Touring Inspiration Temple

Emerald merges with incense haze;
The temple's calm in colored glaze.
Dragon Hall with the roofs aligns;

Tiger Den with the eaves combines.
The vales so calm, only pines sigh;
The hills so deep, no birds will cry.
The jade peaks open to the door;
The gold brook thru the grove does pour.
The road to Ying thru all clouds goes;
The stream from Ch'in beyond rain flows.
The wild goose king offers fruit sweets;
The deer daughter amid flowers tweets.
Shaking off, I leave the poor lane
And come off to live in this fane.
Under the hedge fungi grow lush;
Nearby the hall hill cherries blush.
A sesame meal or green wild rice,
Fresh greens or bamboo shoots nice.
With the monks chanting a sutra,
I'd sit, musing for Nirvana.

* Inspiration Temple: name of a temple, which is probably on Mt. Blue Field.
* incense: an aromatic substance in the form of a stick that exhales perfume during combustion, burnt before a Buddhist, Wordist or any religious or ancestral figure as an act of worship, usually offered with a prayer or vow.
* Dragon Hall: an imaginary palace under water, where dragons live. A metaphor for a building in this poem, probably with dragons on the ridge or eaves.
* Tiger Den: a metaphor for a building, probably with tigers on the ridge or eaves.
* Ying: the capital of the State of Ch'u in the Eastern Chough dynasty, and an alternative name for the lands in present-day Hupei and northern Hunan.
* Ch'in: Ch'in (221 B.C.- 207 B.C.), the first unified empire in Chinese history founded by the State of Ch'in in the late Warring States period.
* wild goose: an undomesticated goose that is caring and responsible, taken as a symbol of benevolence, righteousness, good manner, wisdom, and faith in Chinese culture.
* deer: a ruminant (family *Cervidae*), having deciduous antlers, usually in the male only, as the moose, elk, and reindeer. Deer are closely related to Chinese life. Deer

hide is a precious gift, especially presented to a female and a deer is usually a symbol of imperial power as it is often a target of pursuit.
* sesame: an East Indian herb, containing seeds which are used as food and as a source of the pale yellow sesame oil, used as salad oil or an emollient, introduced from Ferghana by Ch'ien Chang (164 B.C. - 114 B.C.), a diplomat, traveler, explorer, and the initiator of the Silk Road.
* wild rice: a tall aquatic grass, the stem of which is used as a vegetable and the grain of which was formerly used as food, now esteemed as a table delicacy.
* bamboo shoots: tender bamboo sprouts, which may be dried for storage, are used as a delicacy in China.
* sutra: a formulated doctrine, often so short as to be unintelligible without a key; literally a rule or a precept. In Buddhism, it is an extended writing usually in verse, and often in dialogue form, embodying important religious and philosophical propositions, sometimes directly, sometimes in highly allegorical or metaphorical language.
* Nirvana: the attainment of complete freedom from all mental, emotional and psychic tension.

临高台送黎拾遗

相送临高台，
川原杳何极。
日暮飞鸟还，
行人去不息。

Ascending the Height to See Off Counselor Li

I see you off now on this height;
The vast plain rolls far out of sight.
Coming back, all the warblers fly;
Going out, all the travelers hie.

辋 川 闲 居

一从归白社，
不复到青门。
时倚檐前树，
远看原上村。
青菰临水映，
白鸟向山翻。
寂寞於陵子，
桔槔方灌园。

Staying Idle at Rimriver

Now I have come to Altar White,
To Blue Gate I'll not go again.
I oft lean on the eaves by tree
And view the village on the plain.
Wild rice shoots I pick by the stream
While white birds to the mountains fly.
Like Sir Crow Ridge in solitude,
By shadoof, I'll water fields dry.

* Rimriver: a place named after the Rim River south of Blue Field County, which is under the jurisdiction of today's Hsi-an, the capital of Sha'anhsi Province. Wei Wang, our poet, had a cottage here, which was bought from Chihwen Sung (A.D. 656 - A.D. 712), another T'ang poet.
* Altar White: name of a lane where a recluse used to dwell, east of Loshine; a metaphor for the poet's villa.
* Blue Gate: the east gate of Long Peace, the capital of T'ang.

* wild rice shoot: sprout or stem of a tall aquatic grass, used as a vegetable.
* Sir Crow Ridge: an important thinker and hermit of the Ch'i State in the Spring and Autumn period.

积雨辋川庄作

积雨空林烟火迟,
蒸藜炊黍饷东菑。
漠漠水田飞白鹭,
阴阴夏木啭黄鹂。
山中习静观朝槿,
松下清斋折露葵。
野老与人争席罢,
海鸥何事更相疑。

Composed at Rimriver Villa in a Raining Season

Smoke curls up late out of the rain-soaked wood;
To the east farmland is sent millet food.
Egrets fly 'cross the plain full of water;
Orioles cheep in the grove lush with summer.
I watch hibiscus in the mountains quiet,
And dine under pines, mallow as my diet.
I've merged with nature and nature with me;
Seagulls, if seeing me, don't have to flee.

* millet: a member of the foxtail grass family, or its seeds, culvivated as a cereal, used as a stable food in ancient times, having been cultivated in China for more than 7,300 years, one of the earliest crops in the world.
* egret: a heron characterized, in the breeding season, by long and loose plumes drooping over the tail, usually white plumage.
* oriole: golden oriole, one of the family of passerine birds, which looks bright yellow with contrasting black wings and sings beautiful songs.

* hibiscus: any of various malvaceous herbs, shrubs and trees of the genus *Hibiscus*, having large, showy flowers of various colors.
* pine: a cone-bearing tree having needle-shaped evergreen leaves growing in clusters, a symbol of longevity and rectitude in Chinese culture.
* seagull: a kind of sea bird, any gull or large tern, a symbol of clean integrity. The seagulls in the Wordist book *Sir Line* (Liehtzu) are particularly sensitive to impurity of motive and will make friends only with the completely guileless and disinterested.

戏题辋川别业

柳条拂地不须折，
松树披云从更长。
藤花欲暗藏猱子，
柏叶初齐养麝香。

A Poem to Rimriver Villa for Fun

Don't break the willow twigs sweeping the ground;
Look at the pine top scraping the clouds blown.
I'll keep macaques in the wisteria shade;
And raise water deer with cypress leaves grown.

* willow: any of a large genus of shrubs and trees related to the poplars, widely distributed in China and most of the world, having glossy green leaves resembling a girl's eye-brow, and generally having smooth branches, and often long, slender, pliant, and sometimes pendent branchlets, which seem to be waving good-bye, or weeping amorously, or drooping for nostalgia. The best image is in Vetch We Pick, a verse in *The Book of Songs*, which is like this: When we left long ago, / The willows waved adieu. / Now back to our home town, / We meet snow falling down.
* macaque: a monkey with a stout body, short tail, cheek pouches, and pronounced muzzle.
* wisteria: any of a genus Wisteria of woody twining shrubs of the bean family, with pinnate leaves, elongated pods, and handsome clusters of blue, purple, or white flowers.
* water deer: normally called Chinese water deer (*Hydropotes inermis*) without antlers, in golden brown colour, interspersed with black hairs, having a white underside, active in the morning and evening and hiding in dense vegetation for the rest of the day.
* cypress: an evergreen tree of the family Cypressaseae, having durable timber, a symbol of rectitude, nobility and longevity in Chinese culture.

归 辋 川 作

谷口疏钟动，
渔樵稍欲稀。
悠然远山暮，
独向白云归。
菱蔓弱难定，
杨花轻易飞。
东皋春草色，
惆怅掩柴扉。

Composed After Going Back to Rimriver

The clear toll from the dale quakes me;
Fishers and woodcutters come home.
Far, farther the hills roll in dusk;
I go back to where white clouds roam.
Water chestnuts float on surface;
Poplar catkins like feathers fly.
East shoreland is live with grass hue;
I shut my brushwood door and sigh.

* Rimriver: a place named after the Rim River south of Blue Field, which flows into the Pa River. Wei Wang, our poet, had a cottage here, which was bought from Chihwen Sung (A.D. 656 – A.D. 712), another T'ang poet.
* water chestnut: the hard horned edible fruit of an aquatic plant.
* poplar: any of a genus (*Populus*) of dioecious trees and bushes of the willow family, widely distributed in the northern hemisphere.
* catkin: a deciduous scaly spike of flowers, as in the willow, an image of helpless

drifting or wandering in Chinese literature.
* brushwood: a low thicket; underwood. A brushwood door is a symbol of country life of a hermit.

春中田园作

屋上春鸠鸣，
村边杏花白。
持斧伐远扬，
荷锄觇泉脉。
归燕识故巢，
旧人看新历。
临觞忽不御，
惆怅远行客。

Spring Comes to the Country

On the roof cooing doves alight;
By the vill apricots bloom white.
With axes they trim mulberries;
Hoe shouldered, a spring he o'ersees.
Swallows back their nest remember;
The host reads a new calendar.
The cup I hold but I can't drink;
Of those who drift sadly I think.

* dove: a pigeon, especially the mourning dove, turtledove, etc., a symbol of peace.
* apricot: a tree or the fruit of the tree of the rose family, intermediate between the peach and the plum. It often appears in Chinese poetry, as a line by Chun Kou (A.D. 961 – A.D. 1023) says: "To the slanting sun apricot blooms fly."
* mulberry: the edible, berry-like fruit of a tree (genus Morus) whose leaves are valued for silkworm culture, and the tree itself.

* swallow: a passerine bird, with short broad, depressed bill, long pointed wings, and forked tail, noted for fleeting flight and migratory habits. In Chinese culture, swallows are welcome to live with a family with their nest on a beam.

春 园 即 事

宿雨乘轻屐，
春寒著弊袍。
开畦分白水，
间柳发红桃。
草际成棋局，
林端举桔槔。
还持鹿皮几，
日暮隐蓬蒿。

Working in the Field in Spring

It rained at night, clogs I put on;
The spring chill, a thick gown I'd wear.
Troughs are dug to drain flood away;
Amid willows peach blossoms glare.
A chessboard's set up amid grass;
A shadoof's worked, a grove beside.
A deer-skin desk I'll bring with me
And at dusk in thistles I'll hide.

* clog: a wooden soled shoe, an inkling of country life.
* willow: any of a large genus of shrubs and trees related to the poplars, widely distributed in China and most of the world, having glossy green leaves resembling a girl's eye-brow, and generally having smooth branches, and often long, slender, pliant, and sometimes pendent branchlets, which seem to be waving good-bye, or weeping amorously, or drooping for nostalgia.
* peach: any of the plant (*Prunus Percica*), bearing a fleshy, juicy, edible drupe,

cultivated in many varieties in temperate zones considered sacred in China, often used as a metaphor for a young woman, as a section of a poem in *The Book of Songs* reads: The peach twigs sway, / Ablaze the flower; / Now she's married away, / Befitting her new bower."

* shadoof: a water-raising device, operating on the principle of a well sweep: used in the Orient for irrigation.
* deer-skin: Deer-skin is a precious gift, especially presented to a female. Deer, closely related to Chinese life, are a ruminant (family *Cervidae*), having deciduous antlers, usually in the male only, as the moose, elk, and reindeer.
* thistle: a prickly plant with cylindrical or globular heads of tubular purple flowers, a metaphor for poor hard conditions.

山 居 即 事

寂寞掩柴扉，
苍茫对落晖。
鹤巢松树遍，
人访荜门稀。
绿竹含新粉，
红莲落故衣。
渡头烟火起，
处处采菱归。

Notes on Mountain Abiding

Quietly, I close my brushwood door
And through the dusk face fading hue.
Crane nests hang on all the pine trees;
Travelers calling on me are few.
The bamboo's put on a new sheen;
The red lotus has shed flowers slack.
The ferry sees fishing lights live;
Water chestnut pickers row back.

* brushwood door: a simple door made of brushwood, a sign of country life.
* crane: one of a family of large, long-necked, long-legged, heronlike birds allied to the rails, a symbol of longevity and integrity in Chinese culture, only second to the phoenix in cultural importance.
* pine: an evergreen tree having needle-like leaves, a symbol of longevity and rectitude in Chinese culture.
* bamboo: a tall, tree-like or shrubby grass in tropical and semi-tropical regions, a

symbol of integrity and altitude, one of the four most important botanical images in Chinese literature, which are wintersweet, orchid, bamboo and chrysanthemum.
* lotus: any of various waterlilies, especially the white or pink Asian lotus, used as a religious symbol in Hinduism and Buddhism. The lotus is a common image in Chinese literature, as two lines of a lyric by Hsiu Ouyang (A.D. 1007 - A.D. 1072) read: "A thunder brings rain to the wood and pool, / The rain hushes the lotus, drips cool."
* water chestnut: the hard horned edible fruit of an aquatic plant.

山 居 秋 暝

空山新雨后，
天气晚来秋。
明月松间照，
清泉石上流。
竹喧归浣女，
莲动下渔舟。
随意春芳歇，
王孙自可留。

The Hills Wearing Autumn Hue

After the rain all hills are new;
The sky is tinged with autumn hue.
The moon bright to the pine trees glows;
The stream clear on the pebbles flows.
The washing girls stir the bamboo;
The lotus blooms sway the canoe.
Spring can take a rest as it may;
Prince and princess may as well stay.

* the moon: the satellite of the earth, an important image in Chinese literature or culture as it can evoke many associations such as solitude and nostalgia on the one hand, and purity, brightness and happy reunions on the other. Philosophically, it is the very germ or source of Shade, and the sun is its Shine counterpart. The moon is celebrated with mooncakes in China on Mid-autumn Day when the moon is at its full glory.
* pine: a cone-bearing tree having needle-shaped evergreen leaves growing in clusters, a

symbol of longevity and rectitude in Chinese culture.
* bamboo: a tall, tree-like or shrubby grass in tropical and semi-tropical regions, a symbol of integrity and altitude. Plankbridge Cheng (A.D. 1693 – A.D. 1765), A Ching poet, speaks of its character in a poem *Bamboo Rooted in the Rock*: "You bite the green hill and ne'er rest. / Roots in the broken crag, you grow, / And stand erect although hard pressed. /East, west, south, north, let the wind blow."
* lotus bloom: lotus flower, flower of a plant of the waterlily family, pink or white in color.

田园乐七首

Farmland Glee, Seven Poems

其 一

出入千门万户，
经过北里南邻。
蹀躞鸣珂有底，
崆峒散发何人。

No. 1

In and out of myriads of doors and gates,
Thru neighborhoods south and north, here and there,
Their horses trot and pendants clink, so what?
Lo, from Mt. Hollow loom immortals fair.

* horse: a large solid-hoofed quadruped (*Equus caballus*) with coarse mane and tail, of various strains: Ferghana, Mongolian, Kazaks, Hequ, Karasahr and so on and of various colors: black, white, yellow, brown, dappled and so on, commonly in the domesticated state, employed as a beast of draught and burden and especially for riding upon.
* Mt. Hollow: a mountain in present-day Kansu Province, famous for martial arts. As is said, people here are brave and skillful at fighting battles. And it is a Wordist sanctuary, where Lord Yellow learned the Word from Sir Goodharvest. *Sir Lush* keeps a record of this inquiry, as reads: Lord Yellow had reigned nineteen years and his orders were carried out all over the land. Having heard that Sir Goodharvest lived on Mt. Hollow, he went to pay him a visit, saying: "I hear that you know the very Word. May I inquire of you about the quintessence of the very Word? I would acquire the essence of Heaven and earth to help five grains and sustain my people. And I also want to govern Shade and Shine so that all things may grow well." Because of this event, Mt. Hollow is esteemed as the first Wordist mountain in China.

其 二

再见封侯万户，
立谈赐璧一双。
讵胜耦耕南亩，
何如高卧东窗。

No. 2

Met two times, he was as high peer knighted;
While talking, with jade discs he was granted.
But I would till and rake the southern farm,
Or sleep in the shade, head reposed on arm.

* jade discs: jewels worn by royal families and nobles. Jade is exclusive to the upper echelon of the society, but gold and silver are not, as a saying goes, "Gold is priced while jade is priceless."

其 三

采菱渡头风急，
策杖林西日斜。
杏树坛边渔父，
桃花源里人家。

No. 3

Wind blows hard at Water Chestnut Pier;
With a stick I go till the sun's west.
Fishermen talk by Apricot Altar;
In Shangrila the folks are well blessed.

* Water Chestnut Pier: unidentified.
* Apricot Altar: a place where Confucius taught his disciples, which is mentioned in *Sir Lush*. The passage reads like this: Confucius strolled to a grove called Black Tent and took a rest on Apricot Altar. His disciples were reading while Confucius was plucking the lute and singing. Before half of the tune was finished, an old fisherman got off his boat and came on. He went along the bank, his beard and eyebrows all gray, his hair drooping down and sleeves flying, and stopped on a high but level ground, his left hand covering his knee, right hand supporting his chin, listening to Confucius plucking and singing. When the tune was over, the old fisherman accosted Sir Offer and Sir Road, who came to him.
* Shangrila: an imaginary Edenesque place, an ideal land free of tyranny and exploitation.

其 四

萋萋春草秋绿，
落落长松夏寒。
牛羊自归村巷，
童稚不识衣冠。

No. 4

Lush spring grass in autumn is still green;
Tall pine trees in summer make one cold.
Sheep and cattle stroll back to their lanes;
Naïve kids do not know jade or gold.

* pine: a cone-bearing tree having needle-shaped evergreen leaves growing in clusters, widely distributed in temperate zones, a symbol of longevity and rectitude in Chinese culture.
* sheep and cattle: referring to country life. Sheep are medium-sized domesticated ruminants of the genus *Ovis* while cattle are large domesticated bovine animals. They were used as a sacrifice in the past in both Western and Eastern cultures.

其　五

山下孤烟远村，
天边独树高原。
一瓢颜回陋巷，
五柳先生对门。

No. 5

Downhill a village afar in haze;
Distant, a tree lonely in the moor.
With his gourd, Hui Yan in his poor lane;
Mister Five Willows by the next door.

* moor: a tract of open, rolling wetland, usually covered with heather and often marshy or peaty. Natural places like moors, glades, coves, hills, rivers, mounts and seas, and so on often allude to reclusion in Chinese culture.
* Hui Yan: Hui Yan (521 B.C.- 481 B.C.) or Yanhui as is called in China, Confucius' most diligent student, one of Confucius' seventy-two established disciples, a thinker in the late Spring and Autumn period. Confucius commended him like this: "What a man Yanhui is! A bowl of meal, a kettle of water, living in a shabby hut. No one can tolerate such poverty, but Yanhui feels happy about it. What a man he is!"
* Mister Five Willows: referring to Ch'ien T'ao, alias Poolbright T'ao (A.D. 352 - A.D. 427), a verse writer, poet, and litterateur in the Chin dynasty, and the founder of Chinese idyllism, who was once the magistrate of P'engtse. Pure and lofty, T'ao resigned from official life several times to live a life of simplicity. There were five willow trees planted in front of his house, so he called himself Mr. Five Willows.

其 六

桃红复含宿雨，
柳绿更带朝烟。
花落家童未扫，
莺啼山客犹眠。

No. 6

The pink peach carries rain from last night;
The green willow holds mist in dawning light.
The fallen red the boy does not broom;
Birds chirp to the sleeper in the room.

* peach: any tree of the genus *Prunus Percica*, blooming brilliantly and bearing fruit, a fleshy, juicy, edible drupe, considered sacred in China, a symbol of romance, prosperity and longevity.
* willow: any of a large genus of shrubs and trees related to the poplars, widely distributed in China and most of the world, having glossy green leaves resembling a girl's eye-brow, and generally having smooth branches, and often long, slender, pliant, and sometimes pendent branchlets, which seem to be waving good-bye, or weeping amorously, or drooping for nostalgia.

其 七

酌酒会临泉水，
抱琴好倚长松。
南园露葵朝折，
东谷黄粱夜舂。

No. 7

Beside the fountain spring we drink wine,
And play the lute neath the pine upright.
In South Field we pick mallow at morn;
Down East Dale we pound millet at night.

* lute: a Chinese lute, a stringed musical instrument, usually placed on a table, played by plucking the strings with fingers or a plectrum.
* pine: a cone-bearing tree having needle-shaped evergreen leaves growing in clusters, a symbol of longevity, solitude and rectitude in Chinese culture.
* South Field: a metonymy for fieldland. As a slope facing south is good for farming, ancient Chinese usually reclaimed farmland uphill or on a slope facing south, hence the term.
* mallow: *Malva verticillata* or any plant of the genus *Malva* with roundish leaves, the first of the five popular vegetables in ancient China.
* millet: a member of the foxtail grass family, or its seeds, tiny and yellow, cultivated as a cereal, used as a stable food in ancient times, having been cultivated in China for more than 7,300 years, one of the earliest crops in the world.

泛 前 陂

秋空自明迥，
况复远人间。
畅以沙际鹤，
兼之云外山。
澄波澹将夕，
清月皓方闲。
此夜任孤棹，
夷犹殊未还。

Boating on the Front Pond

In the autumn sky, the moon's far,
Let alone it's beyond the crowd.
I'm happy like a crane on sand,
Besides, I row beyond Mt. Cloud.
The water rolls on to the dusk;
Much at leisure is Luna bright.
So composed, no one has gone back;
Their boating they enjoy tonight.

* crane: one of a family of large, long-necked, long-legged, heronlike birds allied to the rails, a symbol of integrity and longevity in Chinese culture, only second to the phoenix in cultural importance.
* Mt. Cloud: a nonce name, a mountain veiled in clouds.
* Luna: the moon, an important image in Chinese literature as it can give rise to many associations such as solitude, purity, brightness and happy reunions.

山　茱　萸

朱实山下开，
清香寒更发。
幸与丛桂花，
窗前向秋月。

Hill Cornels

The cornels bloom below the hill;
In fragrant chill a lot they blow.
Together with the laurel flowers,
By the shade they see the moon glow.

* cornel: a kind of dogwood carried or worn on Double Ninth Day, as it can exorcize evil spirits, as is traditionally believed.
* laurel: *laurus nobilis*, an evergreen shrub with aromatic, lance-shaped leaves, yellowish flowers, and succulent, cherry-like fruit, a symbol of glory usually in the form of a crown or wreath of laurel to indicate honor or high merit, especially when one had passed Grand Test in ancient China. In Chinese mythology, there is a laurel tree that is more than 1,500 meters tall on the moon, and it would never fall even though Kang Wu, a banished immortal, kept cutting it.
* the moon: the satellite of the earth, a symbol of solitude or happy reunion in Chinese culture. Luna, the goddess of the moon and of months in Roman mythology, is in Chinese culture the imperial concubine of Lord Alarm (2,480 B.C.- 2,345 B.C.), one of five mythical emperors in prehistorical China. The moon is celebrated with mooncakes in China on Mid-autumn Day when the moon is at its full glory.

酬虞部苏员外过蓝田别业不见留之作

贫居依谷口，
乔木带荒村。
石路枉回驾，
山家谁候门。
渔舟胶冻浦，
猎火烧寒原。
唯有白云外，
疏钟闻夜猿。

To Counselor Su of Forestry Office Who Visits My Cottage in Blue Field but Does Not Stay

I live at the mouth of the dale;
Tall trees surround the village small.
You come to visit me in vain
I'm not in, not knowing your call.
The cold stream keeps a fishing boat;
Hunting fire lights up the plain chill.
Out of the white clouds floating there,
A night toll echoes monkeys' shrill.

* monkey: any of a group of primates having elongate limbs, hands and feet adapted for grasping, and a highly developed nervous system, including marmosets, baboons, and macaques, but not the anthropoid apes, though monkeys and apes are used alternatively in Chinese.

蓝田山石门精舍

落日山水好，
漾舟信归风。
探奇不觉远，
因以缘源穷。
遥爱云木秀，
初疑路不同。
安知清流转，
偶与前山通。
舍舟理轻策，
果然惬所适。
老僧四五人，
逍遥荫松柏。
朝梵林未曙，
夜禅山更寂。
道心及牧童，
世事问樵客。
暝宿长林下，
焚香卧瑶席。
涧芳袭人衣，
山月映石壁。
再寻畏迷误，
明发更登历。
笑谢桃源人，
花红复来觌。

Stonegate Vihara at Mt. Blue Field

The landscape gilds the setting sun;
In the wind my boat rows at will.
You ne'er feel too far to explore
Where the source begins from a nil.
The cloud wood far away is green,
I might go astray I first doubt.
Great, I can get there from the hill,
As with the waves I turn about.
I moor my boat and take my stick
To go where'er I feel it fine.
Lo, four or five old monks are there
Idling in the shade of the pine.
Monks chant sutras before dawn breaks;
They meditate as night's still as such.
The Word can shepherds influence;
The world but woodcutters know much.
As dusk falls I'll sleep in the wood;
Incense burnt, I spread my mat fine.
A scent from the creek lures my robe;
To the stonewall the moon does shine.
If searching on, I might be lost;
Tomorrow I'll come for more sight.
To thank those in Eden I smile;
I'll come back when red flowers blush bright.

---

* vihara: dwelling place literally, usually referring to a temple or a place for teaching Buddha's messages and meditation.

* Mt. Blue Field: a mountain 15 kilometers away from Blue Field County under today's Hsi-an, Sha'anhsi Province, famous for jade mined there, called Bluefield Jade.
* sutra: a formulated doctrine, often so short as to be unintelligible without a key; literally a rule or a precept. In Buddhism, it is an extended writing usually in verse, and often in dialogue form, embodying important religious and philosophical propositions, sometimes directly, and sometimes in highly allegorical or metaphorical language.
* the Word: referring to Tao if transliterated, the most significant and profoundest concept of cosmology and axiology in Chinese philosophy. The Word is fully elucidated in *The Word and the World*, the single book that Laocius wrote all his wisdom into. Its importance or implication can be seen in this verse: "The Word is void, but its use is infinite. O deep! It seems to be the root of all things."
* shepherd: a person who herds and takes care of seep, a metaphor for a leader of a group, especially a minister.
* incense: an aromatic substance in the form of a stick that exhales perfume during combustion, offered to a Buddhist, Wordist or any religious or ancestral figure as an act of worship, usually with a prayer or vow.
* Eden: the garden that was the first home of Adam and Eve, used as a metaphor for any delightful region or abode or an elysium, a paradise.

山　中

荆溪白石出，
天寒红叶稀。
山路元无雨，
空翠湿人衣。

In the Hills

White rocks in the Chaste Stream appear;
Red leaves so sparse, it's coldly drear.
On the mountain road, there's no rain;
Green air wets my clothes as it's fain.

* the Chaste Stream: a river originating from northwest of Blue Field County and flowing into the Pa River.
* red leaves: probably maple leaves, which turn red in late autumn.

赠刘蓝田

篱间犬迎吠，
出屋候荆扉。
岁晏输井税，
山村人夜归。
晚田始家食，
馀布成我衣。
讵肯无公事，
烦君问是非。

To Magistrate Liu of Blue Field

At the hedge my dog barks aloud;
I come out and by the door wait.
The folk who's gone to pay farm tax
Has come back at night, now so late.
What is left o'er will be my food;
Remanent cloth is for my wear.
All I've done is for the public,
Dear friend, is it fair or unfair?

* Blue Field: Blue Field County under today's Hsi-an, Sha'anhsi Province, famous for the relics of ape men (pithecanthropus) excavated and jade mined, called Bluefield Jade.
* dog: a domesticated carnivorous mammal (*Canis familiaris*), of worldwide distribution and many varieties, noted for its adaptability and its devotion to man. The dog was domesticated in China at least 8,000 years ago and was often used as a hunter, as a poem in *The Book of Songs* says: "The dog bells clink and clink; / The hunter's

handsome, a real pink."

* farm tax: tax peasants paid to the court in kind. Taxation in the State of Lu was first recorded in 594 B.C. according to *Spring and Autumn*.

山 中 送 别

山中相送罢，
日暮掩柴扉。
春草明年绿，
王孙归不归？

Parting in the Hills

In the hills, I see off my peer;
At dusk, I close my brushwood door.
When grass greens everything next year,
Will you come to me any more?

* brushwood door: a simple door made of brushwood, often used as a symbol of country life.

早秋山中作

无才不敢累明时,
思向东溪守故篱。
岂厌尚平婚嫁早,
却嫌陶令去官迟。
草间蛩响临秋急,
山里蝉声薄暮悲。
寂寞柴门人不到,
空林独与白云期。

In the Hills on an Early Autumn Day

Not worthy, I won't let down a good age;
At the East Stream on my old hedge I'll wait.
I don't think Shang got married too early,
But think Ch'ien T'ao's resignation too late.
Crickets by the shack cheep to autumn fast;
Cicadas in the hills to the dusk croon.
Before the brushwood door, there is no soul
But me in the glade greeting clouds alone.

* the East Stream: also known as the Ying River, originating from the east peak of Mt. Tower, a Buddhist sanctuary.
* Shang: referring to P'ing Shang, a hermit in the Eastern Han dynasty, highly respected by Bright Chuke, the great premier of Shu in the Three Kingdoms period.
* Ch'ien T'ao: referring to Poolbright T'ao (A.D. 352 – A.D. 427), Yüanming T'ao if transliterated, a verse writer, poet, and litterateur in the Chin dynasty, and the founder of Chinese idyllism, who was once the magistrate of P'engtse. T'ao resigned

from his official post four times to live in seclusion.
* cricket: a leaping orthopterous insect, with long antennae and three segments in each tarsus, the male of which makes a chirping sound by friction of forewings, a common image of a quiet night in Chinese literature.
* cicada: a homopterous insect that sings its song of summer and shrills in autumn, a symbol of death and resurrection in Chinese culture because of its metamorphosis and recycle. Therefore, in ancient China, a jade cicada figure was put in the mouth of a dead body with such an intention of eternal life.
* brushwood door: a sign of country life, a common image in Chinese idyllic literature.

林园即事寄舍弟紞

寓目一萧散，
销忧冀俄顷。
青草肃澄陂，
白云移翠岭。
后浦通河渭，
前山包鄢郢。
松含风里声，
花对池中影。
地多齐后疟，
人带荆州瘿。
徒思赤笔书，
讵有丹砂井。
心悲常欲绝，
发乱不能整。
青簟日何长，
闲门昼方静。
颓思茅檐下，
弥伤好风景。

To My Younger Brother Tan from Wood Land

A look at this natural sight
Will make my worries go away.
The grass is calm by the clear pool;
White clouds float to the ridge to stay.

The stream behind flow to the Wei;
The hills in front hold Yan and Ying.
The pines green are part of the sough;
The flowers to the pool their shade bring.
Many are ill with Lord Ch'i's sore;
In Chaste's mountains many grow gall.
Since none can get a sacred book,
Is there cinnabar, a cure-all?
Desperate I oft feel, so sad;
I can't straighten out my toused hair.
On my green mat, I feel time's long;
The room is calm, as is the air.
As fretted, I sit neath the eaves,
But the good sight to me more grieves.

* the Wei: the Wei River, the largest branch of the Yellow River, originating from today's Mt. Birdmouse in Kansu Province, flowing through Precious Rooster, Allshine, Long Peace, and meeting the Yellow River at T'ung Pass.
* Yan and Ying: two capital of the State of Ch'u, the former southwest of today's Eeton (Yich'eng), Hupei Province and the latter northwest of today's Chaston (Chingchow), Hupei Province.
* pine: an evergreen tree with needle-shaped leaves, a symbol of longevity and rectitude in Chinese culture.
* Lord Ch'i: referring to Lord Scene of Ch'i (? - 490 B.C.), a hegemon, in the Spring and Autumn period, both ambitious and epicurean.
* Lord Ch'i's sore: Lord Scene of Ch'i was ill with scabies and diarrhea for a few years.
* Chaste: a prefecture in the Han dynasty, Chaston as its town of administration, present-day Chaston (Chingchow), Hupei Province.
* gall: an excrescence on plants caused by insects, bacteria, or a parasitic fungus. The galls of commerce are produced by a gallfly which lays its eggs in the soft twigs of an oak. Galls contain tannin, and are used in inkmaking, dyeing, etc.
* cinnabar: a crystallized red mercuric sulfide, HgS, the chief ore of mercury, the raw mineral material for elixir in Wordist alchemy.

酬诸公见过

嗟予未丧,
哀此孤生。
屏居蓝田,
薄地躬耕。
岁晏输税,
以奉粢盛。
晨往东皋,
草露未晞。
暮看烟火,
负担来归。
我闻有客,
足扫荆扉。
箪食伊何,
簋瓜抓枣。
仰厕群贤,
皤然一老。
愧无莞簟,
班荆席藁。
泛泛登陂,
折彼荷花。
静观素鲔,
俯映白沙。
山鸟群飞,
日隐轻霞。
登车上马,
倏忽云散。
雀噪荒村,

鸡鸣空馆。

还复幽独，

重欷累叹。

Thanks to the Lords Who Visit Me

Oh my God, I did not die;
To my poor life I sigh.
In Blue Field I dwell now;
The barren field I plough.
The year o'er, I pay rice
For public sacrifice.
At dawn eastward I go
Thru grass with undried dew.
At dusk in smoke that's black
From fishing I come back.
I hear my guest will call,
I clean my room and hall.
What's in the basket, what?
Melons, dates and a lot.
I admire all those sage
And respect the old age.
Sorry, I have no mat,
We can use stalks like that.
To the pond we can row;
Let's pick lotus flowers, go.
Look at the sturgeons bright
Shining to the sand white.
The hill birds fly anon
To the clouds dimly shone.

I get aboard the cart;
And the clouds go apart.
To the lane sparrows row;
To the hall roosters crow.
Go back to peace I'd try;
I heave a long, long sigh.

* God: the one Supreme Being, ever-existing and eternal; the infinite creator, sustainer and ruler of the cosmos with the attributes of being omniscient, omnipotent and omnipresent, or else called Father in Heaven or with a natural propensity, the Word, the One, Heaven and so on.
* Blue Field: Blue Field County under today's Hsi-an, Sha'anhsi Province, famous for jade mined there, called Bluefield Jade.
* melon: a trailing plant of the gourd family, or its fruit. There are two genera, the muskmelon and the watermelon, each with numerous varieties, growing in both tropical and temperate zones.
* date: an oblong, sweet, fleshy fruit of the date palm, enclosing a single hard seed, a symbol of early fertility in Chinese culture.
* lotus: any of various waterlilies, especially the white or pink Asian lotus, used as a religious symbol in Hinduism and Buddhism. The lotus is a common image in Chinese literature, as two lines of a lyric by Hsiu Ouyang (A.D. 1007 - A.D. 1072) read: "A thunder brings rain to the wood and pool, / The rain hushes the lotus, drips cool."
* sturgeon: a large genoid fish of northern regions, with coarse, edible flesh. Sturgeons are the common source of of isinglass and caviar.
* sparrow: a small, plain-colored passerine bird related to the finches, grosbeaks and buntings, a very common bird in China, a symbol of insignificance.
* rooster: the male of the chicken that struts with pride and crows at dawn.

别辋川别业

依迟动车马，
惆怅出松萝。
忍别青山去，
其如绿水何。

Good-bye to My Cottage at Rimriver

I hesitate to start my cart,
Though I leave the pines with a sigh.
From the green hill we go apart;
The blue stream feels hard to say bye.

* Rimriver: a place named after the Rim River south of Blue Field, so named because it looks like a rim of an old-fashioned wheel. Wei Wang, our poet, had a cottage here, which was bought from Chihwen Sung (A.D. 656 – A.D. 712), another T'ang poet.
* pine: a cone-bearing tree having needle-shaped evergreen leaves growing in clusters, a symbol of longevity and rectitude in Chinese culture.

辋 川 别 业

不到东山向一年，
归来才及种春田。
雨中草色绿堪染，
水上桃花红欲燃。
优娄比丘经论学，
伛偻丈人乡里贤。
披衣倒屣且相见，
相欢语笑衡门前。

My Cottage at Rimriver

It's a year since I came to the East Hill;
Back here, it's time to the vernal field till.
The green of grass rain-washed can be a dye;
The peach blossoms in water to flame vie.
The great monks discuss sutras so profound;
The elders respect worthies from around.
He comes to greet me, shoes front at the back.
They talk and laugh by the door of the shack.

* the East Hill: the East Hills, 27.5 kilometers southwest of Shangyü County, Shaohsing, a place for reclusion, where An Hsieh (A.D. 320 – A.D. 385) used to live.
* sutra: a formulated doctrine, often so short as to be unintelligible without a key; literally a rule or a precept. In Buddhism, an extended writing usually in verse, and often in dialogue form, embodying important religious and philosophical propositions, sometimes directly, sometimes in highly allegorical or metaphorical language. The best example is a dialogue between two monks, Hsiu Shen and Neng Hui. The former's

verse is like this: "The body is a Bodhi tree; /The mind's like a mirror stand bright. / Make it clean, as oft as can be, / In case dust should on it alight." And Neng Hui replied, bettering the former: "There's nothing like a Bodhi tree, / Nor such things as a mirror stand. / There is nothing that you can see. / Where can dust find a place to land?"

郑 果 州 相 过

丽日照残春，
初晴草木新。
床前磨镜客，
树下灌园人。
五马惊穷巷，
双童逐老身。
中厨办粗饭，
当恕阮家贫。

A Visit from Cheng, Magistrate of Kuochow

The bright sun shines in fading spring;
Plants and grass turn out a new sheen.
Mirror-honers would come to call;
Field-waterers would make trees green.
Your five horses startle the lane;
To meet you, two pages with me trot.
In the kitchen coarse food we make;
Please excuse me for having not.

* Kuochow: today's Nanch'ung, Ssuch'uan Province.
* sun: the heavenly body that is the center of attraction and the main source of light and heat in the solar system, a representation of Shine in contrast with Shade, the moon, in Chinese culture, a symbol of hope, life, strength, vigor, and youth.
* Mirror-honer: referring to an immortal whose job was to hone mirrors for very little money.
* Field-waterer: referring to an immortal who waters a field with a shadoof.

酬张少府

晚年唯好静，
万事不关心。
自顾无长策，
空知返旧林。
松风吹解带，
山月照弹琴。
君问穷通理，
渔歌入浦深。

Thanks to Chang, a County Sheriff

In my late years I love quietude
And about nothing do I care.
I think I have no good plan,
But retire to the old wood there
The pine wind will untie my lash;
The hill moon will shine to my string.
If you ask me about the truth,
To the deep moor a song I'll sing.

* old wood: referring to hermitage like the East Hills, deep moor, mounts and seas and other such natural surroundings.
* pine wind: a wind blowing through a pine forest, usually soughing.
* moor: a tract of rolling wasteland, usually covered with heather and often marshy or peaty, often used as a metaphor for hermitage away from the noise of the world. Natural places like coves, glades, hills, moors, rivers, mounts and seas, and so on often allude to reclusion in Chinese culture.

题 辋 川 图

老来懒赋诗,
惟有老相随。
宿世谬词客,
前身应画师。
不能舍馀习,
偶被世人知。
名字本皆是,
此心还不知。

Dedication to the Painting of Rimriver

Old, to compose poems I'm not fain,
Only old age staying with me.
A painter I should have but been;
A rhymer I have strayed to be.
What I'm used to I can't give up,
So to the world now I am known.
My name suggests I should be true;
My heart sticks to fame all alone.

* My name suggests I should be true: Our poet was named Wei Wang (A.D. 701 - A.D. 761 or A.D. 699 - A.D. 761), styled Vimalakirti and dubbed Vimalakirti Buddhist. As his name suggests, he should be away from the vainity of the world and pursue truth like Buddhist fathers.
* Rimriver: a place named after the Rim River south of Blue Field, which flows into the Pa River. Wei Wang, our poet, had a cottage here, which was bought from Chihwen Sung (A.D. 656 - A.D. 712), another T'ang poet.

崔濮阳兄季重前山兴

秋色有佳兴，
况君池上闲。
悠悠西林下，
自识门前山。
千里横黛色，
数峰出云间。
嵯峨对秦国，
合沓藏荆关。
残雨斜日照，
夕岚飞鸟还。
故人今尚尔，
叹息此颓颜。

To Brother Chichung Ts'ui, Magistrate of P'ushine, at the Front Hill, with Zest

The autumn fills us with great zest,
And on your pool you're free at will.
Free, and so free in the west wood,
All you know is your front hill.
Dark green spreads for a thousand miles;
Several peaks the clouds override.
They face Ch'in Land in ragged piles,
Among which Chaste Pass seems to hide.
The eve sun gilding lefto'er rain,
Touched with mist, the warblers fly back.

My friend, you have not changed at all;
I but sigh to my face so slack.

* P'ushine: once the capital of Dark Crown's kingdom, the birthplace of the Dragon, a cradle of Chinese civilization, in today's Honan Province.

山 中 示 弟

山林吾丧我，
冠带尔成人。
莫学嵇康懒，
且安原宪贫。
山阴多北户，
泉水在东邻。
缘合妄相有，
性空无所亲。
安知广成子，
不是老夫身。

To My Younger Brothers in the Hills

In the wood I forget myself;
In the world a grown-up you'll be.
Don't learn from Chi, a lazy one;
Like Hsien Yüan poor, you may be free.
In the mountain shade, many dwell;
A spring gurgles through the east end.
By Dharma, all is form, all void;
No such things as dear one or friend.
Sir Goodharvest, how do you know,
Is not myself that does here show.

* Chi: Chi Juan (A.D. 210 - A.D. 263), a poet of the Three Kingdoms period and one of the Seven Sages of the Bamboo Grove.

* Hsien Yüan: Hsien Yüan (515 B.C.-?), from the State of Sung, Confucius' disciple, one of the seventy-two sages from Confucius' school.
* Dharma: the ideal state of truth and righteousness in Buddhist terms.
* Sir Goodharvest: a legendary immortal who is said to have lived 1,200 years when Lord Yellow visited him.

菩提寺禁裴迪来相看说逆贼等凝碧池上作音乐供奉人等举声便一时泪下私成口号诵示裴迪

万户伤心生野烟，
百僚何日再朝天。
秋槐叶落空宫里，
凝碧池头奏管弦。

I'm Jailed in Boddhi Temple and Ti P'ei Comes to See Me, Telling of Lushan An's Party at Deepblue Pool for Musicians While I Am Shaken to Tears with this Oral Impromptu To Ti P'ei

Ten thousand households mad with the wild haze,
When can my mates see the sky from the land?
To the vacant palace fall locust leaves,
While at Deepblue Pool there plays a string band.

* Lushan An: Lushan An (A.D. 703 - A.D. 757), a powerful general-governor in the T'ang dynasty. He, of foreign extraction, was descended from a family of Iranian warriors and his mother was a Turkish witch. He distinguished himself in fighting against his own tribes, won the favor of Jade Ring and the confidence of Emperor Deepsire. His promotion being rapid, he was ennobled as a count, and made the governor of the border provinces of the north, where he held under command the best armies of the empire and nursed an inordinate ambition to own the empire.

* locust: a tree of the bean family widely distributed in the temperate zone, with a rough bark, odd-pinnate leaves, and loose, slender racemes of fragrant, white flowers,

which are a seasonal delicacy.
* Deepblue Pool: a pool in Forbidden Park in Loshine, T'ang's east capital. Lushan An occupied Long Peace and Loshine, the two capital of T'ang, and he gathered a dozen officials and hundreds of musicians for a party to show his trophies. The musicians felt sad with tear in their eyes, and Lushan An would kill those who dared to cry. A musician called Sea Clear was dismembered at Horseplay Hall and was publicly exposed because he, flying into a rage, had thrown his instrument to the ground and cried to the west.

口号又示裴迪

安得舍罗网，
拂衣辞世喧。
悠然策藜杖，
归向桃花源。

Another Oral Impromptu To Ti P'ei

How can I shake off all the traps
And strip myself of the world's din?
Now slowly, I take up my stick
To go to Peach Source I begin.

* the world's din: a place like Vanity Fair, symbolic of worldly folly, frivolity, and show.
* Peach Source: Peach Blossom Source. According to Yüanming T'ao's writing, a group of Ch'in people fled to Peach Blossom Source to keep away from the turbulent days, and the people and their offsprings had lived an idyllic and isolated life for 500 years before a fisherman of Chin stumbled into the village.

既蒙宥罪旋复拜官，伏感圣恩窃书鄙意，兼奉简新除使君等诸公

忽蒙汉诏还冠冕，
始觉殷王解网罗。
日比皇明犹自暗，
天齐圣寿未云多。
花迎喜气皆知笑，
鸟识欢心亦解歌。
闻道百城新佩印，
还来双阙共鸣珂。

When Pardoned and Given Back My Post, I Fall Prostrate to Express My Gratitude to His Majesty with this Poem and Copy the Verse in Letters to the Lords Rehabilitated

Sudd'nly, I'm pardoned and given my post,
Feeling King of Yin's grace of freeing most.
The sunlight, compared with our Lord, is dim;
Who could live longer than the sun, than him?
All the flowers to greet the happiness smile;
All the birds sing loud our hearts to beguile.
I hear all the prefects have their new seal;
To Twain Towers their trinkets clink a great deal.

* King of Yin: Hotspring (cir. 1670 - 1587 B.C.), the fist king of Shang. He, originally Lord of the State of Shang under Hsia, launched eleven expeditions, wiped out vassal states of Hsia one by one and finally annihilated Hsia before the founding of the Kingdom of Shang.

* Twain Towers: a metonymy for a palace; Grand Bright Palace in this poem.

和贾舍人早朝大明宫之作

绛帻鸡人报晓筹,
尚衣方进翠云裘。
九天阊阖开宫殿,
万国衣冠拜冕旒。
日色才临仙掌动,
香烟欲傍衮龙浮。
朝罢须裁五色诏,
佩声归到凤池头。

In Reply to Secretary Chia's Poem: the Levee at Great Bright Palace

The red-scarfed watchman heralds the new day;
The wardrobe keeper sends in His cloud gown.
The sky-high gates of the court open now;
Envoys from all kingdoms bow to the crown.
The plumed fans sway towards the morning sun;
Incense near His dragon robe wafts around.
Hued edicts you'll draft now ends the levee;
Phoenix Pool hears your pendants' clinking sound.

* Secretary Chia: referring to Chih Chia (A.D. 718 – A.D. 772), a poet and official who met Pai Li at Paridge after being degraded.
* levee: a morning reception or an assembly at the court of a sovercign or at the house of a great personage. In ancient China, a levee at court was held every five days.
* incense: an aromatic substance in the form of a stick that exhales perfume during combustion, burnt slowly from upward to downward before a Buddhist, Wordist or any

religious or ancestral joss as an act of worship, usually offered with a prayer or vow.
* edict: a public ordinance emanating from a sovereign and having the force of law.
* Phoenix Pool: alias of the Secretariat the poet Chih Chia chairs.

晚春严少尹与诸公见过

松菊荒三径，
图书共五车。
烹葵邀上客，
看竹到贫家。
鹊乳先春草，
莺啼过落花。
自怜黄发暮，
一倍惜年华。

Visited by Shaoyin Yan and Other Lords in Late Spring

So bleak, but pines and mums in here,
I have five carts of books with me.
I cook mallows to treat my guests;
I'm poor, but bamboo you can see.
Magpies feed chicks when spring grass grows;
Orioles chirrup to fallen flowers.
My hair grows gray I sadly sigh;
You should all enjoy your best hours.

* pine: a cone-bearing tree having needle-shaped evergreen leaves growing in clusters, a symbol of longevity and rectitude in Chinese culture.
* mum: chrysanthemum, a symbol of elegance and integrity in Chinese culture, one of the four most important images in Chinese literature, which are wintersweet, orchid, bamboo and chrysanthemum.
* mallow: any plant of the genus *Malva* with roundish green leaves, the first of the five

most popular vegetables in ancient China.
* bamboo: a tall, tree-like or shrubby grass in tropical and semi-tropical regions, a symbol of integrity and altitude, one of the four most important botanical images in Chinese literature, which are wintersweet, orchid, bamboo and chrysanthemum. Plankbridge Cheng (A.D. 1693 – A.D. 1765), A Ching poet, speaks of its character in a poem *Bamboo Rooted in the Rock*: "You bite the green hill and ne'er rest. / Roots in the broken crag, you grow, / And stand erect although hard pressed. /East, west, south, north, let the wind blow."
* magpie: a jaylike passerine corvine bird, having a long and graduated tail and featured with black-and-white coloring, which often makes loud chirps to report good news, as is believed by many Chinese.
* oriole: golden oriole, one of the family of passerine birds, which looks bright yellow with contrasting black wings and sings beautiful songs.

酬严少尹徐舍人见过不遇

公门暇日少，
穷巷故人稀。
偶值乘篮舆，
非关避白衣。
不知炊黍谷，
谁解扫荆扉。
君但倾茶碗，
无妨骑马归。

Thanks to Shaoyin Yan and Secretary Hsu, Who Visit but Fail to See Me

You have few days free from office;
In this poor lane I have friends few.
But I'm out in bamboo sedan,
Not intending to shun you two.
I don't know if you've stayed to dine,
Or who has cleaned the brushwood door.
You may just have a cup of tea;
Just gallop back or come on once more.

* bamboo sedan: a sedan chair made of bamboo stems.
* brushwood door: a simple door made of brushwood, a symbol of country life.
* tea: an evergreen Asian shrub or small tree (*Thea sinensis*), having a compact head of leathery, toothed leaves and white or pink flowers. The cured leaves of this plant or an infusion of them are used as a beverage. There are four major types of tea in Chinese culture, namely black tea, green tea, dark tea and white tea, and a large variety of

subtypes or brands. Tea, first cultivated in China about 4,700 years ago, is a household necessity, as is shown by an idiom — For a family seven things there need to be: firewood, rice, oil, salt, soya sauce sugar and tea.

同崔傅答贤弟

洛阳才子姑苏客,
桂苑殊非故乡陌。
九江枫树几回青,
一片扬州五湖白。
扬州时有下江兵,
兰陵镇前吹笛声。
夜火人归富春郭,
秋风鹤唳石头城。
周郎陆弟为俦侣,
对舞前溪歌白纻。
曲几书留小史家,
草堂棋赌山阴墅。
衣冠若话外台臣,
先数夫君席上珍。
更闻台阁求三语,
遥想风流第一人。

In Reply to You and Fu Ts'ui

Talents from Loshine come here to Kusu;
The laurel garden's different from your lane.
The maples here have turned green many times;
Yangchow's five lakes surge white once and again.
Insurgent troops in Yangchow you oft see;
From Orchid Ridge army flutes you can hear.
Soldiers with fires flee to Richspring at night;

A chilly wind to Stone Town blows, so drear.
With Chou and Lu, you're of the same kind;
You dance to *Stream* and *Ramie* all the same;
You leave your script on a desk to strike all;
Betting on the cottage, you play the game.
If recommenders talk about prefects,
A bright pearl on the mat, you are the best.
If Three Departments need good officials,
Of all brilliant talents, you are the crest.

* Loshine: Loyang if transliterated, the eastern of the two great cities that served as capitals in the early Chinese dynasties, and the second largest city of the Empire in T'ang times, when it had about 800,000 inhabitants.
* Kusu: an alternative name for Soochow, the capital of Wu, an important city of today's Chiangsu Province. Aged 2,500, it is the birth place of Wu culture, eulogized as Heaven on Earth and Eastern Venice, bristled with waterways gardens and pagodas.
* laurel: *laurus nobilis* in Latin, an evergreen shrub with aromatic, lance-shaped leaves, yellowish flowers, and succulent, cherry-like fruit, a symbol of glory usually in the form of a crown or wreath of laurel to indicate honor or high merit.
* maple: any of a large genus (*Acer*) of deciduous trees of the north temperate zone, with opposite leaves that turn red in autumn and a fruit of two joined samaras, a symbol of cordial love and good luck because of its brilliant fiery color.
* Yangchow: alias Broadridge, a land of Wu in the Spring and Autumn period, belonging to Stripfour (576 B.C.- 484 B.C.), who declined the throne and farmed in Broadridge. It became the most prosperous port city in the T'ang dynasty because of the Peking-Hangchow Canal dug by the previous dynasty and it was a waterland like today's Venice, attracting businessmen, travelers, monks and courtesans from every part of the country and the world.
* Orchid Ridge: Orchid Ridge County, in today's Ch'angchow, Chiangsu Province.
* Richspring: Richspring County on the lower reach of the Richspring River in present-day Hangchow, Chechiang Province.
* Stone Town: referring to Nanking, one of the most well-known ancient capitals in China. This city has had more than twenty names such as Forgeton, Fodder Ridge, Build-gain, Gold Hill, River Peace and so on since the Spring and Autumn period.
* Chou and Lu: Yü Chou and Yün Lu: two talented young men, compared with the

young men the author is writing about. Chou was a general of Wu and Lu, Chi Lu's younger brother, was a litterateur.
* *Stream* and *Ramie*: the two famous conservatoire tunes the two young men dance to.
* pearl: a lustrous, calcareous concretion deposited in layers around a central nucleus in the shells of various mollusks, largely used as a gem, regarded as a treasure, and given as a gift to represent love and friendship in Chinese culture.
* Three Departments: Triune Dais, the official system in the T'ang dynasty, which includes Privy Council (Central Secretariat Department), Censorate (Undergate Department) and Executive (Administration Department).

和宋中丞夏日游福贤观天长寺寺即陈左相宅所施之作

已相殷王国，
空馀尚父溪，
钓矶开月殿，
筑道出云梯。
积水浮香象，
深山鸣白鸡。
虚空陈伎乐，
衣服制虹霓。
墨点三千界，
丹飞六一泥。
桃源勿遽返，
再访恐君迷。

Touring Heaven Long Fane and Blessed Sage Temple Donated by Left Premier Ch'en with Magistrate Sung on a Summer Day

Defected to Kingdom of Shang,
He's left the Father Stream in vain.
On the fishing stone is Moon Hall;
From the rock steps is Ladder Cane.
On the pond floats Elephant Balm;
In the deep hills crow roosters white.
From the void loom painted dancers
So dressed in plumage rainbowed bright.
A dot holds three thousand giant worlds;

Cure-all is made with six-one clay.
Don't return so soon from Peach Source;
Next time here, you may go astray.

* Left Premier: in contrast with Right Premier. Left Premier is a deputy prime minister while Right Premier is a prime minister.
* Defected to Kingdom of Shang: insinuating Lushan An's defection of T'ang. In the spring of A.D. 755, under the pretext of ridding the court of Kuochung Yang, the prime minster, Lushan An raised the standard of rebellion. He quickly captured the city of Loshine, occupied the entire territory north of the Yellow River, and was soon marching eastward on Long Peace. He had proclaimed himself the Emperor of Great Yan. This rebellion led to a loss of a large number of people and a sharp decline of T'ang's national power, a turning point of the T'ang Empire.
* Kingdom of Shang: Shang (cir. 1600 B.C.- 1046 B.C.) for short, founded by Hotspring (cir. 1670 B.C.- 1587 B.C.), the fist king of Shang after he wiped out vassal states of Hsia one by one and finally annihilated Hsia.
* the Father Stream, the Pan Brook, where Great Grand went fishing. A butcher at his young age, Great Grand remained diligent in hardship, expecting to display his ability for the country one day, but he did not make any achievement before he was 70 years old. He went west at the age of 72, fishing as he waited for King Civil, and finally won his appreciation.
* Moon Hall: Moon Palace, where Son of Moon (Mahasthamaprapta) lives in Buddhism.
* Ladder Cane: a ladder wherewith an immortal goes to Heaven.
* Elephant Balm: one of the elephants mentioned in Buddhist sutras.
* rooster: the male of the chicken that struts with pride and crows at dawn.
* A dot holds three thousand wide worlds: the relativity of smallness and largeness. Three thousand wide worlds are large but they are contained in a tiny dot.
* Peach Source: Peach Blossom Source. According to Yüanming T'ao's writing, a group of Ch'in people fled to Peach Blossom Source to keep away from the turbulent days, and the people and their offsprings had lived an idyllic and isolated life for 500 years before a fisherman of Chin stumbled into the village.

春夜竹亭赠钱少府归蓝田

夜静群动息,
时闻隔林犬。
却忆山中时,
人家涧西远。
羡君明发去,
采蕨轻轩冕。

To Ch'ien, a County Sheriff, Back to Blue Field at Bamboo Pavilion on a Spring Night

The night quiet, all creatures still stay,
But from across the wood dogs bay.
When I was in the mountains then,
Some households were west of the glen.
I admire you're leaving at dawn
To pick ferns in defiance of crown.

* Blue Field: Blue Field County under today's Hsi-an, Sha'anhsi Province, famous for jade mined there, called Bluefield Jade.
* dog: a domesticated carnivorous mammal (*Canis familiaris*), of worldwide distribution and many varieties, noted for its adaptability and its devotion to man. The dog was domesticated in China at least 8,000 years ago and was often used as a hunter, as a poem in *The Book of Songs* says:"The dog bells clink and clink; / The hunter's handsome, a real pink."
* to pick ferns: alluding to a hermit's life. The fern is any of a widely distributed class of flowerless, seedless pteridophytic plants, having roots and stems and feathery leaves (fronds) which carry the reproductive spores in clusters of sporangia called *sori*. Its young stems and root starch are table delicacies to Chinese now as well as in the past.

送钱少府还蓝田

草色日向好，
桃源人去稀。
手持平子赋，
目送老莱衣。
每候山樱发，
时同海燕归。
今年寒食酒，
应是返柴扉。

Seeing Off Chien, a County Sheriff, Back to Blue Field

The grass shines under the sun bright;
From Peach Source it seems all have gone.
You are leaving with *Go Home* verse
For your parents as a good son.
When cherry blossoms start to bloom,
Swallows from overseas come back.
When Cold Food Day comes on this year,
I should be leaving for my shack.

---

* Blue Field: Blue Field County under today's Hsi-an, Sha'anhsi Province, famous for jade mined there, called Bluefield Jade.
* sun: the heavenly body that is the center of attraction and the main source of light and heat in the solar system, a representation of Shine in contrast with Shade, the moon, in Chinese culture, a symbol of hope, life, strength, vigor and youth.
* Peach Source: Peace Blossom Source. According to Yüanming T'ao's writing, a group

of Ch'in people fled to Peach Blossom Source to keep away from the turbulent days, and the people and their offsprings had lived an idyllic and isolated life for 500 years before a fisherman of Chin stumbled into the village.

* *Go Home*: a verse by Heng Chang (A.D. 78 – A.D. 139), an astronomer, philosopher and litterateur in the Eastern Han dynasty. He wrote *Go Home* and would go back home when he felt unfulfilled.
* cherry: any of various trees (genus *Prunus*) of the rose family, related to the plum and the peach and bearing small, round or heart-shaped drupes enclosing a smooth pit; especially the sweet cherry, the sour cherry and the wild black cherry.
* Cold Food Day: one or two days before Pure Brightness Day (the third day of the third moon each year), the festival in memory of Chiht'ui of Chieh (? – 636 B.C.) without cooking for a day. In the Spring and Autumn period, Double Ear, a prince of Chin, escaped from the disaster in his state with his follower Chiht'ui. In great deprivation, Double Ear almost starved to death, and Chiht'ui fed him with flesh cut off his thigh. When Double Ear was crowned Lord Civil of Chin, Chiht'ui retreated to Mt. Silk Floss with his mother when feeling neglected. To have him out, Lord Civil set the mountain on fire, but Chiht'ui did not give in and was burned with his mother.

左 掖 梨 花

闲洒阶边草，
轻随箔外风。
黄莺弄不足，
衔入未央宫。

Pear Blossoms at Undergate Department

The step-by grass does them admire!
With wind from out the screen they fly.
The orioles send them to Non-end,
As they cannot keep them all by.

* Undergate Department: a supreme organization of inspection, one of the three most powerful administrative organizations of the T'ang Empire, the other two being Central Secretariat Department and Administration Department.
* screen: a curtain which separates or cuts off, shelters or protects as a light partition, usually made of bamboo, a common image in Chinese literature. A poem in *The Book of Songs* reads like this: "You wait for me before the screen; / Your hat-rings white do tinkle clean, / And your rubies brilliantly sheen."
* oriole: golden oriole, one of the family of passerine birds, which looks bright yellow with contrasting black wings and sings beautiful songs.
* Non-end: the main imperial palace of the Han House, built on the basis of Chapter Height, a Ch'in palace, in 200 B.C., monitored by Premier Ho Hsiao (257 B.C.- 193 B.C.), located on Dragonhead Plateau, the highest vantage of Long Peace. It was the political center of the Han Empire for 200 years and was made a part of the Forbidden Park in the Sui and T'ang dynasties. Non-end, six times as large as today's the Forbidden City or Imperial Palace in Peking, existed for 1,041 years, the longest-lived palace in Chinese history.

送韦大夫东京留守

人外遗世虑，
空端结遐心。
曾是巢许浅，
始知尧舜深。
苍生讵有物，
黄屋如乔林。
上德抚神运，
冲和穆宸襟。
云雷康屯难，
江海遂飞沉。
天工寄人英，
龙衮瞻君临。
名器苟不假，
保釐固其任。
素质贯方领，
清景照华簪。
慷慨念王室，
从容献官箴。
云旗蔽三川，
画角发龙吟。
晨扬天汉声，
夕卷大河阴。
穷人业已宁，
逆虏遗之擒。
然后解金组，
拂衣东山岑。
给事黄门省，

秋光正沉沉。
壮心与身退,
老病随年侵。
君子从相访,
重玄其可寻。

Seeing Off Grandee Wei to East Capital as a Stay Guard

Out of the world you still show care,
With an immortal's heart in vain.
It's Freedom and Nest who were shoal;
How Mound and Hibiscus did gain.
How can the world remain like this?
The king's hood shades all souls the best.
Upper Virtue runs like a mill,
Sending air to the sovereign's chest.
Cloud and Thunder dispels all banes;
Seas and rivers all run their way.
God's Will's found in the human ace
Behold Most High in full array.
Titles and vessels kept in hand,
Peace can be assured out and in.
White all o'er from collar to train,
A gleam from his grandiose hair pin.
With gratitude to the royals,
Remonstrance is given with ease;
Banners like clouds shade the vast plain;
A painted horn will Huns appease.
At dawn T'ang's power is shown to all;

At dusk the River's swept across.
The cornered rebels have no way
But surrender, destined to loss.
Then you're disarmed for a new post
To safeguard East Capital now.
You serve Undergate Department,
The autumn hue makes all grains bow.
My old age has failed my strong will
Illness comes to me more and more.
E'en if you call on me to join,
The profoundness I can't explore.

* Freedom and Nest: referring to Freedom (Yu Hsu) and Father Nest (Fu Ch'ao). They both were hermits of talent and declined to be king when Mound intended to abdicate the throne to them.
* Mound: Mound (2377 B.C.- 2259 B.C.), Yao if transliterated. Divine and noble, Mound has been regarded as one of Five Lords in ancient China.
* Hibiscus: Shun if transliterated, an ancient sovereign, a descendant of Lord Yellow, regarded as one of Five Lords in prehistoric China.
* Hun: a nomadic people north and west of China, regarded as invaders in the long history of China.
* T'ang: the T'ang dynasty (A.D. 618 - A.D. 907) or the T'ang Empire. The three hundred years of the T'ang dynasty witnessed a most brilliant era of national power, culture and refinement, unsurpassed in all the annals of the Middle Kingdom.
* the River: the Yellow River, the second longest river in China, the birthplace of Chinese civilization. It is the second longest river in China, the cradle of Chinese civilization. As legend goes, the river derived from a yellow dragon that, couchant on Midland Plain, ate yellow soil, flooded crops, devoured people and stock, and was finally tamed by Great Worm, the First King of Hsia (21 B.C.- 16 B.C.), and its fertile valleys were turned into fields of rice, barley and oscillating corn, amid gleaming streams and lakes.
* East Capital: Loshine, the second large city of T'ang, with a population of eight million in that period.
* Undergate Department: the imperial Censorate, one of the three most important departments of the T'ang Empire.

瓜　园　诗

维瓜园高斋,俯视南山形胜,二三时辈,同赋是诗,兼命词英数公,同用"园"字为韵,韵任多少;时太子司议郎薛璩发此题,遂同诸公云。

余适欲锄瓜,
倚锄听叩门。
鸣驺导骢马,
常从夹朱轩。
穷巷正传呼,
故人倪相存。
携手追凉风,
放心望乾坤。
蔼蔼帝王州,
宫观一何繁。
林端出绮道,
殿顶摇华幡。
素怀在青山,
若值白云屯。
回风城西雨,
返景原上村。
前酌盈尊酒,
往往闻清言。
黄鹂啭深木,
朱槿照中园。
犹羡松下客,
石上闻清猿。

A Poem of Melon Field

My melon field on the height overlooks the scenes of the South Hills; a few friends of mine write on the same topic, and all are required to include the word "field", not limited to length. Chü Hsüeh, corrector under Crown Prince, suggests the title, hence my friends and I start to write.

Ere I go to the melon field,
My hoe hears a knock on my door.
The retinue leads the green steed;
With the scarlet carts they all pour.
Calls and shouts all thru the poor lane,
Are they my friends coming to call?
Hand in hand, they chase the cool air,
Looking above, not worried at all.
Prosperous our emperor's land,
Temples and fanes make a great sight.
A criss-crossing road from the wood,
Flags o'er the palace flow, so bright.
As I've a heart for the blue hills,
White clouds come and above remain.
A rain from west town with wind whirls
Sunlight to villages on the plain.
I set table and prepare wine;
We have free talks of a pure sort.
Orioles chirrup in the deep wood;
China roses flame in my court.
A recluse I admire alone:
He hears monkeys trill on a stone.

* melon: a trailing plant of the gourd family, or its fruit. There are two genera, the muskmelon and the watermelon, each with numerous varieties, growing in both tropical and temperate zones.
* oriole: golden oriole, one of the family of passerine birds, which looks bright yellow with contrasting black wings and sings beautiful songs.
* China rose: a cultivated rose (*Rosa chinensis*) of Chinese origin or a large hibiscus (*Hibiscus rosa-sinensis*) with showy flowers.
* monkey: any of a group of primates having elongate limbs, hands and feet adapted for grasping, and a highly developed nervous system, including marmosets, baboons, and macaques, but not the anthropoid apes, though monkeys and apes are used alternatively in Chinese.

送杨长史赴果州

褒斜不容幰，
之子去何之。
鸟道一千里，
猿声十二时。
官桥祭酒客，
山木女郎祠。
别后同明月，
君应听子规。

Seeing Off Vice Governor Yang to Kuochow

The Gifttilt can't allow a cart;
Where are you going now you start?
Three hundred miles rolls the bird way;
Monkey shrieks resound night and day.
On the bridge sacrificed is wine;
In the wood there looms Maiden Shrine.
Though we part, the same moon we share,
And you'd hark to the cuckoos there.

* Kuochow: today's Nanch'ung, Ssuch'uan Province.
* the Gifttilt: a dale in Ch'in Ridge, an important but very narrow mountainous road.
* Maiden Shrine: a temple on Mt. Maiden in Paoch'eng County, in today's Mid-Han, Sha'anhsi Province.
* cuckoo: any of a family of birds with a long, slender body, grayish-brown on top and white below, a symbol of sadness in Chinese culture. As is said, during the Shang

dynasty, Cuckoo (Yü Tu), a caring king of Shu, abdicated the throne due to a flood and lived in reclusion. After his death, he turned into a cuckoo, wailing day and night, shedding tears and blood.

慕容承携素馔见过

纱帽乌皮几，
闲居懒赋诗。
门看五柳识，
年算六身知。
灵寿君王赐，
雕胡弟子炊。
空劳酒食馔，
持底解人颐。

Ch'eng Mujung's Visit with Vegetarian Food

My gauze cap, my desk, I repose;
Now idle, a verse I compose.
Five willows at door I behold,
Now nearly seventy years old.
My Senior Stick granted by Lord,
Pupils offer wild rice for board.
Great thanks, you give me food and wine;
So pleased, we can happily dine.

* gauze cap: usually known as black gauze cap, a cap made of gauze, a symbol of an official position. Gauze caps were first made in the Sung dynasty (A.D. 420 – A.D. 479) of the Southern Dynasties period, and used as an official wearing from the Sui dynasty. "losing the black gauze cap" means "losing the official position" in Chinese culture.

* five willows: an allusion to Ch'ien T'ao (A.D. 352 – A.D. 427), a verse writer, poet, and litterateur in the Chin dynasty, and the founder of Chinese idyllism, who was once the magistrate of P'engtse. Pure and lofty, T'ao resigned from official life several times to live a life of simplicity. There were five willow trees planted in front of his house, so he called himself Mr. Five Willows.

* Senior Stick: a symbol of great honor, a stick granted to old senior people by an emperor, usually to Crown Prince's Teacher.
* wild rice: a tall aquatic grass, the stem of which is used as a vegetable and the grain of which was formerly used as food, now esteemed as a table delicacy.

酬慕容十一

行行西陌返，
驻憩问车公。
挟毂双官骑，
应门五尺僮。
老年如塞北，
强起离墙东。
为报壶丘子，
来人道姓蒙。

Thanks to Mujung Eleven

While going, from west they turn back;
Cart stopped, there inquires the man great.
He has official guards with him,
And has tall boys keeping his gate.
In advanced years, he goes northbound;
Off his immortal dream he'd rush.
To requite him, a worthy man,
I would say: my name is Sir Lush.

* Lush: Sir Lush, Chuangtzu (369 B.C.- 286 B.C.) if transliterated, an important philosopher in the Warring States period, one of the representatives of Wordism (Taoism). One of the most important Chinese classics is *Sir Lush*, a book of philosophical allegories written by Sir Lush.

饭覆釜山僧

晚知清净理,
日与人群疏。
将候远山僧,
先期扫敝庐。
果从云峰里,
顾我蓬蒿居。
藉草饭松屑,
焚香看道书。
燃灯昼欲尽,
鸣磬夜方初。
一悟寂为乐,
此生闲有馀。
思归何必深,
身世犹空虚。

Treating Monk of Reversed Pot with Food

Now old, I know the truth of Zen,
Each day, kept off the world so mean.
Waiting for the monk to come on,
Now my lodge I begin to clean.
He appears from clouded peaks
And call at the thatch I abide.
We cook with grass and piny flowers
And read sutras, incense beside.
We light the lantern when dusk falls;

At night we strike at the stone chime.
In musing, Nirvana's the best;
Then this life we have all free time.
One need not to be so intense;
In calmness, your mind is void hence.

* Zen: a kind of performance of quietude in a form of meditation or contemplation. When Sanskrit jana was spread to China, it was translated as Zan or Zen for this kind of practice. In the T'ang dynasty, educated Chinese were imbued with Zen, and many of them were associated with Zen monks and spent much time in Zen monasteries.
* thatch: any of tall, coarse grasses (genus *Spatina*) widely distributed in temperate zones, usually referring to a hermitage in Chinese culture.
* sutra: a formulated doctrine, often so short as to be unintelligible without a key; literally a rule or a precept. In Buddhism, an extended writing usually in verse, and often in dialogue form, embodying important religious and philosophical propositions, sometimes directly, sometimes in highly allegorical or metaphorical language. The best example is a dialogue between two monks, Hsiu Shen and Neng Hui. The former's verse is like this: "The body is a Bodhi tree; /The mind's like a mirror stand bright. / Make it clean, as oft as can be, / In case dust should on it alight." And Neng Hui replied, bettering the former: "There's nothing like a Bodhi tree, / Nor such things as a mirror stand. / There is nothing that you can see. / Where can dust find a place to land?"
* incense: an aromatic substance in the form of a stick that exhales perfume during combustion, burnt before a Buddhist, Wordist or any religious or ancestral figure as an act of worship, usually offered with a prayer or vow.
* Nirvana: the attainment of complete freedom from all mental, emotional and psychic tension, the ideal and goal of all religious effort.

叹 白 发

宿昔朱颜成暮齿，
须臾白发变垂髫。
一生几许伤心事，
不向空门何处销。

Sighing to My Gray Hair

So shortly, a blooming face does decay;
Very soon, a silk fringe turns into gray hair.
A string of sorrows darken my whole life;
Without void, where could I shun them, o where?

* silk fringe: a symbol of youth or prime. When one is young, his or her hair is black and shining, and when one gets old, his or her hair becomes gray, and as time goes on, becomes white.
* void: the state of quietude, free of offense, free of reason, an ideal state pursued by Wordists. Void is regarded as the ultimate being or noumenon that encompasses everything, real as if none, true as if empty.

和陈监四郎秋雨中思从弟据

袅袅秋风动,
凄凄烟雨繁。
声连鹊鹊观,
色暗凤凰原。
细柳疏高阁,
轻槐落洞门。
九衢行欲断,
万井寂无喧。
忽有愁霖唱,
更陈多露言。
平原思令弟,
康乐谢贤昆。
逸兴方三接,
衰颜强七奔。
相如今老病,
归守茂陵园。

In Reply to Ch'ien Ch'en Four's Missing My Cousin Chü in Autumn Rain

Sough, sough, the autumn wind blows fast;
Slash, slash, there falls a misty rain.
The sound whoops into Magpie Shrine;
The cast darkens all Phoenix Plain.
By the tower willow twigs sway sparse;
To the doors locust leaves dried fall.

The boulevards see no more souls;
In the fields there's no noise at all.
Sudd'nly there rings *Sad Autumn Rain*,
With the reminder of "Ware, ware".
Like Chi who did love his brother,
Like Glee who his cousin did care.
You have the zest to meet three times
And when old you will the foes sweep.
Like Hsiangju so bright you're now old;
Back home, Lushridge Tomb you may keep.

* Magpie Shrine: in Sweet Spring Palace on today's Mt. Sweet Spring, Purification (Ch'unhua) County, Sha'anhsi Province.
* Phoenix Plain: a plain on Mt. Black Steed, where, as is said, phoenixes alight to gather.
* locust: a tree of the bean family widely distributed in the temperate zone, with a rough bark, odd-pinnate leaves, and loose, slender racemes of fragrant, white flowers, which are a seasonal delicacy.
* *Sad Autumn Rain*: a poem composed by Chan Hsieh (A.D. 385 – A.D. 421) to Poolbright Hsieh.
* Chi: referring to Chi Lu (A.D. 261 – A.D. 303), a renowned litterateur and calligrapher in the Western Chin dynasty.
* Glee: Poolbright (A.D. 352 – A.D. 427), Ch'ien T'ao or Yüanming T'ao if transliterated, a verse writer, poet, and litterateur in the Chin dynasty, and the founder of Chinese idyllism. He was once the magistrate of P'engtse, but he resigned four times to live in reclusion. All in all, he can be remembered as a complex figure and a poet of complex poems, as has been termed by J. P. Seaton.
* Hsiangju: referring to Hsiangju Ssuma (179 B.C. – 118 B.C.) in full name, a representative verse writer in Chinese literary history. He and his wife, Wenchün, a brilliant woman poet, were equally famous in Chinese history.
* Lushridge Tomb: one of Five Mausoleums of Western Han, the tomb of Emperor Martial of Han, the largest of all Han mausoleums, located in Lush Township, hence the name.

冬晚对雪忆胡居士家

寒更传晓箭，
清镜览衰颜。
隔牖风惊竹，
开门雪满山。
洒空深巷静，
积素广庭闲。
借问袁安舍，
翛然尚闭关。

Reminiscing Hu, a Lay Buddhist on a Snowy Night

The hourglass leaks, a cold night passed;
The mirror shows my face downcast.
Out of the blind, wind sways bamboo;
My door does face the hills of snow.
Calmness prevails in the deep lane;
My court's so white, free of a stain.
May I ask Yüan in his quiet hut:
Why calmly is your door fast shut?

* lay Buddhist: one who believes in Buddhism and practises Buddhism at home instead of being a monk in a temple. Many poets in the T'ang dynasties were lay Buddhists like our poet Wei Wang, who was accorded Buddha of Poetry, and Pai Li, who was esteemed as Fairy of Poetry.

* hourglass: a vessel used for measuring the passage of time by the running of water or sand from the upper into the lower compartment, also used as metaphor for the elapse

of time.
* bamboo: a tall, tree-like or shrubby grass in tropical and semi-tropical regions, a symbol of integrity and altitude, one of the four most important botanical images in Chinese literature, which are wintersweet, orchid, bamboo and chrysanthemum.
* Yüan: An Yüan (? - A.D 92), a magistrate in the Eastern Han dynasty, a filial son, very strict with his officials but having their respect.

胡居士卧病遗米因赠人

了观四大因，
根性何所有。
妄计苟不生，
是身孰休咎。
色声何谓客，
阴界复谁守。
徒言莲花目，
岂恶杨枝肘。
既饱香积饭，
不醉声闻酒。
有无断常见，
生灭幻梦受。
即病即实相，
趋空定狂走。
无有一法真，
无有一法垢。
居士素通达，
随宜善抖擞。
床上无毡卧，
镉中有粥否。
斋时不乞食，
定应空漱口。
聊持数斗米，
且救浮生取。

To Hu, a Lay Buddhist, Who Gives Me Rice When I Lie Ill

The Four Great Causes you know well;
Where do their productive powers dwell?
With no fancies or fantasies,
There'd be no falls or fallacies.
Six forms are objects of all sort;
Who in this world does these support?
The lotus eyes can see through all,
Caring not birth, death, rise or fall.
Since on sesame food I can dine,
I may do without meat or wine.
Real and nil and pursuits are vain;
Birth and death in all dreams remain.
Obstinance, ideas, void profound,
All go through the none without bound.
No true Dharma does here remain;
No true Dharma incurs a stain.
A lay Buddhist can all cares doff,
So free thanks to his Shaking-off.
No felt on his bed to lie on;
No meal in his pot ready done.
When fasting, he begs not for food;
When musing, rinse his mouth he would.
He's just a few buckets of grain,
The floating life he could sustain.

---

* lay Buddhist: a non-professional Buddhist who practices Buddhism at home, usually

meditating and reading sutras or burning incense to a joss on a regular basis.
* the Four Great Causes: Earth, Water, Fire, and Wind, the four basic elements of forms and phenomena.
* lotus: any of various waterlilies, especially the white or pink Asian lotus, used as a religious symbol in Hinduism and Buddhism. The lotus is a common image in Chinese literature, as two lines of a lyric by Hsiu Ouyang (A.D. 1007 – A.D. 1072) read: "A thunder brings rain to the wood and pool, / The rain hushes the lotus, drips cool."
* sesame: an East Indian herb, containing seeds which are used as food and as a source of the pale yellow sesame oil, used as salad oil or an emollient, introduced from Ferghana by Ch'ien Chang (164 B.C. – 114 B.C.), a diplomat, traveler, explorer, and the initiator of the Silk Road.
* void: the state of quietude, free of offense, free of reason, an ideal state pursued by Wordists. Void is regarded as the ultimate being or noumenon that encompasses everything, real as if none, true as if empty.
* Dharma: truth and righteousness in Buddhist terms.
* Shaking-off: getting rid of worries in meditation, translated from Sanskrit Dhuta.

秋 夜 独 坐

独坐悲双鬓,
空堂欲二更。
雨中山果落,
灯下草虫鸣。
白发终难变,
黄金不可成。
欲知除老病,
唯有学无生。

Sitting Alone on an Autumn Night

Sitting, I rue my sideburns white
Till my bare room sees off the night.
In the hills fruits fall in the rain;
Beneath my lamp insects complain.
To grey hair nothing one can do;
No dream of elixir comes true.
From age and illness if you'd stay,
Nirvana is the only way.

* elixir: a kind of cure-all, all alchemists in Chinese history have tried to make and all Wordists hope to find.
* Nirvana: the attainment of complete freedom from all mental, emotional and psychic tension, which is the goal and ideal state of all religious effort.

与胡居士皆病寄此诗兼示学人二首

To Hu, the Lay Buddhist, Who Is Ill like Me and For Other Learners, Two Poems

其 一

一兴微尘念,
横有朝露身。
如是睹阴界,
何方置我人。
碍有固为主,
趣空宁舍宾。
洗心讵悬解,
悟道正迷津。
因爱果生病,
从贪始觉贫。
色声非彼妄,
浮幻即吾真。
四达竟何遣,
万殊安可尘。
胡生但高枕,
寂寞与谁邻。
战胜不谋食,
理齐甘负薪。
予若未始异,
讵论疏与亲。

No. 1

Once the idea of dust comes through,
Your body dries like morning dew.
Hades, it seems, I can now see;
Where could ego and others be?
If stillness at real does prevail,
The approach to void will not trail.
Is Heart-washing Getting-away?
Knowing the Word, one goes astray.
To love, one's destined to get ill;
In greed, one's certain to have nil.
Form and sound leads you not astray;
Fantasies are Truth where we stay.
What will Four Thoroughfares attain?
Nothing on earth can be a stain.
My friend, do relax, be care-free;
Can loneliness your neighbor be?
Triumph o'er your greed, do not lust;
A woodcutter's life is our must.
If we've no sense of out and in,
We won't care what's feud or who's kin.

* lay Buddhist: one who believes in Buddhist doctrines and practises Buddhism at home instead of being a monk in a temple.
* Hades: the abode of the dead, and a euphemism for the netherworldor hell.
* ego: self, considered as the seat of consciousness, the permanent real being to whom all the conscious states and attributes belong.
* void: the state of quietude, free of offense, free of reason, an ideal state pursued by Wordists. Void is regarded as the ultimate being or noumenon that encompasses everything, real as if none, true as if empty.

* Heart-washing: getting rid of evil thoughts, greediness and craftiness from one's mind.
* Getting-away: the other way of saying relief. As is said in *Sir Lush*: This is what was called relief in ancient times. If one cannot be relieved, he's bound by things. The binding, however, cannot last too long, why should I hate it?"
* the Word: referring to Tao if transliterated, the most significant and profoundest concept of cosmology and axiology in Chinese philosophy. The Word is fully elucidated in *The Word and the World*, the single book that Laocius wrote all his wisdom into. Its importance can be seen in this verse: "The Word is void, but its use is infinite. O deep! It seems to be the root of all things."
* Truth: the state of being as it is in Wordism.
* Four Thoroughfares: the four ways to transcend Cause-effect relationship so as to attain Nirvana..

其　二

浮空徒漫漫，
泛有定悠悠。
无乘及乘者，
所谓智人舟。
讵舍贫病域，
不疲生死流。
无烦君喻马，
任以我为牛。
植福祠迦叶，
求仁笑孔丘。
何津不鼓棹，
何路不摧辀。
念此闻思者，
胡为多阻修。
空虚花聚散，
烦恼树稀稠。
灭相成无记，
生心坐有求。
降吴复归蜀，
不到莫相尤。

No. 2

Floating Void stretches without bound;
Drifting Real turns round after round.
No means to take or means to take,
To the other bank they can make.
Whether you are ill or in need,

It's Flow of Life and Death indeed.
Do not liken me to a mare,
Or with me an ox you compare.
Do revere Kasyapa for bliss;
Do laugh at Confucius like this.
Which sea to cross, you need no oar?
Which way to go, you get no sore?
Wisdom you hear, wisdom you learn;
But why are there blockades so stern?
All blossoms bloom, all blossoms fall;
Worries are thorns low and thorns tall.
Extinguish all and don't judge;
Ideas are stains, and lust a smudge.
To Wu or to Shu there is no way;
If I'm wrong, excuse me you may.

* Floating Void: the boundless state of nothingness.
* Drifting Real: whatever exists as Form or Phenomena.
* mare: a fully mature female horse, mule, donkey, burro, etc., especially a female horse that has reached the age of five.
* ox: any of several bovid ruminants as cattle, buffaloes, bison, gaur, and yaks; especially a domesticated bull (Bos taurus), used as a draft animal, a symbol of diligence in Chinese culture.
* Kasyapa: Kasyapa Buddha, one of the ten disciples of Sakyamuni (565 B.C.- 486 B.C.), the founder of Buddhism.
* Confucius: Confucius (551 B.C.- 479 B.C.), a great educationalist, ideologist and the founder of Confucianism from the State of Lu (770 B.C.- 476 B.C.). Through his righteousness, optimism and enterprising spirit he has greatly influenced the character of the Chinese people from generation to generation.
* Wu: the State of Wu (12 Century B.C - 473 B.C.), a vassal state of Chough in the lower reaches of the Long River. It was one of the most powerful states in the Spring and Autumn period and was finally annexed by the State of Yüeh, its neighboring state.
* Shu: one of the earliest kingdoms in China, founded by Silkworm according to legend. In the Three Kingdom period, a new Shu was established by Pei Liu, hence one of the three kingdoms in that period.

恭懿太子挽歌五首

Five Elegies to Crown Prince of Respecting Virtue

其 一

何悟藏环早，
才知拜璧年。
翀天王子去，
对日圣君怜。
树转宫犹出，
笳悲马不前。
虽蒙绝驰道，
京兆别开阡。

No. 1

He had acumen as a child,
But deceased a premature one.
Like the crane rider, he's away;
His Majesty grieves to the sun.
His hearse rolls out of palace there,
The steeds pause at the flute in gloom.
He has the same status with Crown;
By officials is built his tomb.

* the crane rider: referring to Prince of Front, a son of King Spirit of Chough, who had been intelligent and courageous since childhood. Though he was Crown Prince, he had few desires and was keen on the Word. In some legends, he knew his mortality and

became immortal.
* hearse: a vehicle which is unvarnished and has four wheels, used to carry the dead usually in a coffin to his grave.
* steed: a horse; especially a spirited war horse. The use of horses in war can be traced back to the Shang dynasty (1600 B.C.- 1046 B.C.), when a department of horse management was established. A verse from *The Book of Songs* tells of Lord Civil of Watch's industriousness: "In state affairs he leads; / He has three thousand steeds."
* flute: a tubular wind instrument of small diameter with holes along the side.

其 二

兰殿新恩切，
椒宫夕临幽。
白云随凤管，
明月在龙楼。
人向青山哭，
天临渭水愁。
鸡鸣常问膳，
今恨玉京留。

No. 2

Orchid Hall basks in His new grace;
Balm Palace cries in deadly gloom.
White clouds go after Phoenix Flute;
The moon shines to his empty room.
People bemoan the mountains blue;
Heaven o'erlooks the saddened Wei;
His servants come at dawn as e'er,
But he's gone, the town bleak today.

* Orchid Hall: an imperial concubine's palace or bedroom.
* Balm Palace: an empress's palace or bedroom.
* Phoenix Flute: the flute Prince of Front played while ascending to Heaven.
* moon: the celestial body appearing at night and revolving around the earth from left to right, with many connotations in Chinese culture, predominantly a symbol of solitude.
* Heaven: the space surrounding or seeming to overarch the earth, in which the sun, the moon, and stars appear, popularly the abode of God, his angels and the blessed, and in most cases suggesting supernatural power or sometimes signifying a monarch.
* the saddened Wei: referring to the sad look of the Wei River, the longest branch of the Yellow River.

其 三

骑吹凌霜发,
旌旗夹路陈。
礼容金节护,
册命玉符新。
傅母悲香褓,
君家拥画轮。
射熊今梦帝,
秤象问何人?

No. 3

The chivalry band starts in frost;
Along the road the banners flow.
The capital chief's the chief guard;
The deceased has a tally new.
His swaddle his teachers bewail;
The peers escort the painted carts.
The bear shot appears in his dream;
The elephant scaler now departs.

* tally: referring to a tiger tally, a token issued to generals for troop movement. It is usually tiger-shaped, with one half kept by the Monarch and the other by local generals, and generals can send troops only if the two halves are matched.
* swaddle: a cloth or bandage used for swaddling, i.e., wrapping a newborn baby.
* the elephant scaler: referring to the five-year-old Ts'ung Ts'ao (A.D. 196 – A.D. 208), who weighed an elephant by standing it in a boat, and then measuring the amount of sinking and at last weighing the same amount of pebbles laid in the boat to make it sink the same length.

其 四

苍舒留帝宠，
子晋有仙才。
五岁过人智，
三天使鹤催。
心悲阳禄馆，
目断望思台。
若道长安近，
何为更不来。

No. 4

Like the prodigy, he's Crown's grace
And like Front, he's gifted and wise.
At five, he outshines all at court;
Three Heavens hasten him to rise.
Her Majesty mourns her lost son;
The Lord peers on the mound with pain.
If Long Peace is not very far,
Why don't you wake and come again?

* the prodigy: Ts'ung Ts'ao (A.D. 196 – A.D. 208), the prodigy who weighed the elephant with a boat, here likened to Shao, the deceased Crown Prince.
* Front: Prince of Front, an ingenious crown prince in of Chough, who died young, likened to the deceased in the poem.
* Long Peace: Chang'an if transliterated, the capital of the T'ang Empire, with one million inhabitants, the largest walled city ever built by man, and a cosmopolis of world religions, Buddhism, Confucianism, Wordism, Nestorianism, Zoroastrianism, and even Islamism represented by Saracens. It saw the wonder of the age that reached the pinnacle of brilliance in Emperor Deepsire's reign: The main castle with its nine-

fold gates, the thirty-six imperial palaces, pillars of gold, innumerable mansions and villas of noblemen, the broad avenues thronged with motley crowds of townsfolk, gallants on horseback, and mandarin cars drawn by yokes of black oxen, countless houses of pleasure, which opened their doors by night all made this city a kaleidoscope of miracles.

其 五

西望昆池阔,
东瞻下杜平。
山朝豫章馆,
树转凤凰城。
五校连旗色,
千门叠鼓声。
金环如有验,
还向画堂生。

No. 5

Bright Pool in the west looks so broad;
In the east, Birch Leaf is flat down.
His mausoleum sees Camphor Fane;
The High Park trees face Phoenix Town;
The field officers hold their flags;
The gates and doors hear the drum sound.
If the golden hoop can forebode,
Frescoed Hall will view him come around.

* Bright Pool: an artificial lake dug for navy training in Emperor Martial's reign of the Han dynasty, 20 kilometers in circumference, between the River Rich and the River Gush southwest of Long Peace.
* Birch Leaf: Birch Leaf Town, southeast of Long Peace, the State of Birch Leaf in the Chough dynasty and a county in the Ch'in dynasty.
* mausoleum: the tomb of Mausolus, king of Caria, at Halicarnassus: included among the seven wonders of the ancient world, a metaphor for a large, imposing tomb or a building with vaults for the entombment of a number of bodies.
* Camphor Fane: a Wordist temple in Bright Pool.

* High Park: an imperial park that Lord Martial of Han built on the site of a discarded park of Ch'in. It was vast and splendid with palaces and woodlands, having various functions and recreational facilities, rolling about 340 kilometers.
* Phoenix Town: referring to Long Peace, the capital.
* Frescoed Hall: a palace frescoed inside, referring to an imperial palace.

河南严尹弟见宿弊庐访别人赋十韵

上客能论道，
吾生学养蒙。
贫交世情外，
才子古人中。
冠上方簪豸，
车边已画熊。
拂衣迎五马，
垂手凭双童。
花醺和松屑，
茶香透竹丛。
薄霜澄夜月，
残雪带春风。
古壁苍苔黑，
寒山远烧红。
眼看东候别，
心事北川同。
为学轻先辈，
何能访老翁。
欲知今日后，
不乐为车公。

Yin Yan from Honan Pays Me a Visit and Stays for the Night in My Lodge, Hence the Score Lines

My honored guest talks on the Word;

I rear myself in darkness dressed.
Our friendship is out of the world;
Of all talents you rank the best.
A unihorned beast on your crown,
A painted bear on your cart hood.
You pat your clothes to meet Five Steeds;
On the two kids rely I would.
Flower wine and pine nuts for your guests,
Tea fragrance wafts in the bamboo.
Frost glistens on the moonlit night;
The spring wind whirls with thawing snow.
The old wall is dim with dark moss;
The cold hills with bonfires flare.
Soon we'll by Eastern Mound depart,
And the Northern Hill I do care.
If young learners despise elders,
How can they call on me in here?
What could I do after you leave?
No one can take your place, I fear.

* the Word: referring to Tao if transliterated, the most significant and profoundest concept in Chinese philosophy. According to Laocius's *The Word and the World*: "The Word is void, but its use is infinite. O deep! It seems to be the root of all things."
* unihorned beast: hsiehchih if transliterated, a legendary strange bull-size animal in Chinese mythology, which can tell right from wrong, good from evil, and will butt the evil one if there is a fight going on, used as a symbol of justice.
* bear: any of a family (*Ursidae*) of large, heavy omnivorous carnivores that walk flat on their soles of their feet and have shaggy fur and a very short tail. Bears are native to temperate and arctic zones.
* Five Steeds: a metonymy for a five-steeded cart for a prefect or a prefect himself.
* flower wine: rice wine brewed with some kinds of flowers like laurel flowers.
* pine nuts: oily pine kernel or seeds enclosed in a brown woody shell, regarded as a delicacy.

* tea: an evergreen Asian shrub or small tree (*Thea sinensis*), having a compact head of leathery, toothed leaves and white or pink flowers. The cured leaves of this plant or an infusion of them are used as a beverage.
* bamboo: a tall, tree-like or shrubby grass in tropical and semi-tropical regions, a symbol of integrity and altitude, one of the four most important images in Chinese literature, which are wintersweet, orchid, bamboo and chrysanthemum. Plankbridge Cheng (A.D. 1693 – A.D. 1765), A Ching poet, speaks of its character in a poem *Bamboo Rooted in the Rock*: "You bite the green hill and ne'er rest. / Roots in the broken crag, you grow, / And stand erect although hard pressed. /East, west, south, north, let the wind blow."
* bonfire: originally, a large fire for the burning of bones, as a funeral pile; referring to beacons for warning of an imminent threat in this poem.
* Eastern Mound: A mound is a pile of earth to mark distance with, one for 2.5 kilometers and two for 5, so Eastern Mound is one of them in east direction.
* the Northern Hill: an allusion to a verse in *The Book of Songs* with the title of *The Northern Hill*, the first lines of which read like this — The northern hill I climb/And pick medlars atop./Those who are right in prime/Run for court without stop.

送元中丞转运江淮

薄赋归天府，
轻徭赖使臣。
欢沾赐帛老，
恩及卷绡人。
去问珠官俗，
来经石劫春。
东南御亭上，
莫使有风尘。

Seeing Off Magistrate Yüan to the Yangtze and the Huai Area as Transportation Director

Taxes and tariffs you manage,
And all provisions you transport.
Privileged are elders you rule;
Favored are outliers of all sort.
In south you see how pearls are reaped;
In east you care how clams are caught.
The Imperial Post's there southeast;
No chaos but peace should be sought.

* pearl: a lustrous, calcareous concretion deposited in layers around a central nucleus in the shells of various mollusks, widely distributed in the world, largely used as a gem or medicine or give as a gift.
* clam: any of various bivalve mollusks, especially the edible quahog, usually served as seafood.
* the Imperial Post: a post established by Ch'uan Sun, Great Emperor of Wu, 69 kilometers from today's Ch'angchow, Chiangsu Province.

早 春 行

紫梅发初遍，
黄鸟歌犹涩。
谁家折杨女，
弄春如不及。
爱水看妆坐，
羞人映花立。
香畏风吹散，
衣愁露沾湿。
玉闺青门里，
日落香车入。
游衍益相思，
含啼向彩帷。
忆君长入梦，
归晚更生疑。
不及红檐燕，
双栖绿草时。

Early Spring

All purple plums are in full bloom;
The orioles chirrup, off and on.
Who's the girl that willow twigs plucks,
Afraid the spring might be gone.
She looks at her dress in water,
Blushing shy, like a rosebud new.
Her scent, she fears, may be blown off,

And her blouse may be wet with dew.
She lives at Blue Gate of the town;
Her cart rolls back with the eve sun.
The vagrant looks more homesick now
And walks to the tent in tears shone.
Yearning, I hold you in my dream;
Your coming late makes me depressed.
Behold the swallows neath red eaves
Can live in pairs in their soft nest.

* plum: any of various trees of the genus *Prunus*, which bear edible drupaceous fruit.
* oriole: golden oriole, one of the family of passerine birds, which looks bright yellow with contrasting black wings and sings beautiful songs.
* willow twig: a small shoot or branchlet of a willow tree, which is any of a large genus of shrubs and trees related to the poplars. The willow, widely distributed in China and most of the world, have glossy green leaves resembling a girl's eye-brow and its smooth branches, and often long, slender, pliant, and sometimes pendent branchlets, seem to be waving good-bye, or weeping amorously, or drooping for nostalgia.
* rosebud: the bud of a rose, a metaphor for a young girl or a debutante.
* Blue Gate: the southern gate of the three gates on the east wall of Long Peace.
* swallow: a passerine bird, with short broad, depressed bill, long pointed wings, and forked tail, noted for fleeting flight and migratory habits. In Chinese culture, swallows are welcome to live with a family with their nest on a beam of a sitting room.

座上走笔赠薛璩慕容损

希世无高节,
绝迹有卑栖。
君徒视人文,
吾固和天倪。
缅然万物始,
及与群物齐。
分地依后稷,
用天信重黎。
春风何豫人,
令我思东溪。
草色有佳意,
花枝稍含荑。
更待风景好,
与君藉萋萋。

To Ch'u Hsüeh and Sun Mujung as I Run My Brush Seated

To fawn on the world no saint will;
The best may in lowness abide.
You inspect all rituals and rites;
I'm with Nature identified.
The cosmos began long ago;
Then all were equal, man and clime.
Land was parted by King of Corn;
Chung and Lee ruled in line with time.

The spring wind is a pleasant king;
Of the East Stream there I now think.
The grass there to me sweetly smiles;
The sprouting sprays await buds pink.
Now let's wait for the glorious scene
And I'll lie by you on grass green.

* cosmos: the world or universe considered as a system, perfect in order and arrangement, opposed to chaos.
* King of Corn: Magic Farmer, one of the Three Sovereigns in the remote ages of China, along with Hidden Spirit and Nüwa, regarded as the father of herb medicine and agriculture.
* Chung and Lee: legendary ancestors of Five Emperors, the forerunners of Chinese civilization.
* the East Stream: also known as the Ying River, originating from the east peak of Mt. Tower.

李处士山居

君子盈天阶，
小人甘自免。
方随炼金客，
林上家绝巘。
背岭花木开，
入云树深浅。
清昼犹自眠，
山鸟时一啭。

The Cottage of Li, a Lay Buddhist

The high all high offices fill;
The low, so low, have a low will.
Like Wordists cinnabar you'd seek;
Behind you is the highest peak.
Inside the hills all blossoms blow;
Into the deep wood there you go.
In the morning you're still asleep;
The warblers sing to you: cheep, cheep.

* lay Buddhist: one who believes in Buddhism and practises Buddhism at home instead of being a monk in a temple.
* Wordists: those who believe in and practice the Wordism, naturalist doctrines advanced and elaborated by Laocius (571 B.C.- 471 B.C.). In the T'ang dynasty, an age of proselytism, while Confucianism remained the guiding principle of state and social morality, Wordism had gathered an incrustation of mythology and superstition and was fast winning a following of both the court and the common people. Laocius,

the founder, was claimed by the reigning dynasty as its remote progenitor and was honored with an imperial title, Emperor Dark One.

* cinnabar: a crystallized red mercuric sulfide, HgS, the chief ore of mercury, which is the raw mineral material for elixir in Wordist alchemy.

丁寓田家有赠

君心尚栖隐,
久欲傍归路。
在朝每为言,
解印果成趣。
晨鸡鸣邻里,
群动从所务。
农夫行饷田,
闺妾起缝素。
开轩御衣服,
散帙理章句。
时吟招隐诗,
或制闲居赋。
新晴望郊郭,
日映桑榆暮。
阴昼小苑城,
微明渭川树。
揆予宅闾井,
幽赏何由屡。
道存终不忘,
迹异难相遇。
此时惜离别,
再来芳菲度。

To Yü Ting Who Likes a Farming Life

In reclusion you wish to live,

And for long go back home you would.
As you often say in the court:
Without my seal, I feel so good.
As cocks in the lanes crow at dawn,
All rise to go about what they do.
Farmers begin to work their farm;
Wives and concubines start to sew.
You open your chest for your clothes
And uncase your book to peruse.
Sometimes, "back to nature" you chant;
Sometimes an idyll you compose.
In new sunshine you look afar;
Beyond the mulberries sets the sun.
The garden town rests in a shade;
The Wei thru trees shimmers to run.
Living in a town, I suppose,
How much can we enjoy the sweet?
We're in the Word we won't forget;
As we're different, it's hard to meet.
We hate to say good-bye, alas,
May we meet soon for flowers and grass.

* cock: the male, usually full grown and full of pride, of the domesticated fowl, having a high red crown, hence an image of a leader or champion.
* concubine: a cohabitant or secondary wife. China was a polygamous society from prehistoric years till the first half of the twentieth century. An ordinary man could have three wives and four concubines and a concubine could be bartered or sold or given as a gift in ancient China. An emperor might have thousands of concubines, for example, Emperor Deepsire had 40,000.
* idyll: a short poem or prose work describing a simple, peaceful and picturesque scene of rural or pastoral life.
* mulberry: a tree (genus *Morus*) whose leaves are valued for silkworm culture, bearing

edible, berry-like juicy fruit.
* the Wei: the Wei River: the largest branch of the Yellow River, originating from today's Mt. Birdmouse in Kansu Province, flowing through Precious Rooster, Allshine, Long Peace, and meeting the Yellow River at T'ung Pass.
* the Word: referring to Tao if transliterated, the most significant and profoundest concept in Chinese philosophy. The Word is fully elucidated in *The Word and the World*, the single book that Laocius wrote all his wisdom into. Its significance or implication can be seen in this verse: "The Word is void, but its use is infinite. O deep! It seems to be the root of all things."

渭川田家

斜光照墟落，
穷巷牛羊归。
野老念牧童，
倚杖候荆扉。
雉雊麦苗秀，
蚕眠桑叶稀。
田夫荷锄至，
相见语依依。
即此羡闲逸，
怅然吟式微。

A Farmer on the Wei

The village touched by the setting sun;
Thru the lane the herds back home run.
For his herdboy the gramp does wait
On his cane by the wicker gate.
Pheasants coo in the wheat field green;
Silkworms sleep on mulberry leaves lean.
Hoe on shoulder, farmers home walk;
With each other, they laugh and talk.
Such an easy life I admire;
It's Dark, now I sing and sing higher.

* the Wei: the Wei River: the largest branch of the Yellow River, originating from today's Mt. Birdmouse in Kansu Province, flowing through Precious Rooster, Allshine,

Long Peace, and meeting the Yellow River at T'ung Pass.
* pheasant: a long-tailed gallinaceous bird noted for the gorgeous plumage of the male.
* wheat: a grain yielding an edible flour, the annual product of a cereal grass (genus *Triticum*), introduced to China from West Asia more than 4,000 years ago, widely used as a staple food in China and most of the world. In its importance to consumers, it is second only to rice.
* silkworm: the larva of a moth that produces a dense silken cocoon, especially the common silkworm from whose cocoon commercial silk is made. The silkworm was cultivated in 3,000 B.C. when Lace Mum, who was Lord Yellow's concubine, began to raise silkworms and made silk.
* mulberry: the edible, berry-like fruit of a tree (genus *Morus*) whose leaves are valued for silkworm culture, and the tree itself.
* *It's Dark*: a verse from *The Book of Songs*, the first stanza reads like this: It's dark, oh nearly black,/Why not go back? /If it's not for you, oh you,/Why do we get wet with dew?

过 李 揖 宅

闲门秋草色，
终日无车马。
客来深巷中，
犬吠寒林下。
散发时未簪，
道书行尚把。
与我同心人，
乐道安贫者。
一罢宜城酌。
还归洛阳社。

A Visit To Chi Li's Residence

Your door is closed to the grass hue,
All day no horses or carts rolled.
Some guests come into the deep lane;
The dogs bark under the wood cold.
Your hair is left undone, unpinned,
A Wordist book you hold in hand.
He who has the same heart with you
Is one who can poverty stand.
Once I have finished drinking wine,
I'll go back to residence mine.

* horse: a large herbivorous solid-hoofed quadruped (*Equus caballus*) with a coarse mane and tail, of various strains: Ferghana, Mongolian, Kazaks, Hequ, Karasahr and so on, and of various colors: black, white, yellow, brown, dappled and so on, commonly in the domesticated state, employed as a beast of draught and burden and especially for riding upon.

* dog: a domesticated carnivorous mammal (*Canis familiaris*), of worldwide distribution and many varities, noted for its adaptability and its devotion to man. The dog was domesticated in China at least 8,000 years ago and was often used as a hunter, as a poem in *The Book of Songs* says: "The dog bells clink and clink; / The hunter's handsome, a real pink."

* Wordist: one who believes in and practices Wordism, the naturalist doctrines advanced and elaborated by Laocius (571 B.C.- 471 B.C.). In the T'ang dynasty, an age of proselytism, while Confucianism remained the guiding principle of state and social morality, Wordism had gathered an incrustation of mythology and superstition and was fast winning a following of both the court and the common people. Laocius, the founder, was claimed by the reigning dynasty as its remote progenitor and was honored with an imperial title, Emperor Dark One.

奉送六舅归陆浑

伯舅吏淮泗，
卓鲁方喟然。
悠哉自不竞，
退耕东皋田。
条桑腊月下，
种杏春风前。
酌醴赋归去，
共知陶令贤。

Seeing Off My Sixth Uncle to Luhun

When you govern Huai and Ssu well,
E'en Chuo and Lu would praise you more.
Free of care, you do not compete,
And you would farm by the east shore.
Trim mulberry twigs in the first moon
And plant apricot before spring.
Drinking wine, you compose *Go Back*;
With Lord Glee you may pluck your string.

* Huai and Ssu: the drainage areas of the Huai River and the Ssu River, the former of which flows through today's Honan, Hupei, Anhui, Chiangsu and Shantung provinces and the latter flows into Lake Wei Hill in Shantung Province.
* Chuo and Lu: referring to Mao Chuo and Kung Lu, two capable magistrates in the Eastern Han dynasty.
* mulberry: the edible, berry-like fruit of a tree (genus *Morus*) whose leaves are valued for silkworm culture, and the tree itself.

* apricot: a tree or the fruit of the tree of the rose family, intermediate between the peach and the plum. It often appears in Chinese poetry, as a line by Chun Kou (A.D. 961 – A.D. 1023) says: "To the slanting sun apricot blooms fly."
* *Go Back*: an allusion to the prose by Lord Glee, about the wish for reclusion.
* Lord Glee: the title Lingyün Hsieh (A.D. 385 – A.D. 433) inherited from his grandfather. Hsieh, once the Prefect of Yungchia, was a highborn poet, Buddhist, idyllist and traveler, famous for landscape poems in particular.

送　别

下马饮君酒，
问君何所之？
君言不得意，
归卧南山陲。
但去莫复问，
白云无尽时。

Good-bye

Dismounting to drink you good-bye;
"Where are you going?" I inquire.
Your aim has been unreached you sigh;
To bide the South Hills you desire.
Go ahead, I will ask no more;
The white clouds there endlessly soar.

* the South Hills: the Southern Mountains, also known as Mt. Great One, Mt. Earthlungs, the mountains south of Long Peace, a great stronghold of the capital, towering in the middle of Ch'in Ridge and rolling about 100 kilometers. It is the birthplace of Wordist culture, Buddhist culture, Filial Piety culture, Longevity culture, Bellheads culture and Plutus culture and is praised as the Capital of Fairies, the crown of Heavenly Abode and the Promised Land of the World.

送张舍人佐江州同薛璩十韵

束带趋承明，
守官唯谒者。
清晨听银蚪，
薄暮辞金马。
受辞未尝易，
当御方知寡。
清范何风流，
高文有风雅。
忽佐江上州，
当自浔阳下。
逆旅到三湘，
长途应百舍。
香炉远峰出，
石镜澄湖泻。
董奉杏成林，
陶潜菊盈把。
彭蠡常好之，
庐山我心也。
送君思远道，
欲以数行洒。

Seeing Secretary Chang Off to
Be Vice Prefecture of Riverton Together
with Ch'u Hsüeh

All come to court wearing a belt;

The reporting secretary is you.
The silver dragon tells time at dawn;
You leave Gold Horses in dusk hue.
Reports received, you're never curt;
You know you'll shortly leave the post.
A good example you have set,
Refined best and cultured the most.
You're dispatched to the river land,
And down the Bankshine you will row.
You'll stay in hotels in Three Hsiangs
And for one hundred days you'll go.
Mt. Censer rises from the peaks;
Stone Mirror shows Blue Lake so grand.
You will have an apricot wood,
And have chrysanthemums in hand.
Lake P'oshine everyone loves much,
And Mt. Lodge catches all my heart.
You are going a long, long way,
Now I feel two strings of tears start.

* Gold Horses: indicating the royal academy, also called Gold Horse Gate.
* Bankshine: an ancient name of present-day Chiuchiang, Chianghsi Province.
* Three Hsiangs: referring to present-day Hunan Province. The Hsiang River flows into three rivers, the Li, the Cheng and the Hsiao, hence the name Three Hsiangs.
* Mt. Censer: a scenic peak of Mt. Lodge, looking like an incense burner.
* Stone Mirror: the stone by Lake Cavehall, which is round and smooth like a mirror.
* Blue Lake: alias P'oshine Lake, the largest freshwater lake of China in present-day Chianghsi Province and the Long River.
* apricot: a tree or the fruit of the tree of the rose family, intermediate between the peach and the plum.
* chrysanthemum: any of a genus of perennials of the composite family, some cultivated varieties of which have large heads of showy flowers of various colors, a symbol of elegance and integrity in Chinese culture, one of the four most important floral images

in Chinese literature, which are wintersweet, orchid, bamboo and chrysanthemum.
* Mt. Lodge: a famous mountain with historic, cultural and religious attractions, an especially sacred place to Wordists, about 5,000 feet high, in present-day Chianghsi Province.

新 晴 野 望

新晴原野旷，
极目无氛垢。
郭门临渡头，
村树连谿口。
白水明田外，
碧峰出山后。
农月无闲人，
倾家事南亩。

An Outlook after a Rain

The fields look far after the rain;
Far you look, there's no dust or stain.
The town gate by the ferry be;
The village trees line to the sea.
Outside the fields white water hies;
Behind the mountains high peaks rise.
In this month no farmer's lazy;
On the south farm all are busy.

* white water: a light-colored water over a shallow area, for example, the water for irrigation.
* south farm: a metonymy for fields. As a slope facing south is good for farming, ancient Chinese usually reclaimed farmland facing south, hence the term.

苦　热

赤日满天地，
火云成山岳。
草木尽焦卷，
川泽皆竭涸。
轻纨觉衣重，
密树苦阴薄。
莞簟不可近，
絺绤再三濯。
思出宇宙外，
旷然在寥廓。
长风万里来，
江海荡烦浊。
却顾身为患，
始知心未觉。
忽入甘露门，
宛然清凉乐。

Smothering Heat

The red sun bakes Heaven and land;
Fire clouds pile up like mountains high.
Plants and grass are all burned to smoke,
Rivers and streams having gone dry.
A light gauze shirt does heavy feel;
The dense trees in dense haze remain.
The bamboo mat I dare not touch,

My linens washed once and again.
I'd rather go out of the space;
Stay in the cool expense of blue.
When from afar a high wind whirls,
Rivers and seas all their mud spew.
I turn back, still bothered by heat,
Like in a state of stuffy wool.
Sudd'nly, there blows a draught of dew,
Refreshing me with fragrant cool.

* red sun: the source of heat as the sun is the heavenly body that is the center of attraction and the main source of light and heat in the solar system.
* Heaven: the space surrounding or seeming to overarch the earth, in which the sun, the moon, and stars appear, popularly the abode of God, his angels and the blessed, and in most cases suggesting supernatural power or sometimes signifying a monarch.
* bamboo mat: a flat bedding made of bamboo, woven or plaited to be laid on a floor or bed, usually used in summer as it feels cool when one sits or lies on it.
* linen: things made of linen which is yarn, thread or cloth made of flax, or of cotton, etc., as shirts, tablecoths, sheets, etc.

燕子龛禅师

山中燕子龛，
路剧羊肠恶。
裂地竞盘屈，
插天多峭崿。
瀑泉吼而喷，
怪石看欲落。
伯禹访未知，
五丁愁不凿。
上人无生缘，
生长居紫阁。
六时自搥磬，
一饮常带索。
种田烧白云，
斫漆响丹壑。
行随拾栗猿，
归对巢松鹤。
时许山神请，
偶逢洞仙博。
救世多慈悲，
即心无行作。
周商倦积阻，
蜀物多淹泊。
岩腹乍旁穿，
涧唇时外拓。
桥因倒树架，
栅值垂藤缚。
鸟道悉已平，

龙宫为之涸。
跳波谁揭厉，
绝壁免扪摸。
山木日阴阴，
结跏归旧林。
一向石门里，
任君春草深。

To Zen Master in Swallow Shrine

In the mountains is Swallow Shrine;
The trail meanders there to creep.
The cracked land reveal crags and cliffs;
The peaks pierce the Heavens, so steep.
Waterfalls and fountains spurt on;
Bizarre rocks would collapse about.
Great Worm came here but lost his way;
Five Giants could not chisel way out.
The monks have the non-life Dharma;
In Purple Turrets they abide.
Night and day they strike the stone chime,
Having one meal, a string on side.
They slash and burn to farm on high;
Their lacquer chops shake the rock crest.
Monkeys for chestnuts follow them,
And back they see pine cranes nest.
Sometimes deities come for a call;
Sometimes fairies come for a game.
For salvation, mercy and grace,
They live their Non-life of no aim.

Merchants from Chough, tired, will stop here;
Products in Shu just there suspend.
Rocks and crags suddenly show up;
Ravines and gullies out extend.
Some trees fallen, bridges are made;
Railings set up, vines climb high.
The bird way is level and smooth;
The dragon pool has now gone dry.
The creeks well drained, no need to wade;
The cliffs toppled, clear is the sky.
The hill trees shade the hills all day;
You can muse deep in the old wood.
Once you have come into Stone Gate,
You'll be free in grass lush and good.

* Swallow Shrine: probably a temple east of Flying Cloud Spring in Long Peace.
* Great Worm: the founding lord of Hsia, who took over the leadership from Hibiscus. When Worm regulated rivers and watercourses, he used to travel all over to check the conditions.
* Five Giants: Since there was no easy way to reach Shu, King of Shu sent five strong men to build an artery to receive the gold bull given by Lord Letter of Ch'in (356 B.C.-311 B.C.). With the help of the artery, Ch'in successfully took over Shu.
* Non-life: a state of complete freedom, what is called Nirvana in Buddhism.
* Dharma: truth and righteousness in Buddhist terms.
* Purple Turrets: a peak on the South Mountains.
* lacquer: a lacquer tree of China and Japan, from which resinous varnish can be extracted.
* monkey: any of a group of primates having elongate limbs, hands and feet adapted for grasping, and a highly developed nervous system, including marmosets, baboons, and macaques, but not the anthropoid apes, though monkeys and apes are used alternatively in Chinese.
* chestnut: a smooth shelled, sweet, edible nut of any of the genus (*Castanea*) of trees of the beech family, growing in a prickly bur.
* crane: one of a family of large, long-necked, long-legged, heronlike birds allied to the

rails, a symbol of integrity and longevity in Chinese culture, only second to the phoenix in cultural importance.
* Chough: the State of Chough (1046 B.C.- 256 B.C.), the third kingdom in Chinese history, comprising Western Chough and Eastern Chough.
* Shu: an area covering approximately today's Ssuch'uan Province, one of the earliest kingdoms in China, founded by Silkworm and Fishbuck according to legend. In the Three Kingdoms period, a new Shu was established by Pei Liu, hence one of the three kingdoms in that period.

羽林骑闺人

秋月临高城,
城中管弦思。
离人堂上愁,
稚子阶前戏。
出门复映户,
望望青丝骑。
行人过欲尽,
狂夫终不至。
左右寂无言,
相看共垂泪。

The Escort Guard's Wife

The autumn moon over the town,
In the town rings a sad flute lay.
The wife looks worried in the hall;
Some children before the steps play.
She comes out, sunrays on the door,
Thinking him ride a green-reined horse.
All passengers have gone away;
His man is for e'er on his course.
She looks around, from left to right,
Her welling tears blurring her sight.

---

* the autumn moon: The cool silvery light of the moon arouses a feeling of loneliness on an autumn night, as the moon is a symbol of solitude in Chinese culture.

* flute: a tubular wind instrument of small diameter with holes along the side. It has long been used in China, as a poem in *The Book of Songs* says: A flute in his left hand, / In his right a plume grand, / Red and red his face rays. / Give him wine the lord says.
* horse: a large solid-hoofed quadruped (*Equus caballus*) with coarse mane and tail, of various strains: Ferghana, Mongolian, Kazaks, Hequ, Karasahr and so on and of various colors: black, white, yellow, brown, dappled and so on, commonly in the domesticated state, employed as a beast of draught and burden and especially for riding upon. Horses have played an important part in human civilization, widely employed in agriculture, transportation and warfare.

早　朝

皎洁明星高，
苍茫远天曙。
槐雾暗不开，
城鸦鸣稍去。
始闻高阁声，
莫辨更衣处。
银烛已成行，
金门俨驺驭。

Morning Levee

Pure and clean, the stars twinkle bright;
In the far east there's dawning light.
From locust trees mist does not go;
On the town wall some ravens crow.
One hears a toll from the bell tower;
Though dim, it is dress changing hour.
The candles are in line displayed;
At Gold Gate wait all lords arrayed.

* levee: a morning reception or an assembly at the court of a sovereign or at the house of a great personage. In ancient China, a levee at court was held every five days.
* locust tree: a tree (*Robinia pseudoacasia*) of the bean family widely distributed in the temperate zone, with a rough bark, odd-pinnate leaves, and loose, slender racemes of fragrant, white flowers, which are a seasonal delicacy.
* raven: a large omnivorous, crow-like bird (*Corvus corax*), having lustrous black plumage, with the feathers of the throat elongated and lanceolate.

* bell tower: a tower in which a bell is hung to tell time at dawn in contrast with a drum tower, which tells time at night. The tolling of a bell tower was initiated in Emperor Martial of Ch'i's reign (A.D. 483 – A.D. 493) to begin the history of bell towers in China.
* candle: a cylinder of tallow, wax, or other solid fat, containing a wick, to give light when burning, first seen in literature in the Eastern Han dynasty. The most famous lines about candles are from a poem by a T'ang poet named Shangyin Li, "Silkworms stop offering silk when they die; / Candles become ash as their tears run dry."
* Gold Gate: implying an imperial academy.

杂　诗

朝因折杨柳,
相见洛阳隅。
"楚国无如妾,
秦家自有夫。"
对人传玉腕,
映竹解罗襦。
"人见东方骑,
皆言夫婿殊。
持谢金吾子,
烦君提玉壶。"

Miscellany

He breaks a willow twig at dawn
And comes across her in the town.
"There's nobody like me in Ch'u,
I have my man, a husband true."
He passes her a cup of brew
And unties her dress neath bamboo.
"All have seen him riding a steed,
Saying he's the best man indeed.
I'd warn you, sir, you should try not,
Please go away with your wine pot."

* willow: any of a large genus of shrubs and trees related to the poplars, widely distributed in China and most of the world, having glossy green leaves resembling a

girl's eye-brow, and generally having smooth branches, and often long, slender, pliant, and sometimes pendent branchlets, which seem to be waving good-bye, or weeping amorously, or drooping for nostalgia.

* Ch'u: a vassal state of Chough, one of the powers in the Warring States period, conquered and annexed by Ch'in in 223 B.C.
* bamboo: a tall, tree-like or shrubby grass in tropical and semi-tropical regions, a symbol of integrity and altitude, one of the four most important botanical images in Chinese literature, which are wintersweet, orchid, bamboo and chrysanthemum. Bamboo shoots, fresh or dried, are widely used in Chinese cuisine, bamboo rats and bamboo worms are regarded as table delicacies.
* steed: a horse; especially a spirited war horse. The use of horses in war can be traced back to the Shang dynasty (1600 B.C.- 1046 B.C.), when a department of horse management was established. A verse from *The Book of Songs* tells of Lord Civil of Watch's industriousness: "In state affairs he leads; / He has three thousand steeds."

夷 门 歌

七雄雄雌犹未分,
攻城杀将何纷纷。
秦兵益围邯郸急,
魏王不救平原君。
公子为嬴停驷马,
执辔愈恭意愈下。
亥为屠肆鼓刀人,
嬴乃夷门抱关者。
非但慷慨献良谋,
意气兼将身命酬。
向风刎颈送公子,
七十老翁何所求。

Song of Ee Gate

The seven powers fought so hard to prevail,
Capturing, killing, all chaos and wail.
Ch'in swept in and to Hantan marched again;
King of Way would not rescue Prince of Plain.
Prince of Faithridge dismounted his cart now,
And took up Hou's rein and to him did bow.
At Ee Gate Hou served as a gate keeper
And his good friend, Hai, was a butcher.
Not only did Hou scheme the arduous strife
But also sacrificed his gallant life.
He cut his throat against the wind, so killed;

At seventy, his mission he'd fulfilled.

- Ee Gate: the eastern gate of Great Beam, the capital of Way, near today's K'aifeng, Honan Province.
- the seven powers: referring to the seven most powerful states existing during 475 B.C. to 221 B.C., including Ch'ih, Ch'u, Yan, Han, Chao, Way and Ch'in. The Warring States period ended in 221 B.C. when Ch'in wiped out the other six states and established the first unified empire in China's history.
- Ch'in (221 B.C.- 207 B.C.): the first unified empire in Chinese history founded by the State of Ch'in in the late Warring States period.
- Hantan: a city more than 3,100 years old, the capital of the State of Chao (403 B.C.- 222 B.C.) in the Eastern Chough dynasty (770 B.C.- 256 B.C.), located in present-day Hopei Province. This city was built as early as the Shang dynasty (cir. 1600 B.C.- cir. 1046 B.C.) and an imperial palace was built here for King Chow (cir. 1105 B.C.- 1046 B.C.) according to *Lonely Bamboo Annals*. The legacies and ruins in and around the town bespeak the splendor of its glorious past.
- King of Way: King Boon of Way (400 B.C.- 319 B.C.), son of Lord Civil of Way and grandson of Lord Martial of Way. The State of Way (403 B.C.- 225 B.C.) was at its best when King of Boon was in power.
- Prince of Plain: Prince Plain of Chao (? - 253 B.C.), one of the Four Childes in the Warring States period, King Spirit of Chao's son, who served as prime minster for two reigns, a great politician and strategist, attracting thousands of hangers-on.
- Prince of Faithridge: Prince of Way, the youngest son of King Glare of Way, a famous militarist and politician in the Warring States period. He was courteous to talents, attracting 3,000 hangers-on.
- Hou: referring to Ying Hou (? - 257 B.C.), a hermit living as a porter of Ee Gate of the State of Way and became Prince Faithridge's hanger-on. When threatened by the troops of Ch'in, Chao asked Trustridge for help. Hou suggested stealing the military tally so that Way's army was under Trustridge's command. In this way, Trustridge successfully saved Hantan.

黄 雀 痴

黄雀痴,
黄雀痴,
谓言青觳是我儿。
一一口衔食,
养得成毛衣。
到大啁啾解游飏,
各自东西南北飞。
薄暮空巢上,
羁雌独自归。
凤凰九雏亦如此,
慎莫愁思憔悴损容辉。

The Loving Siskin

The loving siskin,
The loving siskin,
It says the chicks are my sons together,
I feed them morsel by morsel,
Now they are all growing feather.
When they chirp, chirp and spread their wings to ply,
East, west, north, south they will by themselves fly.
Now dusk falls on the nest so soon;
A stray bird comes back all alone.
A phoenix has nine sons, all like this,
Do not worry, do not pine, do not go amiss.

* siskin: a finch, related to the golden finch, olive-green and yellow barred with black.
* chick: young chicken or birdling, sometimes used as a metaphor for a child (a term of endearment), and a young woman.
* phoenix: a legendary bird of heavenly beauty, unique of its kind, which was supposed to live five or six hundred years before consuming itself by fire, rising again from its ashes to live through another cycle, a symbol of immortality and sovereignty, a totem of Chinese as well as the dragon. In Chinese mythology, the phoenix only perches on phoenix trees, i.e. firmiana, only eats firmiana fruit, and only drinks sweet spring water, and this mythic bird appears only in times of peace and sagacious rule.

赠 吴 官

长安客舍热如煮,
无个茗縻难御暑。
空摇白团其谛苦,
欲向缥囊还归旅。
江乡鲭鲊不寄来,
秦人汤饼那堪许。
不如侬家任挑达,
草屩捞虾富春渚。

To Officials from Wu

Your capital room is like baking sand;
Without tea porridge the heat you can't stand.
You sway your white fan all in vain, alack;
You'd take your blue brocade bag and go back.
Fresh crucians, salted carp aren't sent from kin;
Cakes, noodles, how can you swallow them in?
In hometown mine all are free, come or go
Doff your sandals, catch shrimps at Rich Spring, lo.

* tea porridge: probably porridge cooked with tea or tea powder as a condiment, which appears only in this poem.
* crucian: crucian carp, fresh water food fish smaller than carp, widely distributed in China.
* carp: fresh water food fish (*Ciprinus carpiao*), originally of China, now widely distributed in Europe and America, a mascot in Chinese culture, symbolizing great success and harmony. An popular idiom "a carp jumping over the Dragon Gate" means

climbing up the social ladder or succeeding in the imperial civil service examination.
* shrimp: any of numerous diminutive, long-tailed, principally marine crustaceans (genus *Crago*), especially the edible shrimp of the northern hemisphere.
* Richspring: an ancient county located in present-day Hangchow.

雪中忆李揖

积雪满阡陌，
故人不可期。
长安千门复万户，
何处蹙蹀黄金羁。

Missing Chi Li in Snow

Snow covers all lanes and fields now;
My friend, to me you have come not.
Tens of thousands of households in Long Peace,
Where do you and your gold-harnessed horse trot?

* Long Peace: Ch'ang'an if transliterated, the capital of the T'ang Empire, a cosmopolis with 1,000,000 inhabitants, the largest walled city ever built by man. It was the center of world religions, Buddhism, Confucianism, Wordism, Nestorianism, Zoroastrianism, and even Islamism represented by Saracens came on the stage here. It was the center of education — There were colleges of various grades and special institutes for calligraphy, arithmetic, music, astronomy and so on. And it was the wonder of the age: The main castle with its nine-fold gates, the thirty-six imperial palaces, pillars of gold, innumerable mansions and villas of noblemen, the broad avenues thronged with motley crowds of townsfolk, gallants on horseback, and mandarin cars drawn by yokes of black oxen, countless houses of pleasure, which opened their doors by night. Such and such scenes made this city a dream world, a kaleidoscope of miracles.
* horse: a large herbivorous solid-hoofed quadruped (*Equus caballus*) with coarse mane and tail, of various colors — black, white, yellow, brown, date-red, dappled, and so on; commonly in the domesticated state, employed as a beast of draught and burden and especially for riding upon. Horses have played an important part in human civilization, widely employed in agriculture, transportation and warfare.

送崔五太守

长安厩吏来到门，
朱文露网动行轩。
黄花县西九折坂，
玉树宫南五丈原。
褒斜谷中不容幰，
唯有白云当露冕。
子午山里杜鹃啼，
嘉陵水头行客饭。
剑门忽断蜀川开，
万井双流满眼来。
雾中远树刀州出，
天际澄江巴字回。
使君年纪三十馀，
少年白皙专城居。
欲持画省郎官笔，
回与临邛父老书。

Seeing off Prefect Ts'ui Five

The stall men come to the gate to meet you;
The red hood and gauze screen now start to go.
West of Yellow Flower spread a nine-turn slope;
South of Sweet Spring rolls a vast plain in scope.
The Gifttilt Valley can't a cart allow;
Only the white clouds float above you now.
In the Meridian Hills sad cuckoos whine;

By the Fine Ridge River on ferns you dine.
Sword Gate sees the two Swords cut thru Shu Land;
Two rivers through the plain to you expand.
Out of hazy trees Swordton one discerns;
From the skyline like a snake the Blue turns.
My friend, you're now more than thirty years old;
A fair-skinned young lad, the whole town you hold.
In Undergate your writing brush you sway
To tell Nearmound folks what the Crown would say.

* red hood and gauze screen: referring to a deluxe cart for a ranking official.
* Yellow Flower: a county named after the Yellow Flower River in its east, in present-day Sha'anhsi Province.
* Sweet Spring: Sweet Spring palace.
* the Gifttilt Valley: name of a narrow valley road.
* the Meridian Hills: the Meridian Valley, a gateway in present-day Sha'anhsi Province.
* cuckoo: the bird of homesickness in Chinese culture. It is said that during the Shang dynasty, Cuckoo (Yü Tu), a caring king of Shu, abdicated the throne due to a flood and lived in reclusion. After his death, he, the human Cucoo, turned into a bird cuckoo, wailing day and night, shedding tears and blood.
* the Fine Ridge River: Chialing Chiang if transliterated, a river starting from the Fine Ridge Valley in Sha'anhsi and joins the Long River in Double Gain (Chungch'ing).
* fern: any of a widely distributed class of flowerless, seedless pteridophytic plants, having roots and stems and feathery leaves (fronds) which carry the reproductive spores in clusters of sporangia called *sori*. Its young stems and root starch are table delicacies to Chinese now as well as in the past.
* Sword Gate: the gateway between Mt. Big Sword and Mt. Small Sword.
* two Swords: referring to Mt. Big Sword and Mt. Small Sword.
* Swordton: alias of Eechow, a large prefecture covering today's Double Gain (Ch'ungch'ing), Yunnan, Kuichow, a large area of Mid-Han and the northern part of Burma.
* snake: an ophidian reptile, having a greatly elongated, scaly body, no limbs, and a specialized swallowing apparatus, a symbol of indifference, malevolence, cattiness, and craftiness in Chinese culture.
* the Blue: an unspecific river in this poem.

* Undergate: referring to Undergate Department, an organization of inspection, one of the three most important departments in the T'ang dynasty.
* writing brush: also called Chinese brush or brush for short, which is used for writing or painting, invented or renovated by Tien Meng (259 B.C.- 210 B.C.), a general in the Ch'in dynasty. It is one of the four treasures in a Chinese study, the other three stationeries being ink, paper and inkslab.
* Nearmound: Linchiung if transliterated, a prefecture in today's Ssuch'uan Province, where Ts'ui would be the prefect.

寒食城东即事

清溪一道穿桃李，
演漾绿蒲涵白芷。
溪上人家凡几家，
落花半落东流水。
蹴鞠屡过飞鸟上，
秋千竞出垂杨里。
少年分日作遨游，
不用清明兼上巳。

Notes on Cold Food Day East of the Town

A brook flows thru a grove called Peach and Plum;
Onto green cattails and white roots ripples come.
With quite a few households the brook does teem;
Flowers fallen chase after the eastward stream.
The football is shot o'er the birds in flight;
The swings are swayed out of the willows slight.
In different groups the youngsters come to play;
They need not wait until Pure Brightness Day.

---

* Cold Food Day: one or two days before Pure Brightness Day (the third day of the third moon each year), the festival in memory of Chiht'ui Chieh (? - 636 B.C.) without cooking for a day. In the Spring and Autumn period, Double Ear, a prince of Chin, escaped from the disaster in his state with his follower Chiht'ui. In great deprivation, Double Ear almost starved to death, and Chiht'ui fed him with flesh cut off his thigh. When Double Ear was crowned Lord Civil of Chin, Chiht'ui retreated to Mt. Silk Floss with his mother when feeling neglected. To have him out, Lord Civil set the mountain

on fire, but Chiht'ui did not give in and was burned with his mother.
* cattail: a perennial aquatic plant (genus *Typha*), with long leaves, flowers in cylindrical terminal spikes, and downy fruit.
* football: a game with a leather ball played by kicking between two parties, which originated in the age of Lord Yellow (2717 B.C.- 2599 B.C.), formally recorded in the Han dynasty and became popular in the T'ang and Sung dynasties.
* Pure Brightness Day: the tomb-sweeping day mourning those who have passed away, which is the third day of the third moon each year.

奉和杨驸马六郎秋夜即事

高楼月似霜，
秋夜郁金堂。
对坐弹卢女，
同看舞凤凰。
少儿多送酒，
小玉更焚香。
结束平阳骑，
明朝入建章。

In Reply to Adjunct Groom Yang Six, Notes on an Autumn Night

O'er the tower shines the moon frost white;
Balm Hall bathes in the autumn night.
A singer there does the flute play;
The dancers a phoenix dance sway.
The waiters serve you with good wine;
A maiden lights an incense fine.
A cavalryman's robe you don;
You'll come to Chapter morrow morn.

* Adjunct Groom: an emperor's son-in-law, usually holding the position of guarding the horses of the adjunct carts, hence the name.
* the moon: the satellite of the earth, a representation of feminity in contrast with the sun, a presentation of masculinity. In a universe animated by the interaction of Shade (female) and Shine (male) energies, the moon is literally Shade visible.
* phoenix dance: a dance danced by a dancer in plumage like a phoenix.

* incense: an aromatic substance in the form of a stick that exhales perfume during combustion, burnt slowly before a Buddhist, Wordist or any religious or ancestral joss as an act of worship, usually offered with a prayer or vow.
* Chapter: Chapter Hall, a magnificent palace of the Han Empire, a metaphor for a T'ang palace.

酬贺四赠葛巾之作

野巾传惠好,
兹贶重兼金。
嘉此幽栖物,
能齐隐吏心。
早朝方暂挂,
晚沐复来簪。
坐觉嚣尘远,
思君共入林。

Thanks to Ho Four, Who Presents Me with a Co-hemp Scarf

The co-hemp scarf is a good gift;
Its worth can be double the gold.
So good is this for a recluse;
An immortal's heart it can hold.
For morning levee, I hang it,
And don it, coming back from court.
Sitting scarfed, I feel dust is far;
With you to the wood I'd resort.

* co-hemp scarf: a long or broad piece of cloth worn about the neck, head or shoulders made of co-hemp fiber.
* levee: a morning reception or an assembly at the court of a sovereign or at the house of a great personage. In ancient China, a levee at court was held every five days.

过福禅师兰若

岩壑转微径，
云林隐法堂。
羽人飞奏乐，
天女跪焚香。
竹外峰偏曙，
藤阴水更凉。
欲知禅坐久，
行路长春芳。

A Visit to Zen Master Bliss in a Temple

The rocky dale turns to a trail;
The wood can Sutra Hall discern.
The plumed man plays a Heaven tune;
The maid kneels to an incense burn.
O'er the bamboo are sunlit peaks;
Neath the vine shade, cool water flows.
You have sat cross-legged for so long;
From fully-grown grass fragrance blows.

* Sutra Hall: a hall where sutras are interpreted. A sutra is a formulated doctrine, often so short as to be unintelligible without a key; literally it is a rule or a precept. In Buddhism, it is an extended writing usually in verse, and often in dialogue form, embodying important religious and philosophical propositions, sometimes directly, and sometimes in highly allegorical or metaphorical language.
* incense: an aromatic substance in the form of a stick that exhales perfume during combustion, offered to a Buddhist, Wordist or any religious or ancestral figure as an

act of worship, usually with a prayer or vow.
* bamboo: a tall, tree-like or shrubby grass in tropical and semi-tropical regions, a symbol of integrity and altitude, one of the four most important images in Chinese literature, which are wintersweet, orchid, bamboo and chrysanthemum.
* cross-legged: a sitting posture in Buddhist meditation, normally with eyes closed.

过香积寺

不知香积寺，
数里入云峰。
古木无人径，
深山何处钟。
泉声咽危石，
日色冷青松。
薄暮空潭曲，
安禅制毒龙。

A Visit to Balm Temple

Where Balm Temple is I don't know;
Miles to the clouded peaks I go.
In the woods there's no trace of soul;
From the mounts there sounds a bell toll.
The creek flows into sobs, stones bold;
All through the pines, the sun looks cold.
Dusk falls upon the abyss then;
What kills Vile Dragon is Still Zen.

* Balm Temple: located in Long Peace, that is, present-day Hsi'an. The ruins have been found in Huangfu Village in today's Long Peace District, Hsi-an.
* pine: a cone-bearing tree having evergreen needle-like leaves, a symbol of rectitude and longevity in Chinese culture.
* Vile Dragon: indicating vicious thought and vain hope in Buddhism.
* Still Zen: a kind of performance of quietude in a form of meditation or contemplation. When Sanskrit jana was spread to China, it was translated as Zan or Zen for this kind of practice. Still Zen is the concentration of calmness.

送李判官赴东江

闻道皇华使，
方随皂盖臣。
封章通左语，
冠冕化文身。
树色分扬子，
潮声满富春。
遥知辨璧吏，
恩到泣珠人。

Seeing Off Judge Li to East of the River

I hear the envoy is gone now
With our officials from the town.
Grants are for the barbarians there,
The tattoos are taught as per Crown.
The Long River's tinted with grass;
The Richspring resounds with the tide.
I know the jade connoisseurs will
Pass Lord's grace to aliens worldwide.

* tattoos: referring to barbarians on the borders of China, with their foreheads tattooed.
* the Long River: the longest river in China, originating from the T'angkula Mountains on Tibet Plateau, flowing through 11 provincial areas, more than 6,300 kilometers long, the third longest river in the world.
* the Richspring: the Richspring River, a river in today's Mid-Chechiang, 110 kilometers long, with many natural attractions.

送张道士归山

先生何处去，
王屋访茅君。
别妇留丹诀，
驱鸡入白云。
人间若剩住，
天上复离群。
当作辽城鹤，
仙歌使尔闻。

Seeing Off Chang, a Wordist, Back to the Hills

Where, master, are you going now?
Mao at the Kinghouse I'll call on.
His wife has the knack for cure-all;
Driving chickens, to clouds he's gone.
How can he stay long in the world?
But in Heaven he feels alone!
May you become a crane in Liao
That to a fairy song has flown.

* Wordist: one who believes in and practices Wordism, naturalist doctrines advanced and elaborated by Laocius (571 B.C. - 471 B.C.). In the T'ang dynasty, an age of proselytism, while Confucianism remained the guiding principle of state and social morality, Wordism had gathered an incrustation of mythology and superstition and was fast winning a following of both the court and the common people. Laocius, the founder, was claimed by the reigning dynasty as its remote progenitor and was honored

with an imperial title, Emperor Dark One.
* Mao: a Wordist who was said to become immortal in legends.
* the Kinghouse: one of the most famous mountains for Wordism.
* Heaven: the space surrounding or seeming to overarch the earth, in which the sun, the moon, and stars appear, popularly the abode of God, his angels and the blessed, and in most cases suggesting supernatural power or sometimes signifying a monarch.
* a crane in Liao: referring to Lingwei Ting, an immortal admired by Wordists. He was born in the east of Liao and transformed himself into a fairy crane and became immortal.

送李员外贤郎

少年何处去，
负米上铜梁。
借问阿戎父，
知为童子郎。
鱼笺请诗赋，
橦布作衣裳。
薏苡扶衰病，
归来幸可将。

Seeing Off Counselor Li's Talented Son

Where are you going now, young man?
With rice, you head for Copper-Beam.
May I ask your father who smiles:
Do you know your son is the cream?
Please compose a poem on the pad,
And sew clothes made of linen crack.
With pearl barley you treat the sick,
And some of it you can bring back.

* Copper-Beam: referring to Tungliang if transliterated, a district in Double Gain (Ch'ungch'ing).
* linen: yarn, thread or cloth made of flax, usually used as material for shirts, tablecoths, sheets, etc.
* pearl barley: a kind of barley reduced to a round shot-like form by pearling, used in soups.

送梓州李使君

万壑树参天，
千山响杜鹃。
山中一夜雨，
树杪百重泉。
汉女输橦布，
巴人讼芋田。
文翁翻教授，
不敢倚先贤。

Seeing Off Prefect Li of Tsuchow

The dales see the trees scrape the blue;
All hills resound with cuckoos' coo.
At night, it rained in the mountains;
From treetops spout myriad fountains.
With tung cloth Han maids pay tribute;
O'er taro fields Pa men dispute.
Do teach like Wen for the new age;
Rest not on the gains of the sage.

* cuckoo: any of a family of birds with a long, slender body, grayish-brown on top and white below, a symbol of sadness in Chinese culture. As is said, during the Shang dynasty, Cuckoo (Yü Tu), a caring king of Shu, abdicated the throne due to a flood and lived in reclusion. After his death, he turned into a cuckoo, wailing day and night, shedding tears and blood.
* tung: tung tree or tung oil tree, a deciduous arbor, *Jatropha curcas* in Latin, having a grey bark, bearing oily kernels or seeds, widely distributed in tropical and subtropical

zones.
* taro: any one of several tropical plants, grown for their corm-like rootstocks.
* Pa: an ancient state referring to an area covering present-day Ch'ungch'ing, the east of Ssuch'uan, the west of Hupei, and north of Kuichow and the northwest of Hunan. Taro was the staple food in this area.
* Wen: Tang Wen (187 B.C.- 110 B.C.), a prefect in the Han dynasty, who made great contribution to education and water conservancy.

送孙秀才

帝城风日好，
况复建平家。
玉枕双文簟，
金盘五色瓜。
山中无鲁酒，
松下饭胡麻。
莫厌田家苦，
归期远复赊。

Seeing Off Showcharm Sun

In Capital it's fine all day,
Let alone with Prince Peace you'll stay.
The jade pillow, the painted mat,
Five-hued melons in gold like that.
In the hills you had no Lu wine
And you ate sesame neath a pine.
A poor farmer's life don't abhor;
Too early to go there once more.

* showcharm: hsiuts'ai if transliterated, a talent recommended for official use through official examinations usually held every three years or a well learned person in ancient China. A showcharm was well respected in the traditional Chinese society.
* Prince Peace: Chienp'ing (A.D. 452 - A.D. 476) if transliterated, Chingsu Liu, a prince, general and scholar, well praised for his righteousness and politeness.
* melon: a trailing plant of the gourd family, or its fruit. There are two genera, the muskmelon and the watermelon, each with numerous varieties, growing in both

tropical and temperate zones.
* Lu wine: referring to weak liquor.
* sesame: an East Indian herb, containing seeds which are used as food and as a source of the pale yellow sesame oil, used as salad oil or an emollient, introduced from Ferghana by Ch'ien Chang (164 B.C.- 114 B.C.), a diplomat, traveler, explorer, and the initiator of the Silk Road.

送方城韦明府

遥思葭菼际，
寥落楚人行。
高鸟长淮水，
平芜故郢城。
使车听雉乳，
县鼓应鸡鸣。
若见州从事，
无嫌手板迎。

Seeing Off Wei, Magistrate of Squareton

I think of the green reeds o'er there;
You're going to Ch'u's land so bare.
Birds fly high, the Huai River blue;
All o'er Old Ying Town grass does grow.
Driving your cart, you'll see chicks fly;
And hear drums to roosters reply.
Soon to your work you will get down;
Don't fear the troubles of your town.

* Squareton: a county under Southshine, in the southwest of today's Honan Province.
* reed: the slender, frequently jointed stem of certain tall grasses growing in wet places or in grasses themselves.
* Ch'u: a vassal state of Chough, one of the powers in the Warring States period, conquered and annexed by Ch'in in 223 B.C.
* the Huai River: one of the seven rivers in China, between the Long River and the

Yellow River, 1,000 kilometers long.
* Old Ying Town: the capital city of Ch'u in the Warring States period.
* rooster: the male of the chicken that struts with pride and crows at dawn.

送友人南归

万里春应尽，
三江雁亦稀。
连天汉水广，
孤客郢城归。
郧国稻苗秀，
楚人菰米肥。
悬知倚门望，
遥识老莱衣。

Seeing Off My Friend Back South

From the vast land spring should be gone;
In Three Rivers wild geese are few.
The Han's so broad, broad like the sky.
Back to Yington you start to go.
The State of Yün grows crops so well;
Ch'u folks have luxuriant wild rice.
Your parents may gaze now at door;
You should serve them with all supplies.

* Three Rivers: referring to the River Yüan, the River Hsiang and the River Li, which flow outside Yüehshine, in today's Hunan Province.
* wild goose: an undomesticated goose that is caring and responsible, taken as a symbol of benevolence, righteousness, good manner, wisdom and faith in Chinese culture.
* the Han: the Han River, the longest branch of the Long River, having an important position in Chinese history.
* Yington: the capital city of Ch'u.

* the State of Yün: a small state located nearby Ch'u.
* Ch'u: a vassal state of Chough, one of the powers in the Warring States period, conquered and annexed by Ch'in in 223 B.C.
* wild rice: a tall aquatic grass, the stem of which is used as a vegetable and the grain of which was formerly used as food, now esteemed as a table delicacy.

送 孙 二

郊外谁相送，
夫君道术亲。
书生邹鲁客，
才子洛阳人。
祖席依寒草，
行车起暮尘。
山川何寂寞，
长望泪沾巾。

Seeing Off Sun Two

Who is the one I now see off?
You are virtuous, gifted with flair.
A Confucian scholar you are
And a talent from Loshine there.
We bid farewell by the cold grass;
At dusk your carriage does dust raise.
How sad the hills and rivers are!
In tears for long and long I gaze.

---

* Loshine: Loyang if transliterated, the eastern capital and the second largest city in the T'ang dynasty, with a population of about 0.8 million. It was first built from 1735 B.C. to 1540 B.C. in the Hsia dynasty as its political center, and in 1046 B.C. Prince of Chough built two cities here in order to control Chough's east territory. In 770 B.C. King Peace of Chough moved to this place when Warmer (Haoching), Chough's capital, was captured by Hounds (Ch'üanjung), hence the Eastern Chough dynasty. Since its founding, Loshine has been a capital for thirteen dynasties.

观　　猎

风劲角弓鸣，
将军猎渭城。
草枯鹰眼疾，
雪尽马蹄轻。
忽过新丰市，
还归细柳营。
回看射雕处，
千里暮云平。

Watching Hunting

Against the wind rings the horn bow;
Wei sees the general hunting go.
The hawk looks sharply thru dry grass;
The hoofs tread lightly on snow to pass.
The steeds bolting thru Newrich Town
Come back to Thin Willow anon.
He looks back to where he has shot;
It's all quiet and clouds there are not.

* Wei: the city of Wei, northeast of Allshine, now a district of it.
* hawk: a diurnal bird of prey, notable for keen sight and strong flight, which are usually used as a metaphor for those who take military means in contrast with doves, those who try to find peaceful solutions.
* Newrich Town: the seat of Newrich County's administration, known for wine brewed there. The county was built by Pang Liu in imitation of his hometown Rich County. Newrich is in today's Lintung County, near Hsi-an, Sha'anhsi Province.

* Thin Willow: a military camp commanded by General Yafu Chou (199 B.C.- 143 B.C.), a general of great reputation in the Han dynasty. Under his command, the troops ran in a rigorous order, and even Emperor Civil had to follow the rules in the tent when he came to visit.

春日上方即事

好读高僧传，
时看辟谷方。
鸠形将刻仗，
龟壳用支床。
柳色青山映，
梨花夕鸟藏。
北窗桃李下，
闲坐但焚香。

Notes on Your Abbot Room on a Spring Day

You oft read *The Book of High Monks*；
In Grain Fasting you are well read.
Your stick has turtledoves carved on；
With tortoise shells propped is your bed.
The willow hue fits the green hills；
In pear blossoms dusk warblers hide.
By the north window neath peach trees，
You sit，incense burning beside.

* *The Book of High Monks*：a history book of Buddhist monks.
* Grain Fasting：a practicing skill of Wordists. In Grain Fasting, they usually take herbal medicine instead of grain, in which way they believe they could stay healthy and live a long life.
* turtledove：a kind of dove (genus *Streptopelia*), noted for its affection for mate and young.

* pear: a plant of the rose family, with glossy leaves and white flowers, bearing greenish or brown, juicy, edible and fleshy fruit.
* peach: any tree of the genus *Prunus Percica*, blooming brilliantly and bearing fruit, a fleshy, juicy, edible drupe, considered sacred in China, a symbol of romance, prosperity and longevity.
* incense: an aromatic substance in the form of a stick that exhales perfume during combustion, burnt for the purification of air or offered to a Buddhist, Wordist or any religious or ancestral figure as an act of worship, usually with a prayer or vow.

游李山人所居因题屋壁

世上皆如梦，
狂来止自歌。
问年松树老，
有地竹林多。
药倩韩康卖，
门容向子过。
翻嫌枕席上，
无那白云何。

Touring Immortal Li's Abode and Writing the Dedication on His Wall

All the world's like a dream to you;
Running like mad, you sing as such.
Asked how old you are, like the pines,
On your rich land bamboo grows much.
Hermit friends your magic herbs sell;
Immortals all go through your door.
The white clouds play with you in bed;
You shoo them and they come once more.

* pine: a cone-bearing tree having needle-shaped evergreen leaves growing in clusters, a symbol of longevity and rectitude in Chinese culture. Pine nuts, oily pine seeds enclosed in a brown woody shell, are served as a dainty.
* bamboo: a tall, tree-like or shrubby grass in tropical and semi-tropical regions, a symbol of integrity, fortitude and altitude, one of the four most important botanical images in Chinese literature, which are wintersweet, orchid, bamboo and

chrysanthemum. A Ching poet speaks of its character in a poem *Bamboo Rooted in the Rock*:"You bite the green hill and ne'er rest. / Roots in the broken crag, you grow, / And stand erect although hard pressed. /East, west, south, north, let the wind blow."

戏题示萧氏甥

怜尔解临池，
渠爷未学诗。
老夫何足似，
弊宅倘因之。
芦笋穿荷叶，
菱花冒雁儿。
郗公不易胜，
莫著外家欺。

Dedication to Hsiao's Nephew for Fun

Hand writing you learn by the pool;
Your father cannot read poems though.
How can I compare with you, sir?
Through my door oftentimes you go.
Sparrow grass pierces lotus leaves;
Wild geese to water chestnuts peer.
A man like Lord Hsi one can't slight;
How could a nephew domineer?

* sparrow grass: asparagus, often used as a metaphor for corruption.
* lotus: any of various waterlilies, especially the white or pink Asian lotus, used as a religious symbol in Hinduism and Buddhism. The lotus is a common image in Chinese literature, as two lines of a lyric by Hsiu Ouyang (A.D. 1007 - A.D. 1072) read: "A thunder brings rain to the wood and pool, / The rain hushes the lotus, drips cool."
* wild goose: an undomesticated goose that is caring and responsible, taken as a symbol of benevolence, righteousness, good manner, wisdom and faith in Chinese culture.

* water chestnut: the hard horned edible fruit of an aquatic plant.
* Lord Hsi: referring to Chien Hsi (A.D. 269 – A.D. 339), a calligrapher and minister of great importance in the Eastern Chin dynasty. He refused to take the advice from the empress' brother and successfully stopped the fights between the clans.

听 宫 莺

春树绕宫墙，
宫莺啭曙光。
忽惊啼暂断，
移处弄还长。
隐叶栖承露，
攀花出未央。
游人未应返，
为此始思乡。

Listening to Orioles in the Palace

Spring trees beside the palace wall,
Orioles toward dawn sing a song.
Now startled, they stop for a while;
Having flown there, they chirp for long.
Tree leaves perch upon the dew cups,
From Non-end show flowers on a vine.
The travelers have not come back yet;
For my hometown I start to pine.

* oriole: golden oriole, one of the family of passerine birds, which looks bright yellow with contrasting black wings and sings beautiful songs.
* dew cups: According to legend, Lord Martial of Han ordered that a bronze man be made to hold a jade cup to collect dew, aiming to be immortal by drinking it with jade filings.
* Non-end: the main imperial palace of the Han House, built on the basis of Chapter Height, a Ch'in palace, in 200 B.C., monitored by Premier Ho Hsiao (257 B.C.- 193

B.C.), located on Dragonhead Plateau, the highest vantage of Long Peace. It was the political center of the Han Empire for 200 years and was made a part of the Forbidden Park in the Sui and T'ang dynasties. Non-end, six times as large as today's the Forbidden City or Imperial Palace in Peking, existed for 1,041 years, the longest-lived palace in Chinese history.

早　朝

柳暗百花明，
春深五凤城。
城乌睥睨晓，
宫井辘轳声。
方朔金门侍，
班姬玉辇迎。
仍闻遣方士，
东海访蓬瀛。

Morning Levee

Willows dark, a hundred flowers bright,
Late spring hours in Capital dwell.
Crows are perched on the city wall;
Windlass sound comes from the court well.
The courtiers wait beside Gold Gate;
The belles greet Lord with Sedan grand.
I hear necromancers are sent
To East Sea to find Fairyland.

* levee: a morning reception or an assembly at the court of a sovereign or at the house of a great personage. In ancient China, a levee at court was held every five days.
* willow: any of a large genus of shrubs and trees related to the poplars, widely distributed in China and most of the world, having glossy green leaves resembling a girl's eye-brow, and generally having smooth branches, and often long, slender, pliant, and sometimes pendent branchlets, which seem to be waving good-bye, or weeping amorously, or drooping for nostalgia.

* crow: an omnivorous, raucous, oscine bird of the genus *Corvus*, with glossy black plumage. It is regarded as an ominous bird, a metaphor for death because it is a scavenger, feeding on carrion. It is a common image in Chinese literature, which can be found in *The Book of Songs* compiled 2,500 years ago: "Crows are all black, it's said, / So as foxes are red."
* Gold Gate: implying an imperial academy. Courtiers and officials would wait here before the court was opened.
* necromancer: a sorcerer who claims to tell the future by alleged communication with the dead.
* Fairyland: an ideal abode for immortals, sometimes thought of as being in the middle of East Sea, sometimes in the sky.

愚公谷三首
Fool's Dale, Three Poems

其 一

愚谷与谁去，
唯将黎子同。
非须一处住，
不那两心空。
宁问春将夏，
谁论西复东。
不知吾与子，
若个是愚公。

No. 1

Who's going with you to Fool's Dale?
Only you, Master Li, my friend.
If we don't go there together,
Our hearts will lonesomely suspend.
Who cares spring will summer become
Or from west one will turn east then?
I don't know if it's you or me,
Who's called a fool, a silly man.

* Fool's Dale: located in present-day Lintzu, Shangtung, named for a foolish man that Lord Pillar of Ch'i met in the dale. When Lord Pillar of Ch'i chased a deer into a dale, he met an old man, asking: "What dale is it?" , the latter replied: "Fool's Dale". the Lord asked why, and the reply was "It was named after me." The lord said: "Judging by your looks, you are not a fool, why were you so named?" The latter replied: "Let me tell you why. Once I reared a cow, which gave birth to a calf. When the calf grew bigger, I sold it to buy a pony." A young man said, "How could a cow bear a pony?" So, he led my pony away. At this, my neighbor laughed at me as foolish, so I named this dale Fool's Dale." The lord commented: "You are really a fool. Why did you let him go with your pony?" Lord Pillar went back and told this to Chung Kuan. Now, straightening his collar, Chung Kuan started: "It's me who is foolish. If Mound were king and Kaoyao the judge, could any one take someone else's pony? If one met such a rough, he wouldn't let him go. The old man knew about the unjust litigation, so he let the rough alone. Please let me go readjust our law." It can be seen that the old man was not a fool but a wise remonstrant.

其 二

吾家愚谷里，
此谷本来平。
虽则行无迹，
还能响应声。
不随云色暗，
只待日光明。
缘底名愚谷，
都由愚所成。

No. 2

Fool's Dale's somewhere I abide;
This dale's not deep from either side.
Although you go, no trace follows,
You can still hear something echoes.
If in mountains there'd be no light,
And you would see no morning bright.
Why do all call it Fool's Dale then?
'Cause of the fool, the silly man.

其 三

借问愚公谷，
与君聊一寻。
不寻翻到谷，
此谷不离心。
行处曾无险，
看时岂有深。
寄言尘世客，
何处欲归临。

No. 3

If you ask me about Fool's Dale,
To chat with you I can now start.
Without searching, you can be there,
Because the dale follows your heart.
Not steep at all if there you wend;
How can it be deep when you peer.
To worldly people I suggest:
Where else should you go except here?

杂　　诗

双燕初命子，
五桃新作花。
王昌是东舍，
宋玉次西家。
小小能织绮，
时时出浣纱。
亲劳使君问，
南陌驻香车。

Miscellany

The two swallows chirp to their chicks;
The five peach trees blossom their best.
Booming's their neighbor in the east;
Handsome abides the cottage west.
A young girl, she can weave brocade;
She does wash yarn and wash again,
Please go send your greetings to her,
Who's in her scent-cart in South Lane.

* swallow: a black passerine bird, with short broad, depressed bill, long pointed wings, and forked tail, noted for fleeting flight and migratory habits. In Chinese culture, swallows are welcome to live with a family with their nest on a beam over the sitting room, as it is believed "Swallows do not enter a saddened door", so swallows bespeak a happy family.
* chick: a young chicken or bird.
* the five peach trees: a metaphor for beautiful blooming girls, an allusion to *The*

Peach, a verse in *The Book of Songs*, the first stanza of which reads: The peach twigs sway,/Ablaze the flower;/Now she's married away,/Befitting her new bower.
* Booming: a handsome man thought to be a man in the Chin dynasty.
* Handsome: referring to Yü Sung, one of the four most handsome men in ancient China, a student of Yüan Ch'ü's and a verse writer in the Warring States period, once an official for King Hsiang of Ch'u.
* scent-cart: a cart made of wood giving off fragrance, a fabulous deluxe cart.
* South Lane: the lane or road in the south, a term often used in poetry.

送方尊师归嵩山

仙官欲往九龙潭，
旄节朱幡倚石龛。
山压天中半天上，
洞穿江底出江南。
瀑布杉松常带雨，
夕阳苍翠忽成岚。
借问迎来双白鹤，
已曾衡岳送苏耽。

Seeing Off Master Fang Back to Mt. Tower

Master, you are going to Nine Dragons Pool;
Yak tails and red banners by Stone Rooms fly.
Through a hole to the Long the water flows,
While Mt. Tower penetrates the middle sky.
Waterfalls and pines are oft washed by rain;
Cypresses in the eve sun all haze don.
May I ask you, are they the two white cranes
That at Mt. Scale saw the immortal gone?

* Mt. Tower: located in the west of present-day Honan Province, one of the Five Mountains in Chinese culture. It is one of the five sanctuaries of Wordism, and the abode of God of Mt. Tower worshiped by Han Chinese, with an area of 450 square kilometers, consisting of Mt. Greatroom and Mt. Smallroom, having 72 peaks, 350 meters above sea level at the lowest and 1,512 meters at the highest.
* Nine Dragons Pool: a pool on Mt. Greatroom, the east peak of Mt. Tower.
* Stone Rooms: referring to Mt. Smallroom and Mt. Greatroom, two main mountains

that make Mt. Tower.
* the Long: the Long River, the longest river in China, originating from the T'angkula Mountains on Tibet Plateau, flowing through 11 provincial areas, more than 6,300 kilometers long, the third longest river in the world, the part of which from Nanking to Shanghai is called the Yangtze River.
* cypress: an evergreen tree of the family Cupressaceae, having durable timber, a symbol of rectitude, nobility and longevity in Chinese culture.
* crane: one of a family of large, long-necked, long-legged, heronlike birds allied to the rails, a symbol of integrity and longevity in Chinese culture, only second to the phoenix in cultural importance.
* Mt. Scale: one of the Five Mountains in China, located in Hunan Province, along with Mt. Ever in Shanhsi, Mt. Arch in Shantung, Mt. Flora in Sha'anhsi, and Mt. Tower in Honan.

送杨少府贬郴州

明到衡山与洞庭,
若为秋月听猿声。
愁看北渚三湘远,
恶说南风五两轻。
青草瘴时过夏口,
白头浪里出溢城。
长沙不久留才子,
贾谊何须吊屈平。

Seeing Off Yang, a County Sheriff, Demoted to Ch'enchow

Morrow you're leaving for Mt. Scale and Cavehall;
How can you bear moonlit apes' cries in plight?
The shoals in Three Hsiangs are so far from here;
Against south wind, your weathercock turns light.
You'll pass Summermouth in grass miasma
And go through the white waves out of Gush Town.
How can Long Sand keep a talent for long?
You aren't Ee Chia who mourned Yüan, feeling down.

* Ch'enchow: located in the southeast of Hunan province, a gateway to the southeastern lands.
* Mt. Scale: south in today's Hunan Province, one of the five especially sacred mountains in China, one for each of the four directions and one at the center. The other four mountains are Mt. Arch, east in Shantung, Mt. Ever, west in Shanhsi, Mt. Flora, north in Sha'anhsi, and Mt. Tower, the central one in Honan.

* Cavehall: Lake Cavehall, one of the largest lakes in China and many cultural attractions.
* ape: a large, tailless primate, as a gorilla or chimpanzee, loosely any monkey.
* Three Hsiangs: referring to present-day Hunan Province. The Hsiang River flows into three rivers, the Li, the Cheng and the Hsiao, hence the name Three Hsiangs.
* Summermouth: an ancient town in today's Hupei where the River Summer (the former name of the River Han) meets the Long River.
* Gush Town: P'ench'eng if transliterated, a town in present-day Juich'ang, Chianghsi, named for a gushing well.
* Long Sand: referring to Ch'angsha if transliterated, the capital city of present-day Hunan Province.
* Ee Chia: Ee Chia (200 B.C.- 168 B.C.), a political commentator, litterateur, who gained his fame when he was young. When he served as an official, he was envied by those higher-ranking ministers.
* Yüan: Yüan Ch'ü (340 B.C.- 278 B.C.), a great patriotic poet and official of Ch'u, the archetype of the incorruptible and faithful minister, repeatedly wronged by the king. His suicide at last by drowning himself in the Milo River is still commemorated every year throughout China by the Dragon Boat Festival.

听 百 舌 鸟

上兰门外草萋萋，
未央宫中花里栖。
亦有相随过御苑，
不知若个向金堤。
入春解作千般语，
拂曙能先百鸟啼。
万户千门应觉晓，
建章何必听鸣鸡。

Listening to Mocking Birds

Out of Forbidden Orchids grass grows lush;
To perch in Non-end Palace mocking birds like.
Some of them oft fly to the royal park;
And one or two will alight on Gold Dyke.
In springtime they can speak a thousand tongues;
At dawn before other birds they will coo.
All households can know it is dawning now,
Why need they hark to cocks in Chapter crow?

* mocking bird: a bird termed *Turdus merula* in Latin, noted for its rich song and the powers of imitating the calls of other birds.
* Forbidden Orchids: name of a Han Wordist temple in High Park, the royal family's recreational resort that was huge, rolling about 340 kilometers.
* Non-end Palace: an imperial palace of the Han House, appearing most often in Chinese literature.
* Gold Dyke: referring to a dyke in High Park, one of the largest recreational parks in

Chinese history.
* cock: the male, usually full grown and full of pride, of the domesticated fowl, having a high red crown, hence an image of a leader or champion.
* Chapter: a palace built by Emperor Martial of Han in 104 B.C., with a suspension passage to No-end Palace in the other part of the capital. This palace was actually a group of different complexes with walls.

沈十四拾遗新竹生读经处同诸公之作

闲居日清静,
修竹自檀栾。
嫩节留馀箨,
新丛出旧栏。
细枝风响乱,
疏影月光寒。
乐府裁龙笛,
渔家伐钓竿。
何如道门里,
青翠拂仙坛。

Counselor Shen Fourteen's Sutra Reading Place in New Bamboo, with Other Colleagues

Reposed so free on a calm day;
The bamboo tall sways their green lush.
Tender shoots out of their coarse sheath,
Under old rails new clusters rush.
Thin branches stir a noisy wind;
Sparse shades sway the moon to shine.
Conservatoire come here for flutes,
Fishers for their fishing rods fine.
With a Word fane yours may compare;
Greenness strokes Fairy Altar there.

* bamboo: a tall, tree-like or shrubby grass in tropical and semi-tropical regions, a symbol of integrity and altitude, one of the four most important botanical images in Chinese literature, which are wintersweet, orchid, bamboo and chrysanthemum. Bamboo shoots, fresh or dried, are widely used in Chinese cuisine, bamboo rats and bamboo worms are regarded as table delicacies.

* Conservatoire: Yüehfu if transliterated, which might be otherwise called Music Hall or Music Bureau. It was an ancient official organization for the management of music and poetry, specifically responsible for the collection, adaptation, composition, and performance of musical and poetic works, initially instituted in Ch'in and formally established in 112 B.C., the age of Emperor Martial of Han.
* Word: of or about the Word, a concept that is closest to God in meaning.
* Fairy Altar: an altar on Mt. Fairy, a fabled place in East Sea, where fairies live and immortals gather.

田　家

旧谷行将尽，
良苗未可希。
老年方爱粥，
卒岁且无衣。
雀乳青苔井，
鸡鸣白板扉。
柴车驾羸牸，
草屦牧豪豨。
多雨红榴折，
新秋绿芋肥。
饷田桑下憩，
旁舍草中归。
住处名愚谷，
何烦问是非。

Farmers

They will finish all grains they have;
The seedlings good are too young here.
The elders can eat thin porridge,
But have no clothes to end the year.
Sparrows hatch in a mossy well;
Roosters crow to the white plank door.
The cart is drawn by a lean cow;
The grass sandal tends a strong boar.
Much rain spoils the red pomegranates;

The new autumn helps taros grow.
Neath the mulberries they rest and dine
And to the shack near they will go.
For Fool's Dale o'er there they may long;
Who cares what may be right or wrong.

* sparrow: a small, plain-colored passerine bird related to the finches, grosbeaks and buntings, a very common bird in China, a symbol of insignificance.
* rooster: the male of the chicken that struts with pride and crows at dawn.
* the grass sandal: a metonymy for the one who wears grass sandals.
* boar: a male hog or a wild pig having sharp buckteeth.
* pomegranate: an Asian and African tree of the *Punica granatum* family, about the size of an orange, having flaming flowers and bearing fruit with a hard rind and subacid red pulp with many seeds, a symbol of fertility and good life in Chinese culture.
* taro: any one of several tropical plants, grown for their corm-like rootstocks.
* Fool's Dale: located in present-day Lintzu, Shantung Province, named for a simple, silly-looking man that Lord Pillar of Ch'i met in the dale. It is often used as a metaphor for a place of reclusion.

哭褚司马

妄识皆心累，
浮生定死媒。
谁言老龙吉，
未免伯牛灾。
故有求仙药，
仍馀遁俗杯。
山川秋树苦，
窗户夜泉哀。
尚忆青骡去，
宁知白马来。
汉臣修史记，
莫蔽褚生才。

Mourning Commander Ch'u

All fantasies will our hearts tire;
Vanity's for one to expire.
All know Old Dragon Auspice still
Can't stop First Bull from being ill.
All those who would cure-all obtain
Could not in reclusion remain.
The autumn trees thru all hills blow;
The window hears a night spring's woe
Now on your mule you've gone away,
Can you hear my horse sadly neigh?
The scholar could *Annals* repair;

No one should e'er eclipse your flair.

* Ch'u: the Ch'u State or the State of Ch'u, a vassal state of Chough, one of the powers in the Warring States period, conquered and annexed by Ch'in in 223 B.C.
* Old Dragon Auspice: a great teacher in prehistoric China, from whom Lotus Sway Sweet and Magic Farmer had their education. A passage from *Sir Lush* tells of Old Dragon Auspice like this: Lotus Sway Sweet and Magic Farmer were classmates at Old Dragon Auspice. Magic Farmer slept at desk at day time with the door closed. Around noon, Lotus Sway Sweet pushed the door open, exclaiming: "Old Dragon died." Magic Farmer rose with his stick in hand, and pop, he threw his stick aground and laughed: "He knew I was short-sighted and absent-minded, and so died, leaving me alone. Finished, my teacher. You died without enlightening me with your words from the Word."
* First Bull: referring to Keng Jan (A.D. 544 -?), a student of Confucius's, whose nick name was First Bull. Confucius went to visit him when he was seriously ill and wailed for his doomed life.
* on your mule you've gone away: referring to the legend of Shaochun Li, a Wordist in the Han dynasty. A hundred days after his death, people saw him riding a mule away. Hearing that, Lord Martial checked Li's tomb and found the body had already gone.
* *Annals*: the first biographical annals with records of 3,000 years' history written by Ch'ien Ssuma (A.D. 145 - A.D. 90) in the Han dynasty.

赠韦穆十八

与君青眼客，
共有白云心。
不向东山去，
日令春草深。

To Mu Wei Eighteen

My friend, from me you now depart;
For white clouds we have the same heart.
To the East Hills why don't we go?
The spring sees the grass there deep grow.

* the East Hills: located in today's Shaohsing, Chechiang Province, the hills where An Hsieh (A.D. 320 - A.D. 385), a statesman and litterateur with high reputation, lived with ease and kept declining official positions until he was in his forties. It is often used as a metaphor for a hermitage, the place for reclusion.

皇甫岳云溪杂题五首
Five Miscellanies at Hill Huangfu's Cloud Creek

鸟鸣涧

人闲桂花落，
夜静春山空。
月出惊山鸟，
时鸣春涧中。

Birds Twitter o'er the Brook

I idle laurel flowers to fall;
Night quiets the vernal hills o'er all.
The moon out, startled birds flutter;
At times o'er the brook they twitter.

* laurel: *laurus nobilis*, an evergreen shrub with aromatic, lance-shaped leaves, yellowish flowers, and succulent, cherry-like fruit, a symbol of glory usually in the form of a crown or wreath of laurel to indicate honor or high merit, especially when one had passed Grand Test, i.e. Civil Service Examinations for selecting government officials, in ancient China. In Chinese mythology, there is a colossal laurel tree that is more than 1,500 meters tall on the moon, and it would never fall even though Kang Wu, a banished immortal, has kept cutting it.
* the moon: the planet of the earth, which appears at night and gives off shining silvery light, an image of purity and solitude in Chinese culture.

莲花坞

日日采莲去,
洲长多暮归。
弄篙莫溅水,
畏湿红莲衣。

Lotus Cove

To gather lotus pods she goes;
She's back from the shoal as dusk grows.
She plies her pole light lest it douse
The flame of her lotus-flower blouse.

* cove: a small bay or inlet. Natural places like coves, glades, hills, moors, rivers, mounts and seas, and so on often allude to reclusion in Chinese culture.
* lotus: one of the various plants of the waterlily family, noted for their large floating round leaves and showy flowers. It is a symbol of purity and elegance in Chinese culture, unsoiled though out of soil, so clean with all leaves green. And because of this, it has become a symbol of Buddhist enlightenment, which requires an alienation from the dust and noise of the world.

鸬鹚堰

乍向红莲没，
复出清蒲飐。
独立何褵褷，
衔鱼古查上。

Cormorant Weir

From the lotus flowers it dives down,
And comes out of cattails, so sleek.
On the raft, it stands fully drenched,
All alone, a fish in its beak.

* Cormorant Weir: the name of a weir in the vicinity of Hill Huangfu's cottage. The cormorant is a large web-footed, voracious aquatic bird of wide distribution and gregarious habits, having a strong hooked bill and large throat gular pouch, having been domesticated for fishing in China for a long time.
* lotus: any of various waterlilies, especially the white or pink Asian lotus, used as a religious symbol in Hinduism and Buddhism. The lotus is a common image in Chinese literature, as two lines of a lyric by Hsiu Ouyang (A.D. 1007 - A.D. 1072) read: "A thunder brings rain to the wood and pool, / The rain hushes the lotus, drips cool.
* cattail: a perennial aquatic plant (genus *Typha*), with long leaves, flowers in cylindrical terminal spikes, and downy fruit.
* raft: a float of logs, planks etc., fastened together for transportation by water. The sheepskin bag raft is a special craft made of 14 to 600 hundred sheepskin bags, varying according to the size of the raft, mainly used on the part of the Yellow River that flows through Lanchow in Kansu Province.

上平田

朝耕上平田，
暮耕上平田。
借问问津者，
宁知沮溺贤？

Upper Field

At dawn you plough your Upper Field;
At dusk your Upper Field you plough.
"May I ask you, who ask the way,
Don't you find hermits sage enow?"

---

* Upper Field: the name of the field that Hill Huangfu (Yüeh Huangfu) tills in reclusion. Hill Huangfu's information was brief and according to *The New Book of T'ang*, he was born into a powerful family, a son of Trust Huangfu (Hsun Huangfu).

萍 池

春池深且广，
会待轻舟回。
靡靡绿萍合，
垂杨扫复开。

Lotus Pool

The spring pool is so deep and wide,
Waiting for her skiff to come back.
The lotus leaves close, slow and slow,
Now the willow twigs start to rack.

* skiff: a light rowboat for fishing or lotus-picking and so on; formerly a sailing vessel.
* lotus: one of the various plants of the waterlily family, noted for their large floating round leaves and showy flowers, a symbol of purity and elegance or Buddhist enlightenment in Chinese culture, unsoiled though out of soil, so clean with all leaves green.
* willow: any of a large genus of shrubs and trees related to the poplars, having generally smooth branches, and often long, slender, pliant, and sometimes pendent branchlets, a symbol of farewell or a metaphor for nostalgia in Chinese culture. The best image is in *Vetch We Pick*, a verse in *The Book of Songs*, which is like this: When we left long ago, / The willows waved adieu. / Now back to our home town, / We meet snow falling down.

红 牡 丹

绿艳闲且静,
红衣浅复深。
花心愁欲断,
春色岂知心?

The Red Peony

Her green leaves stay free and serene;
Her red blouse does glisten and sheen.
The sadness cuts her through, so smart;
Do the hues of spring know her heart?

* peony: a plant of the crowfoot family having large, handsome, crimson, rose or white flowers, a symbol of fecundity and dignity in Chinese culture, esteemed as the king of all flowers. It is a common image in Chinese literature, the earliest of which is probably from *The Book of Songs* two thousand years ago: "Of each oth'r they make fun; / His gift of peony is a nice one."

杂 诗 三 首
Three Miscellanies

其 一

家住孟津河，
门对孟津口。
常有江南船，
寄书家中否。

No. 1

Nearby First Ferry I abide

First Ferry is faced with my door.

Can I receive a letter now

As the boat from south is to moor?

---

* First Ferry: a county in the west of today's Honan Province, 134 kilometers from Chengchow, the provincial capital of today's Honan Province and 10 kilometers from Loshine, the second capital of T'ang and an important cultural city under Honan Province. It is one of the birthplaces of Chinese civilization with many historical attractions.

其 二

君自故乡来，
应知故乡事。
来日绮窗前，
寒梅著花未？

No. 2

Now from our hometown you have come;
What has happened there you must know.
The day you left, by the window there,
Did you see the wintersweets blow?

* wintersweet: *Armeniaca mume Sieb* in Latin, a plant or shrub about 4 to 10 meters tall, bursting into bloom in winter to herald spring with small yellow or red flowers giving off thick fragrance. It is a symbol of elegance, solitude and pride in Chinese culture for its blossoming and fragrance in the coldest season while all other plants are still bare. It belongs in "Four Gentlemen", the other three being the orchid, bamboo and chrysanthemum, and one of the "Three Cold Weather Friends", the other two being the pine and bamboo.

其 三

已见寒梅发，
复闻啼鸟声。
心心视春草，
畏向阶前生。

No. 3

Now I see the wintersweets blow;
Now I hear the cuckoos do coo.
I watch the vernal grass in woe,
Afraid to my steps they may grow.

* wintersweet: a cold-resistant plant having small yellow or red flowers, a symbol of elegance, solitude and pride in Chinese culture for its blossoming and fragrance in the coldest snowy winter while all other plants are still dry and bare. It is an important image in Chinese literature because of its solitude and fragrance in winter, especially in snow. Four most favored plant images with rich cultural associations in Chinese literature are wintersweet, orchid, bamboo and chrysanthemum.
* cuckoo: any of a family of birds with a long, slender body, grayish-brown on top and white below, a symbol of sadness in Chinese culture. As is said, during the Shang dynasty, Cuckoo (Yü Tu), a caring king of Shu, abdicated the throne due to a flood and lived in reclusion. After his death, he turned into a cuckoo, wailing day and night, shedding tears and blood.

书　事

轻阴阁小雨，
深院昼慵开。
坐看苍苔色，
欲上人衣来。

The Sight Before Me

The light murk stops the drizzle fine;
My sloth lets my yard closed remain.
I sit and see the green moss shine;
Come onto my clothes it would fain.

* moss: a tiny, delicate bryophytic plant growing on damp decaying wood, ground, rocks or trees, producing capsules which open by an operculum and contain spores. Under a poet's writing brush, it may arouse a poetic feeling or imagination.

崔兴宗写真咏

画君年少时，
如今君已老。
今时新识人，
知君旧时好。

Portraying Hsingtsung Ts'ui

When I painted you, you were young;
Today you've already grown old.
Although a new person I know,
The past of yours was just like gold.

* Hsingtsung Ts'ui: a T'ang poet from Broadridge (today's Tingchow, Hopei Province), who lived in reclusion in the South Mountains south of Long Peace in his early life and used to hang out with Wei Wang, our poet and painter, drinking, writing and playing the zither. The position he held in the dynasty was Left Alternate and he finished his career as Secretary of Jaochow Prefecture, in today's Chianghsi Province.

寄河上段十六

与君相见即相亲，
闻道君家在孟津。
为见行舟试借问，
客中时有洛阳人。

To Tuan Sixteen on the River

Now I have met you, we are dear;
You live by First Ferry I hear.
Seeing a boat, I would make sure:
Is there one from Loshine on tour?

* First Ferry: the name of a ferry and the county which was named after it, in the north of Loshine, located in the west of today's Honan Province.
* Loshine: Loyang if transliterated, the eastern of the two greatest cities that served as capitals in the early Chinese dynasties, and second largest city of the Empire in T'ang times, when it had about 800,000 inhabitants, now a major city under Honan Province.

送王尊师归蜀中拜扫

大罗天上神仙客，
濯锦江头花柳春。
不为碧鸡称使者，
唯令白鹤报乡人。

Seeing Off Master Wang to Mid-Shu for Tomb Sweeping

The immortal from Grand Clude in Heaven,
On the Silk, in the spring willows does sport.
You are not Emerald Rooster's envoy;
A white crane rider, to folks you'll report.

* Mid-Shu: referring to present-day Ssuch'uan Province. Shu was one of the earliest kingdoms in China, founded by Silkworm and Fishbuck according to legend.
* Tomb Sweeping: an activity of making sacrifice to ancestors after sweeping their tombs, observed on Pure Brightness Day, which is fifteen days after Vernal Equinox. This festival started in the Chough dynasty 2,500 years ago and merged with Cold Food Day, which is one day earlier, in the Sui and T'ang dynasties (A.D. 581 – A.D. 907).
* Grand Clude: the highest of the thirty-six skies in Wordist mythology. The thirty-six skies in Wordist mythology were fabricated based on the cosmology that the Word begets everything. The thirty-six skies include nine layers of sky and each layer covers four directions that in turn represent four seasons.
* Heaven: the space surrounding or seeming to overarch the earth, in which the sun, the moon, and stars appear, popularly the abode of God, his angels and the blessed, and in most cases suggesting supernatural power or sometimes signifying a monarch.
* the Silk: referring to the present-day Min River, a tributary of the Long River flowing in Ssuch'uan Province.

* Emerald Rooster: a mythological creature according to *The Book of Han*, usually offered as a sacrifice.
* white crane rider: a metonymy for an immortal. Literally, the white crane rider refers to Prince of Front (567 B.C.- 549 B.C.), the first son of King Spirit of Chough. He was an intelligent and courageous young man. Though high as a prince, he had few desires and was keen on the Word. As legend goes, after his early death he rose, astride a white crane, to the sky, hence an immortal.

送沈子福归江东

杨柳渡头行客稀，
罟师荡桨向临圻。
惟有相思似春色，
江南江北送君归。

Seeing You Off Back to East of the River

By Willow Ford now passengers are few;
The fisherman to the cove plies his oar.
Only my lovesickness is like spring hue;
All see you off from south shore or north shore.

* East of the River: referring to the drainage area of the lower reaches of the Yangtze River.
* Willow Ford: an old ferry of the Yellow River in today's Tung-o County, Shantung Province.
* cove: a small bay or inlet. Natural places like coves, glades, hills, moors, rivers, mounts and seas and so on often allude to reclusion in Chinese culture.

剧嘲史寰

清风细雨湿梅花，
骤马先过碧玉家。
正值楚王宫里至，
门前初下七香车。

Jeering at Huan Shih

The wintersweets wet with a drizzle fine,
With a draught your horse trots near to her.
Just now King of Ch'u arrives at the door;
Behold, he lights from his cart with a whir.

* wintersweet: a plant having small yellow or red flowers, a symbol of elegance, solitude and pride in Chinese culture for its blossoming and fragrance in the coldest winter while all other plants are still dry and bare. The Four most favored plant images with rich cultural associations in Chinese literature are wintersweet, orchid, bamboo and chrysanthemum.
* horse: a large solid-hoofed quadruped (*Equus caballus*) with coarse mane and tail; commonly in the domesticated state, employed as a beast of draught and burden and especially for riding upon. The horse is very important in ancient China, there are about hundred names for various strains, such as Black Steed, Bownie, Dragon Colt, Red Bolt, Wind Chaser, Shade Trotter and so on.
* King of Ch'u: a metaphor for a certain prince of T'ang.
* Ch'u: a vassal state of Chough, one of the seven powers in the Warring States period, conquered and annexed by Ch'in in 223 B.C., covering the regions covering present-day Hunan and Hupei and neighboring areas.

秋 夜 曲

桂魄初生秋露微,
轻罗已薄未更衣。
银筝夜久殷勤弄,
心怯空房不忍归。

A Tune of Autumn

The moon is new and the autumn dew light;
Tho chill, she does not change her costume thin.
She plucks the lute into the depth of night,
For she can't bear her vacant room therein.

* the lute: a stringed musical instrument, usually placed on a table, played by plucking the strings with fingers or a plectrum.
* Luna: the moon, an important image in Chinese literature or culture as it can evoke many associations such as solitude and nostalgia on the one hand, and purity, brightness and happy reunions on the other. Philosophically, It is the very germ or source of *Shade*, and the sun is its *Shine* counterpart. What is "moon" in Chinese has at least two hundred names, like Shade Spirit (yinp'o), Jade Mound (yaot'ai), Fair Lady (ts'anchüan), Jade Hare (yüt'u), White Hare (pait'u), Silver Hare (yint'u), Ice Hare (pingt'u), Gold Hare (chint'u), Hare Gleam (t'uhui), Laurel Soul (Kuip'o) and so on.

译 者 简 介

赵彦春教授致力于中华经典典籍的翻译和传播。他持表征之神杖,舞锐利之弧矢,启翻译范式之革命,将诗歌之"不可译"变为"可译";将"译之所失"变为"译之所得";将中华五千年的语言、哲学、诗学和美学的智慧融为一体,进行大胆尝试而细腻创新;他坚持译诗如诗,译经如经,从音韵形式、思想内容和文化意蕴上完美诠释了音美、形美和意美的统一;他相信语言与宇宙同构,将翻译的"诗学空间"不断延伸和拓展。

为了讲好"中国故事",引领中国文化"走出去",他带领一批志同道合的专业人士兢兢业业,孜孜不倦,锐意进取。从编辑、出版经典译著到举办国学外译研修班,从召开经典外译与国际传播学术研讨会、举办中华文化国际翻译大赛到创办 Translating China(《翻译中国》)国际期刊,他和同仁将忙碌的身影融入到了中华文化复兴的背景之中。

他带着"赵彦春国学经典英译系列"等一大批优秀的翻译成果走向世界,向世界展示中华文明的无尽魅力。

他无愧为中华典籍传统文化的传承者和传播者。

About the Translator

Professor Yanchun Chao devotes himself to the translation and transmission of Chinese classics. To inherit the traditional Chinese culture, he holds the divine scepter of Representation and sways the sharpness of bow and arrow to initiate a paradigm revolution out of fallacies, turning "untranslatability" of poetry into "translatability", "losses of translation" into "gains of translation", integrating the wisdom of five thousand years of Chinese language, philosophy, poetics and aesthetics to make bold attempts and exquisite innovations; he insists on translating Poesie into Poesie and Classic into Classic, perfectly interpreting the beauty of sound, form and sense from prosodic features, ideological contents and cultural implications; he also believes that language is isomorphic to the universe and constantly expands the "Poetic Space" of translation.

To tell good "Chinese stories" and lead them to "go global", he guides a group of like-minded specialists to work with diligence and fortitude, editing and publishing classic translations, convening seminars on English translation of Chinese culture, holding conferences on Classic Translation and International Communication, organizing "CC CUP" International Chinese Culture Translation Contest and editing an international journal *Translating China*, their busy figures silhouetted against the background of the revival of traditional Chinese culture.

With "Yanchun Chao's English Translation Series of Chinese Classics" going global, he shows to the world the endless appeal of the Chinese civilization.

He is a true inheritor and promoter of Chinese classics and traditional Chinese culture.